"GAVIN, WHAT ARE YOU GOING TO DO?" ANNA ASKED.

He took a long swallow of beer. He carefully placed the bottle down on the counter before he crossed powerful arms over a broad chest and leaned back against it. Judging by the muscle playing in his taut jaw, she recognized he was struggling to hold his temper.

"I've got to make it right," he said tiredly.

"How are you going to do that?"

"That's up to you."

"Me?"

"Mmm-hmm." He took both her small hands in his larger ones. "I need your help, Anna Mae Prescott."

Unforgettable

BETTE FORD

HarperTorch
An Imprint of HarperCollinsPublishers

This is a work of fiction. Names, characters, places, and incidents are products of the author's imagination or are used fictitiously and are not to be construed as real. Any resemblance to actual events, locales, organizations, or persons, living or dead, is entirely coincidental.

❦

HARPERTORCH
An Imprint of HarperCollins*Publishers*
10 East 53rd Street
New York, New York 10022-5299

Copyright © 2003 by Bette Ford
ISBN: 0-06-053307-2

First HarperTorch paperback printing: December 2003

HarperCollins ®, HarperTorch™, and ❦™ are trademarks of Harper-Collins Publishers Inc.

Printed in the United States of America

Visit HarperTorch on the World Wide Web at www.harpercollins.com

10 9 8 7 6 5 4 3 2 1

I give thanks to my Heavenly Father.
Through Him all things are possible.

To my cousins,
whose love and support mean so much.
Growing up an "only" can be lonely,
but not for me, thanks to all of you.
Diane Short, Marsha P. Carter,
Debra W. McCane, Judy C. Norris,
Cheryl M. Mays and Audrey Brown.
Dennis Porter, Larry Porter,
David Carter, Kevin Moton,
John Moton and Nathaniel Clark.

To the ladies in my Reading Group.
In the three years we've read and laughed together
we've also become good friends.
Ann Casey, Pat Frazier,
Michelle Hill, Gail Porter
and Debbie Sims.

To my agent, Nancy Yost.
You are the best!

To Jeanette Osborne Morris,
with all my love.
It has been a joy to watch you grow into
a warm, confident and lovely young woman.

ACKNOWLEDGMENTS

Special thanks to Jessica B. Harris, author of *Iron Pots and Wooden Spoons: Africa's Gifts to New World Cooking*.

The northern city was green and lush from a long, sizzling hot summer and recent bounty of rain. September first had begun as a cool, crisp day with bright sunshine, but as the day progressed, it warmed enough for air conditioning or ceiling fans to be turned on.

Only one of the trees that surrounded Anna Prescott's modest two-bedroom home showed hints of the rich russet and scarlet foliage yet to come. The house was situated in a residential area dotted with brick homes, schools, and a park on the east side of Detroit, Michigan.

"This is the last one," Anna said as she sealed, then labeled the last of the aluminum containers lining her kitchen workstation.

"Good, it looks like I'll be able to keep my promise this time. Carl is expecting me home in time to go out tonight for dinner and dancing," Janet Raye-Matthews said with a wide smile.

The two African-American women owned Prescott-Raye Catering. Their business had been growing faster than either woman expected when they started three years ago. They worked out of Anna's professionally equipped kitchen with one assistant, Krista Moore.

It was the big kitchen that had won Anna's heart, with its double deep sinks, separate prep areas, and center island. It had been decorated in golden yellow with cream tiled counters, open shelves, and a large picture window that overlooked a spacious backyard.

They prepared twelve complete meals with very generous portions five days a week for their bachelor clientele, all members of the Detroit Lions football team. Not only did the meals have to be tasty but they also had to be nutritionally balanced, rich with rice or pasta, vegetables and fruits, an assortment of whole grains, meat, and dairy products.

The meals were being transferred in stainless-steel racks to the van specially equipped with both a warming unit and refrigerated drawers. Each lid was carefully labeled with the client's name, contents, and heating instructions.

"Well, it would be nice, considering this is your first wedding anniversary," Anna teased. "You should have spent the day pampering yourself in a spa instead of here cooking."

The two women were opposites in looks and personality. Janet had a quick wit and ready temper, while Anna was level-headed and seldom ruffled. Janet was five-six, slim and shapely, with small features and soft, light brown skin. Her brown shoulder-length hair was pulled back into a ponytail.

Anna, on the other hand, was tall, five-ten, full-figured, with generous breasts and hips, and a small waist. Her soft black hair had been styled in thin, tightly coiled dreadlocks that flowed past her shoulders. She kept them pulled back into a high ponytail when she was working. Her skin was a rich and creamy mocha brown. She had inherited her height from her father and her dark gray eyes from her mother.

"Carl and I should wait and celebrate this weekend. We don't have an event scheduled. Honestly, Anna. Why can't he ever see that my work is just as important as his law practice?" Janet carried another rack of dinners out to the van.

Anna was right behind her, her hands, like Janet's, covered by protective oven mitts. Together they fitted the last two trays inside the van's heating unit.

"I'm sure if you just talk to him calmly about it, he'll understand."

"And whose side are you on?"

Anna smiled. "Yours, of course. But sometimes you let your temper get the best of you."

Janet laughed. "You know me too well."

"I should hope so. We've been friends and partners for years." Shaking her head, Anna added, "I sure hope Sam likes the rack of lamb we made today. You know, I still can't get over what happened the other day when he was entertaining his new lady friend." She laughed. "I'm just the hired help. My outfit was hardly eye-catching." After locking the van's side door, they went back to the house.

Anna had recently made changes in her appearance. Instead of the loose-fitting pants and oversize tee-shirts she used to wear, she now wore form-fitting jeans and knit tops that skimmed her lush curves.

Anna had been referring to the time she'd been delivering defensive lineman Sam Roger's meal and she'd run into his newest ladylove. The woman had gone into a jealous fit at the idea of another woman having a key to his place and threatened to dump the carefully prepared meal in the trash.

"I don't blame her for being upset. A pretty lady in her man's kitchen is a problem," Janet teased. "Girl, you've changed your whole look over the summer. When are you going to tell me what or who caused this change? I don't care what you say, it has to be a new man."

Anna shook her head. "Wrong, wrong, wrong. How many times do I have to tell you? The change is all about me, no one else."

"Why are you keeping secrets?" Janet tried another tactic.

They'd been super busy since the team had returned from their training camp. They'd added two new bachelor clients while maintaining their weekend catering jobs, which included weddings and an occasional baby or bridal shower.

"I'm not. Besides, this incident isn't about me, but Sam's lousy taste in women."

Anna had quickly grown bored with the subject. It was all so simple, but others insisted on complicating the matter. One day she'd looked in her mirror and decided she was in a rut. She did something about it. End of subject.

Janet laughed, "No sense wasting time worrying about her. We both know he changes his women every other week."

"After two years of cooking for these guys, nothing, and I mean nothing, surprises me anymore."

They had started by catering weddings, luncheons, and banquets, and then they'd gotten lucky. With the help of Anna's oldest brother, Wesley Prescott, and his best friend, Gavin Mathis, both Detroit players, Prescott-Raye Catering was soon catering team events. That was only the beginning.

Anna came from an athletic family. Her father, Lester Prescott, was a physical education teacher who also coached high school football, while both her older brothers were pro football players. Devin, two years younger than Wesley, was the starting quarterback for the St. Louis Rams. Even her little brother, Wayne, at fourteen, was already crazy about football. He was working hard to make his high school varsity team next year.

Only her cousin Ralph Prescott, who was like another older brother, wasn't fascinated with football. He at one time had played basketball for the University of Detroit, where he now coached his old college team. His pro basketball career had ended after five years due to injury.

Anna was the only girl in the family. Although she looked like her pretty and petite mother, Donna, Anna had been five-seven by the time she was ten. She had been self-conscious about being taller than all the other kids in her fifth-grade class, even the boys. But thanks to her mother, over the years she'd grown comfortable with herself.

She couldn't help being a tomboy, growing up with her rough-and-tumble cousin and brothers. It was only after her twenty-seventh birthday that she had taken the time to bother with clothes. Yet she'd always enjoyed floral-scented perfumes and bath products, as well as silky underthings.

Her mother, who had always given her form-fitting, feminine gifts, had been very pleased by the changes Anna had made, but like Janet, she was full of questions.

"Do you think she's the one?" Janet asked, eager for a bit of gossip.

"Sam's new lady?"

"Who else?"

"I have no idea and I'm not about to lose sleep worrying about who will end up with any of our bachelor clients."

"You would be interested if it was Gavin Mathis we were discussing," Janet tossed back.

"Why?"

"He's your brother's best friend. And it was his bragging about your food that started this."

"Yes, we owe him. But what does one thing have to do with the other? Gavin is like a brother to me, as you well know. Besides, if he were seeing someone special, I'd know about it. Gavin wouldn't keep a secret from the family."

"They're confirmed bachelors only until the right woman comes along," Janet teased.

"I don't know. Gavin claims it's for life. He dates and probably sleeps around, then leaves as soon as he gets what he wants," Anna surmised.

"Are you talking from personal experience?"

"Just speculating." She laughed. "I'd better get these meals delivered. Forget about the kitchen and get out of here early. I'll clean up when I get back."

Anna gave her friend a quick hug. "Enjoy yourself. Bye."

Gavin Mathis lived west of Woodward Avenue in the Palmer Park section of the city. His place was always last on her list. It was after six when Anna paused outside the high wrought-iron fences that enclosed the lush acreage surrounding his large, beautiful home.

When Anna had bought her own house, she'd done so because she knew she would have no independence living in her parents' home. Her father, cousin, and older brothers were down right overprotective of her. Old-fashioned wasn't the term to describe her father's attitude when it came to his only daughter—he was antiquated. He'd gone so far as to teach not only his sons but also the nephew who grew up in his home to always look out for Anna, no matter what.

After Anna punched in the security code, the electronic gates swung open. As Anna recalled Janet's questions about Gavin, she recognized that she had no idea how she would react if she ran into one of his lady friends at his place. Gavin, like her brothers and cousin, had his share of women.

It had only been since Wesley had met and married Kelli Warner that his life had changed for the better. And when sweet little Kaleea had been born, he became a proud father with hints of becoming as protective of his little girl as his own father.

What Anna couldn't figure out was why Janet would doubt her claim that Gavin was like a brother to her. She'd known him since she was in her teens. Gavin and Wesley had been close friends since they played football together at Michigan State University.

Gavin had been invited to so many holiday meals over the years that she thought of him as family. After the men turned pro, Gavin and Wesley had become business partners as well. They jointly owned several sporting goods stores across the country.

Anna shook her head, bewildered by why her best friend believed there was anything between them other than friendship. It was ridiculous. Gavin was no more romantically interested in her than she was in him.

Anna didn't need to look into a mirror to verify that she was nothing like the petite and exquisitely beautiful women Gavin dated. Besides, she was beginning to believe that there wasn't a woman alive who could captivate that man's attention for long.

She certainly wasn't stupid enough to get in that very long line of hopefuls, even though Gavin was one of the few men she could actually look up to, even in three-inch heels. At six-foot-four with wide shoulders and powerful biceps, he was big enough to make even a big woman like her feel small. Not that it mattered, of course.

The house was set back from the road. Anna followed the paved drive, taking the curve to the right that brought her to the side entrance. She parked in front of the four-car attached garage done in the same pale beige brick as the impressive house.

Collecting the last covered containers, Anna let herself inside Gavin's side door. She called out a hello, making her way past the laundry room, bathroom, and into the large, sunny kitchen. It was a kitchen that any professional cook would love. She should know, since she'd planned and decorated it at his insistence. He'd been too busy playing football to be bothered about the details.

The kitchen was painted a warm cream with long, hunter green granite counters and back splash. The floor was a beautiful gold-veined marble. Pale maple cabinets were placed around the room but there were no overhead cabinets to block the row of windows that overlooked the extensive garden beyond. A double-door, stainless steel paneled refrigerator stood beside the built-in desk, and the sinks and drawer-pulls were also stainless steel.

There were built-in convection and conventional ovens, as well as a six-burner stovetop built into the large circular center island with additional sink and prep areas. The island also sported a raised counter that served as a breakfast bar.

A cream marble counter for working with pastry was positioned in front of one of the wide windows, with two built-in refrigerator drawers underneath for cooling dough and storing cream and butter. The kitchen also contained every modern appliance on the market, such as built-in deep fryer, microwave, and KitchenAid mixer.

Gavin had lived in New York while he played for the Giants. His home back then had been decorated by an interior designer, and he hated it. When he moved to Detroit three years ago to play for the Lions, he had asked Anna and her mother to do the decorating. His only instruction was to make it feel like a home.

Anna had taken special joy in designing the spacious kitchen. It turned out to be her dream kitchen, and she often teased Gavin, telling him that it was completely wasted on him. He'd only laughed, inviting her to use it any time she wanted.

She was putting the food away in the refrigerator when Gavin Mathis walked in. He was a handsome man whose strong features spoke of his African ancestry. His skin was a deep copper brown. His wide mouth framed by a mustache was his most striking feature. His lips were well shaped, but the bottom was lush, blatantly seductive.

"Hey, Short Stuff," he said, using the nickname her cousin and brothers insisted on calling her. As tall as she'd been growing up, her cousin and older brothers were taller. And they loved to tease her. "Looking awfully cute today," he tossed out the compliment. "You goin' to tell me his name?"

"Nope." She did her best to ignore his dark brown gaze. She teased, "You're looking good your own self."

Anna was not about to admit that she'd never cared enough about any one of the men she dated to want more than friendship. She'd never figured out if it was because she'd been busy with school and later getting her business established, or if there was something missing deep inside. She'd never even come close to falling in love.

Gavin laughed. "I'm serious. Who is he?"

"Honestly, you're getting as bad as Janet with these questions. Enough already."

He had a towel draped over his neck, and his smooth dark skin glistened from perspiration, indicating he had been working out in his home gym. His muscular shoulders, deep chest, and lean midsection were covered in a gray Lions tee-shirt, and his heavy muscled thighs were encased in tight shorts. His long feet were in the brand of athletic shoes he endorsed.

Although he was a big man, he was extremely fast, making him one of the NFL's most sought-after and highest-paid wide receivers for two major reasons. His superb cutback ability and his powerful thighs allowed him to pass the thousand-yard rushing mark each season, and to obtain three rushing titles.

It was his straightforward, no-nonsense style that both the fans and the advertisers adored. Gavin lent his name only to products and causes he believed in. He headed the Eloise Mathis Foundation, named for his deceased mother. The foundation's single aim was to make a college education possible for minority and low-income teens.

"Keeping out of trouble?" He was always teasing her about her boyfriends, certain she was keeping them hidden because they wouldn't get past the men in her family.

"Always." She grinned. "I brought a crisp cucumber and green salad, new jacket potatoes in a garlic and butter sauce, pot roast, homemade rolls, and pineapple upside-down cake," she rattled off the menu, then reminded him of the heating instructions.

Like most of the bachelors she cooked for, Gavin didn't care what she brought as long as there was plenty of it and it was good. The only two foods on his no-no list were cheesecake and brussels sprouts. He hated both.

"Are you busy tonight?" He removed a bottle of spring water from the refrigerator drawer.

Just for a moment her heart rate accelerated, and she blushed as if she thought he was asking her out on a date. Thank goodness, common sense took over. As her pretty dark gray eyes met with his dark brown troubled gaze, she cautioned herself to calm down and use her head. His eyes had not lingered on her curves or caressed her small features. She could tell by his creased forehead and tight lips that something was wrong.

Before she could question him, a painfully thin teenaged boy walked into the room. He shared the same warm copper skin tone and eye coloring as Gavin. He looked as if he hadn't had a haircut in weeks, and his jeans and tee-shirt were threadbare. He took one look at Anna, ducked his head, and turned to leave.

"Wait, Kyle. There's someone here I want you to meet," Gavin said in his deep baritone voice.

"I only came for something to drink. I can come back later."

"No need. Anna, this is Kyle Reynolds, my brother. Kyle, this is Anna Prescott, a good friend. She's a chef and brought our dinner."

Having no idea Gavin even had a sibling, Anna struggled to hide her dismay. She smiled as she moved toward the boy but stopped when she realized he was backing away.

"Hello, Kyle. Nice meeting you. I have a brother about your age. Maybe you'll have a chance to meet him while you're here."

Kyle nodded, yet shifted uncomfortably from one foot to the other. He didn't lift his eyes from the tops of his dirty sneakers.

"Kyle," Gavin promoted.

"Hi," he muttered before he ducked out of the room without his drink.

Once she was certain they were alone, she said, "Okay, Gavin. What's going on here? I didn't know you had a brother."

"Neither did I until last night when our father showed up with him. George spent the night, got his handout, but when I came in from practice today, he had left without Kyle." His voice was tight with anger.

"What?"

"Yeah. That was my reaction."

"How could you not know you had a brother?"

"It's a long story."

"How old is he? He looks to be about the same age as Wayne."

"Fourteen. Can you stay for dinner? There is something I'd like to discuss with you later."

Anna studied him, seeing controlled fury mixed with a

touch of desperation. She nodded. "I'll stay. What time do you want to eat?"

"As soon as you can get it on the table. As you can see, Mrs. Tillman set the table before she left for the day." He mentioned his housekeeper, who did a wonderful job of keeping the house spotless but was a terrible cook.

He walked over to squeeze her hand. "Thanks, kiddo. I'll be right back. I need to take a shower. It will only take a few minutes, then I'll help you dish up the food."

"Take your time."

Anna went to the refrigerator and removed the food she had just put inside. She paused when she realized that her hands weren't exactly steady from his casual touch. She was annoyed with herself, disturbed by the way she had felt when she thought Gavin had asked her out. For a single moment her heart had gone wild and she'd barely been able to catch her breath.

It was crazy, but her reaction was what scared her. What had happened to her brain? Hadn't she just told Janet that Gavin was like another brother to her? She had no business taking note of his deep chest and washboard stomach. So what if he was all male? He was a good friend, and she would be better off concentrating on what she understood—food.

As Gavin walked away he had to stop himself from really giving in to his curiosity over the changes in Anna's appearance. She had always been pretty, but recently she was downright sexy. Despite what she said, she had to be seeing one of the guys on the team. It wouldn't surprise him since she was in and out of their homes on a daily basis. What surprised him was how much he detested the idea. He didn't need to remind himself that it was none of his damn business.

He wouldn't be male if he hadn't taken note of the way her

jeans hugged her luscious hips and her top followed the sweet curves of her ripe breasts. His male parts had strained toward all that was female in her. Had he lost his mind? He had no right to notice anything about her other than her eye color and shoe size. It was safer that way. Evidently he'd been sleeping alone for too blasted long. The pulsing of his shaft reminded him just how long it had been since he'd been inside a woman.

He quickly ran up the wide, bronze marble staircase. At the top of the stairs his feet sank into the thick, beige carpeting. He walked past three closed guest bedroom doors before he paused to knock on the fourth door on the left. He waited for a response before opening it. Kyle was propped up on the bed, his eyes on the television set.

"You okay, kid?"

"What's it to you?" Kyle answered without looking at his older brother.

Gavin ignored the attitude, saying, "Look, Anna is staying for dinner. It will be ready in fifteen minutes."

"Not hungry," the boy mumbled.

"I want you at the table. Got it?"

"I heard."

Gavin sighed wearily, closing the door. He'd tried talking to the boy when he'd gotten home and realized their father was gone. It had been like trying to hold a conversation with a concrete wall.

He continued down the hall to the double doors at the end of the corridor. As he walked into the master suite, he didn't even glance around the sitting room with its twin, oversize tan leather sofas and matching armchairs positioned in front of a fireplace.

He didn't stop, but continued on into the connecting bedroom. Passing his custom-made oversize bed, built to comfortably accommodate his two-hundred-and-ten-pound, hard-muscled frame, he went into his private oasis. The bronze and gold-veined marble bathroom was complete with double sinks, an oversize whirlpool tub, and glass-enclosed large multihead shower stall.

He grumbled to himself as he stripped in front of the heated towel bars and tossed his things into the hamper before going into the shower. He hung his head as hot water rushed over him, wondering if he had ever felt more helpless.

Neither the practice today nor the workout in the gym later had eased the tautness in his back and neck. The tightness in his heart couldn't be eased by physical exertion. It had nothing to do with his high-pressure job and everything to do with a deep, churning resentment that had been a part of him for as long as he could remember. The resentment was directed at George Reynolds, his pitiful excuse for a father.

The only thing he'd gotten right was causing Eloise Mathis, Gavin's sweet, loving mother, to fall in love with him. She'd defied her very conventional and religious parents by moving in with the man she adored, believing in his promise of marriage. When George learned that Gavin was on the way, he'd disappeared, leaving Eloise unmarried, pregnant, and unable to take care of herself or her baby. Her parents had relented enough to give Eloise money until after the baby was born. They'd never welcomed her back into their home or recognized their illegitimate grandson.

Gavin grew up watching his mother work herself into an early grave, striving to give him the best care. She didn't want him to do without, considering he had suffered enough by not having his father's name. As soon as Gavin was old enough, he'd gotten after-school jobs to help out as much as he could, until his mother put her foot down, insisting his schoolwork came first, even before sports.

George hadn't been kind enough to stay out of their lives.

He would pop up every few years and expect things to be as if he had walked out hours ago. He stayed long enough to keep Eloise emotionally involved with him. Then he'd leave again, unconcerned that Eloise had a broken heart and an empty wallet. Even back then his gambling came first.

Gavin knew he was lucky, not only because of the love his mother had given him but because of the pride and determination she'd instilled in him. He'd wanted to someday give her the things she'd missed over the years, but unfortunately, it hadn't worked that way. Even though he'd won the Heisman Trophy in his junior year at Michigan State and drawn the attention of the NFL scouts, his mother hadn't lived to see him graduate from college or sign his first multimillion-dollar contract.

His father hadn't bothered to attend her funeral. His best friend, Wesley, and his college coach and teammates had helped him through the most difficult day of his life. Thanks to national news coverage, George had been there to cheese for the cameras when Gavin became a New York Giant. Gavin had been sure he'd seen the worst when his father's hand was held out for his share. That didn't compare to the stunt George had pulled with Kyle.

Over the years George never failed to appear when his pockets were empty. Gavin had always forked over a check, not because he wanted to, but because he knew that was what his mother would have expected. He could almost hear her saying, "No matter what, George Reynolds is your father and deserves your respect."

This last stunt was too much. Gavin could only imagine how bad it was for Kyle being tossed from one uncaring relative to the next. Was it any wonder the boy was so resentful? Kyle didn't know Gavin. He had no idea what to expect from this newly discovered brother. And Gavin didn't have a clue how to reassure him that somehow it would all work out.

Kyle was the reason he needed Anna's help. At least she

had a fourteen-year-old brother and knew more than he did about taking care of a teenager.

It didn't lift Gavin's mood when he later knocked on Kyle's door and was greeted by a guarded look filled with bitterness. At that moment, if Gavin could have gotten his hands on George Reynolds, he wasn't sure he'd be able to stop himself from going after him with his fists. The kid didn't deserve to be treated so callously. Somehow Gavin had to find a way to clean up George's mess.

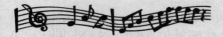

2

"**E**verything looks great. Thanks," Gavin smiled as he held Anna's chair for her. He had changed into navy slacks and a blue knit shirt.

"No problem. Kyle, I hope you're hungry," she said with a smile.

The boy said nothing, nor did he bother to lift his eyes from his plate. After Gavin said grace, she noticed Kyle's badly bitten nails and dirty hands.

"Before we get started, Kyle, I'd appreciate it if you'd wash your hands again."

Gavin looked on, his surprise evident, but he didn't say a word. When Kyle sent Anna an angry glare, Gavin intervened, "Anna's right. We'll wait while you wash up." He pointed to the bathroom off the kitchen.

"What difference does it make? I'll only be here until you

find good old George." Kyle glared. "Neither one of you give a damn about me,"

"Watch your mouth," Gavin warned. "You don't talk that way in front of a lady. As far as what difference it makes, take my word for it, it matters. Now go."

The boy pushed back his chair, then left for the bathroom. He slammed the door behind him.

"I didn't mean to embarrass him," Anna whispered.

"Don't worry about it. I'm glad you noticed. The kid is either mouthing off or sullen." He sighed. "This entire situation is a new one for me." It was all he was able to say before the resentful teen returned.

Throughout the meal both Gavin and Anna tried to include Kyle in their conversation. He made no effort to respond to any inquiry and limited himself to shrugs. His single comment was made when Gavin asked Anna about the private high school where her father worked and her younger brother attended.

"I'm not goin' to school here. I'm not gonna be here that long."

Both Gavin and Anna shared a worried look, but it was Gavin who said, "Son . . ."

"You're not my father."

"You're right," Gavin said, releasing a slow breath. "I'm not, but as long as you're here, you're going to school."

Kyle didn't look pleased but he kept his thoughts to himself. Just as soon as he'd eaten his fill, he excused himself and left the table.

Shaking her head, Anna confessed, "I must be slipping. My cousin and brothers eat anything I put in front of them and always ask for seconds, sometimes thirds." She looked pointedly at Gavin's plate. "You haven't eaten very much either."

"Sorry, Anna. It has nothing to do with this wonderful meal."

"Gavin, what's going on?"

"It's a result of what my unbelievably selfish, bastard of a father pulled today."

Having known Gavin for a number of years, she knew about his strained relationship with his remaining parent.

"I didn't realize he was in town. I didn't see him when I dropped off your dinner yesterday."

"He showed up last night with Kyle. Believe me, he wasn't expected."

"Do you have any idea where he might have gone?"

"I wish I knew. He could be in any state with a casino. He's a gambler." He shook his head, revealing his frustration. "I can't say who was more surprised when I learned we're brothers, Kyle or me. George was the only one enjoying his little surprise." Gavin's voice was edged with disgust.

"Oh no," she whispered in shock.

Their meal had been forgotten.

"Yeah." Scowling, he continued, "George comes around when he's low on funds, only this time it was different. I wrote the check late last night, certain that was the end of it. I expected him to be gone sometime during the day. He was gone, all right, but without Kyle. Can you imagine my reaction when I came home from practice? That sorry bastard hadn't felt the need to explain a thing to me or Kyle. The kid has no idea why he was left behind or for how long."

Gavin pushed away from the table, carrying his and Kyle's plates to the sink. He pulled two imported beers from the refrigerator and held one up for her. When she refused, he put it back inside.

"I'm so sorry, Gavin. What are you going to do?"

He took a long swallow of beer. He carefully placed the

bottle down on the counter before he crossed powerful arms over a broad chest and leaned back against it. Judging by the muscle playing in his taut jaw, she recognized he was struggling to hold on to his temper. And she couldn't blame him.

"Gavin?" she prompted.

"I wish I knew. Other than calling Paul Carter, my lawyer, and hiring a private investigator, both of which I have already done, there isn't a lot I can do."

"What about Kyle's mother?"

"She died of a drug overdose soon after she'd dumped Kyle on her only relative, a great-aunt. He lived with her until she died a few months ago. That was when George took over. Rather than let Kyle go into foster care, like George had been, he felt he could do better. He's been dragging the kid while moving from one city to the next. From what Kyle told me, he has missed more school than he's attended since he's been with George." Gavin was scowling when he said, "It looks as if the kid has spent his entire life being passed from one relative to the next. Evidently I'm last on a very short list."

"That's terrible. Poor Kyle, no wonder he's so angry and resentful."

Gavin nodded. "He's been tossed around like a damn football his whole life. No one deserves that kind of treatment."

"And now he's landed in your lap. It's not fair to either one of you."

"Too bad I didn't have a vote when my mother chose George Reynolds to be my father," he said sarcastically.

Anna laughed. "This is true. At fourteen, Kyle's not equipped to deal with any of this. All he knows is that he's not wanted. I don't know many adults who would be able to cope with that . . . including me."

"I've got to make it right," he said tiredly.

"How are you going to do that?" Her heart went out to both the man and the boy . . . brothers.

No wonder Gavin never talked about his father. There wasn't much good he could say. Anna was only beginning to understand why Gavin was such a private man, allowing few people to get close to him. Trust didn't come easy to him.

"I wish I knew. But I'm all he has at the moment. If I hadn't taken him in, he'd be out on the streets. And I'm not about to let that happen. I can just imagine my mother's reaction if I did something that lowdown."

"Are you letting your father off the hook?"

"Hell no. Kyle knows I'm trying to find him. The problem is, I don't have a clue as to how to get my hands on the bastard. The son of—" Gavin stopped abruptly, before he said, "I mean, he never stays in one place for long." He sighed. "Sorry, Anna. I don't mean to swear, but I'm so frustrated by this whole stinking mess."

"I know. He has to have a mailing address, doesn't he?"

"If he does, he hasn't shared it with me."

"I hate to say this, but some folks need to keep their pants zipped and their skirts down. This doesn't make a bit of sense." Understanding his frustration, she walked over to him and gave him a hug. Easing away, she questioned, "How are you going to manage?"

"That's up to you."

"Me?"

"Mmm-hmm." He took both her small hands in his larger ones. "I need your help, Anna Mae Prescott."

Determined to ignore the tingle of awareness that raced along her nerve endings, she forced herself to concentrate on what he was saying. She could see it coming, but didn't know how to ignore the desperation in his dark eyes.

"You want me to take him home with me?" she whispered.

He grinned, "You're a sweetheart, but no. What I would like is for you to work for me as my personal chef. I need someone I can trust. That's you." He paused before he went on to say, "I'll need you here during the day to cook for us and to be available in the afternoon when Kyle comes in from school. You know my schedule.

"I'm facing night games and charity events. Naturally, there will be times I have to be on the road. When I'm gone, I'll need you to stay over to look after things for me until I get back."

"What about Mrs. Tillman? Or Gretchen Hamilton?" Gretchen helped with both the sporting goods stores and his foundation. Anna knew she was reaching when she named his secretary. "Or Vanessa Grant?"

"Mrs. Tillman does a wonderful job of keeping the place clean, but I need more than that. And Gretchen has enough to do taking care of my business interests and the foundation, and keeping on top of my public appearances. Plus she also has a family of her own to take care of. And Vanessa is raising her teenaged sister and younger twin brother and sister." He paused before he said, "Please, Anna. You're the one I know I can trust to care for Kyle, especially while I'm away. I need to know he is with someone I have complete faith in. That's you, Short Stuff."

What you need is a wife, Anna thought, but wisely didn't say. "It sounds as if you're planning on keeping Kyle with you."

Even though she was deeply touched by his faith in her, she was determined to keep her feet planted firmly on the ground. This was not personal, and she had to remember that. For the last few months, she hadn't been able to control her awareness of him. Being around him every single day was bound to make it worse. She valued their friendship. She wasn't about to jeopardize that.

"I don't know. It's clear our father doesn't know what it means to be a man. That means it's up to me to make certain Kyle gets a fair shake. We're brothers."

Gavin instinctively knew that if George had brought Kyle to his mother to care for, she would never turn her back on the boy. If nothing else, he was his mother's son.

Anna stood on tiptoe to brush her lips against his cheek. "You're one of the good guys, Gavin Mathis." Their eyes locked for a long moment.

"Well?"

"Well, what?" she hedged

"You know what."

"Gavin, I wish I could help you out, but how can I? You know I have a business to run."

"Anna, you can cook anywhere. You always said you loved my kitchen and how it's been wasted on me. Be my guest. Use it. I promise to make it worth your while."

"This isn't about money, and you know it."

"What is it about, Anna? Friendship and family? We're both. And I sure as hell need your help."

"Have you talked to Wesley?"

"No. This all happened too fast. I don't need your big brother's permission to ask for your help."

She couldn't look away from his dark eyes. He was a man she respected. He was straightforward and honest in all his dealings. He always kept his word, but like her brothers, Gavin was a pro football player, which meant he spent a fair amount of time away from home. Travel was a necessary part of the job.

She knew that now that he'd accepted Kyle as part of his family, he would do everything within his power to take care of his brother for as long as the boy was in his home. Unfortunately, there was no way of knowing how long this situation would go on . . . it could be months, not weeks.

"I respect what you're trying to do, but Janet is my business partner, and any decision I make affecting the business has to be discussed with her. It's not as if I've forgotten that I owe you for your help in getting our business going." She went on to say, "You gave me the money I needed without questions. I could have gone to my father or brothers and cousin. But I wanted to do it my way. I appreciated your faith in me."

"You don't owe me anything. We're family. Besides, you paid me back that loan with interest." He ran a hand over his close-cut natural. "Look, I understand about you having to talk to Janet. But before you decide, let me put all my cards on the table." He named an incredibly generous figure that anyone would have a difficult time turning down.

She pointed a menacing finger into his deep chest. "How many times do I have to tell you, Gavin Mathis, this isn't about the money?"

"Maybe I said that badly." He grinned. "Let me try again. Ms. Prescott, I'm willing to compensate you for the inconvenience this job will no doubt cause. I have no idea how long it's going to take to locate my father. You'll have part of each day to do what you like. Perhaps work on that cookbook you've been talking about doing for so long. Kyle and I will even volunteer to eat anything you come up with."

Laughing, she shook her finger at him. "That's so wrong." Gavin knew about the summers she'd spent while growing up with her namesake, her great-grandmother Anna-Mae Lewis in rural Georgia.

Grandma Anna-Mae was determined to maintain their family history going back as far as slavery. They came from a long line of strong black women, many of whom supported their families by their wonderful cooking. Some of their stories had been passed down in their diaries and oral histories. The only written records for some were recipes that had been passed on through their daughters. Each new generation of women made a point of adding to the collection.

Her great-grandmother had filled young Anna's head with the wonderful stories as the two tended her large garden and cooked in the big, old kitchen. Even as a girl, Anna had taken notes and started her own diary. But now that her great-grandmother was gone, Anna had inherited the wonderful collection.

She had long held the belief that it was up to her to safeguard her family's rich history. She'd longed to develop and publish a special cookbook of both the stories and the recipes of these remarkable women. She also longed to include her mother's and her own story and their favorite recipes. Unfortunately, the demands of owning a business had gotten in her way.

Anna was frowning when she asked, "For how long?"

"A few weeks, if we're lucky."

"And if we're not?"

"I honestly don't know." He hesitated then said, "Give yourself a few days before you decide. Talk it over with Janet. In the meantime, I've got to get Kyle enrolled in school."

"Gavin," she cried in frustration.

"Anna," he mocked.

"You don't know a thing about raising that boy," she said with her hands on shapely hips. "You can't enroll him in school without becoming his temporary guardian. Without that, you can't even get medical care for him."

"You're right. I hadn't even thought of that. I've got a lot to do and learn in a hurry." Thoughtfully he smoothed his mustache, and then added with firm resolve, "I can't be like the others. I can't let that kid down."

Anna had seen that determined look before. It meant his mind was set. "Look, I'm not trying to talk you out of this, but aren't you seeing someone? What's she going to think about this new arrangement? Maybe she won't like the idea of another woman staying in your home while you're away."

"I know how to handle my sex life, and I know how to keep it private. Besides, I am not involved at the moment, if that's what you're worried about." He quirked a questioning brow.

Embarrassed, Anna turned away. She wasn't surprised by his response. Other than his assistant, his secretary, and his housekeeper, she had never run into any of his lady friends in the two years she'd cooked for him. Discounting what was printed in the society columns and tabloids, she knew next to nothing about his women. It was only from overhearing her brothers talking that she knew Gavin enjoyed women as much as the next man, but he had no interest in settling down. He valued his freedom too much to even consider giving it up.

She only had to look at him to know why women found him so attractive. He was one-hundred-percent male. But he wasn't what she considered the "typical" pro ball player. He wasn't loud or showy, but a private, intense man who kept his thoughts to himself. His income alone was an enormous incentive that kept women flocking to him. In her opinion it was his intense masculinity that caused women to wake up and take notice.

Gavin brought her back to the problem at hand when he said, "Just think about it."

Anna hadn't expected Janet's car to still be parked in front of her house when she got home. She found her seated at the kitchen table. After hanging her jacket in the tiny back hall, she walked into a spotlessly clean kitchen. Janet's butterscotch coloring was decidedly flushed. She had opened a bottle of red wine and was sipping from a crystal wineglass. Judging from the look on her face she wasn't enjoying it.

"Hi," Anna said as she joined her at the table tucked in

front of the window. "What are you still doing here? Didn't you have a date with your husband, Miss Lady?"

"Not me."

Anna took her friend's hand and tugged her along with her into the small but cozy burgundy and cream living room. She pointed to one of the twin deep-cushioned, velvet burgundy armchairs. "Sit." Anna took the matching chair and propped her feet on one side of the oversize button-tucked ottoman positioned in front. "Okay, tell me what happened."

"There is nothing to talk about. I just didn't want to go home. Can I sleep on your couch?" Janet had managed to hang on to her wine and lifted the glass to her lips to sip.

"First Gavin, now you. Is everyone I know in a crisis?"

"So that's where you've been," Janet surmised.

"Yes, but that's another can of worms. Well? Did you and Carl have a fight?"

"No fight. I just may never speak to him again, that's all."

"Mind telling me what we're talking about?"

"I stared working on a new menu and forgot the time. I called to tell him I was running a little late. Asked him to call the hotel and move back our dinner reservation. Before I could get the words out of my mouth, he tells me to forget it. It was already after six and he'd canceled. It's a good thing," she hissed, wiping angrily at a tear. "I don't want to go any-where with that opinionated fathead." Janet was forced to bite her bottom lip to hold back a tremor.

"Oh, honey, I'm so sorry. Surely if you go home now, you and Carl can talk this over. Maybe it isn't too late to go out? This is your first wedding anniversary."

Janet let out an impatient snort. "I have nothing to say to that man. He doesn't appreciate me or my career goals. He gets ticked every time I'm late."

"But why?"

"He decided *after* we were married that he wanted a full-time wife. I work just as hard as he does. Why shouldn't I have a career? Our business is doing better than either one of us imagined. We're making good money. He should be proud of me, not trying to get me to quit. He knew all this when he married me."

"Janet, you two love each other and need to talk this out."

Anna couldn't believe how they could let something as stupid as a dinner cancellation stop them from being together. Just knowing a man felt the way Carl felt about Janet had to be a dream come true. Anna had never been that lucky. It seemed to Anna that all the men she met were more interested in meeting her wealthy cousin and brothers than in getting to know her.

Janet stubbornly stuck out her chin, "No, I'd much rather hear about you and Gavin."

"Very funny. You know as well as I do that there is no 'Gavin and me.' He invited me to stay and have dinner with him and his brother, Kyle."

"I didn't know he had a brother. Younger or older?"

"Much younger. He's fourteen. And the dinner was full of surprises. Gavin will be taking care of his brother for a while." Anna went on to tell Janet about how George Reynolds had left without his son.

"You are kidding, aren't you?"

"No. Gavin has no idea how to take care of a kid, especially a sullen, withdrawn boy like Kyle."

"I don't envy him."

"Neither do I. He asked for my help."

"What can you do?"

Anna took a deep breath before she confessed, "He offered me a job as his personal chef. Besides cooking, he wants me to be there when Kyle comes home from school and stay over on the nights he's late or on the road." Anna went on to tell her how much he offered to compensate her for the inconvenience.

"Wow."

"Is that all you can say?"

"Well, yeah. What are you going to do?"

"I haven't a clue. I told him I had to talk to you. He offered the use of his kitchen whenever we need it."

"That dream kitchen you designed when he bought the house?"

"That's the one. What do you think?"

Janet studied her for a moment before she said, "I can see that you want to do this as a favor to Gavin."

"I'm that transparent?"

"No, but you care about the man."

"As a friend," Anna emphasized. "We owe him. Without his help, we couldn't have made it."

"True. He helped get the bachelor clients, and Wesley helped us get several events scheduled for the Lions' head office."

"I'd like to be able to help Gavin."

Janet rose and began pacing across the Oriental carpet. She paused to ask, "Will you have to move into his place?"

"No. If I do this, I'll have to be there to cook their meals and stay until Gavin comes home. I only have to stay late if he's tied up or playing a night game and naturally when he's out of the city."

"You've been giving this some thought," Janet said as she returned to her chair.

"With the salary he's paying me, we can afford to hire a new chef."

Janet agreed. "Got anyone in mind?"

They looked at each other and simultaneously said, "Krista."

"It would be a promotion for her."

"And a lot easier for us to work with someone we know and can count on." Janet wondered aloud, "Think she'll agree?"

"I do. She could use the extra money with that little boy to raise on her own."

They smiled at each other.

It was Janet who asked, "What if she wants to buy into the business?"

"We'll have to think about it."

"Anna, you don't have to pay her out of what you're going to make working for Gavin. We make enough to give her a raise and still have enough to hire a replacement for Krista."

"That's true. And I can put the extra money back into the business."

"There is no need. We'll still clear enough after our expenses, as long as you can help us out with the special events. We have the Ellis wedding next weekend and the Grant wedding at the end of the month. Then there's the Lions banquet in October."

"That shouldn't be a problem. And you still have my kitchen to work out of every day. For special events, when we need more room, we can use Gavin's kitchen. Naturally I'll clear it with him first." Anna was beaming when she added, "This will mean that I'll have the time to work on my family cookbook while Kyle is in school. Gavin even volunteered to sample some of the recipes."

"Fantastic. I know how much that cookbook means to you."

Sporting wide grins, the two hugged each other.

"It's going to work out. And I'll be able to help Gavin and Kyle."

"So has Gavin noticed the change?" Janet teased.

"I don't know what you're talking about," Anna hedged.

"Oh yes, you do. I will assume by that blush that he has noticed," Janet said with a smug grin.

Exasperated, Anna frowned. "He's just curious, like someone else I know. Can't a girl make a simple change that has nothing to do with a man?"

"Yeah, it can happen," Janet admitted with some reluctance. "So Gavin noticed. Isn't that nice?"

"And your point?" Anna drummed her fingers impatiently on the armrest.

3

"The man is available."

"You need to quit. You've some crazy idea that Gavin will . . . What? All of a sudden notice me? Or worse, I'll fall into his lap like a ripe plum. Get over it. This is business."

"Okay, okay. I'm stretching. But tell me what do you know about his love life? Is he—"

Just then the doorbell rang. Anna was grateful. She wasn't about to waste time speculating on Gavin's sex life. She didn't even want to think of him as anything other than what he was . . . a good friend.

"Be right back." Anna hurried to the front door. Switching on the outside lamp, she wasn't surprised to see Carl Matthews on her porch. There was a welcoming smile on her face as she unlocked both the storm and front doors.

"Hi. Come on inside."

She had liked him from the very beginning. There was no

doubt in her mind that he was the right man for her friend and business partner.

"Hi." He kissed her cheek. "Think she'll talk to me?"

"I sure hope so," Anna whispered back. "Come in." Crossing the small foyer, she said, "Will you look who's here? I think I'll make some coffee. Excuse me." She left the couple staring at each other.

Smiling to herself, she moved across the small hallway and through the kitchen's swinging door. She took her time brewing a fresh pot of coffee. Stalling for more time she turned on the portable radio she kept on top of the refrigerator, then sat down to sort through her mail that Janet had left on the table. She glanced at her watch before she began flipping through the new issue of a favorite cooking magazine. Her mind wasn't on the magazine, nor was she worried about the newlyweds in the next room. There was no doubt that those two were very much in love.

Anna couldn't seem to concentrate on much beyond what had happened at Gavin's. It was clear that he had a long way to go to shatter that protective shell Kyle had placed around himself. Trust was something the boy was not willing to offer.

Then there was the problem with Gavin's father. But she had enough faith in Gavin to know he'd do everything in his power to help the boy.

She thought about the hints Janet had made concerning her friendship with Gavin. But Anna was reluctant to admit to even her best friend that she felt vulnerable where Gavin was concerned. It wasn't as if she thought he was interested in her . . . she knew better. No, there were other issues.

As a teenager, she'd had a secret crush on Gavin. Even her family didn't know. She'd longed for him to notice her back then. It hadn't happened. It was something she had never quite managed to forget. Gavin thought of her as Wesley's baby sister. That hadn't changed. And it had stopped bothering her years ago.

Gavin kept so much of himself hidden, yet tonight he had opened up to her. She'd been heartened when he admitted he trusted her and needed her help.

Was it her imagination, or had he looked at her in a different way? Recently he'd been questioning her about her love life. What she couldn't figure out was why. She'd made some changes to her appearance, certainly nothing drastic. Why should it matter? Their friendship was solid, and they both intended to keep it that way.

She wasn't fooled. Janet's teasing was nothing more than wishful thinking on her part. What she wanted was for Anna to fall in love and be happily married the way she was.

Janet called her name before she walked into the kitchen, followed by her husband. She was beaming. "Just wanted to tell you to forget the coffee. We're on our way home."

Judging by the way they couldn't take their eyes off each other, Anna assumed all was well in the Matthews household. "Are you sure? It won't take a minute," she teased.

"You drink it. I'll see you in the morning. We can talk to Krista when she comes in at eight."

"Okay. I'll walk you two to the door." She hid a smile as she watched Janet grab her tote bag and jacket from the hook near the back door. Carl was grinning enough for both of them.

Janet gave Anna a quick hug. "Thanks for putting up with me."

"Don't be silly. Good night." Anna waved after them and locked up. Returning to the kitchen, she poured the coffee down the sink before flicking off the light.

Curling up in her favorite chair, she hummed to herself as she began writing out a "to do" list. The first thing that needed to be done was an inventory of Gavin's kitchen and pantry. She had to admit she was excited about working in his fabulous kitchen. If Krista agreed to take over Anna's job, then all they had to do was find Krista's replacement. How hard could it be?

For the next few days Anna and Krista Moore worked together, from menu planning to learning the routine. Krista went with Anna and was introduced to all their clients. There was so much to do, and both Janet and Anna wanted to ensure that the transition was smooth.

The hardest problem was finding a new assistant, but that was finally resolved when Lori Fleming, a recent culinary arts graduate, answered their newspaper ad. Janet and Krista would continue to work out of Anna's kitchen. For the most part, Anna would be available to help with their upcoming weekend catering jobs.

Anna's mother welcomed her with a hug when she surprised her family by coming for dinner in the middle of the week. She was working alongside her mother when her father arrived home.

"Whom do I owe for this treat, precious?" Lester Prescott grinned as he closed the back door. "You're home for dinner on a Thursday night? What happened to all those hungry bachelors?"

He pulled his daughter into his arms for a hug. He was tall, six-foot-two inches with dark, caramel brown coloring and a youthful, handsome face despite the flecks of gray in his hair.

"Hi, Daddy." Anna reached up on tiptoe to kiss his cheek. "I have the night off, so I thought I'd come by and eat all your food," she teased. "I brought an apple cake with caramel and pecan topping."

He was grinning when he said, "You didn't have to do that." He gave her a hard squeeze before he let her go. "But

I'm glad you did. Isn't that right, sugar," he said as he leaned down to place a lingering kiss on his wife's lips.

"That's right." Donna Prescott smiled up at her husband, her dark gray eyes sparkling with love. "You're kinda late, aren't you, honey?" Even after four children, she was as petite and slim as the day she married. Her soft black, shoulder-length hair had touches of gray at the temples, but her ready smile and mocha brown skin was as smooth and unlined as her daughter's. She was only five-foot-two inches, and all her children towered over her.

"Had to stop by a student's home to talk to his mother. He's been goofing off in his classes. Sorry. I didn't realize it was so late."

Lester and Donna Prescott smiled at each other, still very much in love after thirty-three years of marriage and four children.

"Ralph stop by?" Lester asked, referring to the nephew he and Donna had raised as one of their own after his parents were killed when he was twelve. Devin and Ralph were the same age, and both were single.

Donna laughed. "Not tonight. He has a class." Although Ralph no longer lived at home with the family, he often showed up for home-cooked meals.

Lester nodded. "I keep hoping he'll go back for his doctorate. Playing pro ball gave him a solid financial base, but now it's time to shore up his career at the university. These days in the academic world, a master's isn't enough." The pride in his voice was evident.

"Lester, you promised." Donna reminded, "Ralph is old enough to make his own decisions."

"I know. I know."

"Anna, call Wayne."

"Mama, don't you want me to help?"

"No, angel. This is your day off. I want you to relax and enjoy yourself. You work too hard."

"Did I hear my name? Dinner ready?" Wayne, like all the Prescotts' children, was tall. He was nearly six foot, but he was still slim, and his hands and feet seemed too big for his body.

"That's all you think about, your stomach. Did you speak to your father, young man?" Donna scolded gently.

"What's up, Dad? Sorry, must be the hunger dulling my brain." Wayne grinned, patting his father on the back.

Laughing, Lester grabbed his son by the nape of the neck and hauled him close for a quick hug.

"Aw, Dad, I'm too old for that kinda stuff."

"You're never too old to give or receive love, son. Come on, let's wash up. How did you do on your math test today?" Their voices trailed away as they headed down the central hall to the bathroom.

Anna laughed, shaking her head as she took a large bowl and began filling it with mashed potatoes.

"Anna," her mother scolded halfheartedly, while filling a platter with slices of meat loaf.

Anna grinned. "That boy is growing so fast. He's already taller than I am." She took the platter and bowl into the dining room.

"That he is. Now, young lady, when are you going to tell me what's going on with you? How come you don't have to deliver dinners tonight? Are you and Janet in financial trouble? If that's the case, then Daddy and I can certainly help. Your brothers and cousin keep tossing money at us after we've told them we have no need for it. Just look at this huge house they insisted on buying."

"Mama, it's nothing like that." Anna kissed her cheek. "Yes, I have news but you have to wait. I want to tell both you and Daddy together."

Her mother lifted a beautifully arched brow. "It sounds serious."

"Not really."

"Well?" Donna prompted as she watched her daughter pull a pitcher of iced tea out of the refrigerator.

"Not even a hint."

Although Donna wasn't pleased by the delay, she followed her daughter into the dining room, carrying a basket of home-made rolls. Donna was an excellent cook and was very proud of her homemaking skills. Once the children came along, she had given up her teaching job to become a full-time mother.

"You sure didn't get that stubborn streak from me. It had to come from your father's side of the family."

Anna laughed, "Mama, everything looks wonderful." She began filling the glasses.

Lester had just said grace when Wesley let himself in through the back door.

"Hey," Wesley called out before he appeared in the dining room. "Something smells good." He was a big man, broad shouldered like their father, but he shared the same eye color and skintone as their mother. "Looks like I'm just in time." He grinned, rubbing his hands together.

"No food without hugs and kisses," said his mother.

Wesley laughed, but kissed his mother and sister before he slapped his dad on the back and squeezed his younger brother's shoulders.

"Looks good, Mom. Be right back." While Wesley went to wash his hands, Wayne drew up a chair from the sideboard and Anna went to get another place setting and silverware.

When Wesley was settled in the chair beside Anna, Lester asked while passing the platter, "What brings you here without your wife and our grandbaby?"

"Kelli is having dinner with two of her girlfriends from college and took the baby with her."

Donna didn't even try to hide her disappointment.

"Don't worry, Grandma. We'll bring Kaleea for dinner on Sunday."

"What do you have to say for yourself, Short Stuff? I heard about your new job," Wesley said to his sister as he filled his plate.

Anna scowled in exasperation. Evidently Gavin and Wesley had spoken. "And they say women can't keep their mouths shut."

"Is that your news?" Donna asked excitedly.

"What new job?" Lester joined in, as both parents looked pointedly at her.

"What's going on? Some kind of secret?" Wayne paused from forking mashed potatoes into his mouth.

"Not at all," Anna replied. "I was planning to tell everyone after dinner, until my big brother opened his gigantic mouth." She sent Wesley a sharp look.

Wesley shrugged as he helped himself to more vegetables. "What's the big deal? You're only going to be working for Gavin."

"Gavin? Doing what, young lady?" her father asked.

Anna kicked her brother under the table. "Cooking, Daddy. What else did you think? Surely you don't think Gavin is interested in me"—she glanced at her youngest brother before she finished—"that way."

Wesley roared with laughter. Anna flushed, clearly upset. "What are you laughing at?"

"I'd also like to know the same thing. Your sister is a very lovely woman. Any man would be lucky to have her." Lester frowned at his eldest son.

Wesley swallowed, taking a sip of his tea before he answered. "I didn't mean a thing. You know I love Anna. I'd never do anything to hurt her."

"Then what do you mean, son?" Donna demanded.

"It's okay," Anna interrupted. "We all know what he means. I'm not the glamourous, petite type that Gavin dates." She didn't wait for a response, but went on to say, "Gavin offered me a job as his personal chef. His younger brother is staying with him now and he needs help. I'll be cooking and will be there when Kyle comes home from school. And I'll stay over when Gavin is on the road."

"I didn't know Gavin had a brother," Wayne said, around a mouthfull of meat loaf. "How old is the kid?"

"Fourteen," Anna and Wesley answered at the same time.

Donna asked, "What about your catering business? Will this leave Janet in a jam?"

"That's right," her father added. "Surely you haven't given up on your business, now that it's been doing so well?"

"Of course not. Janet and I have talked it over. We've promoted our assistant, Krista Moore. You've met her. She has taken over my duties and we're making enough to increase her salary and hire another assistant. It won't be a problem. Gavin has offered me a very generous salary."

Anna couldn't explain the custody issue with Wayne sitting there. It had taken a while for Gavin to obtain temporary custody in order to be able to enroll the boy in school. Monday was a day of new beginnings. Anna would start her new job, and Kyle would start school.

"I'll be able to help him out, and while Kyle's at school, I'll have a chance to work on the family cookbook."

"Oh, that is wonderful." Her mother beamed with tears in her eyes. It was a project that she'd been longing to see completed. She jumped up and kissed her daughter. "I'm so proud of you. Your great-grandmother would have loved to see it come to fruition."

"It's a dream that's a long time coming," her father said. "Well, well. It looks like you're going to have to get serious about finding a publisher."

"Congratulations, sis." Wesley kissed her cheek.

Anna laughed, "Thanks. I admit I'm excited. Gavin has volunteered his kitchen for any additional cooking I might have to do for the business and the book. All he wants is regular meals on the table so Kyle can feel comfortable and at home."

"How long will his brother be staying?" Wayne asked as he helped himself to yet another serving of meat loaf.

"Indefinitely," Anna said quietly. She and Wesley exchanged a look of understanding.

It wasn't until later as Wesley and Anna were cleaning up the kitchen that he had an opportunity to say, "I'm sorry about what I said earlier. I didn't mean to hurt your feelings."

Placing a clean, wet plate into the draining rack, she shook her head, before saying, "You didn't hurt my feelings. Growing up with you all, I learned early to grow a thick skin. Besides, I knew what you meant. And I've seen some of the beautiful women Gavin dates. They're petite and drop-dead gorgeous."

"Any other man would be lucky to have you," Wesley persisted as he dried and put another glass in the cupboard. "Unless the guy is offering a ring, he'll have to go through me first."

"Surprise, surprise, brother. I don't need your approval to date." Anna scoffed at the idea.

"Please. You'll always be my baby sister. When you're ninety-six and I'm a hundred, you'll still be the baby," he teased.

She pushed his shoulder. "Time you got over yourself." More than ready to change the subject, she asked, "What do you think of this Kyle situation? Do you think their father is coming back for him?"

Wesley swore beneath his breath before admitting, "I think Gavin is on his own with this one."

"I do too. He's going to end up dragging that pitiful excuse for a man back here to take care of Kyle. But then there's no guarantee that old George will do right by the boy. Gavin is determined to see that Kyle gets a fair shake, but he certainly can't follow his father around every minute of the day."

"You got that right. I still can't believe that sorry son of a bitch left his own child." Realizing what he let slip, Wesley offered a hastily apology before he added, "Gavin doesn't know how lucky he is that his parents never married. George Reynolds isn't my idea of a decent man, let alone a good father."

"Mine either. Both Kyle and Gavin deserved better," Anna agreed as brother and sister exchanged an understanding look.

It was Anna who said, "I feel bad for Gavin, but poor Kyle is the one who's suffering the most. He is so resentful . . . so alone. It's almost as if the kid expects Gavin to turn his back on him as well."

Wesley shook his head, "That won't happen. Gavin believes in family. Look how much he respects Mama and Daddy."

"We were lucky, weren't we?" She smiled as she finished rinsing the last pan.

"Yeah," he replied. "I'm glad you're going to be able to help Gavin with this one. He's a good man."

"That he is." Drying her hands, she said, "Looks like we're all done. Now tell me all about my pretty little niece. Did you bring any new pictures?"

"As a matter of fact, I have a few on me." Wesley grinned as he reached for the sports jacket he'd left hanging over one of the kitchen chairs. He removed a bulky envelope from the inside pocket.

"A few?"

They both laughed.

Only after obtaining temporary guardianship status was Gavin able to enroll Kyle in school. It was the same high school where Anna's father coached and her brother attended.

Anna soon fell into the new routine. She arrived at six-thirty, prepared breakfast for Gavin and Kyle, and packed Kyle's lunch. She had a snack waiting for Kyle when he came home from school and prepared their evening meal. Her schedule allowed time for her to work on her cookbook.

Even though it wasn't expected of her, she often prepared something for his staff or Gavin, if he happened to be in during the day. No one was going hungry on her watch.

The nights Anna stayed over, she used the guest room across from Kyle's room. And she didn't mind taking Kyle to school or picking him up when Gavin wasn't available.

She especially enjoyed the part of the day when she worked at the kitchen desk on the computer, writing her family stories or testing one of her family recipes. The recipes often involved making adjustments for the modern cook. She had to remake a recipe until she felt certain she'd come up with the final one. She arranged for Janet to test each one in her own kitchen before she would consider it ready to be put in the cookbook.

"Mmm, smells really good." Gavin smiled as he watched Anna ladle a thick, fragrant, tomato-based stew into the huge soup tureen. A few weeks had passed since she started working for Gavin full-time.

She smiled, "It's Kedjenou de Langouste, one of my family's oldest recipes. It's generally eaten with rice." She handed him the tureen and a huge bowl of fluffy, long-grain rice to place in the center of the table.

She carried over a warm loaf of homemade, dark, crusty sourdough bread she'd baked that morning and a crisp salad.

"What's in it?" he asked as he held her chair for her.

"This one is made with chicken, onions, ripe tomatoes, a Geinea pepper, and garlic, ginger, and bay leaf. It's one of my great-great-great-grandmother Ella Mae's recipes. According to her diary, she was a cook for the McAdams family in Alabama before the Civil War around 1851. We know she was one of the few slaves who could read and write. Ella Mae learned to make this recipe from her mother in the Motherland. We think my mother's side of the family was taken from the Ivory Coast in West Africa."

Gavin flashed a smile. "Fascinating. Which country?"

"We're not sure, but we think Ghana."

"Well, this looks good. Doesn't it, Kyle?" Gavin asked.

The French doors had been opened to let in the crisp late-afternoon air, but now they were closed. The floor-to-ceiling glass wall of the Florida room overlooked the grounds, which consisted of a garden, tennis court, and swimming pool, as well as a jogging track and a fully equipped guest cottage.

On the evenings when she had nothing planned, Anna had dinner with Kyle and Gavin. Tonight she was only going home to an empty house and a romance novel.

Seated in his usual place, Kyle muttered, "If you say so."

Anna glanced up in time to see Gavin's mouth tighten. She'd been amazed at the changes he'd been willing to make to provide a wholesome home for his younger brother.

Gavin ate breakfast with Kyle each morning and drove him to and from school. Gavin stayed home most evenings unless he had a charity or business dinner. Then he either took Kyle with him or asked Anna to stay until he got back. There was no doubt in her mind that Gavin was determined to provide the stability he felt Kyle badly needed.

Gavin had taken his brother shopping to furbish his meager wardrobe. He'd also completely changed the room Kyle had been using. He let Kyle pick out his own bedroom furnishings, including a new desk, laptop computer, and stereo equipment. Yet nothing he did seemed to make much of a difference to the boy. Kyle was as angry and belligerent as the day he arrived. He spent as much time as he could get away with alone in his bedroom.

Anna often wondered how Gavin was going to gain the boy's trust. It quickly became a custom for Anna and Gavin to keep the conversation going during meals while Kyle did his best to ignore both of them.

She was delighted when she discovered Kyle loved baked ham, macaroni, and a three-cheese casserole, as well as her triple-layer chocolate fudge cake. She made a point of serving one or more of those dishes often. Kyle never said much, but he did clean his plate on those days.

Despite her best efforts the teen was, in her estimation, still too thin, although his dark skin and trimmed black hair were beginning to glow from good health.

Kyle didn't say he enjoyed the stew, but he emptied his plate and helped himself to a second serving. Gavin insisted that Kyle clean the kitchen after dinner, but today he surprised Anna when he excused Kyle from kitchen duty. Once the boy had left to finish his homework, Gavin began clearing the table.

Curious, she asked, "What was that about?"

"I'd like to talk to you before you take off, and I didn't want him to overhear."

4

"Sounds serious," she murmured as she began to fill plastic containers with leftovers.

"What am I doing wrong? I can't get the kid to open up," Gavin voiced his frustration.

"Give it more time, Gavin," she encouraged. "It's only been a couple of weeks."

When he passed her the soup tureen he'd just rinsed, their fingers touched. Anna felt a tingling all the way up her arms, and only careful handling prevented her from dropping it on the floor. Her hands were still trembling when she placed it in the bottom rack of the dishwasher. Despite her best efforts to ignore it, each day she was a little more aware of him than the one before.

"I'm out of my league and I know it," he grumbled. "I don't know a damn thing about raising a kid. What I know is football. Ask me how to get the pigskin in the end zone"—he snapped his fingers—"no problem. I'm a jock, not a child psychologist."

"You're more than a jock. You have a successful foundation that provides scholarship money for needy kids. Besides, you're also a successful businessman." She paused. "Have you heard anything from that private investigator?"

"So far he's found nothing worth reporting. I wish I knew where that sorry son of a—" He stopped abruptly. "Sorry, I shouldn't have said that. I know you weren't brought up around rough language. Lester would never stand for it."

Anna understood the pressure he was struggling with. And he was right. Her father had always insisted that the boys respect their mother and sister. He held to the belief that there were some things a man shouldn't say around a lady.

"I know you're frustrated, but you've been doing your best. Obviously it's going to take more time. And it's not just you. Kyle doesn't trust me either. It's understandable considering that he hasn't had one adult in his entire life that he could depend on. It was so different for both of us. I had my parents and you had your mother. That poor kid has never known the kind of love or security we've taken for granted all these years."

"You're right," he said thoughtfully. "Even though my mother died young, she was always there for me growing up. I know I'm fortunate."

"How old were you when she passed?"

"Nineteen. I was in my second year at State."

"I'm sorry."

"Me too. She made the difference for me. George had been out of my life more than he'd been in it. He'd come around long enough to break my mother's heart yet again, and then he'd leave. My mother was a loving, hardworking woman, yet I never understood what she saw in my father. He took her money and never respected her enough to give her his name. I asked her once why, and she told me I'd understand the day I fell in love. If that's love I want no part of it."

She suspected that his mother wasn't the only one hurt by his father's callousness, not that Gavin would admit it. Anna, her cousin, and her brothers had never lacked for love. Gavin, on the other hand, had grown up not knowing his father's love or support, just like Kyle.

A father in the home was what she'd always believed every child needed, especially a boy. Her own father had helped shape her brothers and cousin into strong, self-reliant men. In spite of the circumstances of his birth, Gavin possessed those qualities in abundance also. He was a man she both respected and admired very much.

"You were lucky because you had someone you could depend on, someone who believed in you. Your mother was responsible for the man you are today." She smiled at him as she admitted, "I'm sure she would be very proud of you."

Gavin grinned. "Thanks."

"You are very welcome."

She was switching on the dishwasher when he pulled her close and gave her a hug. Thoughtful for a moment, he asked in all seriousness, "How come no guy has hooked you yet? Or are you keeping secrets?" he teased. "That would explain the makeup and new clothes."

Unnerved by his closeness, Anna dropped her lashes. She took a step back because she enjoyed the feel of him a little too much. She longed to press suddenly heavy breasts into his muscular chest. She had to stop whatever this was . . . now.

Trying to make a joke out of it, she said lightly, "What does my love life have to do with anything?" Then holding up her hand, she snapped, "No. Don't bother answering that. You, Gavin Mathis, are as bad as the men in my family. News flash. I'm old enough to have a man if I want one." Frustrated, she asked, "Did that ever occur to any of you at all?

That I might be in need of a change? Or that I simply got bored? Enough already. I'm so sick of that question."

"Calm down, Anna. I didn't mean to make you angry." He ran soothing hands up and down her arms, unwittingly causing chills to race up and down her spine.

She closed her eyes as if trying to calm herself. "I apologize. I'm the one that overreacted." Deciding a change of topic was in order, she said, "Answer something for me. Why did you finish college before turning pro? So many guys do just the opposite."

He lifted a brow as if surprised by the inquiry, but he answered, "Too many. With me, however, it was what my mother wanted. And it was also what your parents encouraged both Wes and me to do. Pro athletes, as a rule, could have a very short career due to injuries."

"Have you every regretted that decision?"

"Never. The offers started coming in when I was still a junior in college. I wasn't ready to handle the money." He was somber when he admitted, "I regret that my mother wasn't able to be at my college graduation. Your family was there . . . that helped."

"It was a wonderful day . . . sunny, not a cloud in the sky."

"Yes, it was. You were still in high school, right?"

She laughed. "It was a day to remember. We all went out to celebrate afterward. Mama and Daddy were so proud of both you and Wes."

He grinned before he said quietly, "I want that for Kyle. He deserves so much better than what he's been given."

She nodded. Kyle didn't know it yet, but he was lucky simply because he had an older brother who genuinely cared about him.

"He needs to know that he's important to you, Gavin. Somehow you're going to have to find a way of showing him. Right now he's busy protecting himself from you."

Anna picked up a sponge to finish cleaning the stove and countertops.

Gavin plunged his hands into soapy water and began scrubbing pots and pans. "What makes you say that?"

"It's obvious. Kyle doesn't want to care about you and then have you toss him out of your life the first chance you get. That would hurt too much."

"I'd never do that."

Drying her hands on a paper towel, she had to tilt her chin up to look into his dark brown eyes. "I know that and you know it, but Kyle doesn't."

"How am I supposed to prove to him that he's wrong? He won't talk to me. Everything I say to him goes in one ear and out the other," Gavin said as he scrubbed the inside of a large pot.

"Doesn't matter what you say. What's important is what you do."

"Like what?" He sent her an impatient look. "I've done everything I can."

"Have you? Gavin, I've heard you say this situation is temporary. Kyle probably heard you too."

"That doesn't mean—" Before he could finish, the buzzer sounded, signaling someone was at the front gates. "Get that, will you? My hands are wet."

"Sure." Anna hurried into the spacious, cathedral-ceiling foyer. Her heels tapped on the marble floor as she paused in front of the intercom and monitor mounted into the wall. "Hello? Mathis residence."

"Natasha Baker here to see Gavin, please."

Anna had no difficulty identifying the petite beauty. She had seen her on Gavin's arm in the *Detroit News* society column on more than one occasion. In addition, Wesley had let slip that Natasha was more than a friend. After releasing the electronic gates, Anna went back into the kitchen where Gavin was finishing up.

"Ms. Baker." Anna went to the built-in desk where she worked. Her laptop had been left open. She began straightening the desk and collecting her notes. Because her back was to him, she missed his frown.

"You leaving so soon?"

"Soon? It's nearly eight." Anna was careful not to let him see her face.

"You don't have to run off. At least stay and meet Natasha."

"Another time." Anna reached for her briefcase.

"It won't take long. Stay," he insisted before going to answer the door.

While he was out of the room, she sank into the chair. She was upset, but why? Why should she care if one of his ladies came around? She and Gavin were friends, nothing more. What was her problem? Had she begun wanting more? Was that what this was about?

When she overheard Natasha's sexy laugh as the two approached the kitchen, Anna quickly stuffed her things inside her briefcase. She was closing the case while he ushered the African-American beauty into the room. She forced a smile.

"Natasha Baker, meet my friend and chef, Anna Prescott."

As the two women shook hands, Anna was uncomfortably aware of the way she towered over the other woman. Natasha was everything that Anna was not. Natasha was about five-one, somewhere around one hundred and five pounds, at the most. Her skin was a flawless, rich toffee tone and she was very beautiful. Her hair had been styled in a short, sassy cut.

"Nice to meet you. Any relation to Wesley and Devin Prescott?" Natasha asked with a generous smile.

"My brothers." Anna turned to Gavin. "I have to go."

"Please don't rush off on my account." Natasha smiled as she linked an arm through Gavin's.

"Excuse me," he said to Natasha before he moved away. He returned with Anna's coat.

"Thank you. See you in the morning." She picked up her case, glad her wallet and keys were in her coat pocket. She was too rattled to have to search for anything. "It was a pleasure meeting you, Natasha. Good night." She rushed out.

It wasn't until Anna was in her car that she realized she was shaking. Why was she so upset? Evidently it was one thing to know Gavin was seeing other women, but it was quite another to see him with one of them. All she'd known for certain was that she had to get out of there.

On the drive, she scolded herself all the way home. She had practically run out of the house. She had no right to be upset. After all, he was an unattached, attractive, and virile man. Just because her awareness of him was growing didn't mean she had any claim on him. It was none of her concern whom he slept with. She'd assumed Kyle was the reason he didn't bring his women home.

She wasn't fool enough to think he was suddenly embracing celibacy. If she wanted to keep herself in check, she had better concentrate on the three things that mattered—helping Kyle, cooking and finishing her cookbook. And forget any romantic fantasy that had crept into her thoughts. Their friendship was too important to put at risk.

Anna stayed over on Sunday night because Gavin was out of town on a road trip. On Monday morning there was no response when she knocked on Kyle's bedroom door. She called his name twice.

"Go 'way. I ain't going to school today. I don't feel good," he yelled.

Undeterred, she warned, "I'm coming in."

He was still in bed. He slept on the top bunk of a bed, the bottom of which was a futon. Beside the bed was his desk, on which sat a stack of textbooks, papers, and his laptop computer.

"What's wrong?"

"I told you I don't feel good." Kyle rolled over, turning his back to her.

"You can do better than that."

"I got a stomachache."

"Okay. I'll get the castor oil. That should fix you right up." She turned to leave.

"I'm not taking that stuff." Kyle yanked the blankets and comforter over his head.

"Then you need to go to the doctor. Get dressed while I call my family doctor."

"No." He sat up and glared down at her.

Anna sighed, determined not to let him get the best of her. Gavin wasn't expected back until the next day. Deciding on a different tactic, she pulled out the desk chair and sat down. "Okay. Tell me why you don't want to go to school."

He shrugged thin shoulders, keeping his face averted. "I just don't want to go."

"Has someone said or done something to upset you? Is there a problem in one of your classes?" When he didn't answer, she asked, "Do you want me to talk to the principal or one of your teachers?"

He looked horrified. "No. I just don't like the place. I don't see why I have to go anyway. I never had to go before, at least not every blasted day."

"Are you having trouble in class?"

All he would say was, "I just don't like it."

"When I was in school, I used to hate having to take swimming, but I got through it. You can too. If you're having trouble in one of your classes, I'll help you study."

"Why do you care? You don't know me."

"I like you, Kyle. You remind me of my second older brother. Devin hated junior high school. My dad had to threaten him to get him to go. We found out later that he was having a problem with some of the guys in his class. He knew my parents would really get on him if he got in a fight."

"So what happened?"

"My parents went to school with him and got it straightened out."

"It ain't that easy. I don't have parents to take up for me. I'm on my own."

"You have Gavin," she gently reminded him.

"For how long? Until he gets tired of me? Or the old man shows?" Kyle threw back the covers. Clad in a tee-shirt and pajama bottoms, he scrambled down and padded barefoot into the connecting bath. Just before slamming the door, he snapped, "I got nobody."

"That's not true," Anna yelled back, but she doubted he heard over the flush of the toilet. When she heard him turn on the shower, she left the room.

Some fifteen minutes later, Kyle, dressed in his customary baggy jeans and sweatshirt, headed for her car. His lunch was in his backpack, and he was munching on a scrambled egg and bacon-filled croissant.

When they stopped in front of his school, Anna placed her hand on his arm. "Have you thought you could be wrong about your brother?"

"I'm not wrong. The only difference between him and the others is money. He buys me clothes and stuff, but he can't wait to find our father so I'll be off his hands." Kyle hurried out of the car, slamming the door behind him.

Anna waited until he was inside the building. Kyle hadn't glanced at the other kids or spoken to even one of them. She began to wonder if the boy had made any friends at all.

Kyle was still angry with her when she picked him up after school and spoke only when asked a direct question. When she inquired about his day, he mumbled a vague reply intended to get her off his back. Yet she had the added assurance of knowing his stomach wasn't upset. He had eaten his breakfast, and both his afterschool snack and his dinner. He refused her offer of help with his homework. After cleaning up the kitchen, he went straight to his room and stayed there.

Anna worked for a while on the computer, transcribing some of her notes about her ancestors. Tired, she stretched and went upstairs. She stopped at Kyle's room to ask if he wanted to watch Gavin's game with her on the large screen television in the media room. He refused.

She went into the guest room and took a hot, fragrant bubble bath. After smoothing lavender-scented lotion on her skin, she changed into peach silk pajamas and a matching silk robe. Then she went down to watch the game.

It was late when Gavin let himself into the dark, quiet house. He was beat, and his body felt as if it had been used for a punching bag. All for nothing. They had lost the game. Everyone was in a foul mood. On top of that, Ronald Grayson, one of their best running backs, had broken a leg. No one put up a protest when the coach decided to return to Detroit that same night.

It was a lousy game. Every time he caught the ball, he got nailed. Wesley had played as bad as he had. The final score was a joke.

His footsteps were absorbed by the thick carpeting as he stopped to look in on Kyle. His brother was asleep. Gavin switched off the television and lamp. Closing the door behind him, he noted that there was no light under Anna's door, so he went on to his own room at the end of the hall.

After dropping his bag on the carpet, tossing his jacket

onto a chair, and kicking off his shoes and socks, he headed on bare feet back down to the kitchen.

He cut himself a big piece of chocolate cake and poured a tall glass of cold milk. He sat at the breakfast counter to enjoy the late night treat. One thing was for sure, he'd have to run a few extra miles on the track and put in some extra laps in the pool to get rid of the empty calories.

Gavin hadn't eaten this well since he left home for college. Home cooking every day was bound to spoil any man. Chuckling to himself, he rinsed out his few dishes and put them in the dishwasher. If he'd had a lick of sense, he would have hired Anna to cook more than one meal years ago. Regular meals weren't the only thing that had changed in the few weeks she'd been in his employ. For some indefinable reason, Anna's presence had made this huge house feel like a home.

He enjoyed sharing a portion of his day with her. Even Kyle seemed to be settling into the new routine, although the boy was far from happy. One thing was for sure, Gavin's progress toward shattering the kid's defenses wasn't enough to spit at. That kid had more walls around him, all designed to keep everyone out.

Deep in thought, Gavin walked barefoot into the softly lit media room. The volume of the television set was on low and Anna was curled up on her side, asleep on the oversize dark green leather sofa. Silently he crossed to the matching leather recliner, then sighed as he stretched out with his feet propped up. Grabbing the remote, he switched to an all-news cable channel. Despite the problems in the world, his assessing gaze wasn't on the screen.

Anna looked tired, making him wonder if Kyle had given her a hard time. Her incredibly long legs were tucked close to sweetly rounded hips.

There was no doubt, at least in his mind, that she was an exceptionally beautiful woman. She had the softest creamy brown skin that glowed with good health, and her black, tightly curled locks hung past her shoulders. She usually wore her hair up in a ponytail or pinned on top of her head, but tonight it was spread over the armrest and several locks rested on her generous breasts. His pulse quickened.

He had no idea why it bothered him that she had begun using makeup to emphasize her dark beauty. Her dark gray eyes were lovely. Her lips were full, naturally tinted pink, and looked as sweet and succulent as ripe strawberries. He couldn't pull his gaze away as she moistened those lips with the tip of her tongue. He frowned at the unexpected way his body reacted to the innocent action. He'd been doing that a lot lately, noticing and reacting to her femininity.

She looked so pretty in those silk pajamas, but the robe was open and hid nothing. His breath quickened even more as he watched the top two buttons come undone as she shifted onto her back, affording him a delectable view of her long, graceful neck down to the swells of full breasts. He couldn't stop himself from wondering if she was as smooth and creamy brown all over.

5

Gavin tried to make himself stop, but his hungry gaze lingered on those plump curves, then on her nipples, beading against the soft fabric. He shifted in his seat as his shaft hardened and lengthened. Her nipples were large, elongated. He not only wondered how she tasted, but he wanted to know the exact hue of those taut peaks.

He was forced to swallow a deep, throaty groan as his penis throbbed, ready to discover all her sweet secrets. His nostrils filled with her enticing scent. A man would have to be stone-cold and six feet under not to be aware of her feminine attributes.

For the past few years she'd been in and out of men's homes five days a week, delivering meals. On more than one occasion she'd refused to discuss her love life, which only caused him to wrack his brain speculating on which one of his teammates was the lucky dog. He hated the thought. She was too good for the lot of them. Yet there was no doubt that she was enough woman to fill a big man's arms.

He moaned as he watched her squeeze her thighs together. What in the hell was she dreaming about? Making love?

He swore softly. What was wrong with him? Had he lost his mind? Anna wasn't some groupie, following the team. This was Lester's daughter and Wesley's little sister he was drooling over. Both of them wouldn't hesitate to come after him if he dared to so much as touch her.

Lester Prescott had always treated him like one of his sons since that first time Wesley brought him home for the Christmas holidays. Wesley was someone he trusted and depended on . . . something that was rare in his experience. They were the two men he loved and respected the most.

The only other man Gavin had ever been close to was his high school football coach, Randolph Williams. Coach Williams had taught him how to dream and convinced him he could some day play pro ball.

When Anna mumbled softly in her sleep, Gavin's hot gaze settled on her parted lips. He swore beneath his breath. He couldn't remember being this horny, even during his rookie year with a fat paycheck in his pocket and a gorgeous woman on each arm. Evidently Gavin had gone without a woman for too damn long. He'd grown so tired of easy women, women who were more interested in what he was worth than in learning what mattered to him.

No matter what Anna thought the night Natasha Baker had dropped by, Natasha was really only a friend. Natasha worked as a counselor at Kettering High School and had insisted on hand-delivering the names of students eligible for his foundation scholarship program.

Although the two of them had gone out a few times, even slept together once, he didn't mean any more to her than she did to him. She, like most of the women he took out these days, had rarely been inside his home. Meaningless sex left him feeling empty inside, so much so that he'd gone without for nearly a year.

What had happened to all the real women? Someone a man could trust and genuinely care for? The kind of woman who would be there for her man, through the worst of it. Women like his mother, like Donna Prescott and Wesley's wife, Kelli. A woman like Anna.

Gavin believed that if Anna ever fell in love, she would give that lucky guy her entire heart. Her man would know that she would be around for the long haul. He would know that even if he lost every dime he possessed, he wouldn't also lose her.

"Hi," Anna said as she stretched and quickly covered a yawn. "Excuse me. I guess I fell asleep. I didn't hear you come in." She slid up to a sitting position, closing her robe and tying the sash around her waist. "We weren't expecting you until tomorrow."

Gavin covered his lap with a sports magazine. "Hey. Believe me, we were ready to practically walk back to Detroit after that game." Hoping the huskiness in his voice hadn't given him away, he focused on the television screen. When he glanced her way again he asked, "Did you see it?"

Unexpectedly he realized just how much she had been in his thoughts. He'd missed her. That truth caused his stomach to knot with tension.

"Yes, I'm sorry you guys lost. Did you get hurt? You took a couple of hard hits."

"Naw. Just a little sore." He smiled, warmed by her concern. "We couldn't get it going tonight," he grumbled. "Devin did a hell of a job against us. His aim was incredible."

"You get a chance to talk to him? How is he?"

"Just fine." He grinned.

Anna smiled, "Wes seemed to be having a bad night too."

"The understatement of the year. It's tough playing against your little brother." Then he teased, "Which team where you pulling for, Short Stuff?"

"Both of them." She laughed. "Do I look stupid?"

Gavin chuckled, enjoying the sparkle in her pretty gray eyes. "How's Kyle? Did he give you any trouble?"

"Physically, he's fine. He pulled a fast one on me this morning."

"Oh?"

"Oh yes. He told me he wasn't going to school today. Said he was sick."

"Was he?"

"I don't think so. He claimed he had a stomachache. When I offered him a choice between castor oil or a visit to the doctor, he decided he was well enough to go to school after all."

Gavin howled with laugher. "Some choice. Smart kid."

Her smile was a bit smug. "Yeah, I thought it was a good one. But I did keep an eye on him to make sure he wasn't really ill. The boy ate his breakfast and didn't bring back so much as a crumb from lunch. I fixed all his favorites for dinner. I figured if he didn't eat then he was really sick."

"And?"

"He cleaned his plate."

They grinned at each other.

Anna sent him a worried look. "Gavin, there's a problem. I asked him if he was having difficulty in school, but he wouldn't talk to me about it. I noticed on his way into the building this morning that he didn't speak to even one of the kids." She paused before she admitted, "I'm worried about him. I really don't think he has any friends. Do you recall him talking about anyone he has met in school?"

"No. He never talks about school. He never says anything about his classes or his teachers."

"That's not good. He keeps too much inside."

"Tell me something I don't know. Like what to do about it," he grumbled.

"I wish I knew. Even when he's home he spends too much time in his room. I think he feels that he's very much alone in the world." Reluctantly she added, "He needs to know that someone cares about him."

"You act like I'm not trying. Anna, I've tried everything I can think of to reach that kid. I've taken him skating, to the movies, tossed around the football, and shot hoops with him. Nothing. Hell, I even stopped in to talk to your dad the other morning at school, hoping to get some advice on how to reach the kid."

Gavin pounded his fist on the arm of his chair. "Nothing works. Can't get him to open up. Do you think I should try to get him some counseling?"

"That's something to take into consideration if all else fails," she whispered unhappily. "Maybe we're expecting too much too soon. Perhaps he just needs more time."

"Maybe." His frustration was evident.

"Gavin, have you tried talking to him? Letting him know he has a place here with you?"

"He knows that."

"Does he? I don't think so. What he knows is that this situation is only temporary until you find your dad. Then you're going to hand him over as soon as it can be arranged."

"He's supposed to be with our father. George is the one who should be raising Kyle, not me."

"Will you listen to yourself?" She glared at him. "One thing is certain, as long as you have that attitude Kyle isn't going to trust you."

"Anna!"

"Don't 'Anna' me, Gavin Mathis. Kyle has never had an adult in his life he can count on. His own mother didn't want him. His father sure doesn't. Tell me one reason why he should believe you're different."

"Because I'm trying to help him," Gavin shot back in frustration. "I'm his brother. I care about him."

"Then it's time to start showing some of that caring," she advised.

He just stared at her as if he could find the answer in her dark eyes. Finally he asked, "How do you know all those things?"

"I don't know for sure. I just know how I would feel in his situation. I don't believe that kid is ever going to open up to you if he thinks he's nothing more than an obligation to you."

"He's my brother."

"Is that supposed to matter?" She lifted a perfectly arched brow. "If you yell at me one more time, I'll pop you a good one."

"Sorry." He rubbed an impatient hand over his unshaven jaw. His voice was filled with regret when he said, "It matters to me."

"Then start showing Kyle that he matters to you," Anna stretched her arms over her head. "It's late. I'm going to bed." After tucking her feet into satin slippers, she stood up.

Gavin wasn't ready to say good night. He wanted answers, wanted to understand what made her so different from the women he dated. She wasn't drop-dead gorgeous, like many of the women he had spent his time with in the past. Yet Anna was attractive and definitely sexy.

She was so much more than her shapely breasts and hips. What made her special was her big heart. She wasn't afraid to extend kindness to others. There was no doubt that the man this woman chose to love would be one lucky man.

No. Her beauty had nothing to do with her dress size. It

had everything to do with the caring woman he was only just getting to know.

None of his thoughts was evident on his face when he said, "Good night, Anna. And thanks."

He didn't consider going to bed. There was too much on his mind for him to fall asleep easily. She was right. He had to find a way to reach his brother. There was too much trouble a kid could get into, especially if he was vulnerable.

Kyle wasn't the only one who suffered from being fathered by George Reynolds. Gavin knew what it was to be a boy longing for a caring father. It was more than missed fishing and camping trips. Gavin's own resentment went far deeper than the bitterness he'd seen in his brother's eyes. Kyle didn't realize it yet, but he had something Gavin hadn't had at fourteen. He had an older brother who cared.

George had no idea what it meant to be a man. He wore a pair of trousers but he certainly didn't know how to fill them. For him fatherhood involved leaving his sperm behind. George was nothing more than a sad, middle-aged boy. Hell, Gavin would have been shocked if the man had ever spent as much as a quarter on diapers or clothes, or even put one crumb of food in his or Kyle's mouth. In short, George was everything Gavin didn't want for himself or his brother.

Evidently it was his turn to make the difference in Kyle's life. How was he supposed to reach his brother? Anna was right. He had concentrated all his efforts on finding their father—not on reassuring his brother that he had a home there with Gavin for as long as he needed it. It was painful but true that Kyle didn't trust him any more than he trusted their father. Gavin couldn't even blame the boy. He had to begin putting his own frustration with this situation aside to help his young brother. Kyle's needs had to be a priority if he wanted to gain the boy's trust.

* * *

"Where are we going? Why aren't we going back to your place?" Kyle questioned his brother on Friday afternoon as he studied the passing scenery.

Gavin took his eyes off the road for a moment. "I thought you'd like to see your school's football game."

"Not me."

"Why not?" Gavin couldn't keep the surprise from his voice. Traffic was just starting to get congested.

"Not interested."

"Well, I'm interested," Gavin replied.

The football games were played on a field a few miles from the campus. They could see the cars from more than a block away and hear the high school band warming up on the side of the field. It was going to be tough to find a parking space in the lot.

"Don't you have better things to do?" Kyle shot back.

"Nope."

Kyle sent him a resentful look. "Then drop me off first."

"No can do. Anna has the evening off. There is nothing to eat at home but leftovers. We can get hot dogs and fries at the game." Gavin could see that Kyle wasn't thrilled but there wasn't much he could do about it.

Gavin had been trying to talk to his brother for nearly a week to no avail. Kyle had effectively shut him out. Cornering the kid in his room wasn't the way to get him to open up. Maybe attending a football game would allow both of them to relax.

Gavin got lucky and found a parking space in the lot. Judging by Kyle's face Gavin's luck was going downhill rapidly. With food in hand, the two looked for seats in the crowded bleachers. Kyle refused to say anything, let alone share any of the excitement in the team or even the pretty cheerleaders shaking it up on the field.

To make matters worse, Gavin received more than his share of attention. While Kyle's classmates didn't have much to say to Kyle, plenty of the kids and their parents recognized Gavin and wanted his autograph or to shake his hand.

Gavin was relieved when he spotted the Prescotts a few rows behind the home team's bench. Anna, her mother, Wesley, and his wife, Kelli, were all there. Wayne and her father were on the field.

"Looks like the gang's here." Gavin greeted them. "Where is Ralph?"

"Had to work," Donna said, waiting expectantly for a hug. "Hi Kyle."

Gavin was glad to comply while Kyle mumbled hello. On the Sundays Gavin played, Kyle spent part of the day with Anna and her family.

"How's it going?" Anna whispered once Gavin had taken the seat next to her. She and her mother had a wool blanket draped over their legs and were sharing a big bag of peanuts.

"Not good," he whispered back.

Anna offered Kyle some peanuts. She jumped to her feet like everyone else when their team was within a few yards of the end zone.

Gavin grinned for the first time that evening.

When their team scored Wesley yelled at Gavin. "Did you see that?"

"Yeah." Gavin laughed. "Your old man still has it."

"Damn straight." For that he received a glare from his mother and wife. "What?"

"You know what, Wesley Allen," Donna said.

Once everyone was seated Gavin patted Kyle on the back. "What do you think of that? I told you they were going to win."

Kyle grumbled, "How much longer?"

"Relax. Want another hot dog?" Gavin asked, spotting the vendor.

"No."

Everyone went wild when their team scored a touchdown, then took the extra point.

"How much longer?" Kyle asked again.

"It's the third quarter, less than two minutes on the clock. It won't be much longer. If you could just loosen up, you might actually enjoy yourself." Gavin quickly shut up, knowing he might as well be talking to himself.

When their team won the game, Gavin asked his brother if he wanted to go down on the field with him to congratulate Coach Prescott and the team, and the boy refused.

As Gavin and Wesley descended, it was Wesley who said, "No sense in asking you how it's going."

"That obvious, huh?" Gavin frowned. There was nothing he couldn't tell this man . . . well, almost nothing. Gavin was not about to share the lustful thoughts he'd been harboring since Anna had come to work in his home. Those thoughts had only grown more intense after the night he came home early and found her asleep on the sofa.

Besides the fact that his best friend would take offense, Gavin hadn't come to terms with what was going on inside his own head and body.

After restless nights due to a relentless hard-on, Gavin tried eliminating his desire in another woman's bed. It hadn't worked. He'd paid a late-night call on a lady he'd dated in the past. He quickly accepted it wasn't going to happen for him. Feeling like a dog, he'd said good night and gone home alone. But when he climbed into his own bed, he lay awake for hours recalling the sweet scent of a particular woman's skin, the long length of her shapely legs, and the feel of her creamy brown skin. Unfortunately for him, the legs, the skin, and the scent belonged to Anna Prescott.

Hell, he'd enjoyed sitting close to her during the game, inhaling her unique fragrance. He'd wasted hours wondering if there was a man in her life that not even her family knew about or trying not to imagine her in his own bed. He wasn't likely to get a chance to learn her feminine secrets. He'd never know how she'd look and feel with her beautiful body bare, waiting for his hands, his mouth, and his arousal.

Was he nuts? Anna Prescott wasn't the kind of woman a man fooled around with, not if he valued his life.

He knew he had to get a handle on this unrelenting hunger. How difficult could it be? All he had to do was keep his zipper up and his hands to himself. He had only imagined Anna staring at his mouth while they were talking earlier. She was not interested in his kisses. The sooner he got that into his head, the better it would be for all concerned.

"It will work out, Gav. Give it time," Wesley advised.

"You have no idea how difficult it was just to get Kyle to the game. Whoever heard of a kid who doesn't love sports?" Gavin grumbled. "I can't seem to reach him, man. He's living in my home, eating in my kitchen, but he won't talk to me, flat out doesn't trust me."

"So that's why you brought him here tonight."

"Yeah. I thought I could get him to relax a little, loosen up. Maybe realize I'm not the enemy."

"Man, you're pushing too hard. He's only been with you a little over a month."

"You sound like Anna. She thinks he'll open up once he realizes he's safe and that I'm not going to throw him out the first chance I get."

"She's right. From what you've told me, the kid hasn't had much stability in his life."

"And that's my fault?"

"Hell, no. He'll open up when he's ready. You're going to have to wait him out."

"Yeah, but the wait is murder," Gavin complained, as they threaded their way through the jubilant crowd to reach Coach Prescott.

6

"Kyle Reynolds, I'd like to see you after class." Mrs. Winston looked pointedly at the teen who was seated in the last row of her English class.

Kyle's heart jumped in his chest. He dropped his head, embarrassed by the snickers from the other students. He knew he was in trouble when she'd passed out everyone's paper but his.

"Class, finish reading your assignment. Be prepared to discuss it in class tomorrow. Anyone who doesn't participate will automatically have his grade lowered."

Kyle waited until the others had filed out of the room before he shoved his book and spiral-bound notebook into his backpack and reluctantly approached the teacher's desk.

Mrs. Winston held up the failing paper. When he took it without comment, she snapped, "Well?"

He shrugged, unable to meet her penetrating stare.

"Did you read the assignment?"

"Yeah."

"You can't prove it by this. This is your third failing paper. If you don't start doing better you're going to end up with an F on your report card." When he remained silent, her mouth tightened even more. "Evidently your schoolwork doesn't matter to you, but I am sure your guardian won't feel the same." She pulled out a manila envelope, folded his paper, and sealed it inside. "I want you to have Mr. Mathis sign this paper and bring it back tomorrow. You're not to come back without his signature. Do you understand?"

Kyle mumbled a confirmation as he took the envelope, shoved it into his backpack, and hurried out of the classroom. He hated the old prune face. Mrs. Winston had no right to give him all those failing grades. She could have given him a D for trying. But then he was not one of her pets, like Wayne Prescott, Anna's brother.

Kyle swore to himself as he moved through the nearly deserted halls. What was he supposed to do now?

Gavin would be waiting for him and would be furious when he learned that he was flunking English. It wouldn't matter to Gavin that he got A's in math and geography. All that would matter was the failing grade.

What was he going to do? So far he'd managed not to make his brother angry, but this was bound to cause him to lose his temper. What would Gavin do? Beat him like his aunt did when she was ticked off? Or put him out, even though Gavin knew he had nowhere else to go? Neither option was worth the risk. The only thing he knew for sure was that he couldn't let his brother find out about the paper.

Until now, no one in his family cared what he did in school. His mother had never cared if he went or stayed home. His elderly aunt had been too old and sick even to notice what he did. The old man dragged him from place to place, not caring what Kyle did as long as he didn't get in his way. He tossed a couple of dollars at him and told him to go buy something to eat as he walked out, headed for the casinos.

It had taken a while to get used to the way Gavin insisted he not miss school unless he was in need of a doctor, and that he do his homework every night. If Gavin didn't bring him and pick him up from school, then Anna did.

It still seemed strange the way Gavin and Anna acted as if they really cared about him. When Gavin wasn't on his case about school or picking up his room, his brother was trying to get him to talk . . . spill his guts. For what? What difference did it make how he felt? Did his older brother think he was stupid? He knew his stay in Detroit was only temporary. As soon as Gavin found their father he would be gone.

Despite his brother's speeches about caring, he wasn't fooling anyone. He'd heard Gavin on the telephone with his lawyer. And he'd also overheard Gavin talking to Anna. No matter what his two-faced brother said, he knew Gavin couldn't get rid of him fast enough. All Gavin wanted was his life back to the way it was before George left him behind. Why else would Gavin even bother to look for George?

Anna was no better than Gavin. She treated him okay, but she wasn't fooling him either. She was being paid to be nice to him.

Kyle was scowling as he walked out of school. He wasn't a punk. There was only one person he'd ever been able to count on—himself. To hell with all of them.

Anna was trying to adjust a recipe when the telephone rang. She paused in measuring dry ingredients to rinse her hands, gave them a quick dry before she grabbed the telephone. "Mathis residence."

She couldn't concentrate on anything since she'd just

learned from Kelli that Gavin had brought someone new when Kelli, Wesley, and Gavin had all gone out to dinner together. It shouldn't have mattered one way or the other. Yet she would be lying to herself if she didn't admit that she'd been upset since hearing the news. Knowing she had no right to care one way or the other didn't seem to change how she felt. Maybe, it was a good thing he was out of town.

"I'd like to speak to Gavin Mathis, please. This is Mrs. Winston, Kyle's English teacher."

"I'm sorry, Mrs. Winston, but he's out of town. I'm Anna Prescott, and I look after Kyle while Mr. Mathis is away."

"I really need to speak to Kyle's guardian."

"Perhaps there's something I can do to help?"

"There is a problem with Kyle. Kyle received an F on his last book report. His third failing grade. I gave Kyle the paper back on Tuesday and he was to return it the next day with Mr. Mathis's signature."

"Mrs. Winston, I had no idea Kyle was having trouble in school. As far as I know, Mr. Mathis hasn't seen this paper, but I will call him and let him know about the problem."

"Ms. Prescott, Kyle has not been in school in three days. Has he been ill?"

Alarmed, Anna gasped. "There has to be a mistake." Anna's heart raced with fear. "Are you saying he's not there?"

"I don't know where he's been, but I've spoken with all his teachers, and he has not been in school since Tuesday."

Anna was shaking so badly she had to sit down. "I don't know what's going on, but I promise you, I'll get to the bottom of this."

"Can I expect either Mr. Mathis or you with Kyle on Monday?"

"Yes."

"Thank you. Goodbye."

" 'Bye." Anna slowly replaced the receiver. "Now what?"

She looked around the messy kitchen, saw the half-finished bread dough, and threw her hands up in the air. "Forget dinner." She grabbed her purse and jacket and headed for the school. It didn't matter that she was two hours early. She intended to wait until Kyle showed up. She considered stopping in to talk to her father, but decided against it. She wanted to be parked in front of the school when Kyle showed his face.

Where had he been going each day? Did he have any idea the trouble a fourteen-year-old kid could get into on his own? Gavin was going to have a fit when he found out about this. Skipping school for three days? Anything could have happened to him.

Right on time, Kyle came strolling out of the building, backpack on as if nothing was wrong.

"Hi," he said as he threw his backpack into the backseat before he got in and buckled himself in the seat beside her.

"How was school?" she asked as she checked the flow of traffic before she pulled out.

"Okay."

"Just okay?"

"Yeah. I did all my homework, turned it in on time. Had a test in English. Can we stop and get a burger?"

"I'm making dinner," she said, recalling the mess she'd left in the kitchen. It didn't matter. None of it mattered, except the trouble this boy had gotten himself into. Anna didn't say another word all the way back to the house.

Kyle looked around the kitchen in disbelief, but instead of commenting he went to the fruit bowl on the counter and picked out a banana and took a small bottle of apple juice from the refrigerator.

Before he could leave the room, Anna said, "Mrs. Winston called today. She asked to speak to Gavin."

"Oh."

"Oh? That's all you have to say? Where have you been for the last three days? Where did you go?"

Kyle's dark eyes had gone wide before he recovered enough to shout, "I don't have to tell you nothin'! You're not related to me. You're not even Gavin's girlfriend. You're just the hired help."

Although disturbed by the angry outburst, she quietly insisted, "I don't like your tone, young man. I might not be related to you, but I'm responsible for you while your brother is away. I'm waiting for an answer. Where have you been all week?"

Dropping his gaze, he reluctantly admitted, "I hung out on the street, then went to the arcade a few blocks from school."

"Why didn't you feel you could tell Gavin or me that you were having trouble in school?"

"Are you going to tell Gavin?"

She shook her head. "No. You're the one who's going to tell him exactly what's going on." She watched his eyes go wide with fright as he put the food down on the counter and shoved his hands into the pockets of his baggy jeans. "What? You didn't think he'd want to know?"

"He don't give a damn about me. And neither do you. I'm just a responsibility." He turned to leave.

"Wait. You're not going anywhere until we've talked." She pointed to the tall chair at the breakfast bar. "Have a seat."

"I don't have to—"

"I said *sit*."

Once he was seated, she took a deep breath before she said, "First, you don't swear at me. Not ever. Second, you are wrong about me and your brother. We both care about you. After I talked to Mrs. Winston I was scared that something terrible had happened to you. As for Gavin, he more than cares about you, he loves you. Third, you are his business. You better believe he will want to know about this."

She went over to the wall-mounted telephone and punched in Gavin's cell phone number that was pinned to the cork board.

"Mathis."

"Gavin, this is Anna. Do you have a moment?"

Anna heard a woman talking in the background before Gavin covered the mouthpiece, and she couldn't make out what he was saying. Then he was back. "Sorry about that. What's going on?"

Did she imagine it, or was there a touch of impatience in his voice? She spoke as calmly as she could manage. "Kyle has something to tell you."

She wasn't about to embarrass herself by revealing her hurt feelings. She had no right to feel anything remotely possessive of Gavin. They both had separate lives.

"Something wrong?"

"Yes, there's a problem. Hold on." She held out the telephone. "Gavin wants to speak to you." Anna could tell by the boy's expression that the last thing he wanted was to speak to his brother.

"Gavin . . ." Kyle swallowed nervously. "I got in trouble in school." He paused before he said, "I got a bad grade in one of my classes. I couldn't go back to class until I showed you the paper and had you sign it."

Anna watched the boy's eyes water before he turned his back on her.

"So I didn't go back. And my teacher called Anna." Then he stiffened as he listened before he muttered bitterly, "Don't know. No." He handed her the telephone and left the room.

"Kyle!" Gavin was shouting into the phone.

"It's Anna. Hang on a second. I need to see where he's

gone." She took off after him. She watched him race up the stairs. She was several steps behind him when she said, "Kyle, that wasn't the best way to handle the situation. It will only make Gavin angry."

"Does it matter? He's not going to listen to me," Kyle tossed over his shoulder before he slammed and locked his door.

"What now?" Anna grumbled to herself as she crossed to pick up the bedside extension in the guest room she used while Gavin was away. "Hi. Sorry about that. I just wanted to make sure he went to his room. He's very upset."

"What did he say?"

"Nothing much. He doesn't think you're going to listen to him and he's defensive."

"He should be upset. Anna, what happened?"

She explained how his English teacher called earlier that afternoon and what happened after she picked up Kyle from school.

Gavin swore under his breath. "I don't like his lying to us. Nor do I like his being on the street. Anything could have happened to him."

"I know. It's scary. What do you want me to do?"

"I'm in the middle of a business meeting. I would take the first flight out but I'm scheduled to speak tonight at a scholarship dinner. Can you handle him for tonight?" There had been a problem in the Atlanta store. Gavin had flown down the day before.

"Yes. Thank goodness tomorrow is Saturday and we don't have to worry about school. His teacher wants to see you on Monday."

"No problem. Thanks for holding things together. I'll see you around noon."

"Okay. Bye." After she replaced the receiver, she remembered that the telephone was off the hook in the kitchen. As she hurried downstairs she reminded herself to concentrate on those things she could do something about. She began putting the kitchen to rights and then prepared dinner.

It had absolutely nothing to do with her if Gavin had been in a business meeting or with a woman. She was here to do a job, nothing more, nothing less.

It had been a long evening and an even longer night. Kyle came out of his room only to eat dinner. She checked on him again before she turned in for the night. The only sound coming from his room was the television.

The next morning she practically had to drag herself out of bed. She'd gotten so little sleep. In hopes of picking up her spirits, Anna dressed in dark pink denim leggings and a pale pink turtleneck sweater. She used a clip to keep her hair off her face, and then applied foundation, a little mascara, a touch of blush, and a cranberry shade of lipstick.

She needed to feel feminine and in control. As long as she held on to her reasons for being in Gavin's home, she would be fine.

Unfortunately, she could no more stop her awareness of him than she could stop breathing. She'd spent too much time noticing the way he filled a pair of tight jeans or the way the turtleneck sweaters he favored showed off his deep chest and powerful arms. The man had a body that a woman couldn't easily ignore, no matter how hard she tried. Lately she'd gone so far as to inhale when he came close. He smelled almost as good as he looked.

Kyle should be her sole concern. But the boy wasn't what kept her tossing, unable to sleep during the night. It was Gavin and the possibility of a new woman in his life. Who was she? How much did she mean to him? She considered asking Kelli, but thought better of it.

No matter how much Anna didn't wish to care for Gavin,

the truth was she did. Too much. She was close . . . too close to falling in love with him. Loving a man like Gavin would only cause her heartache.

After knocking on Kyle's door, she called, "I'm starting breakfast. Want anything special?"

"Not hungry."

She didn't waste time arguing. "It will be ready in twenty minutes. I expect to see you at the table."

The first thing she'd learned about Kyle was that he had a healthy appetite. Regardless of his mood, he never missed a meal

Generally, she didn't work at Gavin's on Saturdays, but with him out of town she had no choice. Kyle couldn't be left alone for days on end. He might think he was all grown up but he was still a child.

What she couldn't figure out was how Gavin was going to handle this situation without alienating the boy even further. Kyle didn't seem to feel any safer here with Gavin than he had with his father. Gavin had been trying, with little success, to gain Kyle's trust. It seemed as if every time Gavin tried to talk to his brother, Kyle managed to keep his protective wall firmly in place. Now with this situation at school, Anna just hoped Gavin didn't lose the little progress he'd made the past few weeks.

She prepared sausage, blueberry pancakes, and a pitcher of grapefruit juice. She was filling his glass with milk and her mug with coffee when Kyle walked into the kitchen. They were finishing breakfast when Gavin let himself in the side door.

Anna's heart started racing by the time he walked into the room, a briefcase in one hand and a leather garment bag slung over a broad shoulder.

"Morning. How was your flight?" She smiled. She watched him drape his leather jacket over a chair.

Gavin's dark eyes journeyed over Anna's features, lingering on her lips. "Hi. You look good. New outfit?"

"Birthday gift from my parents. Mama picked it out, and Daddy paid the bill."

"Good system if you can get it." He grinned. Gavin's eyes moved to his brother, seated at the breakfast bar. "Hey. Did you give Anna a hard time last night because you were ticked at me?" he asked as he removed a glass from the cupboard and helped himself to what was left in the pitcher of juice.

Gavin saw the boy flinch, as if he expected to be hit as he reached past him. "What? You think I'm going to hit you? Yes, I'm angry with you, but I'd never hurt you."

"That's not what I thought."

"Who hit you, Kyle?"

"No one."

"Kyle? Was it George?"

"No. It was my aunt when she got angry," the boy reluctantly admitted.

Gavin was frowning when he asked Anna, "Did Kyle give you a hard time last night?"

"No problem," she assured Gavin. "Would you care for breakfast?"

"No thanks." His gaze lingered on his young brother.

"How was the flight?" she asked again.

"Uneventful." Gavin must have noticed the way his brother had stopped eating the moment he entered the house, because he urged, "Finish your breakfast."

"Did your meetings go well?" She could almost feel the boy's tension. His hands were shaking as he waited for Gavin's reaction.

"Yes. We plan to open two more stores. Another one in Atlanta, the other in LA." Gavin referred to the chain of sporting good stores that he and Wesley jointly owned. With the new additions, they would own six stores across the country.

Leaning back against the counter, he suddenly said, "I'd like to see that paper, Kyle."

"It's in my room."

"Get it."

Once Gavin was alone with Anna, her eyes locked with his. "Gavin, please don't be too hard on him. He's already scared."

"This is something I have to do if we're going to move forward. I can't let him get away with skipping school," Gavin said tightly. "Then he really would have a reason to believe I didn't care about him."

"You're right." She carried their plates to the sink and began rinsing them.

Kyle's steps were dragging as he approached his brother with the manila envelope clutched in his hand.

She quickly dried her hands. "Excuse me. I'll finish later."

"No," Kyle pleaded with Gavin. "Can she stay?"

"Anna?" Gavin said.

Although surprised, she nodded her agreement.

"Sit." Gavin pointed his brother toward a vacant chair at the breakfast bar.

Anna and Kyle waited while Gavin read Kyle's assignment. When he finished, he was scowling.

"I can see why your teacher was upset with you." Gavin tapped the failing grade at the top of the page. "Are there others like this one?"

"Two more," Kyle mumbled.

After passing the paper to Anna, Gavin asked, "Was this worth the fear you caused Anna, having her wondering where you were and if you were safe?" He didn't wait for an answer but went on to ask, "What about your teacher? What about me? You lied to all of us."

Kyle's eyes went wide with fright.

"Did you even think about anyone other than yourself?"

"I didn't know what else to do."

"You could have come to me or Anna. You think we don't care, is that it?"

The boy shrugged his slim shoulders, but his face was tight with tension, and his eyes were suspiciously moist.

"Talk, Kyle. Do you believe Anna and I don't care about you?"

"I don't know."

"Well, you should know. Anna had no idea where you were. She assumed you were at school trying to learn something. How do you think I felt when my brother turned out to be a liar, just like our old man?"

"Don't know." He bit his lip, hanging his head.

"Well, let me tell you how I felt. Betrayed . . . disappointed. You lied to me as if I didn't care about you and as if you weren't living in this house."

"You don't care. Nobody does," Kyle shouted, tears streaming down his face. "The only reason I'm here is because you don't have anywhere else to send me. I'm a responsibility. You're no different than he is. You're his son, just like I am."

Gavin was shaking with anger. Being compared with George Reynolds was an insult. "Yeah, George fathered us both. That makes us blood. I've done my best to be a better man than he'll ever be. I want the same for you." He rubbed a hand over his unshaven jaw. "But this is about you. Why didn't you come to me with this? Or Anna? Let us know you were having a problem in school?"

"Leave me alone." Kyle pushed back from the breakfast bar so hard that his chair crashed to the floor.

Anna, seeing Gavin struggle to hold on to his temper, reached over and placed her hand on his arm, but her eyes remained on the trembling boy fighting back tears.

"Kyle, we would have found a way to help you. If you

need a tutor in English, we'll get you one. Neither Gavin nor I can help you if we don't know about the problem. Do you understand what I'm saying? All of this could have been avoided, if only you had trusted us to do what was best for you. It's all about trust."

"Why should you care what I do? No one else ever did." His thin frame was taut with tension, his hands clenched at his sides.

"You and I are brothers," Gavin insisted quietly, having gained some control over his temper. "Nothing and no one can change that. We're family."

"Gavin trusts you to go to school and do your best," Anna said as she moved to place her arm around the boy's shoulders and was relieved that he didn't immediately pull away. "But you're going to have to trust him to do right by you."

Gavin looked his brother in the eye when he said, "She's right. I plan to be here for you, whenever you need me. Even if I'm on the road, remember I'm only a phone call way."

She asked, "Are you having trouble in any of your other classes?" When he didn't answer, she added, "It's easy enough for Gavin to find out. All he has to do is visit each of your teachers. Is that the way you want it?"

The boy's eyes were incredulous as he met his older brother's gaze. "You would do that? Go to school to check on me?"

"You can count on it." Gavin folded his arm over his chest.

"But you don't have time to be—" Kyle stopped abruptly. "I mean—"

"I know exactly what you mean. Yes, I'm busy, especially during football season. But to me family always comes first. I will take time to visit your school and talk to your principal and every one of your teachers if that's what it takes to make sure you're doing your best. That's what I want, for you to do your best in every single thing you do from now on."

Kyle seemed genuinely shocked by the revelation.

"I want better for you than the kids you hung out with on the street for the past three days. I intend to make sure that you have a better life. Kyle, in this house, everyone has a job to do.

"Anna has her work, Mrs. Tillman, Gretchen, and Vanessa all have their work to do. I have mine and you, Kyle, have yours. Your job is to do well in school. This won't happen again. Do we understand each other?"

Even though he was upset, Kyle studied Gavin as if he was searching for the truth in his face. Eventually he said, "Yeah."

"Good. Now I want you to go to your room and redo this book report. In fact, I want you to redo the other two you received failing grades on."

"Mrs. Winston didn't ask for all that."

"I'm asking for it. Did your teacher give a list of questions to answer that might help you do this report?"

"Yeah."

"Did you use them?"

"No."

Gavin shook his head. "This time when you do the report use the guide she gave you. And I suggest you read those books again. So get busy because there will be no television or computer games until the work has been done to my satisfaction."

"Oh man. That's not fair."

"Before you leave, you owe Anna an apology for scaring her yesterday."

Kyle looked at her when he said, "I'm sorry I scared you."

She smiled. "I know."

Gavin waited until Kyle was in the archway that led toward the central hall before he warned, "You might as well prepare yourself. Before the weekend is over I want to see all the papers you've been graded on this semester."

It was all Ann could do not to laugh at the look of pure outrage on the boy's face.

"Oh man!" he said as he stomped off toward his room.

7

"**W**ell?" Gavin said once they were alone.

Anna quirked a brow at him. "What?"

"Do you think anything I said sank in?"

"I think it will. There is no doubt that you care about him. It's only a matter of time until he believes it."

"I hope so."

"What you did surprised him. You took the time to find out what he had done wrong, and you called him on it. I'd bet no one has ever done that for him."

"He had a mother and an aunt."

"But did they care about him? You saw how he flinched when you reached past him. And look at his reaction to you. He wouldn't have been so shocked if he'd been treated to that same kind of discipline when he acted up before. Growing up, we both knew what was coming if we messed up in school. But for Kyle, school was just a place he had to go. I get the feeling that what he did there didn't matter."

"I suspect you're right." He frowned, crossing his arms over his wide chest. "I nearly lost it for a moment there when I heard he'd been hit for acting up. And then, when he compared me to George. Talk about an insult."

"Yes, I could see that." She smiled, then realized her gaze had lingered on his mouth. If she wasn't careful, she would give herself away. She spent far too much time wondering how his lips would feel against her skin.

He caught her hand before she could move past him. "Anna, thank you for helping me with Kyle."

"That's what you pay me to do," Anna tossed back as she pulled free. Going to the sink, she busied herself with rinsing the dishes.

"You went way beyond a paycheck, and you know it."

"Gavin, you don't have to thank me."

She purposefully kept her back to him. She didn't want him to see how much his gratitude hurt. It wasn't what she yearned for. Trembling from both disappointment and fear, she was just recognizing that she hungered for so much more than she was likely to get. Gavin was an attractive, virile man. He had many women in his life.

"I was this close to telling Kyle exactly what I think of our father." He held his thumb and forefinger less than an eighth of an inch apart. "I'm afraid of what could happen, if I ever opened up. The kid doesn't need to know what I really think of the bastard. I had to remind myself that it's only because he fathered my brother that he's entitled to my respect and not my disgust."

When she remained silent, Gavin came to stand behind her. Cupping her shoulders, he asked, "Is something wrong? I mean, more than the obvious?"

"I'm just trying to finish up here. I promised Janet I'd help with the wedding reception this evening. It takes a lot of work to pull these things off smoothly," she hedged.

"No, it's more than that." Gavin turned her around to face him. Ignoring her wet hands, he lifted her chin. "What is it, Anna?"

He studied her eyes for a long moment before his gaze moved to her mouth. Gavin's breath seemed uneven as his head slowly dropped toward hers. His nostrils flared as if he were inhaling the lavender scent of her perfume.

She dropped suddenly heavy lids, unwittingly lifting her lips toward his. Then she felt the warm brush of his mustache before the heat of his mouth brushed each cheek, then the corners of her mouth.

"What are you doing?" she barely got out, her heart pounding like a drum.

"I think you know," he said, an instant before he covered her lips with his own.

He released a husky groan as he slowly enjoyed her soft mouth. Before she could formulate a coherent thought, let alone a protest, Gavin traced the outline of her full mouth with the tip of his tongue. She moaned, pressing her aching breasts into his firm chest while her arms encircled his taut waist. She needed more. When she let out a sigh, Gavin deepened the kiss, sliding his tongue into her mouth. They both groaned as he explored the interior, rubbing her tongue with his own. She held on to his powerful frame, feeling small against his large, hard-muscled body as she relished the heady taste and the smell of his dark skin. The kiss went on and on until only the need for air broke the seal of their lips.

"Oh, sweetheart," he moaned breathlessly.

She was quivering all over when she finally managed to move away from the heat of his big frame and the relentless pressure of his hard shaft.

"Gavin . . ." She struggled to sort out her emotions. "Why?"

"If you expect an apology, I can't give you one." He sighed heavily. "I'm not sorry. I did what I've wanted to do for some time."

Anna shook her head as she recalled the woman's voice she'd heard in the background when she called him yesterday. Was she yet another woman wanting his attention? And what about the woman Kelli mentioned? And she couldn't forget the lovely Natasha Baker. Anna was not prepared to have her name added to the long list of eager females vying for his attention.

She said tightly, "Excuse me. I have to get my things together. I'm due at home in less than an hour."

"Anna? Do you have to leave now? We should talk."

"I do. And there is nothing to talk about. Let's both forget this ever happened."

She nearly ran out of the room. The crazy thing was, he'd done exactly what she'd been longing for him to do. But it had been a colossal mistake. How could she want his kisses, especially when she knew he wasn't likely to ever settle for one woman? No thanks!

Suddenly furious with herself and him, she increased her pace. She was out of breath when she reached the guest bedroom. No way she was interested in sharing any man, even one as attractive as Gavin Mathis. She'd been a fool to welcome his kiss. Never again.

She was relieved that she didn't run into him on her way out. By the time she arrived home, she'd nearly convinced herself that his kiss was nothing more than a thank you for helping him out.

"Girl, what is your problem?" Janet whispered. "The serving tables are filled with delectable dishes while flowing champagne tinkles from the fountain. Except for the wedding cake waiting to be cut, everything is ready. The bride and groom are pleased, and the guests seem happy. Why are you standing here scowling?"

Anna released a sigh. "I'm just a little tired."

"Uh-huh. Keep your secrets, see if I care. I can find a hundred things that need to be done. Excuse me . . ."

Anna caught Janet's hand, whispering, "I'm not trying to keep secrets. I just don't know how I'm feeling."

"Tell me what happened to upset you."

"Gavin kissed me. I didn't expect it, and now I don't know what I should do about it. Janet, the man has women all over the city chasing him."

Janet blinked twice before saying, "I have one question. Did you kiss him back?"

"Janet!"

"Simple question. Simple answer."

Anna nodded, unable to hide the truth.

"Then you don't have a problem."

"How can you say that?" Anna demanded, and then blushed because she realized she'd raised her voice.

"Easy. Nothing happened you didn't want to happen." Before Janet could say more, Krista motioned for them. "Come on, we need to help Krista and Lori refill those side dishes. They're going faster than I expected. I hope we have enough food."

They didn't have a free moment until hours later when the four of them returned to Anna's house. Once her kitchen was clean, the women sat down for a much needed cup of hot tea.

"Today wasn't much of a day off, at least for you." Krista smiled at Anna.

"I survived." Anna smiled. "Congratulations, ladies. Everything went well tonight. Janet, that wedding cake was out of this world."

"It sure was," their new assistant, Lori Fleming, added.

"Thanks, you all. And I think Krista is right. We'd better get out of here and let Anna get some rest. You have to work tomorrow, don't you?" Janet asked as she stretched tired muscles.

"Not really. Since Gavin has a game tomorrow, I'll pick Kyle up for church and take him with me to my folks for dinner."

"Good work if you can get it," Krista teased. "I will see you ladies on Monday. Enjoy the rest of your weekend."

"I should be going too." Lori rose to her feet.

"You were both a great help. Thanks." Anna waved as they went out the back door.

Janet began collecting their teacups to rinse and put in the dishwasher.

Anna asked, "You have to go?"

"Carl is expecting me, but if you need to talk I can stay a few minutes," Janet offered.

"No, I don't need a babysitter. First I'm going to take a hot bath, and then I'm going to bed. I didn't sleep well last night."

"I can stay."

"No need. I'm fine, really."

"Okay, then." Janet collected her tote bag and coat. " 'Bye." She let herself out the back door.

After locking up, Anna went into her bedroom, her private sanctuary. The velvet, dark raspberry comforter and pillow shams on her queen-size bed were trimmed in pale-pink cording and the hardwood floor was covered in a thick, floral rug on a cream background.

Anna had a tough time relaxing, even after a soothing bubble bath. Her head was full of thoughts of Gavin. Why had he kissed her? It had come out of nowhere.

What had brought on the change? Certainly she hadn't said or done anything to make him think she'd welcome his kisses. Or had she?

There was no denying, she had seen it coming. He hadn't rushed the kiss. His movements had been slow, even deliberate. She moaned unhappily, recognizing that she shared some of the blame. She'd welcomed that kiss. Before her common sense had kicked in, she'd been caught up in the heat and sheer pleasure of the kiss. She hadn't wanted it to end.

Anna covered her face with her hands as she let out a sad little moan. It all boiled down to one single fact. She had no business responding to his kiss. What had happened to her brain? She knew he was involved with other women. Stupid, stupid. She had no one else to blame. With her luck she was bound to fall flat on her face the instant he showed up with any one of the women who followed him around like sheep. Where was her pride?

It was best if she did exactly what she'd asked him to do . . . forget it ever happened.

"Why didn't you tell me that you and Wayne are in some of the same classes?" Anna asked Kyle the next evening as she drove away from her parents' home.

"Didn't matter." Kyle shrugged. "We only see each other at school."

"But you've been coming with me on Sundays whenever Gavin has a game."

"What's the big deal? It's not like we're friends."

Anna said no more. She was just glad dinner had gone well, despite the fact Kyle never said much. For once the boy wasn't so guarded, even managing to laugh at one of her father's corny jokes. He certainly enjoyed the meal, judging by the amount of food he put away, and he seemed to take Ralph's good-natured teasing in stride.

She had been pleasantly surprised when Kyle accepted Wayne's invitation to go to his room to listen to a new CD and play a video game. The boys had been gone so long that she had been forced to call him and let him know it was time she got him back home. Both boys had school in the morning.

Anna had anxiously waited to see if Gavin might stop by after the game, especially since Wesley had come by to eat and visit. Of course Kelli and the baby were already there. Perhaps Gavin had a date? She'd never know for sure because she was not about to ask Wesley, who was bound to know Gavin's plans.

Gavin had scored the last touchdown with less than a minute to go. The Lions had won the game. Even Kyle seemed pleased by his big brother's success.

"Did you know Wayne does well in English but has problems in math?"

Kyle looked surprised. "I thought a kid like him would do well in everything."

"What do you mean 'a kid like him'?"

"You know. He's always had a mother and a father . . . a real family."

"Everyone has problems." Suddenly she had an idea. "Since you're so good in math, how do you feel about tutoring Wayne? In exchange he can help you out with English. What do you think?"

"Don't know." Kyle was thoughtful for a time before he asked, "Do you think he would want to help me?"

"I can ask him. This would be a two-way deal. Are you willing to help him?"

"Sure."

"Good. I'll talk to Wayne and let you know what he says."

"Your folks won't mind?"

"Why should they? As long as you two spend time studying and not goofing off, I don't see why they would."

"What about Gavin?"

"You're going to have to ask him." She turned into Gavin's drive, stopped at the gates to punch in the security code before she followed the curve to the right. She slowed to a stop at the side of the house. She spotted Gavin's Lincoln Navigator parked in front of the garage. The outside lamps had been turned on.

"Looks like Gavin's home," Kyle said as he unfastened his seat belt. When she made no move to get out of the car, he asked, "You coming in?"

"Not tonight. It's late. I'll see you in the morning. Congratulate your brother on the win for me."

"Okay. Bye." Kyle shoved his hands into his pockets as he made his way to the side door.

"Good night," she called, but waited until Kyle had gone inside before she turned the car around and headed home, calling herself every kind of coward she could think of.

Anna felt as if she had her emotions under control as she let herself into Gavin's house on Monday. This morning was no different from any other, she assured herself as she put her things away. She tied a floral bib apron around her waist before she scrubbed her hands and nails with a small brush. After filling the coffee maker, she assembled and measured the ingredients for waffles. She quickly had the batter ready to go. Using the juicer she made a morning energizer by juicing fresh oranges, pink grapefruit, carrots, and a touch of ginger root.

Some twenty minutes later, Gavin said, "Good morning. Something smells good." He smiled as he walked up behind where she was working at the center island.

"Good morning," she said as she removed another batch of waffles from the waffle iron. When he leaned down to kiss her cheek, she stepped out of reach before he could make contact. She tried not to notice how nice he looked or how good he smelled.

"Everything is ready. Have a seat." She set a full plate in front of him at the breakfast bar.

"What's wrong?" He crossed his arms over his chest.

"Nothing. Your breakfast is getting cold."

"You're angry."

"Hi," Kyle said as he came into the room. He took the pitcher out of the refrigerator and filled both his and Gavin's glasses before taking his seat.

Anna smiled at him. "Morning. Did you sleep well?"

Kyle grinned sheepishly. "Yeah."

Gavin moved to fill the coffee mugs before taking the tall chair beside Kyle. It was then he noticed only two place settings. "You're not joining us?"

"No, I've already eaten." She busied herself with filling Kyle's plate.

"Looks good." Gavin smiled at her.

"Thanks." Grabbing a carton of milk from the refrigerator, she poured Kyle a glass. "Kyle, did you finish all your schoolwork?"

"Yeah." He glanced at his brother. "He's going with me to talk to Mrs. Winston."

"Good." Anna turned away from Gavin's searching gaze to begin filling the sink with hot sudsy water.

There was so much tension in the room, or at least it felt that way to Anna. She was relieved when first Vanessa, Gavin's secretary, and then a few minutes later Gretchen, Gavin's assistant, arrived. Yet she couldn't seem to breathe until Gavin left with Kyle.

She'd clearly made a fool of herself. If she couldn't face him, why hadn't she called in sick? What was she afraid of? All he'd done was kiss her. If she didn't want his kisses, all she had to do was tell him. Gavin wasn't the type to take advantage of women. He didn't need to, considering the women chasing after him.

What was with him anyway? Had he been trying to smooth things over? Or had he been trying to pretend nothing had happened on Saturday morning? Pretending seemed like a pretty good idea to her. It was what she'd been trying to do. She would much rather do that than deal with her own alarming awareness of him.

She sat down at the desk and turned on her laptop. It didn't take long before she found she couldn't do that either. She couldn't concentrate. Frustrated, she reached for the telephone even though it was only just after eight. Her feet tapped against the flooring as she waited for the telephone to be picked up on the other end.

"Prescott residence."

"Morning, sis. You busy?"

"Hi, Anna. I like it when you call me that." Kelli, her brother's wife, laughed. "No, I'm not busy. Who can sleep with a baby in the house? What's up?"

"Can I stop by? I need to talk."

"Sure. You can help with the laundry."

"I'm on my way."

Gavin was relieved that the interview with Kyle's teacher and the principal had gone so well. Most importantly Kyle seemed to fully grasp the gravity of the situation. The boy wasn't pleased to be the center of so much attention.

There was no denying that Gavin had been scared when he learned that his little brother was essentially on the streets for three days. It was clear the boy was used to solving his own problems. It infuriated Gavin that Kyle had had no one he could depend on for most of his young life.

It was good Gavin hadn't run into George in the past few days because he doubted he could stop himself from going after the bastard with his fists. What kind of life was that for a kid? Growing up with no security, no one he could trust? Kyle deserved better. And it was up to him to make sure that his brother got what he needed, with or without their father's cooperation.

He'd been late for practice but that couldn't be helped. By the time he headed back home, it was early afternoon. During the meeting with the principal and Mrs. Winston, Gavin wished Anna had been with him. He could have used her support. Judging by the way she had moved away from him that morning, she didn't want him anywhere near her. If that was the case, it was time she told him to his face.

He had a little over an hour and half before he needed to pick up Kyle. Time enough for that long-awaited talk with Anna. His brow immediately creased as he noticed the cars parked in the drive. Everyone's but Anna's.

"Where is Anna?" he said to his assistant as he walked into the drawing room that had cleverly been converted into an office.

Gretchen glanced up from the computer screen. "She had to go out but will be back in time to prepare dinner. She left a tray in the refrigerator if you're hungry. Anything I can do for you?"

He shook his head. Rather than tackle the paperwork waiting on his desk, he turned toward the stairs.

"Mr. Mathis," Vanessa called. She'd been at her desk on the telephone when Gavin came in. "You had a call from your lawyer. Paul wants to discuss the changes you want to make in the foundation's scholarship program. There was another call from Carl Johnson. He left his cell phone number, and there was also a call from Dexter Washington, the director of the Malcolm X Community Center. They want to schedule a football clinic in April with you and Wesley."

"Anything else?"

"That's it."

"Thanks, Vanessa. Leave the messages on my desk." Gavin continued on upstairs to his rooms.

Anna knew he wanted to talk to her. What the hell kind of game was she playing with him? Then he stopped suddenly. Game? What was he thinking? That was not her way. She didn't play games with anyone.

She'd agreed to be his personal chef, not his lady. He was the one in the wrong. He had no business letting his erection do his thinking for him. He had no idea how it had happened. All he knew was that the more he was around her, the more intrigued he became by the woman rather than what she placed on his table each day.

To make matters worse, he'd started dreaming about her. Images of her soft and curvy beneath him filled his dreams night after night. Anna was family, just as much a part of his life as Wesley and their folks, Devin, Ralph, and Wayne. Gavin didn't need to be told that his best friend and business partner would come after him with both fists swinging if he had any inkling of the erotic fantasies Gavin entertained about his baby sister day in and day out.

Gavin had been fighting this need to taste her full lips for weeks now. If he was brutally honest with himself, he'd admit that he wanted more than one taste. He ached for the woman.

The other day he'd been so damn needy when he had taken her into his arms that he'd lost it. Before he knew what hit him, he'd been captivated by the luscious shape of her lips. His control shattered the instant she'd parted her lips and made no effort to push him away. He'd been aroused from the moment he'd touched her and had known he couldn't wait to sample her incredible sweetness.

He groaned, recalling that one sip from her lips and he was powerless to stop himself from tightening his hold until her curves rested against him. Her breasts had been unbelievably soft, her nipples hard against his chest. He wanted . . . oh how he wanted to taste every inch of her. And those beautiful long legs of hers . . . all he could think about was imagining them locked around his waist. Before he realized what was happening, he had deepened that kiss, craving more . . . so much more.

That one incomparable kiss had changed everything between them. It had certainly allowed him to know what he'd been missing. He'd been paying for it every day since.

Gavin didn't need to look into her eyes to know he'd shocked her, possibly frightened her. Hell, she'd jumped a foot when he attempted to kiss her nape and cheek. Why was she acting like a virgin? He knew Anna had dated all through college and after.

"Where is she?" he grumbled to himself as he chanced into exercise clothes.

They needed to talk privately and soon. Maybe he needed to back off, leave well enough alone? If she wasn't interested in more than friendship, who was he to force the issue? Anna was Wesley's baby sister, after all. Yet, he couldn't forget her sweet responses. She felt so good in his arms.

8

"You've been here a half hour and you haven't said one word about what's bothering you." Kelli Warner-Prescott was a beautiful woman with full curves and long, thick, black hair she wore in a French twist. She'd been a plus-size model doing print ads and fashion shows in New York, London, and Paris before she married Wesley. These days, she concentrated on her husband and their six-month-old daughter, Kaleea.

"I know." Anna smiled down at her little niece snuggled in her arms. Kaleea's tiny thumb was firmly wedged in her mouth.

"I hate when she does that. It's going to ruin her teeth."

"What teeth? She doesn't have any yet."

"So? Here, let me take her and put her down for a nap. Wes already has her spoiled. I've told that man a hundred times that

I don't want a rotten kid, but will he listen? No," Kelli said with a sparkle in her eyes. There was no hiding her happiness.

"In our family, you're not a Prescott unless you're spoiled. . . . that's called love," Anna teased. "Please, let me put her down. I hardly ever get to."

Once they had the baby settled in her crib, they tiptoed out of the beautiful pink and cream room.

"Okay, now tell me what's going on. You hate your new job? Or you love it, but Janet can't handle the business without you?"

They sat side by side on the sectional sofa in the maple-paneled room.

"No, this has nothing to do with my job." She studied her hands before she confessed, "I'm scared, Kelli. I think I've gone and done something I promised myself I'd never do."

"What?" Kelli reached for Anna's hand and gave it a squeeze.

"You promise not to breathe a word of this to Wes?"

Kelli hesitated a moment. "We don't keep secrets from each other."

"I know. I wouldn't ask, but I don't want him to know. You know how he is about me."

"He's overprotective." Kelli reluctantly nodded. "I promise. What have you gone and done?

"Fallen in love," she muttered miserably. "All I can think about is him."

"It happens to the best of us." Kelli smiled.

"Not to me. I'm old enough to know better."

"Nobody's that old. Who is it? Is it someone I know?"

Anna was scowling when she admitted, "It's Gavin. Don't laugh."

"Believe me, I'm not laughing." Kelli was thoughtful for a time before she asked, "Are you sure? How long has this been going on? You've only been working for him for a few weeks."

"Nothing is going on. And I've been working for him for almost three years."

"Yeah, that's true. If nothing is going on, then what are we talking about?"

"I have no idea what's wrong with me. Nothing like this has happened to me before. Why now, when I just got this ideal job, where I have time to work on my cookbook while helping a friend? I'm going to have to quit." Anna wiped at a sudden rush of tears,

"Oh honey. Don't cry. It's nothing to cry about."

"Oh yes, it is. You were the one who told me he's seeing someone new."

"Taking a new woman out to dinner doesn't necessarily constitute seeing someone new. As far as I know it was one date," Kelli insisted. "Now start from the beginning. What makes you think you are in love with Gavin?"

"I was attracted to him before I started working out of his home. Seeing him day in and day out hasn't helped. If anything, my feelings have gotten stronger. I've been helping him figure out how best to take care of his brother, but you know all that."

"Yes, I do. What I don't know is how you get from helping with Kyle to falling in love."

"I first realized that I had a reason to worry when one of his lady friends stopped by the house one evening. Natasha Baker. Do you know her?"

Kelli nodded. "I've met her. She works for the Detroit school system. She and Gavin went out a while back."

"He mentioned that they were old friends, and that she was bringing over a list of students eligible for his foundation's scholarship program. He insisted that I stay and meet the woman. Believe me, that was the last thing I wanted to do.

Kelli, I was so upset when I saw how tiny and gorgeous she was . . . just his type. When he introduced us, I smiled and nearly broke my neck trying to get out of that house."

Anna covered her face as if she could hide the embarrassment she couldn't get away from. "You don't have to tell me it's none of my business who he's seeing. I know that. The point is, I care too much."

"Is that it?" Kelli asked. "You think you're falling in love with him because you don't like him seeing other women?"

"There is more. He came home unexpectedly from a road trip while I'd been staying overnight with Kyle. I was asleep on the sofa wearing nothing more than silk pajamas and robe when he came in. When I woke up, I realized he'd been watching me sleep.

"We started talking about ordinary things. Kyle and the game. The next thing I knew, I couldn't take my eyes off him. I'm suddenly fascinated by his mustache, the shape of his lips, his body . . . everything. It was as if I took a hard look at the man and really liked what I saw. I couldn't stop staring at him. I ached for him. Kelli, I've been longing for him to kiss me. It's crazy."

"Gavin is a good-looking man. There is nothing wrong with being attracted to a man. It could have been Samuel Jackson"

"It wasn't Samuel Jackson. Gavin is my friend and my brother's best friend and business partner. The same man I've known since I was in my teens."

"Anna, this isn't the end of the world."

"Easy for you to say. It's not going away. In fact, it gets worse. Kelli, I caught him looking at my breasts, at my butt."

"Well, he is a man. There is nothing wrong with his hormones. Honey, that's his job to look," Kelli teased. "But it doesn't necessarily mean anything."

"So, why did he kiss me?"

"He kissed you?"

Anna nodded. "What's worse, I kissed him back."

"Well now." Kelli blinked in surprise. "He's attracted to you."

"Sure. Just like the cow jumped over the moon. Come on, Kelli, that's not likely."

"Why not? You act like there's something wrong with you."

"There is something wrong with me if I want that one man. Gavin Mathis has half the women in Detroit after his gorgeous behind."

"Will you listen to yourself? So what? It doesn't count unless he's doing the chasing. What if he's attracted to you, Ms. Anna Prescott?"

"Don't I have enough problems without look for more?"

Kelli shook her finger at Anna. "The problem is, you're scared that he is attracted to you. You don't even want to find out if it's true. You're too busy running the other way."

"I'm not."

"Okay. Would you care for something to drink?" Kelly rose and walked across to the large sunny kitchen.

Anna was clearly annoyed as she followed. "Okay? Is that all you have to say?"

"What do you expect me to say? You made it very clear that you don't wish to be interested in the man. It's not like you're asking for my advice on how to attract the man, now is it?"

"No." Was that what she'd been doing? Was she running as fast and as far away as she could get?

"So that's the end of it." Kelli hid a smile as she watched Anna beneath the fall of her lashes. She took a pitcher of lemonade from the refrigerator. "If Gavin tries to kiss or touch you, and you don't care for it, all you have to do is tell Wesley and let him handle it."

"Are you nuts?" Anna nearly shouted. "I don't want Wesley to even know about this."

"Why not? You know he adores you and would love to stick his nose in your business." Kelli laughed.

Anna shook her head vehemently. "Stop teasing, Kelli. I mean it. Why do you think I came to you and not him? Besides, you know how protective the men in our family can be." Anna sighed tiredly. "It's ridiculous. I often wondered if one of the reasons I couldn't seem to find a boyfriend in high school was that my brothers and cousin were scaring them off."

"Now that wouldn't surprise me." Kelli filled two glasses. "So what are you going to do?"

"Nothing. He isn't going to touch me. I'm surprised Gavin hasn't apologized for the kiss."

"Is that what you want?"

"No," she stammered. "I mean . . . yes."

Kelli leaned back against the counter. "You mean yes, but you're not ready to admit it."

"How can you say that?"

"Easy. Evidently he really looked at you in those silk pajamas. And you liked him watching," Kelli grinned. "So that's why you bought a new wardrobe . . . Gavin."

"No, he isn't the reason. I needed a change. It had nothing to do with him."

"Well, you got more than you expected from the new look. You caught Gavin's eye. He saw a beautiful woman. There isn't a thing wrong with that."

"Oh, Kelli." Anna sighed. "What am I going to do?"

"Simple. You're going to do what any red-blooded American woman would do. Girl, we're going shopping."

"I don't know why I let you talk me into this," Anna complained, as she took her eyes off I-75 and they approached the exit for the Sommerset Mall in Troy. "What is a new outfit going to do? And we lied to my mother."

"We didn't lie," Kelli replied. "We told her the absolute

truth. I needed her to watch the baby while we went shopping."

"My mother is not stupid. She knows it's not like me to take part of a workday off to shop for clothes. She had to wonder why I came along."

"Who said anything about clothes? She assumes I'm planning a special dinner for Wesley for our anniversary next week. Naturally I'd drag you along to help."

"When did you tell her that?"

"While you were setting up the playpen for Kaleea."

"Oh."

"You are going to help me plan a special menu for our anniversary, aren't you? And you can help me pick out a leg of lamb on the way back."

"We don't have time for all that. I have to get back and cook tonight."

"Girl, please. I know you've got something in that freezer. We've got things to take care of. You do have your credit card, don't you?"

Anna laughed. "I do."

"Good," Kelli said as Anna pulled into the parking lot near Saks. Within minutes they were in the dress department and Kelli was fanning the racks. "What do you think of this one?" She held up a short and sassy black dress.

"Where are the sleeves? And there's no back."

"Anna, please. As much as we work out, we are both toned . . . we're just big girls. Now get serious. Do you like it?"

Anna reluctantly nodded, "Yes. But I doubt I can get one thigh in the thing."

"Sure you can . . . it stretches, darlin'." Kelli giggled.

"It's too tight," Anna shook her head.

"Honey lamb, that's the idea. What do you think of this

one?" She held up a midnight blue, strapless, floor-length silk sheath.

Anna shook her head. "Where will I wear that?"

"You never know. This one shows enough leg to knock him on his head. I might have to get one in green. Wesley has been a bit too complacent lately. I may need to shake him up a bit. I think both the navy and black velvet will look great on you." Kelli set them aside before starting again. "Oh, look, they have this one in red. You could wear it to one of those charity dinners Gavin is always invited to. Now all we have to find is the right accessories."

"There are no straps on either one of them. Besides, I have too much for that top," Anna complained even as her heart raced at the possibility of setting Gavin on his head.

"You don't have to worry about keeping it up. Girl, who needs straps with your glorious bustline? We're giving that man something to look at and wish for."

Anna just stood there with her mouth open, wondering if she would ever have the nerve to put any of them on.

"You go try these on while I run down to the lingerie department and get some serious underwear. What size bra?"

Anna told her, then said, "Wait, you need my credit card."

"This is on Wes and me. Be right back."

"I thought we were getting everyday clothes."

"We'll get to them later." With that, Kelli gave her a push in the general direction of the dressing rooms before she took off.

A smiling saleslady said, "I'll just place these in the first dressing room for you."

"Thank you," Anna mumbled, but was anything but appreciative. What had she put into motion?

How two dresses turned into six Anna didn't have a clue, but there were six dresses waiting for her to try on. Dresses she would never under normal circumstances consider wearing. Yet there was nothing normal about what was going on inside her whenever Gavin came within kissing range.

She knew she had no right to be shocked, but she was when Kelli returned with two filled shopping bags. "Is all that underwear?"

"You asked for my help. Besides, this is my favorite store. What's a nightie or three between sisters. You can't go wrong with me along. Put on that black one while I go look for a cashmere shawl. Let's pick up some casual things, too."

Anna lost every bit of modesty she had left with both Kelli and the saleslady sticking their heads into the dressing room. Anna admitted she was pleased when they finally walked away from the shopping center.

"It's astounding how fast you can spend money when you really try. We can't get all this stuff into the trunk. Some of it's going to have to go in the backseat."

Kelli grinned, thoroughly pleased with herself. "That was fun. We have to do this again. So, sis, what are you going to wear tomorrow?"

"Your guess is as good as mine," Anna said vaguely as she closed the trunk.

"Just as long as it hugs your curves, it doesn't matter. Do me a favor and get rid of all your old things. Show some cleavage."

"Kelli, he's going to notice."

"Darlin', he has already noticed, remember? He may need glasses after he sees that navy number."

"I don't want him to think I'm chasing him."

"Why would he think that unless you're crazy enough to tell him what's going on?"

"Everyone will know something is up," Anna nibbled on her lower lip as she maneuvered the car out of the crowded parking lot.

"So what? It's time for you to show off what the Lord gave you."

"Kelli Prescott."

"Kelli nothing. Let the man wonder. It worked on your brother. It will work on Gavin." She searched in her purse until she pulled out a business card. "This is the number for the hairstylist at my salon. They provide the works from hair, massage, manicure, and pedicure as well as makeup. It's wonderful. I called and asked them to fit us in. Your appointment is at ten tomorrow morning."

Anna would have glared at her sister-in-law if she dared to take her eyes off the busy expressway. "You're taking me too fast."

Kelli patted her knee. "You'll be fine. We can stop at the market now. What do you think of rack of lamb? Should I marinate it? In what? And what about dessert? I've been thinking about a caramel crème brûlée, but you are going to have to explain every step . . . slowly."

Conversation turned to food, something Anna knew she could handle. When they left the market, they were loaded down with even more bags. Anna was alarmed when she checked her watch. It was nearly four-thirty.

"Don't worry about taking me and the baby home. Drop me off at your folks. Wesley can pick us up later and I can visit with your mom. You don't have time to cart us back across town and get to Gavin's place to make dinner."

"Thanks. Do you think I'm overdressed?"

"Hardly. You look pretty, yet stylish."

After pulling into her parents' drive, Anna leaned over and gave Kelli a big hug. "Thanks, sis. I couldn't have done it without you. I would have quit halfway."

"It was fun. If you get shaky, call me."

* * *

Both Kyle and Gavin were home when she arrived. She went to work without delay.

"Hi." She smiled when Gavin walked into the kitchen and took a deep breath to calm her nerves. "Everything is ready. Why don't you call Kyle?"

"Hi yourself. How was your day?" He followed what he could see of her figure that was covered from neck to knee in an apron.

"Busy." She avoided looking at him as she carried two covered serving dishes to the table.

"Want to talk about it?"

"No, thanks. I'm sorry I wasn't here when Kyle got home from school. Everything go all right with his teacher?"

"Yes. I talked to both the principal and Mrs. Winston," he said with a frown. "Anna . . ."

"Everything is all set." She took off her apron. "Dessert is cooling on the stovetop." She pointed to the peach cobbler. "There is homemade vanilla ice cream in the freezer in a plastic container. It's marked."

"Looks good." Gavin wasn't looking at the pot roast, creamed potatoes, carrots, or home made biscuits.

"Good. I'll see you in the morning." Briefcase in hand, she headed to the hall to collect her shoulder bag and coat off the peg near the side door.

"You're leaving?" He followed.

"Yes. Did I forget something?"

"Yes . . . I mean no. You're welcome to join us."

"No thanks. I have plans."

"Is that why you're all dressed up?"

"I'll see you in the morning. Tell Kyle goodbye for me. Good night." With that, she hurried out the door before he could ask about her plans. She intended to fill as many garbage bags as she could with her old things and donate them. She intended to take care of it tonight before she lost her nerve.

Gavin stood in the open doorway.

If Anna had bothered to look, she would have seen his scowl as he watched her start her car and take off down the drive.

9

As Anna dressed for work the next morning, she studied herself in the mirror. She needed something, she just didn't know what. The most she could get right with makeup was a little powder and lipstick. Her base tone didn't seem right but she was uncertain why. In half a minute she was done but not thrilled by the results. She gathered her heavy dreadlocks into a ponytail, using a coated elastic band to secure it.

She hoped this trip to the salon today wasn't a complete waste of time and money. She waved to Janet, who was just pulling up to the front of the house as she backed out of the drive.

When Anna arrived at work, the house was quiet. Vanessa, Mrs. Tillman, and Gretchen weren't in yet. She quickly put her things away and began breakfast. She soon had ham slices on the grill, banana nut muffins warming in the oven, oatmeal with honey on the stove, and a pitcher of carrot, mango, and apple juice.

"Mornin'." Gavin's deep voice startled her.

She looked up from where she stood at the stove. "Good morning. It's a pretty day. Sun's out. If the weather holds, it will be great for the big Thanksgiving game day."

"We still have a few weeks." He watched her closely. "You and your mom planning a big meal as usual?"

"Of course. You and Kyle are coming by after the game, aren't you?"

"Yeah. I plan to, but I have to figure out what to do about him while I'm playing."

"That's not a problem. He can hang out with me and my family until you get there."

"I've imposed on you enough these past few weeks."

"It's not an imposition."

"You don't mind?"

"No, why should I?" She put his meal in front of him. "Need anything else?"

"Thank you, no. It looks wonderful." When she turned toward the refrigerator he caught her hand. "Wait a minute."

"Do you need me to drop Kyle off this morning?"

"No, I have the time. I want to ask you about your evening. Did you have a nice time?"

Anna turned away. "Yes, I did." She began filling another plate.

Gavin shocked her when he asked, "Who is he?"

"He? I never said anything about a man."

"No, you didn't. But something is going on with you."

"Where is this coming from?"

"I care about you. I always have. And since we've been seeing so much of each other, I've started to notice things I never had before."

She avoided his eyes. "You sound so serious."

"Nothing stays the same. I kissed you the other day. And we've both done a bit of pretending it didn't happen. Well, it happened, Anna. Are you expecting an apology?"

"You're making too much out of it."

"Am I? I don't think so. I'd like—"

"Hi," Kyle said as he walked into the room and joined Gavin at the breakfast bar.

"Morning." Anna smiled at the boy, grateful for the interruption. "I'll get your breakfast. Got your homework done?"

"Yes."

She didn't want to discuss that kiss . . . not now . . . not ever. And she certainly didn't want him to apologize for it. She didn't need to be reminded that he was way out of her league. She had no business letting her imagination take over.

"If you guys need anything, just holler," she said before she went over to the desk, pulled her laptop out of her briefcase, and got to work. It was all she could do to keep her mind on the list of ingredients needed for the dishes she'd planned to prepare for dinner.

Gavin sent Kyle ahead of him before he quietly said, "I'd like to finish this conversation when I get back. Are you going to be busy around one? I'd like to take you to lunch."

Anna just stared at him in disbelief.

"Anna, I said—"

"I heard you. And you're going to make Kyle late for his first class."

"About lunch . . ."

"I'm sorry. I have an appointment."

"Anna," he said impatiently, "what's with you? Every time I try to talk to you—"

"Hey, Gavin. I'm going to be late," Kyle called.

"Be right out." To Anna he warned, "We're going to have this talk."

It took her a good ten minutes before she had herself under control enough to clean the kitchen. He couldn't still want to talk about the kiss. They both knew it shouldn't have happened. Why was he pursuing this?

Anna jumped when her sister-in-law buzzed from the front gates. "You're early," she accused when she stepped back to let her into the front foyer.

"I don't want to be late for our appointment. Grab your coat," Kelli urged.

Anna hesitated for a few moments.

"You haven't changed your mind, have you?"

Anna shook her head. "I'm going. Hold on, I have to leave a note and get my coat and purse." Within a few minutes, they were inside Kelli's bright red SUV and on their way. "Where is the baby?"

"Visiting with my mother. Now tell me what happened. Something has you on edge. Did you and Gavin have that talk?"

"Absolutely not. I've been such a coward, I managed to avoid any serious conversation with him."

"Something happened."

"Nothing worth talking about."

Kelli took Woodward north toward Birmingham. She took her eyes off the road long enough to ask, "You mean to tell me that Gavin pretended that nothing happened? I can't believe that."

"Okay . . . okay. He wanted to get it out in the open. Kelli, I don't want him apologizing for it. I just know that's what he plans to do and I am not having it."

"I can understand that. There is nothing to apologize for. You are both consenting adults who apparently are attracted to each other. What is wrong with that?"

Anna blinked away tears of unhappiness. "He dates so many women. They all look like chocolate Barbie dolls . . .

beautiful, petite, and perfect in every way. Wherever he goes, someone is eyeing him. It isn't just his body and good looks. His income is a huge draw. How can any woman stand to know she's just one of many and can be easily replaced?"

"Since I happen to be married to an equally handsome jock, I know it's not easy to deal with. Yes, he can probably have anyone he wants. And it's true that you aren't like the tiny women he normally dates. But it's also possible he wants you, Anna Prescott. Don't forget, there is nothing tiny about me, and Wes came after me."

"My brother has good sense. Unfortunately, I can't say the same for his best friend. Gavin doesn't want to jeopardize our friendship. I tell you, he's going to apologize as soon as he can corner me long enough to get it out."

"He kissed you," Kelli reminded her as they circled the block near the beauty salon, looking for a parking place.

"A temporary loss of sanity."

"Who knows what can happen if you give him a little encouragement."

"He asked me out," Anna revealed.

"He did? Well, well." Kelli was beaming as she found space a few yards from the salon. "Give me details."

"He asked me out to lunch. I turned him down."

"Anna, what more do you want? An engraved invitation?"

"I told him the truth. I do have an appointment this morning. At the best black-owned, head-to-toe beauty salon in Birmingham, Michigan." She waved her hand in the general direction of the salon.

"Why didn't you ask for a rain check? Or go anyway? You can get the works another time."

"It was too late to cancel."

"Wait one minute." Catching her hand before she could get out of the car, Kelli said, "Let's start over. If you had said yes, what is the best thing that could have happened at lunch?"

"I could have enjoyed myself and had a great meal," Anna acknowledged.

"And the worst?"

"I could have made a complete fool of myself. What difference does it make?"

"Now you know the best and the worst. Do you think either scenario will give him cause to fire you?"

"No."

"End your friendship?" Kelli quizzed.

"Nope."

"So either way, you two will come out of it friends, right?" After Anna nodded, Kelli asked, "So what is the real reason you're running scared?"

Anna bit her lip before she said barely above a whisper, "I lied. The absolute worst thing that could happen is I could lose my mind and tell him how I really feel about him." She got out of the car, slammed the door, and began walking toward the salon.

"Anna," Kelli called, scrambling to catch up. When she caught her arm, she slowed her down. "Why are you running off? There is nothing wrong about the way you feel. Gavin is a wonderful man. And yes, there will always be women chasing him down. Accept that. I have."

"I can't. Maybe it wouldn't be so hard if I believed he could care for me the way I care for him, but I don't. And I don't want him to know how I feel. I wish I didn't know. It would make it easier."

"So you're giving up?"

"Yes. Kelli, I'm sorry I dragged you into the middle of this and asked you to keep secrets from Wesley."

"You have nothing to apologize for. Just because Wesley

and I fell in love and got married doesn't mean I don't remember how scary it can be to love and not know if that love is returned."

"Thanks."

"Anna, I also believe that you could be cheating yourself out of a fabulous relationship. We both know Gavin cares about you. But let's forget all about that for a while," Kelli said as they started walking again. "Let's concentrate on enjoying ourselves. After all, there is nothing wrong with showing the world that we are two exceptionally lovely women."

"Yes, let's."

Kelli laughed, "Besides, Gavin won't know what's going on, unless you tell him. Trust me, men aren't naturally intuitive when it comes to women. More often than not, they don't have a clue."

Anna laughed, as she held the door to the salon open for Kelli. "I like how you think."

Several hours later when they were buckled inside the car, Kelli lifted a brow, saying, "Well? Do I take you back to your place so you can wash it all off? Or do I take you back to Gavin's?"

Anna laughed, knowing she'd never looked better in her life. Not only had she gotten her locks refreshed and curled, she also had her makeup and nails done by experts. She'd bought a whole new set of cosmetics and was confident that she could recreate the look on her own.

"Take me home."

"Anna!"

"I want you to help me load the car with those bags of old clothes I packed up last night. If we do it together, I can get them dropped off before I chicken out."

"Good idea." Kelli beamed. As they picked up I-696 Expressway going east, she surprised Anna when she asked, "Well, Miss Lady, what are you going to do if he asks you out again?"

"If he asks me again I'm going."

"Good girl."

"Now tell me about Kaleea. She is such a sweet baby. When are you going to let me babysit?"

Kelli laughed. "Don't worry. You'll get your turn." She began telling Anna about Wesley's attempt to bathe the baby. "He had water everywhere and very little on the baby. She loves her daddy."

Anna laughed, imagining her big lug of a brother trying to bathe his tiny daughter. There was no doubt Kaleea had won his heart the moment she entered the world. "I just hope he mellows some before she grows up. If he is half as bad with her as he has been with me, she'll be lucky if she goes on a date before she's twenty-five."

"I'm going to have to start working on him now. He is such a wonderful man, but he is so painfully old-fashioned." Kelli eased the car to a stop in Anna's driveway, behind the catering van. Both Janet and Krista's cars were parked in front of the house. "You have company."

"Not really. Janet and our two associates work out of my kitchen. We still have the meals to deliver to the players. Right now we can't afford to equip a separate facility. That's our next goal."

"Is this going to be awkward for you?" she asked Anna as they got out of the car.

"No. Besides, if I want to keep this look, I'm just going to have to deal with the comments." Anna carried a small tote bag of beauty products that she had purchased at the salon. "It shouldn't take long."

Lori was chopping vegetables at the center island, Janet was basting prime rib in the oven, and Krista was rolling out dough for the pie tins lining the counters.

"Hi, ladies. Smells good in here." Anna made the introductions. "Janet, you and Krista remember Kelli. Lori Fleming, this is my sister-in-law, Kelli Prescott."

The ladies exchanged smiles.

"You both look great. What's the occasion? And how come I wasn't invited?" Janet teased.

Kelli volunteered. "We decided to indulge ourselves. We had facials, manicures, makeup . . . the works."

"I can see. Where did you go? That great new salon in Birmingham?" Krista laughed.

"Yes, it was fabulous." Anna smiled.

"Next time, we all have to go," Lori said.

Janet teased Anna. "What? Can't stay away from us? No problem; we'd love to put you to work." She washed her hands and dried them on a paper towel.

Anna laughed. "Very funny. No, I needed to pick up a few things. Kelli came to help me. Don't let us interrupt. I know you guys are on a tight schedule. Come, Kelli, we have to get going or I will never make it back to prepare dinner." She ushered her sister-in-law down the hall toward her bedroom.

It wasn't until they were inside with the door closed that Kelli said, "See, I told you it wouldn't be bad."

"You were right." Anna went into her walk-in closet where she had left the bags of clothes.

"You've been busy."

Anna went over to the row of new clothes that she had hung up the night before and pulled out a pair of teal denim leggings and a white knit top trimmed in teal around the deep vee neckline and long sleeves. "This was what I planned to wear today, but I hung it back up before I got out the door."

"Perfect. Nothing fancy, but they do fit nicely. Not too

tight or clingy but follow the lines of your body. You change while I start dragging these out to the car." Kelli had a bag in each hand.

Anna went into her bathroom to change. It didn't take long. She also grabbed two bags and headed for the car.

As Kelli passed her on her way back into the house, she said, "You look great."

"Thanks. Give me a minute, and I'll get the last two and lock up." She carried the bags through the living room into the front foyer before she called, "Janet. We're gone."

"Okay." Janet followed her to the front door. "Will you look at you? Is that new?" Then she laughed, "It has to be. Okay, partner, talk to me."

Anna shook her head. "Not now. I've got to go. We'll talk later. Okay?"

Janet lowered her voice so she wouldn't be overheard. "Does this have anything to do with what happened between you and Gavin?"

"Not really. It has to do with how I feel about me. I might as well tell you that I've bought an entire new wardrobe and I'm giving all my old things away. And I'm glad I did. I feel so much better. Be happy for me."

Janet kissed Anna's cheek. "You know I am. We'll talk later."

Anna waved before letting herself out.

10

"**W**hat in the hell is wrong with you, Mathis?" Wesley yelled, with equal amounts of frustration and concern. "I practically handed you the damn ball, and you still missed it."

They were the last ones off the Lions' state-of-the-art indoor practice field. Since college the two played so well together that Gavin instinctively knew where Wesley was going to throw the football, and he more often than not was there ready for it. They fed off each other's enthusiasm for the sport they both loved. Time after time they flawlessly executed every play.

Gavin was known in the NFL as a star receiver. Their opponents never failed to target him, but his legs were so long and strong that more often than not they couldn't catch him. Today the practice session had gone badly and it didn't bode well for the upcoming game on Sunday afternoon. Wesley's aim was not the problem. Gavin's concentration was shot.

"Get out of my way, Prescott." Gavin pushed past his friend. "I've had as much of your mouth as I plan to take." He certainly didn't need to be told that his mind hadn't been on what he was supposed to be doing, that was for damn sure.

He had an excuse, but he sure as hell couldn't tell Wesley that his little sister was the problem. It wasn't like him to let his personal life interfere with his game. He had been ticked off by her refusal to go out with him, so much so that he could think about little else.

Wesley caught his arm. "You're not going anywhere until you tell me what's going on. Don't make me have to whip your behind, boy."

Gavin grinned. "You haven't whipped my ass since we were juniors at Michigan State. And you got lucky because I'd had too much to drink." As the two walked toward the locker room, he said, "It was over Cheryl Bradon, wasn't it?"

"Yeah. Little hussy was sleeping with half the team." Wesley laughed before he said, "Talk to me, Gav. Is it Kyle?"

"Naw. The kid messed up pretty bad last week in school, but I straightened it and him out. He seems to finally be settling down."

"Any news from Reynolds?"

"Tracked him to St Louis. Then he took off again before I could get there. He could be anywhere. It was bad enough that I had to go to court to get temporary guardianship."

"Is that the problem?"

Gavin knew from experience that Wesley wouldn't give up until he had some answers. "The old man is making it tough on all of us, especially Kyle. How is he going to take it if I have to drag our father back here to do what he should have done all along? I can't make him act like a man. That kid has missed so much school that if he wasn't so smart, he would have been held back a grade."

"That's what you think it will come down to?"

"Looks that way to me." Gavin averted his gaze.

He felt as if he was lying to the one man who was more like a brother than a friend . . . and he didn't like it one bit. As if he was going behind Wesley's back because he hadn't come right out and told him what was on his mind. Gavin knew that he wasn't ready to tell what Wesley certainly wasn't ready to hear.

Wesley punched Gavin playfully on the arm. "Has Kyle put a crimp in your love life? That would explain you're less than pleasant mood, my man."

Gavin didn't miss the women he normally dated because they no longer held the appeal they once had. He'd done without for nearly a year. Sex for sex's sake had lost its appeal. There was no true satisfaction, only a lingering emptiness deep inside, as if something vital was missing. He hadn't even been tempted, until recently.

"Not that it's any of your damn business but I'm not seeing anyone special."

"What about Carol that you took out with us?" Wesley grinned.

"What she liked was my income. Thanks, but no thanks."

The single reason he had taken her out was to get his mind off Anna. It hadn't worked. What he couldn't understand was why Anna had her defenses so firmly in place. Did it have anything to do with the fact she knew the men in her family were so protective that she feared no man could meet their exacting standards? Or was she interested in someone else? But she had denied that time and time again. What was he to think?

Gavin and Anna had been friends for a long time. Perhaps

the huge gap between friends and lovers caused her hesitation. Whatever her reason, Gavin sure as hell couldn't tell Wesley. If a man wanted her, he had better be offering marriage. Nothing less was going to fly with the Prescott men.

Unfortunately, Wesley knew that Gavin had decided a long time ago that marriage was not for him. Gavin would rather remain single for the rest of his days than to hurt any woman the way his father had hurt his mother, or a child the way his father had hurt both his sons. No one deserved that kind of pain.

Gavin knew he wasn't like his father. He'd worked hard to ensure it. Yet there had to be a reason that he had never even come close to falling in love. He preferred experienced women. Nothing serious. That way no one got hurt and he could look at himself in the mirror in the morning.

"Why doesn't that surprise me? What you need is to stop playing around and look for what I have with Kelli. When the Prescott men marry, they stay married. Look how long my folks have been together."

"You had a great example while growing up. I never had that. Besides, I like my freedom. I don't want someone trying to control my life and finances."

Before Gavin could walk through the locker room door, Wesley placed a restraining hand on his shoulder. "It's not about control. It's about love and sharing."

"Yeah? How am I going to do that when you got the last good one?"

"Excuses won't work. If you think you're like your father, you're wrong. He isn't a quarter of the man that you've become," Wesley said seriously as he went inside the locker room.

Deep in thought, Gavin didn't follow for a moment. Although he hadn't said it, he was touched by the compliment coming from a man he respected and loved as a brother. Was

Wesley right? Was he comparing himself to his father? He certainly didn't plan to repeat his old man's mistakes. He'd decided early on not to marry, unwilling to risk becoming less than an exceptional husband and father. Too bad life didn't offer any guarantees.

Just then, he recalled the way Anna had looked curled up on the couch the night he'd come home early. Her skin looked as soft and creamy as the peach silk she wore. He didn't need to be told that she was the kind of woman who would want more than he was able to give. Yet that knowledge didn't change the fact that he ached every minute of every day to be inside of her.

Nor did the knowledge that she would want more stop his heart from pounding with need whenever he looked at her. Nothing worked. Nothing altered the way blood hardened his shaft whenever she was within touching distance.

For the first time in memory he had lost control of his head and taken Anna into his arms. At least he was no longer driving himself nuts wondering about her taste . . . he knew the tantalizing flavor of her mouth. Unfortunately, it had left him hungry for more. He wouldn't be appeased until he had sampled every sweet inch of her shapely body.

Since that moment of weakness she had avoided him. His mouth tightened. She might not have anything to say about what they shared, but he had plenty.

Gavin discreetly watched Anna as she passed a serving dish to Kyle. She'd been teasing the boy about the amount of food he could put away and never seem to gain an ounce.

"He's still growing." Gavin added, "I wouldn't be surprised if he tops me one day by a couple of inches."

Kyle flashed a quick grin. "You really think so?"

"I don't see why not. You're taller than Anna already. Now, you'll have to go some to outweigh me, bro."

Anna laughed. "I'm beginning to feel downright short."

Kyle was clearly pleased by the comment.

Gavin grinned. He liked Kyle's smile. It was the first he'd seen on his brother's face. And he knew he had Anna to thank. Her presence added a normalcy that he found refreshing.

As yet he hadn't managed to have a private word with her, but she'd stayed for dinner tonight. He had no idea why, yet she seemed more relaxed this evening. Something had happened. Her eyes sparkled with humor, and he suspected she was wearing one of her new outfits. The slacks and pretty sweater gently followed the curves of her shapely figure.

When he'd invited her to lunch she'd said she had an appointment, but it was clear to him that she'd rather drink poison than spend time alone with him. He didn't plan to waste time or energy wondering why she had changed her mind but he was grateful for it.

He'd done his best not to pressure her. He'd been surprised and appreciative when he invited her to stay for dinner and she consented. Gavin wasn't about to question his good fortune. She'd let him know that he'd overstepped the imaginary line she placed around herself when he kissed her and again when he'd asked her out. Although disappointed, he planned to try not to force the issue.

"Another great dinner, Anna. Right, Kyle?"

"Right."

"Thanks, gentlemen." She began collecting the dishes.

"Hold it. That's Kyle's job."

Kyle surprised him by asking, "When do you get a turn?"

"Me?"

"Yes . . . you," Anna jumped in.

Gavin chuckled. "You two ganging up on me?"

"Why not? Kyle's been doing better in English, keeping his room clean and helping out." Leaning over, she playfully pulled Kyle's ear.

"True," Gavin hedged as he rubbed his chin thoughtfully. "Okay. I'll do them for one week, if you beat me at air hockey."

"That's a great idea." She clapped her hands. "My money is on Kyle."

The boy's eyes were twinkling. "Okay. I'm game."

Gavin wasn't about to argue. He was thrilled by the happiness in his brother's face. "Let's go." He pushed back his chair. He glanced back at Anna. "You coming?"

"Someone has to keep you two honest." She draped an arm over Kyle's slim shoulders. "Isn't that right?"

"Yeah. He might cheat." Kyle laughed as the three of them headed for the game room.

The room was equipped with a pool table, air hockey game, and Ping Pong table, as well as a shuffle board and a chess board, plus pinball and slot machines. Gavin found his quick reflexes helped, but he couldn't stop Kyle's youthful enthusiasm. Kyle whipped him two out of three games.

"I don't believe it," Gavin groaned, not the least bit put out. He was so relieved to see Kyle relaxed and enjoying himself for a change that losing a hundred games would be worth it.

"Believe it. You lost," Anna teased.

"That's right. Get to work. That kitchen has to be spotless before you can leave," Kyle instructed with a big grin on his face.

"Congratulations," Gavin gave his brother a rough hug. "You're the man."

Kyle was all smiles. "I think I'll go watch some TV while you get to work."

"Yeah, right," Gavin grumbled for good measure as he followed Anna down the main hall to the kitchen. His mind wasn't on the task at hand, but on the seductive sway of her shapely hips.

She was such a beautiful woman, both inside and out. She

didn't need the makeup. She was downright sexy with her incredibly long legs and tempting smiles. Why had she been hiding her beauty all these years? More important, why hadn't he noticed?

When they were out of earshot in the kitchen, Anna beamed. "Did you see those smiles?"

Gavin grinned. "It was great to see him happy. It's about time." He walked to the table and began collecting dishes.

"I don't know if you planned to lose or if it just happened, but I'm so glad." She surprised them both when she came over to him and brushed her lips against his. It was such a light touch that for an instant he wondered if he'd imagined it.

"So was I," he said casually, determined to conceal his delight. He had no idea why she'd kissed him, but he wasn't about to offer a single complaint. He asked as he placed the serving bowls on the counter. "Got to go?"

She shook her head. "But I should." She gathered her things, a soft smile on her face. "See you in the morning."

Gavin had to bite his tongue to keep from calling her back, determined not to pressure her.

Two weeks later, Gavin was stretched out on a bench lifting weights in his home gym when Anna walked into the room. She waited until he placed the three-hundred-and-ten-pound weight on the bar holder above his head before she said, "Do you have a moment?"

He sat up, grabbing a towel to wipe perspiration from his face and upper body. "For you, I've got two. What's up?"

"Has Kyle told you that he'd like to invite my brother Wayne over during the week, after school?"

"Nope. He hasn't mentioned it. Are the boys friends?" Gavin noted the way she quickly looked away from his bare chest and muscular legs.

"Getting that way. It started with them doing their homework together on Sundays. Wayne helped Kyle out in English and Kyle has helped Wayne in math. Kyle wanted to ask Wayne to stay over, but he wasn't sure you'd agree."

"Why would I mind? Kyle spends too much time as it is alone in his room. In fact, I've been considering taking the television out of his room. He claims he can't sleep if the thing isn't on. Why didn't he ask me?"

"He's reluctant to ask in case you say no."

Gavin absently smoothed his mustache. "I don't like it that he feels he can't come to me. Anna, I'm trying. I don't want my brother to be afraid of me."

"I know you don't," she said softly. "But he still needs time to really get to know you and your moods."

"All right." He caught her hand. "You've been looking awfully pretty these days." His gaze slowly moved over her lush curves.

"Thank you. Excuse me . . ."

He didn't release her hand when she tugged. "Kyle isn't the only one reluctant to be near me. Ever since that kiss, you practically run when you see me coming. If you'd like an apology, I'll give you one. Is that what you want?"

Anna's chin shot up a notch. "I never asked for an apology."

He searched her eyes before he said, "I hope you're saying nothing happened between us that we both didn't want to happen. Sweetheart, we both know that I want you. But it takes two." He gently rubbed his thumb over the back of her soft hand.

"Why are you saying these things?"

He tugged her hand, drawing her off-balance. She landed across his splayed hard-muscled thighs. He dropped his head until they were practically nose to nose. "It needs to be said. I don't want you to have any doubts where I'm concerned."

He vowed every single day not to pressure her but the instant he saw her, the hunger started all over again. Didn't he have enough on his mind without having to contend with feeling guilty because he ached to make love to his best friend's baby sister? No matter what he told himself, he yearned to discover all her feminine secrets.

"What about Natasha?" Anna said in a whisper.

"What about her? There's nothing going on between us. She's an old friend and a business associate. Natasha works with high school students who need the scholarship program we provide through the foundation."

"She didn't act like she was just a friend, when I met her."

"We dated a few times more than a year ago. And it's been over for a long time."

"And the others?"

"What others?"

She forced herself to say, "I heard a woman in the background when I called about Kyle. Was she just a friend also?"

"Who?"

"How should I know?"

"Sweetheart, I was in one of our stores. There are women who work for us. But I'm not involved with anyone. Is that what you thought? That I wanted to add you to some list?"

She glared at him. "I am not interested in being your latest toy."

"No, Anna. You have it wrong. First of all, I would never treat any woman like a toy. Second, I've been celibate for nearly a year. I was so tired of the games, and sick of not knowing what the women I dated really wanted. Believe me, the attraction was not me, but what they assumed came with being my lady."

He pressed her hand against his bare chest. "Anna, I want you . . . only you. Feel my heart racing. It happens every time you enter a room. It's nothing I planned."

Anna studied his dark eyes for a long moment before she

released a whimper as she pressed her lips to the base of his throat. She breathed deeply, filling her lungs with his scent.

He groaned low in his throat at the sweetness of the caress. All the reasons that he should not be holding her like this suddenly didn't matter. He dropped his head, pressing tender kisses from her forehead down to her beautiful throat and then he covered her mouth with his own.

"Oh, Anna . . ." Gavin groaned as he kissed her again.

He followed the outline of her lips with the tip of his tongue. When her body melted against his, he gathered her even closer, pressing her lush breasts into the hard wall of his deep chest. When she parted her lips, offering even more, he sponged her bottom lip with his tongue, only to take it into his mouth to suckle.

Anna shivered as Gavin slid his tongue into her mouth. Eventually the need to breathe forced them to part. As she stared up at him, his heart pounded with excitement.

He smoothed a thumb over her kiss-swollen lips. "Do you still doubt that I want you?"

"No." She blushed.

As close as they were, she had to feel his sex, heavy with need. He longed to caress her soft length, discover all her sweet secrets.

"Good." He smiled, pressing a kiss on her throat, close to her ear. When she trembled, he smiled. "The question is, how badly do you want me?"

Her eyes went wide, but she remained silent as she searched his dark eyes.

"Are you ready to be honest with me? To tell me the reason you turned me down when I asked you out?" The ringing telephone didn't prompt him to make a move to answer it.

"You know the reason. Natasha and the others."

"And the reason for the makeup and hair?"

Anna eased away and rose to her feet. Rather than answer that question, she asked one of her own. "What about it?"

"That's not an answer." He surged to his feet.

She smiled. "At the moment, it's all I'm prepared to say."

He grinned. "Maybe I can persuade you to—"

"Gavin, telephone," Kyle said as he walked into the exercise room.

"Thanks."

While Gavin went to the extension mounted on the wall, Anna turned to leave, intending to give him privacy. It would also give her an opportunity to sort out how she felt about what had just happened and what had been said. He wasn't involved with anyone else. It was up to her. Was she ready to take the next step? Ready to be honest about her feelings for him?

Kyle was right behind her. "Did you ask him? What did he say?"

"I asked him." She smiled. "Now it's your turn."

"What?"

"Gavin said you're the one who has to do the asking." She patted his arm reassuringly. "Don't worry. He'll probably say yes."

Kyle didn't look convinced.

"Go on," she urged. "Ask him as soon as he gets off the telephone. See you guys in the morning."

Kyle caught her hand, stopping her. "Will you stay until I ask?"

"You don't need me. This you can handle on your own." She kissed his cheek. "See you in the morning. Good luck."

11

Anna had just hung up the telephone when it rang again. Assuming it was her mother calling her back, rather than saying hello, she said, "I told you I didn't mind doing the cranberry bread. It will be a treat, especially with all the other fixings."

"Sounds great to me. How are you?"

That deep baritone voice didn't belong to her mother. "Gavin?"

"Yes, darlin'."

She was glad he couldn't see that she was grinning like crazy. She made herself ask, "Is something wrong?"

"Not a thing. Are you busy?"

"No. I just got off the phone with my mother. We were planning the Thanksgiving dinner. You and Kyle are invited."

"Good. Can't wait. You got your cooking talent from that

sweet mother of yours, and your soft voice. On her it's decidedly Southern, on you it's downright sexy."

"Hmm. Are you and Wes donating the turkeys to the soup
kitchens around the city this year?"

"Absolutely. I also plan to take Kyle along with me to volunteer on Thursday morning before the game."

"Good." She smiled. The Prescotts and Gavin had been
volunteering their time and food to the area's homeless and
needy for several years. "Tell me, why are you calling?"

"You've been on my mind."

She wasn't ready to discuss anything personal . . . especially those kisses they shared. She still hadn't figured out
how she felt. The only thing that she was clear about was that
she was scared. He was a passionate man and used to dealing
with more experienced women. If she became involved with
him, she knew she was risking having her heart broken.

Switching the topic, she asked, "Did Kyle ask about
Wayne coming over to study?"

"Took a while but he finally got up the nerve. He wants
Wayne to come over on Thursday to study for a math test.
And he wanted your brother to stay for dinner."

"And?"

"You know I said yes. I want him to have a normal life that
includes friends. I warned him that your folks also have to
agree and since it was a school night Wayne has to be back
home by eight."

"You're getting good at this. What did my folks say?"

"I'm surprised your mom didn't tell you that we talked.
The answer was yes. I'll pick them up after school."

"I can drop Wayne off on my way home," she volunteered.

"You don't mind?"

"Not at all. I'm glad for Kyle. He has been doing so well
lately. I'm keeping my fingers crossed that it continues."

"And saying a few prayers, I hope?"

"Naturally." She leaned back against the cushion of her couch, her bare feet tucked under her.

"Anna, I didn't call about Kyle. This is personal. I've asked you to go out with me several times. Tell me what I have to do to spend some time with you away from my home."

"Gavin—"

He interrupted, "I'm putting you on the spot, but I never met a woman so hard to feed."

"It's my job to feed you," she said flippantly.

"Very clever, but I'm serious. I'd like to take you out."

"I'll think about it," she hedged.

"Answer the question."

"What was the question again?"

"Anna Mae Prescott, I'm not fooling around. I'd really like an answer."

She'd have gladly answered if she could think of anything to say but the truth. It wouldn't be long before he recognized her vulnerability to him.

Gavin's voice was deeper when he added, "You have all the answers, sweetheart." After a lengthy pause, he sighed before saying, "Will you at least answer this one for me? Are you involved with another man?"

"What do you mean by 'involved'?"

Gavin grumbled something beneath his breath before he said quietly and evenly, "You know exactly what I mean but if you want me to break it down, okay . . . fine. Are you dating another man?"

"No."

"Are you sleeping with another man?"

"No."

"That's a relief. So why won't you date me?"

"I didn't say I wouldn't. It's just that we've known each

other forever. Dating involves getting to know each other. I know your favorite color and the food you hate. I know about your stubborn streak, even though you pretend you don't have one. I know about your growing-up years. You know the same things about me.

"Gavin, do you realize that I've met most of the women you've dated in the last three years? You like them petite and drop-dead gorgeous. I also know you have a thing against dating out of the race. What else is there?"

He laughed, "You've made your point. Anna, there are lots of things I'd like to learn about you. You are a very special woman, and I'd like to spend some time with you . . . alone."

"Thank you." Considering all that stood between them, she persisted. "You see me almost every day."

"I didn't plan any of this, but that doesn't stop me from wanting more. As I told you today, I'm not seeing anyone else. You're the one I want to spend time with, the one I can talk to about anything. I never would have survived the problems with Kyle without your help."

"Maybe you're confusing friendship for something more?"

"There's no confusion on my part, sweetheart. I enjoy the feel of you in my arms and the taste of you on my tongue." His voice deepened even more. "Make no mistake, I want you. I suspect that feeling may be mutual. Has someone hurt you? If that's the case, I imagine you're not eager to rush into a relationship. You obviously want to take it slow . . . so we'll do it your way."

She confessed, "I'm scared of making a mistake."

"I don't want either of us hurt, but I am not willing to put my head in the sand and pretend that there is nothing going on between us just because you're Wes's baby sister."

"There is that. You know what the men in my family are like."

"Anna, you're entitled to a life of your own. The Prescott men aren't having any problems living their lives, why should you?"

"Gavin, if this is about sex . . ." She trailed off.

"Hardly. It's about the two of us finding out what is between us. Please just give us a chance. That's all I'm asking."

She was quiet for so long that he prompted, "Anna?"

"Okay, but Gavin—" she stopped abruptly.

"Yes?"

"I want whatever this is between us to stay that way . . . between us."

"Why?" he joked. "You ashamed of me?"

"You know better. I need a little time to get used to the idea of the two of us being involved."

"Why, sweetheart?" Gavin didn't sound as if he liked that idea.

"It's not as if we have anything to hide, but what happens with us is private. I want to keep it that way, just for now." She insisted, "We don't even know if there will be an us."

"I know. And I suppose I understand. I'm just not crazy about this idea, but I am crazy about you, Anna Prescott. Okay. Whatever's going on between us will remain between us until you're ready."

"Thank you."

Anna's cousin and older brothers had grown up with her father's insistence that they take care of her . . . no exceptions to that rule. She didn't have to be told that they would blame themselves if she got hurt. As far back as she could remember, all three had watched over her. And she hated it.

"How about dinner on Saturday night?"

Anna laughed. "We can have dinner every night of the week."

Frrustrated, he urged, "Okay, give me a minute here. How

about a play on Saturday night? There is bound to be something interesting at the Fox and Fisher Theaters."

"Who's going to look after Kyle?" She reminded him, "I can't be in two places at once."

Gavin let out an exasperated sound. "I could ask Mrs. Tillman, but I don't think it's a good idea to leave him right now with someone else. I don't want him feeling as if he's in the way or not welcome. It would undo what we've both been trying to do for weeks."

"I think you're right. For now Kyle has to come first," she agreed.

"What about a late lunch when I can get away? What do you say?"

"I'd say yes. I'd like that."

"Good." Gavin surprised her when he said, "Kyle's birthday is next Friday. Do you think he'd like a party?"

"I don't know. I honestly don't think he has enough friends to invite. Maybe you should ask him. There might be something else he'd rather do, like a movie and pizza with a few of his classmates."

"You may be right. Thanks."

"You're welcome."

"It's getting late. I should let you get some rest." He said softly, "An occasional lunch isn't much. If you think of something you'd like to do, let me know. Maybe in the spring we can share a week in the islands? Or Rome?"

"You don't have to try to impress me, Gavin. I have simple tastes. I know what matters in life. How much money you can spend on me isn't the way, not for me."

"I'm glad of that, Anna. It means a lot to me. Good night, sweetheart."

"Night, Gavin."

*　*　*

On Thursday, Anna was pleased by the way Wayne and Kyle buckled down and actually did their homework at the kitchen table. Afterward they played pool with Gavin in the game room. And after dinner the boys complained when she insisted she had to get Wayne home, since it was a school night.

She was very proud of her little brother. Wayne was easygoing, much like their father. He had always been outgoing and didn't need prompting to make friends with Kyle. Wayne genuinely liked the quiet, almost shy Kyle. Despite their diverse backgrounds, the boys had things in common, including older brothers in the NFL. They also had to be careful that others didn't use them to get to know their famous relatives.

Kyle opted not to have a birthday party but asked if Anna would fix a special dinner with all his favorites. He asked if Wayne could come and stay over the weekend.

Kyle's birthday party was a great success. Anna made macaroni and cheese, baked ham, collard greens, and homemade rolls, as well as a chocolate fudge, triple-layer birthday cake served with homemade vanilla ice cream. Kyle sported a huge grin. He was thrilled with the Playstation-2 he got from Gavin, the sweater that Anna gave him, and the latest Harry Potter novel that he received from Wayne.

Anna had to blink away tears at the genuine happiness she saw in the boy's eyes. She was touched when he confessed that this was the first birthday party he'd ever had. She saw the shocked look on Gavin's face that he quickly managed to conceal, and was so glad that Wayne was mature enough not to comment. He, like all the kids in their family, had had birthday celebrations with family and friends every year of his life.

Later, when Gavin walked her to her car, she didn't even offer a token protest when he took her into his arms and kissed her good night. Even though she worried that the boys might see, she didn't pull away. Gavin laughed softly and kissed her again, explaining the boys were in the media room watching a movie on the wide-screen television.

Anna was glad her catering company didn't have an event scheduled on Saturday and she could sleep late. When she finally got up, she began her weekend cleaning. She'd finished her bedroom and the bathrooms and had started vacuuming the living room when the doorbell rang.

"Just a minute." Turning off the machine, she hurried to the front door.

She hadn't expected to see Gavin on her front porch but there he stood, all six-foot-four inches of him, handsome in faded jeans and a blue, pullover sweater and a butter-soft gray leather jacket.

"What are you doing here?" Her hand went to the scarf that covered her hair. She hadn't bothered with makeup and wore her oldest pair of jeans and one of her brother's old college sweatshirts. "What did you do with the boys?"

It was a windy and cold October day. The trees were nearly bare, having lost much of their autumn colors.

"Hi." He smiled at her, leaning down to place a kiss against her mouth as he backed her into the tiny foyer and closed the door behind them. "Mmm," he moaned as he gathered her against his chest.

"Hi yourself." She sighed, wrapping her arms around his taut midsection.

"I missed you. I've gotten used to seeing you every morning." Gavin placed a tender kiss against her throat before he pulled back. "Did you get any sleep last night?"

"Plenty." Anna took his hand, pulling him into her living room. "So?"

"So what?" he said, once they were seated side by side on the sofa.

"Where are the boys?" Her dark gray eyes sparkled with laughter.

He released a deep, throaty chuckle. "They're at the mall. They've gone to see a movie and then pick out shoes they both claimed they had to have before I pick them up at the main entrance."

"How did it go last night?"

"No problems. They both seemed to be having a good time, especially Kyle." Gavin played with her fingers.

"That's wonderful. I'm glad Kyle is enjoying himself. Wayne's a good kid, even if I do say so myself."

"Yeah. He is."

Even though she hadn't expected him, she was vain enough to want to look her best whenever she saw him. "You have to excuse the place and me. I was doing some cleaning."

"You are beautiful . . . all the time. You don't mind me stopping by unannounced, do you?"

She shook her head. "Thank you. The flowers are lovely." Anna referred to the spectacular arrangement of roses, lilies, and daises he'd sent that morning . . . all in shades of pink.

"Glad you like them. That's the least I can do, since I can't seem to take you out on the town." He ran a knuckle over her cheek. "You have such beautiful skin . . . soft, flawless, and so smooth."

She whispered her thanks, uncomfortable with his attention. She wasn't used to it and wondered if she would ever be the kind of woman who took a man's interest for granted.

Anna rose, asking, "Would you care for something to drink?"

He reached for her hand and pulled her down across his muscular thighs.

"Gavin," she exclaimed.

He tilted her chin until her eyes met his. "What I want I have . . . you in my arms."

Unable to look away from the raw need she saw there, she slid her arms up over his shoulders and locked her fingers behind his strong neck. "You have beautiful eyes," she whispered. "So dark and mysterious."

"Anna . . ." He moaned as he warmed her plump bottom lip with his tongue. She trembled, then opened for him, allowing him access to her sweetness. Gavin didn't hesitate, he slid his tongue inside. He took his time, savoring her honeyed depths. "Oh sweetheart," he groaned huskily. She was as delectable and inviting as a succulent peach.

"What are you doing to me?" he asked urgently. "I can't stop wanting you."

Anna whispered his name, cushioning her full breasts on the solid wall of his chest. She ached deep inside; the hard tips of her breasts verified her longing for him. She moved against him, causing yet another ache to bloom, this one deep inside her feminine center. She moaned, pressing her thighs tightly together.

She said against his generous mouth, "I can't stop thinking about you."

Gavin groaned huskily, pulling back. "Please . . . don't tell me that. I'm already half wild for you as it is. All I can think about is being inside of you."

She placed kisses down his warm, scented throat.

"Do you mean it?" He stared into her pretty eyes.

"Yes." She slid her hand under his cashmere sweater, enjoying the heat and feel of his heavily muscled chest. When she caressed his hair-roughened chest and then worried the tight little peaks, he rasped her name from deep in his throat.

He hungrily devoured her soft lips. When he pulled back

and rested his forehead against hers, his voice was hoarse with need, "We've got to stop while I can still think straight."

"Don't think."

"Sweetheart . . ." he growled, moving his hand from her back to the soft swells of her breasts. Then he pulled up her shirt and unclasped her bra, and he buried his face in the scented valley between lush breasts. "You're beautiful," he whispered huskily. "So soft . . . perfect." Gavin cradled her full breasts in his big hands, gently squeezing before he rubbed her large, dark brown nipples.

"Please . . ." She moaned as she unwittingly moved her hips against his arousal.

"Don't . . ." His hands dropped to her waist after he'd pulled her shirt down as he kissed her forehead. When he could speak, he said tightly, "I need you to push me away."

"I can't . . ." She trembled from sizzling hot need. "I've never felt like this before."

Gavin stiffened. "What are you saying? You can't be—"

She interrupted, "I'm not completely without experience."

He stared into her eyes. "You were involved in college, then again last year, right? Wes said something. I can't remember the details. Tell me."

Anna dropped her lids, crossing her arms over her tender breasts. "I dated in college."

"Tell me what happened?"

Anna stroked his jaw. "It doesn't matter now." She kissed his chin, his cheek and then his full lips before she ran her fingers over his mustache.

He held her away, keeping their upper bodies apart. "It does. Talk to me, sweetheart."

"What do you want to know?"

"Everything," he said, taking both her hands into his big one.

"Wes was mistaken. There is a big difference between dating and having your heart broken. First there was college, then culinary arts school and finally getting the business going. I've been too goal-oriented to get serious about one guy."

"And now?" He caressed her cheek. "With me?"

"It's different with you. I care about you," she confessed as she nestled against his chest.

"Good." He admitted, "I'm not interested in casual sex anymore, Anna."

"I know."

"I want more, and you deserve more. Honey—" he stopped when his cell phone began to ring. "Sorry. I have to get that." He searched his jacket before he dug it out of an inside pocket. "Mathis. Kyle. Okay. I'm on my way. You fellows know where to wait? Yeah. Bye." To her, he said, "Anna, I'm sorry. I have to pick up the boys."

She pressed her fingertips against his mouth. "No need to apologize."

"Can we finish this talk later? If it's all right with you, I will call tonight, after the boys have turned in."

"I'd like that."

"Good. I promised the boys I'd take them to one of the stables outside Livonia. They want to go horseback riding this afternoon. Walk me to the door?"

She nodded, as she rose and linked her hand with his. "Sounds like you three have a full day. Are you cooking?"

He chuckled. "Naw. We'll order pizza." He pulled her close, dropping his head until their lips brushed lightly. "Sorry about the interruption."

She kissed him. "It's fine."

"I'll call you later."

She nodded. "Goodbye."

* * *

Gavin's deep voice sent chills of excitement racing down her spine. "Did I wake you?"

"No, I was reading. You and the boys have a good time?"

He chuckled. "Teaching them how to ride and then later letting them beat me at pool wasn't my idea of a good time, but the important thing is that they're having fun, especially Kyle. I've never seen him more relaxed and less guarded."

"That's what important. How about Wayne? Is he homesick?"

"Nope. Wayne's talking about having Kyle spend Thanksgiving weekend with him. I don't know how your folks will feel about that. A three-day weekend sounds a bit much to me."

"Wayne will just have to do the asking. He's got several weeks to work on them." Gavin was silent for so long that she asked, "Something on your mind?"

"Yes. I've got to go out of town on business."

"Oh?"

"New Orleans."

"Coach is going to let you go?"

"He agreed. I leave Tuesday after practice."

"That soon." She sighed. "I'll miss you."

"I wish you were going with me. I like the idea of taking you out to dinner and dancing on Bourbon Street."

"I like the sound of that. But someone has to stay with Kyle."

He sighed. "Anna, we haven't had any time alone. I want that, sweetheart. Don't you?"

"Yes. How long will you be away?"

"Just overnight. I'd like us to take a romantic trip, but I can't leave Kyle."

"I understand."

"It will happen," he said as if he were trying to convince himself. "Just not now."

Anna closed her eyes. The thought of spending a few days alone with him was very appealing.

"A few kisses aren't nearly enough," he said huskily. "You felt so good in my arms. I didn't want to leave."

"I didn't want you to leave either. Next time you drop in give me a little warning will you?"

"Why?"

"I wanted to look my best. Is there anything wrong with that?"

"Absolutely. You looked good to me, sweetheart, except for that sweatshirt you were wearing. Whose is it?"

"I have no idea. Why?"

"If you want to wear a man's jersey, it should me mine."

Anna chuckled. "Is that right?"

"Yes. Will I see you tomorrow?"

"Maybe. I'll come by around seven-thirty to pick the boys up for early-morning service."

"They'll be ready." His voice was rough with need when he said, "I don't mean to press you, sweetheart. I know it's going to take us both a little time to get used to the idea of being a couple. About our keeping it a secret from your family—"

"We agreed," she cut in.

Gavin was silent for a time. "I know. For how long? Sooner or later they will find out."

"Than I'd rather it be later. What happens between the two of us is no one else's concern." Anna reminded him, "You promised."

"I did, reluctantly." Gavin was ready to admit that he wanted her so badly that he was willing to agree to just about anything in order to have her in his life. "And I'll keep that promise. Our relationship will stay between us until you're ready for your family to know."

"You said, 'our relationship,'" she whispered. "Is that what we have?"

"It's what I want. How about you?"

"Yes. It's late. I should go. Good night, Gavin."

"Night, sweetheart."

12

"Where is Gavin?" Anna asked as she slid two perfectly cooked ham and cheese omelets onto warmed plates.

"He's not coming. He's sick. He asked if you could drop me off at school this morning."

She frowned. "Of course. Did he say what was wrong?"

"Naw, but he's coughing bad. He sounds like he has the flu to me. You think we should call a doctor?" Kyle asked with concern.

"I don't know, but you go ahead and eat while I run up to check on him."

Anna quickly prepared a tray of coffee and juice and dry toast before she left the kitchen. It was not like Gavin to stay in bed. She passed Mrs. Tillman in the hallway.

"Coffee is ready," Anna said with a smile. "And there's a pecan coffee cake in the warmer if you care for some."

"Just what I need." Mrs. Tillman laughed as she patted her ample hips. "Where you going with that tray? Mr. Mathis sick?"

"That's what Kyle said. I thought I had better check on him. It's not like him to still be in bed," Anna said, as she climbed the stairs.

The door to his sitting room was open when she reached the end of the hall. "Gavin, you decent?"

"Anna, don't come in here. I might give you this bug," he said around a hoarse cough.

Anna crossed to his spacious bedroom and moved on to the oversize four-poster bed. She found him buried under a bronze down-filled comforter. He was unshaven and bare-chested while sneezing and coughing up a storm.

"How do you feel?" Placing the tray on one of the night tables, she switched on the bedside lamp.

"Like hell. How do I look?" he grumbled, his voice so hoarse that it was hard to understand him.

"Not good. Drink this." She handed him a large glass of mixed juices and then placed her hand on his forehead. "Honey, you're burning up. Have you taken your temperature?"

"You shouldn't have come in here," he moaned. "You could catch something."

"Stop worrying about me. You really are hot. I know you aren't going to practice today."

"Naw. I couldn't make it even if practice was in the next room. The farthest I've gone today was to the bathroom and that wore me out. I talked to the coach. He's sending over the team doctor." He sipped the juice. "I need a favor. Can you take Kyle to school?"

"Of course, but you also need to put something on your chest. Your teeth are chattering. You do have pajama bottoms on, don't you?"

He put down the juice. "Why? Want to check?" Then he started coughing until he groaned weakly.

"See, that's what you get for being such a smart mouth. Seriously, you need to cover your chest."

"Is it cold in here?"

"No. It must be the fever. Where do you keep your pajamas?"

He motioned toward the heavy mahogany dresser. "Third drawer down."

Anna found a stack of silk pajamas that looked like they were all brand-new. She handed him a pair of dark green pajamas. "Where are your socks?"

"Second drawer on the left," he said around a groan.

She found a thick pair of athletic socks and tossed them over to him.

"You put something on while I go look for a thermometer. Drink all that juice and the coffee. You need all the liquids you can get."

"I never knew you were so bossy." He complained, "I never get sick." He just lay there, too tired to move.

When she returned with the thermometer both articles of clothing were on the bed beside him.

"Oh honey. I'm sorry. Let me help you."

She sat down beside him and began helping him dress while pretending she was not aware of the broad, hard-muscled lines of his large body. She tried but failed not to look at his muscular thighs or length of his relaxed shaft. There was nothing little about this man. She bit her lip, determined to hide her appreciation of his male beauty. Instead she forced herself to focus on helping him into the bottom half. He was heavy and alarmingly weak.

"Does your body ache?" When he nodded, she said, "Honey, I bet you have the flu."

"I can't have the flu. I never get the flu." He lay back with his eyes closed as she pulled the socks on his long narrow feet.

"Tell that to someone who is willing to listen." Covering him with the flannel sheet and comforter, she asked, "Are you warm enough?"

"Yes, thanks."

"You hardly touched the juice."

"Not sure I can keep it down. Besides, you're not supposed to take care of me. I mean it, Anna. Get out of here before you catch something."

"I've already had my flu shot. Did you get one?"

"Naw. I never get sick," he mumbled. "Go away."

"I'm going as soon as you eat at least a bite of toast."

"Not hungry."

"You need vitamins. I'll juice some carrots tops, apples, turnips, and watercress with garlic clove. It's a great antiviral cocktail."

"I like real food, not ground-up stuff." He coughed, then groaned from the effort. "That is, if I could eat. Nothing for now. I know it won't stay down."

She smoothed a hand over his unshaven cheek. "Okay. What if I make some chicken noodle soup for lunch? Hopefully, your stomach will be better by then."

"That is what my mother always made when I got sick," he said tiredly.

"Well, if it was good enough for her, then it's good enough for me. Is there anything I can get you before I take Kyle to school?"

"No. Just leave me alone . . . to die in peace," he said with his eyes closed.

"Not a chance. I'll see you, later. I'll tell Mrs. Tillman to send the doctor up when he gets here. Try to sleep. I'll be back later." He mumbled his thanks as he dropped off to sleep.

* * *

"How is he? Did the doctor stop in?" Anna asked as soon as she came into the kitchen. After she dropped Kyle at school, she had stopped at the market to pick up a few ingredients. She hung her jacket by the door and dropped her purse on the desk.

Mrs. Tillman and Vanessa were seated at the breakfast bar enjoying cups of coffee and coffee cake.

Mrs. Tillman said, "Mmm, the doctor just left. Said it was definitely the flu. He called a prescription in to the drugstore." She shook her head. "I don't know how we're supposed to keep that man in bed."

Vanessa and Anna laughed.

"Good question." After scrubbing her hands with the antibacterial soap she kept beside the kitchen sink, Anna began pulling out the fixings for chicken noodle soup. "I want to put the chicken on before I go and pick up his prescription. How's the coffee cake, ladies?"

"Wonderful. As if you didn't know," Vanessa said with a shy smile. "Gretchen and I have both gained a few pounds since you've been working here full-time. Oh, speaking of Gretchen, she isn't coming in today. Something to do with her son's school event. She called while you were out."

"Thanks. I'll be sure and tell Gavin." After taking a block of chicken stock out of the freezer and putting it in the Dutch oven to heat, she cleaned and washed the chicken. She seasoned the chicken pieces and put them on to brown in a bit of olive oil and then began chopping onions, celery and carrots.

"It may be a good thing. She doesn't want to bring anything home to her little boy and husband," Mrs. Tillman said.

"You two don't seem worried," Anna observed as she added the vegetables to the chicken along with minced garlic and rosemary.

"No, dear. I hardly ever catch a thing. I have to take care of my babies." Mrs. Tillman smiled.

Anna nodded, knowing how fond the older woman was of her cats. She had three. Her husband had died a few years back, and they hadn't had children. The housekeeper had worked for Gavin ever since he began playing for the Lions. When Mrs. Tillman started, she took care of the house and cooked Gavin's meals, but it soon became apparent that while she was an exceptional housekeeper, her cooking left a lot to be desired.

Vanessa Grant was a very quiet young woman who was raising her teenage sister and much younger twin brother and sister alone. Their mother had died when Vanessa was barely eighteen. From what Gavin had told Anna, she had given up her own dreams of a college education to care for her younger siblings.

After adding the simmering stock to the chicken and vegetables, Anna added a package of egg noodles to the mix.

Anna asked, "Mrs. Tillman would you mind keeping an eye on the soup while I run to the drugstore?"

"No problem, darling. I'm going to clean in here anyway. Today is the day I usually clean Mr. Gavin's rooms, but I don't want to disturb him." She shook her head.

"I can go for you," Vanessa volunteered.

Anna smiled. "Thank you, but if you take care of the telephones calls and manage the office so that Gavin can rest, that will be a big help. You know he would be lost without you."

Reaching for her coat, Anna said, "Mrs. Tillman, the house always looks wonderful. You do a marvelous job, and I am sure Gavin appreciates your hard work. Ladies, it looks as if we're going to have a few rough days until he feels better."

"Maybe you should stay over. What if Mr. Mathis takes ill during the night? I would stay but who would look after my cats? Vanessa has her brother and sisters to look after."

"Maybe for a few days," Anna said absently. "I'll talk it over with Gavin. Excuse me, but I need to get going. I'll be right back with that medication."

"Of course. The sooner Mr. Mathis gets his pills, the sooner he'll be back to normal," Mrs. Tillman replied.

As Anna turned her car around, she accepted that just the thought of sleeping down the hall from Gavin, even if only for a few days, caused her heart to flutter. Mrs. Tillman's suggestion had been innocent enough. Gavin would need another adult in the house to keep an eye on Kyle while he was confined to his bed.

Later, when Anna brought Gavin his lunch and medication, he surprised her when he asked if she would mind staying over for a couple of days, just until he was over the worst of it.

Anna nodded reassuringly, "Of course I will. You shouldn't worry about anything but getting well."

All he could manage to get down was a little soup and a few crackers before he pushed the tray away. He was clearly exhausted.

"You need to get some rest." She reached out to run her hand down his unshaven cheek but pulled back just in time. "Don't worry about Kyle. I'll pick him up from school and then stop at my place to pick up a few things."

Catching her hand, he murmured, "Thank you." Giving her hand a gentle squeeze, he settled against the pillows with his eyes closed.

She tiptoed out of the room with the tray on her hip. She was worried. He had eaten so little.

It was later that night after Anna said good night to Kyle that she took a long hot bath. She changed into a pair of lavender satin-jacquard pajamas, matching robe and slippers before she went to check on Gavin.

His sitting room and bedroom doors had been left open in case he needed something. She softly called his name as she paused in the entrance of his bedroom. His bed was empty, but it was the sound of his retching that had her hurrying into the connecting bath.

"Oh no!" she cried out when she found him on the cool, marble floor on his knees bending over the commode.

"Go away," he moaned, leaning his head on his upraised knees.

Anna flushed the toilet before she soaked a washcloth in cool water, wrung it out, and gave it to Gavin. He covered his face with it as she soothingly rubbed his back and shoulders. "Feel any better?"

"Yeah. I can't keep anything down, not even the medication."

She filled a glass with water. "You might want to rinse your mouth and get that terrible taste out."

"Thanks."

"What can I do to help?"

"Get Kyle to help me up."

"I can do it."

"No . . . I might hurt you. Go on."

"All right. Be right back." She ran out into the thick carpeted hall. Knocking on Kyle's door, she called out, "Are you awake?"

"Come in."

She stuck her head inside the dark room. "Can you help me get Gavin off his bathroom floor?"

"What happened?" Kyle hurried out of bed in his pajama bottoms and an old tee shirt.

"He was sick in the bathroom, and I'm not sure I can get him up by myself."

"Okay. He's that weak?" There was real fear in his voice.

"It's just the flu. Don't worry. He's going to be all right." She patted his shoulder as they hurried down the hall.

"Once the medication starts working, he should feel much better."

Gavin was right where she'd left him. He looked up when Kyle entered with Anna. "Sorry, kid. I know you were in bed, but I can't get up on my own, and I'm afraid I'd hurt Anna."

"No sweat," Kyle said, going over to his brother's side.

"You get on one side of him and I'll get on the other." Anna ducked under his shoulder and tucked hers under his armpit, bracing her arm around his waist.

"I'm too heavy. I can't believe this. I'm as weak as a baby."

"Hush, and try to push up with your feet," she urged, aware that he was two hundred and ten pounds of solid muscle. "Ready, Kyle?"

"Ready." Like Anna, he'd tucked his shoulder under Gavin's armpit and wrapped his arm around his brother's waist on the opposite side.

With Gavin's help, they were able to get him on his feet and back to bed. He released a weary moan once he was settled.

"Thanks, little brother."

"You're welcome." Kyle stuck out his chest. "Need anything else?"

"No, I'm going to be fine. You'd better go back to bed. You have school in the morning."

" 'Night."

"Good night," Anna called after Kyle. "Gavin, are you going to call your doctor, or should I?"

"No. It's late. And there isn't much he can do."

"Maybe he can give you something that will help you keep something in your stomach."

"Not tonight. If I'm not better in the morning, I'll call, okay?"

She didn't like it, but she knew it was his decision. "I'm going to make some herbal tea."

"No tea."

"How about hot apple cider and some saltine crackers?"

"I'm not sure I can keep it down."

"You have to try, or you're going to be dehydrated."

"Okay."

It didn't take long to prepare the tray. Anna was every bit as worried as Kyle but tried not to show it. She debated if she should call the team doctor.

"Here we are." She smiled. After propping a few more pillows behind his back, she handed him the mug of hot cider. "Maybe you better eat a few crackers first."

Gavin nodded, eating slowly, then sipped the hot drink. "What I need is a shower."

"Surely you can wait until tomorrow." She sat beside him on the bed. "Do you think you can keep down another dose of the medication?"

He frowned, but he did manage to keep the crackers down. When she gave him the medication along with a glass of water, he insisted on sitting on the side of the bed until the medication had settled. Finally he was able to lie down and rest.

Certain he was asleep, Anna rose to leave, but he held on to her hand. "Don't go. Come lie down beside me for a while."

The bed was a California King so there was no question about it being roomy enough for both of them.

"I don't think that is a good idea."

"Why? No one will know. Besides, Kyle is asleep by now. If you don't believe me you can go check." When she hesitated, he urged, "Please, sweetheart."

"Just until you fall asleep," she agreed, moving to the foot of the bed. She paused to remove her robe, draping it over the bronze padded bench, before going to the opposite side of the bed.

"Thank you." He flicked back the down comforter and top sheet.

Once Anna was comfortable, Gavin turned off the lamp. The only light came from the bathroom. He shifted before easing her backward against his front, his arm over her waist. She didn't offer even a token protest.

He said into her ear, "I've fantasized about having you in my bed. I just never imagined I'd be too weak to do more than hold you."

"Shush. Don't worry about anything except getting better."

Soon he was sound asleep. Only then did Anna try to rise without disturbing him.

Gavin stirred; his arm tightened around her waist. "Where are you going?"

"I was only going to turn off the light in the bathroom."

"Leave it. I want you with me."

"I'll stay," she promised, realizing that she couldn't fight him and herself as well.

Anna had told herself that she was only going to close her eyes for a few minutes, but when she woke a glance at the bedside clock revealed it was almost six in the morning. She had also shifted during the night and rested with her head on Gavin's shoulder, her face against his copper brown throat and her breasts against his chest. His hand rested on her stomach, his long fingers close to her feminine mound. She trembled as she imagined the heat of his caress cupping her sex.

What was she thinking? She berated herself, determined to ignore the heat burning inside her feminine core. Real or fantasy, it made no difference because she ached with desire. Careful not to wake Gavin, Anna cautiously slipped out of his arms.

He let out a deep breath, and his arms tightened around her, holding her in place. "What time is it?"

"Good morning. It's nearly six. I'm going back to the guest room to shower and dress. Then I'll wake Kyle and fix breakfast. How are you feeling?"

He sighed tiredly.

"Gavin?" She pressed a hand against a beard-roughened cheek. He was still too warm but much cooler than the day before.

"Better. Thanks to you." He kissed her temple.

"Gavin, why don't you try to go back to sleep? I'll send up some breakfast before I take Kyle to school."

"I'll wait until after you've taken Kyle to school. I'm not hungry." He ignored his grumbling stomach. "I'm more tired than hungry."

"Go back to sleep." She kissed the tip of his chin as she got up. He mumbled something, but Anna couldn't quite make it out because he had gone back to sleep.

Even as she showered and dressed, she couldn't put the fact that she'd slept beside Gavin out of her mind. Yes, he was ill, but she also knew she would be lying to herself, if she didn't admit that she enjoyed being near him. Enjoyed it too much for her own peace of mind. There was no question that she would welcome his kisses and yearn for more.

She was already on shaky ground where he was concerned. Gavin was a good man but he wasn't right for her. They wanted different things from life. Her dreams included marriage while his did not. He wanted a relationship, she wanted a lifetime. Yet the knowledge didn't alter the facts. She still wanted him.

If she wasn't careful, she would wind up brokenhearted and alone. With that decided, she vowed to keep her dress tail down and her feet on solid ground. As long as he kept his hands in his pockets, she had nothing to be concerned about.

She sent up a pot of herbal tea and more crackers with Kyle before she turned her attention to making breakfast.

When she came back from driving Kyle to school, she made Gavin's breakfast.

She was stirring honey into cream of wheat when the bell sounded. Racing to the foyer to check the monitor, she was pleased to see her oldest brother. By the time Wesley parked by the garage, she was waiting at the side door.

"Hi, big brother." She smiled as she wrapped her arms around his waist for a hug.

"Hi, yourself, Short Stuff." He kissed her cheek. "I thought I'd check on Gav on my way to practice. How's he doin'? Have you seen him this morning?"

Anna averted her face in hopes of hiding a blush as she ran to rescue the toast from burning. "He's better this morning. He was so sick yesterday that I decided to stay over to take care of both him and Kyle. It was a good thing I did.

"He hasn't been able to keep anything down. Last night I found him in his bathroom on the floor. Wes, I was really scared. He was so sick that he couldn't get up on his own. I had to call Kyle to help. Between the two of us, we got him back in bed. I wanted to call the doctor, but he wouldn't let me."

"You should have called me." Wesley frowned. "Talk about stubborn. I would have brought Joe, the team doctor, with me. Has Gav been able to keep anything down today?"

"Tea and a few crackers. I don't think he's tried taking the medication. In fact, I made cream of wheat with honey and a stack of dried toast for him." She gestured to the breakfast tray.

"I'll take it up."

"Good. You can help him take a shower and freshen up."

"No problem. If he's not better, I'll call Joe." Wesley squeezed her shoulder. "Don't worry. He's not going to let the flu get the best of him."

After her brother left, she began cleaning the kitchen. It was better than giving in to the unacceptable need for a good cry. Her oldest brother was the last person she wanted to find out that she was falling for Gavin. She had her doubts that Wesley believed there was a man alive good enough for his precious sister, including his friend and business partner.

It wasn't that he didn't want her to be happy. He just didn't want her involved with a confirmed bachelor and jock, like he had once been. Wesley and Gavin's friendship went back years. Certainly long enough for Wesley to know Gavin's pattern with women. Wesley didn't have a problem with it as long as none of those women were members of his family.

Too restless to work on her cookbook, she began gathering the ingredients for oatmeal and raisin cookies, one of Gavin's favorites. Anna was pulling the first batch from the oven when Gretchen arrived.

"Something smells good," Gretchen said with a smile. "How the boss?"

"He's better than yesterday," Anna answered as she placed the cookies on the rack to cool. "The cookies will be ready in a minute. Can I pour you some coffee?"

"Girl, you're spoiling us around here," she said with a grin. She was a few years older than Anna, and both she and her husband had worked for Gavin when he lived in New York. They had no problem relocating to Detroit since both of them also had family in the area.

Anna smiled, but she was only half listening. Her thoughts were on Gavin as she scooped out mounds of cookie dough onto the cookie sheet. He had had such a rough night. What if Wes had to call the doctor? What if it had turned into something worse, like pneumonia?

"Wasn't that Wesley's car in the drive?"

"Yes. He's up with Gavin." Anna told her about his problem keeping food down. Naturally, she omitted the part about her sleeping with Gavin. She ended with, "I can just imagine how Gavin's going to take it if Wesley decides to send for the doctor again."

"Lots of kicking and screaming would be my guess. Men are such babies when they get sick." Gretchen managed to get a laugh out of Anna. "I'll be in the office if you need me. Is Vanessa in yet?"

"She's been in since nine. If you two get hungry later, there will be a sandwich tray in the fridge."

Gretchen shook her finger at Anna. "Girl, you are dangerous. My stomach is starting to stick out and it's not even Thanksgiving. I can't get any bigger without losing my husband's affection. Mrs. Tillman and I both have gained at least five pounds since you've been here."

When Wesley returned, Anna had another batch of cookies cooling in a refrigerator drawer and was preparing the sandwiches.

"Good news," he said with a grin as he placed the empty tray on the counter near the sink. "He ate everything, took the medication, and was able to keep it all down."

"That's wonderful. So you didn't have to call the doctor?"

"Nope." Checking his watch, Wesley said, "Look, I've got to run. Call me if you need me. You have my cell number, right?"

"Yes, thanks, Wes."

"No, thank you for taking such good care of my buddy. We both know it isn't part of your job description." He kissed her cheek. "Can I have a few of those for the road?" He pointed to the stack of cookies she had placed in a clear cookie jar.

She smiled, grabbed a Ziploc baggy, and began filling it. She held them out, "For you."

"Thanks. Love you. Bye." With that Wesley was on his way.

Anna wanted to go up to check on Gavin but decided

against it. All she wanted was to look at him, assure herself he was better.

"You have got it bad," she whispered to herself as she finished up the sandwiches for the staff.

Her feelings were like a runaway train. No matter how hard she tried she couldn't seem to shut them down. It was scary. One minute she was helping a friend, the next she was falling in love with the man. Anna didn't need to be told that she was treading down a very slippery slope.

Last night Gavin had asked her to stay with him, just until he fell asleep. She had ended up spending the rest of the night in his arms. When it came to that man, her brain stopped working and her feelings took over.

Anna wasn't kidding herself. She wasn't a little girl anymore. It was time she faced hard facts. If they became lovers, nothing between them would remain the same. There was only one way to keep their friendship intact, and that was to stay as far away from an emotional involvement with him as she possibly could.

He wasn't going to take this about-face well. He'd gone after her like he was charging down the football field with the pigskin tucked under his arm. There was no stopping him once he'd made up his mind. He claimed he wanted her. Anna knew the one thing that would stop him cold.

When he asked about her experience with other men he assumed she was more experienced than she was. And she purposely held back, not ready to reveal the truth. If she had told him, he'd be making tracks in the other direction. And with his looks and income Gavin wouldn't be alone for long. There were plenty of women willing to console him.

Suddenly Anna couldn't stop her disappointment. As tears slipped past her lashes she hurried into the bathroom, closed and locked the door behind her. It was a while before she had her emotions under control. She knew what had to be done. All she had to do was find the courage to do it.

After blotting her face with a cool washcloth, she was ready. She heated the soup and took it to Gavin's room, along with more crackers and a mug of hot cider.

She knew she had found the only solution he couldn't get around. She reminded herself she would be doing what was best for everyone. Gavin and Wesley's friendship wouldn't be in jeopardy. Gavin would find someone else, someone more sophisticated. And she would survive, a bit worse from the disappointment.

She knocked on the open door and walked in. Gavin was sound asleep.

13

Anna was amazed how quickly Gavin regained his strength in the next few days due to lots of rest and good food.

"You guys certainly don't need me to stay over any longer," she told Gavin as she handed Kyle her empty dinner plate. It was Gavin's first day out of bed. They'd just finished the evening meal and Kyle was clearing the kitchen. "When do you plan to go back to work?"

Gavin was dressed in jeans and a white sweatshirt. He'd lost weight and looked tired, even though he'd been up only a few hours. It was clear he was still fighting the effects of the flu although his fever was gone. "Tomorrow. I want to be at the game even if I can't play on Sunday."

"You can't be serious," Anna exclaimed. "You're exhausted right now."

He said in a low, husky voice, so as not to be overheard, "Why are you in such a hurry to leave?"

"You don't need me here at night." She avoided his gaze as she pushed back her chair. "Excuse me. I'll go pack my things." She went over to remind Kyle to put the leftovers in plastic containers and not store the pots in the refrigerator.

As she ascended the stairs she did her best not to focus on the disappointment she'd seen on Gavin's face. While his health had been steadily improving, her resolve hadn't diminished.

She needed to get out of there. Needed to think about what was best for all of them, including Gavin. She couldn't bear it if his friendship with Wesley ended because of her.

She had stayed to care for Gavin, but staying hadn't been wise for either of them. One night of sleeping beside him had left her longing for more. It had always been so easy to say no to the others, but nearly impossible to say no to Gavin.

Gavin was different. He was a strong man, not afraid of responsibility. He was committed to his team and to caring for his young brother. He had also made a commitment to the low-income youngsters who depended on him to help ease the financial burden of building a better life for themselves through his foundation's scholarship program.

What if she was wrong? What if she couldn't make him understand? He could be stubborn, determined to have his way. If he ever devoted himself to going after a woman the way he did everything else, there was no doubt he could change her mind. She couldn't let that happen. She could never be his woman, not without causing difficulties for everyone concerned. She didn't want that.

Recalling the look on his face when she told him she was leaving had been upsetting. She'd hated disappointing him. There was no help for it. As Anna was zipping her garment bag, there was a knock on the open bedroom door. She glanced up, her surprise evident on her face.

"Gavin?"

"All packed," he noted, yet his dark eyes moved over her delicate African features. "I didn't come to give you a hard time but I want you to know I will miss you. I've enjoyed having you here. More important, I'm grateful that you were willing to come and stay."

Anna's heart hammered in her chest. She could either become more deeply involved with him and, in the process, hurt him and her brother, or stay away from him, and then only she would be hurt.

She forced a smile. "You're very welcome. I'm just glad you're better."

"Me too. Anna, I still want to take you out. I hope very soon."

"Gavin, you don't have to repay me for staying."

"I'm not talking about repayment." He walked over to her, stopped so close that she had to tilt her chin to look at him. His voice was filled with frustration and impatience when he asked, "You've changed your mind about us?"

She hesitated. "About being more than friends?"

"That's exactly what I'm talking about. I want more, and I thought you felt the same."

Anna folded her arms under her breasts. "I've been thinking. And I'm not sure if wanting more is worth losing what we've always had." She didn't add that it wasn't worth losing what he had with Wesley.

"It wasn't my *friend* who returned my kisses last Saturday, and it wasn't my *friend* who slept beside me the other night." Before she could formulate a response, he wanted to know, "Why didn't you come to me these past few nights?"

Her heart was pounding when she said, "You know why. It would be wrong with Kyle right down the hall."

He frowned but didn't argue the point. He ran his knuckles gently down the slope of her cheek, then dropped his head until he could rest his forehead against hers. "Kyle was the only reason I didn't come to you." Then he grinned sheepishly. "Besides, I was too weak to get much further than my bedroom door. Sweetheart, I liked having you here, liked knowing you were just down the hall."

"Gavin, don't. It's complicated. We can't talk about this now."

"When then?"

She stepped beyond his reach. She collected her purse and garment bag. "I have to go."

He took her bag. "Let me get that for you."

"But you're not well enough to—"

"You're a lady and my mama taught me a long time ago that ladies are special and must be treated with tender care."

Anna smiled and then walked past him, conscious of the way her body brushed his. How could she keep her defenses in place when she was so vulnerable to him? One glance from his dark brown eyes and her pulse quickened. One brush of his hand against her skin and she tingled from head to toe.

She'd enjoyed her stay, enjoyed it too much. She was no fool. They were way beyond the friendship she'd counted on for years and moving toward something that was both uncertain and frightening. She wanted to hold on to the past with both hands, yet at the same time, she yearned for more, fantasized about it; and her nights were filled with dreams of it. If only there was a way for them to be together without hurting anyone else. Why couldn't it be only about the two of them?

As they descended the staircase, she asked, "What about the new store? Are you still going to New Orleans?"

"No. Since I couldn't go and Wes can't get away at all, Gretchen will go in my place and Kelli will go for Wes." When they reached the main floor, he took her hand to stop her from moving on. "Anna, I need to know why you're having second thoughts. Do you think I can't convince Wes to be openminded about the two of us dating?"

"It's not just Wesley. The men in my family have this anti-quated idea that I can't decide for myself who I want to be involved with. Besides that, they know you too well. They all know you're a die-hard bachelor."

She took a breath before adding, "Gavin, my reluctance isn't only about my family. It's also about me. I'm not sure of anything. We've been friends for so long. This change could be a huge mistake, and I don't think either one of us wants to lose what we have."

"No. What it's about is that I'm willing to take the chance and you aren't. Life is full of risks. There are no guarantees. As for the men in your family, they will have no choice but to accept that you're not a little girl anymore."

"I'm not trying to be difficult. I don't want to come between you and Wesley. As long as my family doesn't know about us . . ."

"I've decided to tell them."

"No. We're not really involved, not yet. It's too soon."

"For whom? You or me? Anna, you don't seem to understand. I care about you. I want to be able to see you openly. I don't like the idea of sneaking behind anyone's back. It's not my way."

Anna walked away and then stopped a few steps inside the kitchen. Gavin was right behind her. She had heard Kyle in the game room a few doors down. She turned and placed both hands against his chest, as if she could hold him still because she was feeling panicky.

"I don't want to rush into anything, certainly not a relationship. You want more than a few kisses. It's going to take time for me to get where you are. If you want me, you're going to have to be patient."

She rushed on, "Gavin, you don't need another distraction right now. You have to deal with Kyle. Then you also have to find your father and try to drag him back here. That's enough without taking on me or my stubborn family members."

"Did it ever occur to you that you're wrong? Your family might not object."

"Believe me they will."

He released a frustrated sigh. Then he dropped his head to press a lingering kiss against the side of her neck and licked the delectable mole that always drove him a little wild. He felt her shivers.

He said into her ear, "Make no mistake. I want you. It's not something we planned, yet it's there. I thought the feeling was mutual. Was I wrong?"

His deep voice sent another quiver racing along her nerve endings. She shook her head, unable to deny the truth. She longed to press the hard tips of her breasts against his chest, conscious of the pressure of his erection.

"Don't play with me, Anna. Talk to me. You don't want me, or the feeling isn't mutual?"

"Oh Gavin. The feeling is mutual, you know it is. This isn't a game to me."

He whispered back urgently, "Then let's start seeing each other. Making time for just the two of us to be together. And let's face your family together. We have nothing to hide."

"I can't." Her dark eyes were filled with doubts. "Please. You're overwhelming. This situation is overwhelming. I guess I'm just plain scared."

"Sweetheart . . ."

She pressed her fingertips against his lips to stop him. Gavin kissed her fingers, nestled a warm kiss in the center of her tender palm, and then caressed the soft skin with his tongue. She jerked her hand away, but she didn't move out of his arms, not yet. She rested her head against his shoulder, inhaling the scent of his dark skin.

"You should be resting, getting better, and I should go home. This argument is going nowhere."

He released a low hiss, as if he were close to losing his patience. "This conversation is far from finished."

Anna smiled. "For now it is. Good night." She reached up and pressed her lips against his.

"Sweetheart . . ." Gavin whispered.

"Please don't. We'll talk later."

Anna had to force herself to not so much as glance at Gavin as she walked to her car.

The flowers started arriving the next evening. Exactly at eight, the florist would drop off a new arrangement. On Friday it was a dozen Golden Fantastic yellow roses. On Saturday it was fragrant Parrot and Painted tulips mixed with two shades of luscious lilacs. On Monday it was a mixture of pinks, Icelandic and Procelina peonies. By the following Wednesday Anna had had enough. Her house resembled a flower shop, and Janet and their catering staff were teasing her nonstop about her mystery man.

Anna stormed into Gavin's office the next evening. They'd shared a quick dinner with Kyle before Anna's father had taken both him and Wayne to one of their classmate's Halloween party. It was the first opportunity she had had to talk to him alone.

Knocking on the open door, she said, "This has got to stop."

Gavin had just replaced the telephone. "What?"

"The flowers. Enough is enough. I told you that yesterday, the day before, and the day before that. Where did you find dahlias, the last day in October? This is Michigan, for goodness' sake. There was frost on the ground this morning."

"You don't like the dahlias?" He leaned back in his oversize leather chair.

"I love them. I love all the flowers, but no more, please. I'd rather you send the money to feed the homeless."

"Okay, I will send a donation in your name in the morning. Anything else?"

Anna shook her head, uncertain of what she saw in his eyes. Was it pain? Disillusionment? Or just plain despair?

"Gavin?"

"Hmm?" he said, absently.

"You gave in too easily. Is something wrong?"

He'd been staring down at the notepad beside the telephone. "Please, come in and close the door."

After doing so, she walked over to him. She leaned against the side of his desk rather than use one of the visitors' chairs in front of it.

"I just got off the phone with Carl Johnson," he explained. "The investigator I hired to track my father. George is in Atlantic City."

"Is he coming back?"

"Not unless I drag him back, and I don't think that's a good idea. Kyle is just beginning to feel comfortable. I don't want him needlessly upset."

Anna nodded. "I'm sorry, Gavin. What are you going to do?"

"What can I do but try and talk some sense into him? I've just chartered a jet for tonight. Can you—"

"You don't have to ask. Of course I'll stay with Kyle."

Gavin nodded, then said quietly as he rose to his feet, "Wish me luck."

"You know I do." Suddenly, she recognized that she needed to hold on to him for a little while, just as she needed to be held in return. She walked around the desk and slid her arms under his jacket and encircled his waist. She let out a soft sigh when his arms wrapped tightly around her.

With her face against his throat, she whispered, "This isn't going to be easy for you, is it?"

His face was buried in her soft, clean smelling hair. "It has never been easy when it comes to being George Reynolds's son."

"How long do you expect to be away?"

"Overnight. Coach will have my head if I miss another practice. I should be home in the morning."

"What are you going to tell Kyle?"

"Nothing. I'd rather he assumed it's a quick business trip." He placed a kiss on her forehead. "Do you mind getting the boys for me?" Gavin was scheduled to pick them up at ten.

"Not at all. I'll stop at home first and pack an overnight bag, and then I'll get the boys."

"Thank you." He tilted her chin before covering her mouth with his own. The kiss was warm, enticing as his tongue briefly caressed hers. "I don't like you driving alone at night." Reluctantly, he let her go.

"It can't be helped. You be careful."

He nodded and then went to pack his own bag.

It was after nine the next evening when Gavin stopped his Navigator in the garage. Grabbing his leather duffel bag from the back, he headed for the side door.

Talk about a wasted trip. The kitchen light was on but the room was empty. He hung his jacket on a hook on the side door and dropped his bag on the bench nearby. He followed the sound of the television into the media room. Anna and Kyle sat on either end of the sofa sharing the wide ottoman and a large bowl of popcorn.

"Hey," Gavin said as he dropped into the recliner, his caressing gaze taking in her soft curves in rose-colored silk blouse and pants. "Pass the bowl."

"Hey yourself." Anna smiled as she reached over to hand

him the popcorn. Her eyes moved over his long length in dark brown trousers and a beige sweater. "You look tired. When did you get in?"

"In time for practice this morning."

"I told Anna you'd be back tonight," Kyle said with a grin. "How was Atlantic City?"

"Fine. How was school today? Did you get the last math test back?" Gavin kicked off his shoes and propped his feet on the footrest.

Kyle beamed. "School was okay. I got an A on that test. Want to see my paper?"

Gavin grinned back. "Yeah, but in a minute. Congratulations. How was English?"

"No test until next week but I got it covered. Wayne and I went over the assignment together this afternoon."

"I'm proud of you, bro."

Kyle smiled, ducking his head. "Thanks."

"Have you eaten?" Anna asked when he handed back an empty bowl.

Gavin could imagine the questions she left unasked. He also suspected she could tell he was disappointed. "More like a snack. Practice went late. Then I had a late meeting at headquarters. My contract is up next year. They're putting out feelers to see which way I might go." When she swung her feet down, he said, "Don't get up. I'll make a sandwich. Want one, Kyle?"

"Naw, I'm cool."

After Gavin left, Anna volunteered, "I'll make more popcorn. Be right back."

When she reached the kitchen, she came up behind where Gavin stood in front of the refrigerator and put her arms around his lean waist. She rested her cheek on his back. "You okay?"

He grunted, turning until he could wrap his arms around

her. "Not really. It was a wasted trip. By the time I arrived last night, good old Dad had checked out of the hotel and disappeared." He swore softly, "We called every hotel in the damn city and couldn't find him anywhere. Believe me, we tried."

"Oh honey. I'm so sorry." She rose on tiptoe to press a kiss against his chin. "I can only imagine how disappointed you are."

He lowered his head, whispering huskily, "Try again."

Anna brushed her mouth against his. He deepened the kiss. After a time, she whispered, "Are you going to tell Kyle?"

Gavin sighed tiredly, dropped his hands to his sides, and moved over to lean a hip against the counter. "What good would it do?" He folded his arms over his formidable chest and then impatiently snapped, "Kyle already knows our father is a bastard. He doesn't need to know how much of a low-life he really is, or that I went to Atlantic City looking for him."

Kyle gasped from where he stood in the doorway.

Gavin swore beneath his breath. "How long have you been standing there?"

"Long enough to know you went to see our father. What happened? You didn't offer him enough to come back to get me?"

"I didn't realize—"

"Yeah, I guessed that much." His hands were balled into fists as he blinked back tears. "Why didn't you tell me?"

Furious by the corner their so-called father had backed him into, Gavin insisted, "I intended to, after I talked to George. I didn't plan on paying him to come back for you. I wanted to talk to him."

"Well? What did he say?" Kyle demanded to know.

Anna mumbled a hasty excuse, but it was Kyle who said,

"No. You don't have to go." His dark eyes were filled with anguish when he asked again, "What did he say?"

"He was gone by the time I got there," Gavin reluctantly revealed.

"It figures," Kyle grumbled, turning to leave.

"Where are you going?"

"To my room. I still have one, don't I?"

Gavin didn't like the boy's attitude, but he didn't call Kyle on it. "Of course." He hesitated, not knowing what he could say to help. He would do anything to take away the pain in his brother's eyes. "You know you're welcome here."

"I wouldn't even be here if he hadn't left me like a bag of garbage."

When Kyle turned to leave, Anna caught his arm before he could go. "None of this is your fault, Kyle. You have nothing to do with your father's behavior."

The boy looked at her with tears in his eyes, and then quickly averted his face. He mumbled a hasty good night and left.

Gavin was fighting the urge to put a fist through a wall.

"Are you all right?"

"Hell no." He quickly said, "Sorry, it slipped out. Every single time that snake's name comes up in conversation, all I can think about is going after him with both fists. He had no right to treat Kyle this way. Now the kid is back to believing I don't want him here. Everything we've done to make sure he's happy and self-assured doesn't amount to a damn thing."

"That's not true."

"It is true," he snapped.

Anna walked over to him until she stood toe to toe with him, her hands on her shapely hips. "I refuse to believe that. Kyle has been a different boy since you went to school and talked to his teacher. I suspect no one has ever shown that much concern for him. Deep inside, he knows you care about him."

"You have no idea how much I want you to be right." He ran an agitated hand over his hair. "You saw how Kyle looked when he heard that our father had disappeared yet again. He believes no one wants him, including me."

"Would you like me to talk to him?"

Gavin shook his head. "He's too upset to listen to anything either one of us has to say tonight," he said tiredly. "It's late. Why don't you stay the night?" At her look of surprise, he hastily added, "You would have stayed if I hadn't come home."

She lowered her lashes. After a prolonged silence she said, "That isn't wise and you know why."

"Do you want me to beg you to stay?"

Anna threw her hands up. "No. That's not what I want. Okay, I'll stay." Anna went to the refrigerator and began taking out the fixings for a submarine sandwich.

"Don't bother. I can—"

"Gavin, sit. You're tired. Maybe a little comfort food will improve your disposition."

"Very funny," he grumbled.

He sat down at the breakfast bar and made an effort to relax, focusing on nothing more demanding than enjoying the sway of Anna's hips as she moved around the kitchen. Oh yes, he wanted her to stay, but for more than one night. If the truth be told, he didn't want her to leave at all.

As he watched her, he couldn't help wondering if she had been as affected by the night she'd slept in his bed as he had. He'd been too damn sick to do more than hold her. Her sweet body felt so right against him.

There was no doubt in his mind that he wanted her in his life and in his bed. He also knew it wouldn't be right to have a woman living with him. Kyle had already seen and experienced too much in his short life. Gavin had no plans for his need to be with her to become part of the kid's education.

Unfortunately, the knowledge didn't eliminate the longing. For now Kyle was his priority. He was responsible for his brother, and he had no choice but to adjust his life accordingly. How had he forgotten one very important detail? Anna was a Prescott.

How much longer was he supposed to pretend that there was nothing going on between the two of them? He swallowed a groan as he acknowledged just how badly he wanted her. Just the thought of holding her all night long, of being able to make love to her the way he'd fantasized doing, caused his penis to throb. He was hard and aching.

Anna wasn't like other women. She was special. She came from a solid family. And they, as well as she, would eventually expect marriage. Marriage was the one thing he couldn't offer. There was no question that she was entitled to so much more than a lengthy affair.

Gavin was selfish enough to admit to himself that he wasn't sure he could let her go. He had no idea how much longer he could keep his hands to himself, because his desire for her grew a bit more potent each day. How many cold showers could he stand before he came down with pneumonia.

"Here you go." Anna placed a plate in front of him.

"Want to share?"

She smiled. "No, thank you."

He concentrated on feeding the need he could appease. The deeper ache was something he couldn't do a thing about.

"How is your cookbook coming?"

"Slowly. I tried a new recipe on Kyle tonight. He ate it, but it's a long way from being ready to go into the book."

Gavin chuckled. "Kyle's not a good tester. A teenaged boy will eat anything."

"That isn't funny."

"Oh, but it's true. I should know. I was once a teenager."

"Then I'll just have to use you as my tester." She flashed him a pretty smile.

She unwittingly brought his gaze to her body. His hungry eyes lingered on the thrust of her full breasts. He could see the way her nipples beaded against the silk of her blouse.

He put down the sandwich he'd taken one bite of and surged to his full height.

"What? Something wrong with your sandwich?"

"There is plenty wrong with me."

Gavin grabbed her by the waist and pressed her soft bottom into his arousal. Just in case she failed to feel his erection, he leaned against her stomach. He dipped his head until he covered her tempting lips with his own.

He groaned at the sweetness he discovered deep inside as he caressed her tongue while cupping her breast in his wide palm. Anna trembled as he used his thumb to worry her nipple through the layers of her bra and blouse.

"Gavin . . ." She clung to his shoulders. No one had ever made her feel this way. So feminine. So incredibly desirable.

"Baby, tell me what you need," he whispered against the side of her sweet scented soft neck. "You can have me any way you want." Only a sliver of control prevented him from rubbing his aching penis against her.

"Gavin . . ."

He smiled against her soft lips as he murmured, "Yes, baby, it's me. Say my name again." He took her tongue inside his mouth and began to suckle.

Anna whimpered.

Gavin moaned heavily as he quickly lifted her up on the counter. He positioned himself between her thighs. His open mouth journeyed along her neck, tonguing her ear, and then sponged the sweet, scented hollow at the base of her throat.

"Anna, let me see you. Let me touch you. Please, baby." His big body trembled with desire as he rested his forehead against hers.

14

"Not here," she barely managed to whisper. "What if Kyle came down for something?"

His kiss was hard, hungry. "Wrap you legs around my waist."

Cupping her soft bottom, he effortlessly carried her down the hall into his office. He used his foot to push the door closed. He put her down on top of his desk, pushing folders, telephone, and everything in the way onto the carpet. He paused long enough to lock the door. His approach was slow and deliberate. He removed the clasp holding her long locks in place, moving his fingers into her cottony black hair.

"What are you doing?"

"You know exactly what I'm doing and why. You're driving me insane with need. I've been aching for you for months," he said an instant before his mouth took hers.

He took his time as he sucked her plump bottom lip before

he stroked her tongue with his own. The hot, honeyed taste of her mouth was too much, yet not nearly enough.

Anna moaned softly, pressing her breasts against his cashmere-covered chest. The sound was both low and sexy, driving him closer to the edge.

"Baby . . ." His voice was raw, raspy.

Yet there were some limits he wouldn't, couldn't cross, not without her consent. As desperately as he wanted to rip her clothes away, he stopped. "Let me . . ." Before he could get the request past his lips she kissed his brown throat, tonguing the male-scented hollow.

"Yes . . . touch me." She buried her face against the place where his neck and shoulder joined.

Gavin whispered, "Where, sweetheart? Where do you need my hands?"

He was determined to ignore his own raging needs even though he was so hard that all he could think about was burying himself in her feminine sheath. More important, he wanted her to need him just as desperately as he needed her.

Anna surprised him when she grabbed the hem of his sweater and yanked it up his chest and over his head. She caressed his dark, hair-roughened skin, her fingertips lingering at his small dark nipples.

After one hungry kiss, he held her still. "I can't take the feel of your soft hands."

His chest was bare but she was still buttoned up tight. He began opening the buttons that lined her blouse before dropping his head to lick her collarbone. Her sob encouraged him to continue down to the sweet scented valley between her breasts. His breath was as uneven as hers.

"Anna, I've waited so long to have you this way." He followed the upper swells of her breasts with the pointed tip of his tongue while filling his lungs with her floral scent.

"Oh yes, please hurry," she whispered.

She didn't have to say it twice. Gavin pushed the blouse off her shoulders and down her arms. He couldn't look away from her lush breasts cradled in an ivory lace bra. Her skin looked so incredibly soft and silky. She was a creamy brown, and all he could think about was tonguing every delectable inch of her shapely frame.

Instantly embarrassed, Anna dropped her long lashes and tipped her head forward so that her long hair flowed over her shoulders and shielded her from his view. When she moved to cover herself, he caught her hands and held them.

"Why, baby?"

She shook her head.

"Please, let me look at you." He nestled his face against her throat, warming the sexy mole he fond there with his tongue.

"I thought . . ."

"What?"

She blushed when she admitted, "You didn't say anything. I thought you were disappointed."

"Disappointed? You can't be serious." He studied her bowed head for a moment. "Anna, you're so beautiful that for a few moments I couldn't find the words to express how perfect you are to me."

Her eyes questioned his. "Really?"

"Yes, really. I've never meant anything more."

Gavin kissed and then licked her soft skin from her collarbone down to the swells of her breasts. He quickly released the clasp behind her back and eased the straps off her shoulders and down her arms.

He released a husky moan as he finally peeled away the lace cups. He hungrily kissed her again and again. She released a sigh when he let her breathe. Then she arched her back, thrusting her large, dark brown nipples forward.

It was Gavin who groaned, as his penis hardened even

more. It was all he could do not to rub his sex against her mound. He reminded himself to go slow. Her experience couldn't match his own.

"Sweetheart . . ." he said as he filled his hands with her breasts.

He gently squeezed her softness, using his thumbs and forefingers to gently tug on the ultra-sensitive peaks. Trembling, she arched her back even more. He growled, eased her back over his arm while he lowered his head. He licked the entire globe from the upper swell to the sensitive underside.

"Your skin is like silk."

By this time, she was more than ready for him. She begged, "Please . . ."

Gavin chuckled throatily. "You want my mouth, sweetheart?" he said an instant before he took one hard nipple into his mouth. As he circled it with the pointed tip of his tongue, Anna cried out her pleasure, which intensified when he sponged the engorged nipple again and again.

"Oh!" Her eyes were tightly closed as she struggled to catch her breath. She pressed her aching mound forward, seeking the firm pressure of his hard-muscled thigh.

He groaned in response as he gave her what she needed. He looked forward to the day when she would be comfortable enough with him to tell him exactly what she needed from him. He took her nipple into the heat of his mouth to apply the exquisite suction they both had waited so long to experience.

He shifted until he could cup her feminine mound through the layers of her clothes. He squeezed rhythmically. He took his time, concentrating on one thing . . . giving her the utmost pleasure. The combination of his mouth and his hand didn't ease until she was sobbing his name. Only then, he slowly moved to the other breast, overwhelming her with the same sizzling hot attention. Anna clung to him as she cried out, quivering all over as she reached a climax.

He assumed that it had been a very long time since she'd known a man's touch and was thrilled that he was the man doing the giving. As much as he relished the taste of her breasts, he longed to taste her feminine core and to hear her scream his name as she reached an even more powerful release.

When Gavin lifted his head, he was forced to accept how close he was to losing control of his own desire. He was needy, hungry for more. He took her mouth in a hot, unrelenting kiss of unfulfilled longing. Then he quickly refastened her bra, threaded her arms into her blouse, and buttoned it. His hands were far from steady when they rested on her waist. He rested his forehead on hers.

"Why did—" She stopped, unable to say the words aloud.

"Why did I stop? Because I was losing control. It's been a long time since I've been with a woman. I don't want to take you here, nor do I want to take you quickly. We both know it's too soon for us to make love. You're still uncertain of how much you want me."

"I do . . ."

"No, I'm not talking about how much you want me at this moment. I genuinely hope you are as wet for me as I am hard for you." He took a calming breath, then said, "I want more than sex from you, sweetheart. And I think you do too. Our timing is lousy. We need to talk about what we want from a relationship and how badly we want it."

He cupped her face in his palm. "Anna, I want you to think about us. Really think about us. I won't hide what's going on from your family. I can't do that and still call myself a man. I won't lie to men that I've grown to both love and respect." He hesitated. "I want your family to know that I care for you."

Her heart was racing with excitement when he said, "You're a very special lady. You've helped me so much with Kyle. Supported me in ways I never expected. You matter to me." He frowned. "Honey, I want to be in your life, and I want you to be a part of mine. We both know we've moved beyond friendship."

Anna bit her lips as she suddenly recalled what she had planned to say to him. The one thing guaranteed to push him away. Only the words wouldn't come. No matter what she thought was best, she couldn't make herself say those words.

"Gavin . . ."

He pressed his fingertips to her lips. "Never mind. Don't say anything for now. Just think about us. Decide if you want me enough to do it openly. Promise me you'll think about it?"

"I will."

"Good. Now I think you better go on up to bed while I'm able to let you go alone."

"Okay." Before she left, she pressed a kiss against his lips.

The next morning Kyle had that chip back on his shoulder. He was every bit as distant as he had been the day he arrived. Gavin tried to give him a few days to settle down. After nearly a week with no progress, he had no clear idea of the best way to resolve the problem. Nothing he did or said made the slightest difference.

They were in Gavin's Navigator en route to school when Kyle asked if he could spend the upcoming Thanksgiving weekend with Wayne at the Prescotts'. Gavin refused outright.

"What do you mean, no?" Kyle threw his brother an angry look.

"You heard me. And you know why I said no. You've been walking around with an attitude since I got back from Atlantic City. I've tried to talk to you half a dozen times and so has Anna. You can hardly open your mouth to say a kind word to anyone. Well, I've had it. Until your attitude changes, don't expect to be going anywhere other than school or church. As far as having company over, the answer is the same."

"That's not fair. Wayne asked his parents and they said yes."

"You have my answer. Get used to it." Gavin warned, "Don't let me get a bad report from your teachers, or you may not be going anywhere until the New Year. You know what it takes to turn things around."

"You're not my father. I don't have to follow your rules."

"You do as long as you're living with me. Do you have enough money for lunch?"

The rest of the trip passed in silence. When Kyle reached for the door handle, Gavin held his arm. "I asked if—"

"Yes, I do."

"Good. You have less than a week to change that attitude if you want to spend Thanksgiving weekend at the Prescotts'."

Kyle nodded and then got out of the car without slamming the door behind him.

Gavin waited until his brother was inside the school building before he pulled out into traffic. He headed toward Allen Park for the team's headquarters.

It had been a rough few days, not all due to Kyle's attitude. He had made a concerted effort not to pressure Anna into giving him an answer. He intended to give her all the time she needed. He'd hoped she would make the decision quickly, but that hadn't happened.

To make matters worse, she hadn't said a word about what had happened between them the other night. He was doing his damnedest to keep his libido under control. It wasn't easy. He was getting sick and tired of cold showers and restless nights. He didn't need a psychic to tell him that he ached to have her in his bed each and every night.

His patience was hanging by a weak thread. It wasn't that

he had any doubts that she was more than worth the wait. Hell, he had been without for too long. Yet, no other woman even came close to her.

He could have easily asked Mrs. Tillman to stay with Kyle while he went out to one of the clubs around the city or to one of his ex-lady friends for some much needed sexual relief. There were plenty of hopeful females willing to do any- and everything to be with a pro player, especially while the team was on the road. There wasn't a player alive who had to sleep alone unless he chose to do so.

The problem was with him. He didn't want to get laid. What he wanted was to make love to Anna. Only she could do what needed to be done to ease the emptiness deep inside. It was her kisses he longed for, her body he wanted desperately to be a part of. Just the taste and smell of her satiny brown skin was enough to keep him hard and needy.

He couldn't forget how her beautiful breasts had filled his hands. Everything about her was soft. When he'd cupped her mound, he wasn't sure if his imagination had taken flight, but he was certain he felt her heat through her clothing.

Given time, he knew he could make her want him the way he wanted her. If only she would give him her trust. He knew that she wasn't as experienced as the women he dated in the past, but she wasn't a virgin. He longed to show her the difference between those college boys she used to date and a man who yearned to pleasure his woman. How he ached to make her his alone.

There was no way Gavin could let himself touch her if she were an innocent. As badly as he wanted her, he would have no choice but to move on. Every woman deserved to be with the man she loved her first time. And regardless of her denial, he knew she had to have cared for the guy, or she wouldn't have given herself to him.

Sweet, sweet Anna. She had no idea how close he'd been to taking her. He had nearly lost control, something that had never happened to him before. It had taken all his willpower not to open her slacks and bare her feminine folds. The next time they were together like that—assuming there was a next time—he would not stop until neither one of them knew where he ended and she began.

Gavin shifted uncomfortably. How much longer would she make him wait for her answer? Kyle wasn't the only one who wanted Thanksgiving to come. He grinned. He too was hoping that Kyle would get his act together and could spend the three-day weekend with Wayne. A few days alone with Anna would be like heaven. Could he convince her to openly go away with him . . . just the two of them? He sighed, knowing it was only wishful thinking on his part.

Although Thanksgiving morning dawned cold and crisp, it was also bright and sunny with no indication of the rain and snow mix that was forecast. Much of the city prepared for the annual Marshall Field's Thanksgiving Day Parade that would make its way along Woodward Avenue. Gavin and Kyle, along with the Prescotts, including Devin, Anna's second oldest brother who had flown home for the holiday, spent the morning volunteering at one of the city's soup kitchens. They pitched in to help prepare the food and the dining room for the holiday meal scheduled for the homeless or anyone in need of a hot meal or just company.

Wesley and Gavin were the first to leave in order to suit up for the upcoming game at Ford Field. When the Prescott men and Kyle left for the game, the ladies headed to the house to prepare their dinner, planned for late that day. Even though a small television that sat on the kitchen counter was tuned to the game, no one was really watching.

"Anna, I want those sweet potatoes whipped not candied," Donna said sharply as she basted the twenty-five-pound turkey.

Anna and Kelli exchanged a surprised look. Kelli's widowed mother, who usually joined the family's holiday meals, had flown out to spend Thanksgiving with her sister in South Carolina's low country.

It was Anna who asked, "What's got you so upset, Mama?"

"I'm not upset," she answered.

"You are," Kelli added, as she made a vegetable and cheese tray. "It's Aunt Ester, isn't it?"

Anna's father's elderly aunt, Ester Prescott, had flown in from Atlanta for the holidays. She had been in the house only four days and already had Donna on edge.

"Nothing I've put in front of that woman has pleased her," Donna said in a frustrated whisper. "The bacon is too salty, the eggs aren't fluffy enough. I tell you, I'm about ready to send her home." Donna sighed heavily, then forced a smile. "Don't mind me. I'm just a little tired. Aunt Ester is really a wonderful person. She's your father's only living aunt, and he loves her dearly."

"If she's so wonderful, how come her daughter Chandra sent her up here for the holidays?" Anna pointed out and had all of them laughing. None of the ladies was paying attention to the action taking place at Ford Field.

"Hush now. We don't want her to hear. She's only taking a nap in the family room. Besides, I don't want her back in here telling me how to cook," Donna said as she went back to shucking corn.

"I told you that you should have sent her home when she made that nasty comment about your rolls. You make wonderful homemade rolls. She just wishes she had your light touch," Kelli defended. "When Wesley and I were over on

Tuesday night, she had plenty to say about everything Donna put on the table. Of course, she never said it in front of Lester."

"You just gave me an idea. Maybe, I'll suggest she visit you two for a few days," Donna teased.

"Please don't do that," Kelli replied.

Donna laughed, her eyes sparkling. "I'd never do that, especially to someone I love."

"What we should have done was send her with Daddy and the guys to the game. Get her out of here for a few hours. Don't get me wrong. I love Aunt Ester, but I love you more." Deciding a change in subject was needed, Anna said, "It's wonderful that Devin was able to fly in last night. I know he's only in St. Louis, but it seems as if he's half a world away. He should have gone to the Lions."

Donna smiled. "He likes playing for the Rams. But I agree with you, it's wonderful to have all our men home for a change. Lester and I were thrilled when he walked through that door last night."

"No new lady friend?" Kelli asked curiously.

"Not that I heard of but then I'm the last to know these things. You, young lady"—she pointed at Anna—"are a prime example of someone keeping secrets."

"Mama, what are you talking about?"

"Your cousin and brothers and Dad may be fooled, but don't try that mess with me. Something is going on with you." Her mother waved a corn cob before she went back to the next ear of corn. "And you"—she motioned to her daughter-in-law—"Miss Know-What's-Going-On, and don't pretend that you don't."

Kelli, realizing that her mouth was hanging open, decided to close it. "I should go check on the baby."

"My grandbaby is fine. You just put her down not twenty minutes ago."

Anna pressed her hands to her hot face. "Mama . . ."

"Don't 'Mama' me. Keep your secrets. But I know these shopping trips and days at the salon have to do with a man. What do you think? My mama dropped me on my head when I was a baby?" Donna huffed.

"Mama, where did you get that expression?"

"Sounds like down on the farm to me." Kelli laughed.

"Humph. You both are stepping on dangerous ground."

"Okay, okay, I do have news. I wasn't trying to keep it from you, but you know how protective the men in this family are. They don't believe there's a man alive good enough for me."

Donna raised a brow. "What does that have to do with me? You're mine. I didn't know we had secrets."

Anna insisted, "Mama, I never meant to hurt your feelings."

"That tells me nothing." Donna turned her attention to Kelli. "And you. I've done everything I can to make you feel like my own. I couldn't love you more."

Kelli brushed back a tear. "Oh, Mama Prescott, don't. If Anna won't tell, I will."

Donna fired questions at Anna. "Who is he? How long have you known him? How come you haven't brought him by the house to meet me? Something wrong with him?"

Anna and Kelli exchanged a look.

"Well?"

Kelli threw her hands up, claiming, "She made me promise."

Anna refused to drop her head as if she had done something wrong. It had been hard enough not letting Gavin guess what was in her heart. She had no idea how long he would put up with her delays. Or if she could convince him to keep what they shared between the two of them. As of yet she had not given him an answer. Now her mother wanted answers as well.

Donna went over and took both Anna's hands into her own. "What's wrong, precious? Why is it so hard to tell me?"

Anna blurted out, "It's Gavin, Mama. I'm falling in love with him."

Whatever Donna had expected her to say, judging by the shock written on her lovely brown features, that wasn't it. "Gavin? Our Gavin?"

Anna nodded, watching as her mother slowly sank into a tall kitchen chair. "Now you know why I didn't tell you. Can you imagine what the others would say if they knew?"

"The football game is over, ladies. Time we got moving. The men will be here soon," Kelli announced.

"It will do them good to wait. If they make too much fuss, we'll go on strike and let them finish up." Donna laughed. She framed Anna's face in her cupped hands, "Does he make you happy?"

"Very much," she said softly.

"He better, or he'll have me to answer to. Okay, Kelli, you check on those greens, and Anna, after you put those potatoes on, get busy frosting that cake. You know how much our men love your carrot cake. And I'm going to scrape down this corn and get it on the stove. Shouldn't take too long. The macaroni and cheese is ready to go in the oven, the chitlins are nearly done, and the rolls are almost ready. I forgot to ask. Who won the game?"

The three looked at each other blankly, recognizing they didn't have a clue. They started laughing.

Kelli said, "We're in trouble. The first thing Wesley is going to do is ask what we thought of the game."

It was Donna who said, "Don't worry, we'll just smile, nod our heads at whatever they say and try not to look too stupid."

While Kelli and Anna were putting the finishing touches on the table, Kelli said, "That wasn't so bad, was it?"

"Bad enough. Did you see how stunned she was? I couldn't have surprised her more if I'd walked across Ford Field during half-time."

Donna, carrying in the apple and cranberry relish her family loved, overheard. "So you surprised me. I'll get over it. Gavin has been happy being a bachelor, while you, young lady, have been so busy building your business that you haven't taken time to even date. Even you have to admit it was a shock."

"I know. Gavin's insisting on telling the family. I'm the one who is holding back. I'm still getting used to the idea myself. I never expected to fall for him the way I have. We've been friends so long and I didn't want to risk losing that. Besides, you know the men in this family." She shook her head, wearily.

"You're both over the age of consent, and you have the right to pick your own man. So tell me, does Gavin know how you feel?"

"That I think I'm falling in love with him? No, I'm not ready to bare my soul. We're still getting used to the idea of being a couple."

Suddenly they heard boisterous male voices coming from the kitchen.

Anna whispered anxiously, "Mama, I don't know how long I can keep this from the others, but for now I'm not ready to share it with them."

"How long do you think that's going to last?" Donna was clearly not happy about the secrecy.

"As long as possible. Promise you won't tell, please?" Anna pleaded.

"Only for now." Donna gave her a quick hug.

15

Gavin followed Wesley into the Prescotts' spacious and noisy kitchen. His eyes moved around the room until they found Anna. She was at the stove, laughing at something her cousin Ralph had said. She looked up at the sound of Wesley's booming voice. Her eyes collided with Gavin's before she blushed and dropped her lids.

"Something sure smells good," Gavin said as he came over to kiss Donna's cheek. "Tell me you made it?" He grinned, forcing himself not to stare at Anna.

Anna was beautiful, dressed in an ivory sweater set and black velvet slacks. Why had it taken him so long to appreciate what was right in front of his face?

Whenever Anna's company catered one of the team's events, she was the one the guys engaged in conversation. He had noticed but he assumed it was because she was in and out of the guys' homes on a daily basis. Besides, what could he say? Anna was her own person. When she started working for him so many things had changed.

Donna broke into his thoughts when she laughed. "Yes, I made collard greens." Patting his lean cheek as she would one of her sons, she said, "Lester and Wayne have been raving about how good you were out there today. Two touchdowns. Congratulations."

Gavin nodded. "Thanks, but it wasn't enough. We lost."

"Nonetheless, you boys did your best. That's all anyone can ask."

"What about me?" Wesley said, coming over to give his mother a big hug.

Donna reached up and kissed his cheek. "You did your best. Next time you'll get them." She set Kyle and Wayne to work filling the water glasses. "Anyone ready to eat?"

There was an uproar from the men. The women filled the serving bowls, but it was a man who brought them out. Lester seated Aunt Ester at the head of the table. Every head was bowed as Ester said the blessing. As always, the table was brimming with good food, and the house was filled with good-natured teasing and laughter.

Time and time again, Gavin had to pull his gaze away from Anna's engaging smile as she laughed at something one of her brothers said or teased Devin because he never brought any of the women he dated to meet the family. Ralph, on the other hand, had brought along yet another one of his many lady friends.

Gavin was decidedly uncomfortable with the fact that he shared a table with people he loved, yet he was forced to pretend there was nothing going on between him and Anna.

He planned to give her as much time as she needed to decide, but the waiting was getting to him. How much longer did she expect to keep him off balance? Gavin had always been a patient man. Evidently that didn't apply when it came to Anna.

"You ladies have outdone yourselves this year," Devin grinned as he patted his flat stomach. "I can't eat another bite."

They received cheers from the men.

"No room for the dessert?" Anna asked as she leaned over to place her hand on her brother's forehead. "Mama, call the doctor. He must be sick."

"Don't let it worry you." Ralph slapped his cousin on the back. "I'll eat his cake and mine."

Devin laughed, "Forget it. I'll make room."

"That's more like it." She crossed to the sideboard where there was an array of delectable treats that included German chocolate cake, carrot cake, sweet potato pie, lemon meringue pie, and wild berry pies.

"Don't force yourself, Dev. I'll eat his, Anna," Wayne offered.

"No, I will," Kyle joined in.

Everyone laughed.

"I can't figure out where you two fellows put it all." Lester shook his head. "But I haven't forgotten how Wesley, Devin, and Ralph ate when they were your age." To his wife he said, "You remember that, don't you, honey?"

"How could I forget?" Donna laughed.

Devin, Gavin, and Wesley began clearing the table while Anna and Kelli started plating the desserts and Ralph served coffee. After the meal, Wayne rinsed the dishes while Kyle filled the dishwasher and Lester and Ralph cleaned the kitchen. The ladies relaxed in the living room. Later Wayne and Kyle went off to play video games and the men went into the family room to watch a college football game.

Anna was just leaving the powder room when she literally bumped into Gavin.

"Excuse me." She smiled, tilting her head back to meet his dark eyes.

"My fault." He'd placed his hands on her shoulders to steady her. "You look very pretty tonight."

"Thank you. How are you?" Anna, who was busy studying his mouth, didn't consider moving away. Her hands were splayed on his deep chest.

"I'm much, much better now that you're almost where I want you." Dropping his head, he nestled her sweetly scented throat. "Kiss me," he whispered. "I have wanted to taste your lips since I walked in the door. Did you miss me as much as I missed you today?"

Anna sighed softly, her breath warming his chin. She held on to the side of his lean waist for balance. "We can't. Someone might see us."

"One kiss," he bargained in a quiet whisper. "Or would you rather I kiss you?"

"Not here," she pleaded, yet was unable to look away from his dark, handsome features.

"Yes." He gently brushed her mouth with his own. "Please . . ."

Anna shivered with excitement and then moaned softly before she gave him the kiss he requested. When he would have pulled away, she teased the corner of his mouth with her tongue. He groaned and opened for her. Anna's tongue slid inside his mouth, mesmerizing them both as she began stroking his tongue with her own. When she would have pulled back, he leaned forward, suckled her bottom lip as he wished to suck her sweet nipples.

"Sweetheart, I need you so badly. Don't make me wait any longer. Please, tell me what you decided." He couldn't resist taking another kiss, this one longer and deeper than the last.

"I'm telling you that Cameron went after you like—" Devin was talking to Wesley as they walked out of the family room. Both men stopped suddenly when they saw Gavin had Anna pressed against the wall, his mouth covering hers.

"What the—"

Gavin jerked his head up and all four of them stared at one another. Shock and disbelief played along both brothers' faces as Gavin put some distance between his and Anna's bodies. He gave her hand a quick, reassuring squeeze.

"What in the hell is going on?" Wesley demanded.

"Are you blind? He was all over her," Devin shouted.

"That is not true," Anna said.

"Like hell. Have you lost your damn mind, man? Going after my baby sister like that." Wesley advanced on them.

Gavin stiffened as he turned to face the other men. "Let me explain."

"I know what I saw," Devin yelled.

"No. You know nothing." Anna stepped in front of Gavin.

"Why don't you tell me what's going on? And it better be good." Devin warned. "Man, I'll break you in half before—"

"Shut up. All of you," Anna yelled.

"What is going on? Why all the shouting?" Lester asked as he came out of the family room with Ralph a few steps behind him.

Anna wished the floor would open up and swallow her whole. This was getting way out of hand.

"Devin and I were on our way back to the kitchen and found Gavin with his hands all over Anna. He had her backed against the wall," Wesley snarled.

"That's not what you walked in on." Anna pleaded, "Will you lower your voices so we can talk about this calmly."

Wesley moved forward and lifted his sister out of the way, as if she weighed next to nothing. "This is between me and Gavin." Wesley gestured toward the end of the hall.

"No." Anna grabbed her brother's arm. "What you saw

was Gavin kissing me and me kissing him back. That's all you saw."

Gavin said to her, "Stop worrying. We're just going outside to talk."

"Let's all talk," Lester said tightly as he walked down the hall and then held open the door to the suite of rooms he shared with his wife. Once they were all inside with the door closed, Lester gestured to the sofa and armchairs positioned in front of fireplace. Only no one made a move to sit down.

"What is this about, Gavin?" Anna's father asked. "Is there something we all should know?"

"This is ridiculous," Anna interrupted. "This has nothing to do with any of you. It's between Gavin and me."

Gavin placed a hand on her shoulder. He gave it a gentle squeeze. "Anna is right. Lester, we care about each other, that's all that should concern any of you."

"If you care about her, why have you kept it a damn secret?" Wesley demanded. "I haven't heard a thing about it, that's for damn sure." Before Gavin could answer, he answered his own question. "I will tell you why—it's because you're using her."

Lester placed a restraining hand on Wesley's arm. "Is that what is going on here Gavin?"

"No," Anna interjected. "Gavin, don't answer that. I've had about as much of this as I'm going to take. You all have no right to gang up on him as if he's done something wrong." She blinked back angry tears. "It was my idea, not his, to keep our involvement a secret."

"Sis, you don't know what kind of man he is when it comes to women," Devin put in.

"Sure I do." She glared at her second-oldest brother. "Gavin is just like you, Devin, Ralph, and Wes before he got married. That's the problem."

"You don't understand," Wesley insisted. "You can't know—"

"I know all I need to know." She went over to her father while fighting to hold on to her control. Giving in to tears would only make her appear weak. Determined to say what was in her heart, she insisted, "Daddy, I'm not your little girl anymore. I'm a grown woman. I've had enough of this double standard you have going on. One set of rules for me, and another set for the guys. It's never been fair, and I won't stand for it any longer."

Her father looked as if she had slapped him. "Whatever I've done has been to protect you, precious."

"You can't protect me from life. I made my choice. I want to be with Gavin." Anna moved back to Gavin's side and slipped her hand into his. "If I choose to sleep with him, that's my business, no one else's."

Wesley snapped, "You're going to end up hurt. He isn't the kind to offer a wedding ring."

Anna had had more than enough. "Let's go." She looked up at Gavin. She could read the hurt in his eyes even though his features were tight with tension.

Gavin wasn't ready to leave but he couldn't ignore the desperate plea in her eyes. Once they were in the hallway, he said, "Why don't you get your things and Kyle?"

"No," she whispered. "You're not going back in there without me. This is my fight as well as yours."

He struggled not to show the despair and hurt he was feeling after being attacked by men he loved and had considered family for so many years. Lester had been more of a father to him than his own ever could be. He and Wesley had shared everything over the years. It was apparent that not one of them felt he was good enough for Anna.

"Please, Gavin, let's go now."

His chin jutted stubbornly. "I have nothing to run from.

You go ahead, explain to your mother and get Kyle. I will be right out."

"No, Gavin."

"Yes. Don't you see, this is something I have to do?"

With large, troubled eyes, she searched his gaze. Eventually she begged, "Hurry?"

He nodded but didn't move until she disappeared down the hallway.

The instant Gavin walked back into the room, Wesley stepped into his path. The two men, best friends and business partners, stared at each other as if they were strangers.

Wesley broke the oppressive silence when he said, "I never expected you to do something like this. I trusted you around my family. I even encouraged her to work for you. Tell me, do you actually expect me to stand back and let you use her?"

"Use her?" Gavin glared at the other man. "You have no idea what's going on between the two of us, or how we feel about each other."

Ralph stepped between them. "It hurts because we trusted you."

"You could have fooled me. I don't see any trust."

Wesley demanded, "What do you want from her? Her body or her heart? You won't get one without the other. She's not that kind of woman. I'm warning you, Mathis, to leave her the hell alone."

Gavin chose to ask his own question. "What have I done other than care about her?"

"All I want to know is one damn thing. Are you planning on marrying her?" Devin interjected.

Taken aback, but not the least bit surprised, Gavin said, "You know how I feel about marriage."

It was Ralph who insisted, "Anna deserves more than a few months of great sex. She deserves to have a home and family of her own."

"Enough." Lester held up his hand. He went over and looked Gavin in the eye. "I love you like family but I won't accept this. Anna is precious to all of us. I've raised my boys to always look out for her. That won't change. We all know that you and Anna are consenting adults. No one here is denying that. This decision is between the two of you, but don't expect anyone here to sit back quietly and accept it. If you want her, then marry her. Short of that, leave her alone. I'd rather see her with hurt feelings than have her spirit crushed and heart broken once you've moved on."

Gavin's eyes were burning from suppressed tears when he candidly admitted, "I can't walk away from her as if what we feel for each other doesn't matter. Believe me, I have tried to stay away from Anna." He looked at each man in turn before he quietly said, "You're the ones hurting her, not me. I have always been straight with her. Know this, you will be sorry if you make her choose between us. Don't let it come to that."

Anna went in search of her mother. She found her in the kitchen making coffee.

"Honey, what's wrong?" Donna asked.

Brushing away tears Anna hissed, "Ask my muleheaded father, brothers, and cousin. They ganged up on Gavin. They actually told him that if he's not interested in marriage, then to leave me alone."

"What? How did that happen?"

"When Wesley and Devin came out of the family room, they saw Gavin and me kissing in the hallway. Wesley and Gavin started arguing, then Daddy and Ralph joined in. I'm surprised you didn't hear them. Mama, they actually told me to stay out of it, as if it's not my life they were talking about. How could they?"

"Oh no. Precious, I'm so sorry. Maybe if I—"

"No, Mama," Anna interrupted. "How could they embarrass me like that? They even had the gall to accuse Gavin of keeping our involvement a secret. That was my idea, not his." She fought to hold back a sob.

"Calm down." Donna came over and gave her a hug. "You don't want Gavin to see you upset by this."

Anna nodded. "I know." She took in deep, calming breaths in hopes of getting a handle on her emotions. "It's my life and no one can live it for me. No one, no matter how well-meaning they are."

"That's right." Donna sighed. "I've got to try and talk some sense into them."

"Please, Mama, don't even try." Anna tucked several locks behind her ear. "I have to go get Kyle. We're leaving."

"You can't leave now."

"We have to. Kyle is going to be so disappointed that he can't stay over the weekend."

"Where is Kyle? Didn't you—" Gavin interrupted, his jaw taut with anger and disappointment.

"He's playing video games with Wayne in his room. Surely he can stay?" Donna pleaded. "They have been looking forward to this visit for weeks. Wayne has made so many plans for them."

Gavin said wearily, "I know, Donna. But after what's been said I don't think it's a good idea to leave him."

"Well, I do." Donna insisted. "Regardless of what was said between you and the others, Kyle is more than welcome to stay. It's not fair to spoil their plans."

"Mama's right, Gavin. Both of the boys have been looking forward to spending time together." Anna touched his arm. "Kyle was so excited this morning. This is his first sleepover."

Gavin looked from one woman to the other. Finally he nodded. "If you're sure. You'll call me if there is a problem?"

Donna reached up and kissed his cheek. "I will take good

care of him. And Gavin"—she paused—"why don't we all give this matter some time? The men will come around. Besides, nothing has to be settled tonight."

Gavin nodded and then smiled. He took Anna's coat out of her hands and helped her into it. He grabbed his own suede jacket from the hook near the door. "Ready?"

Anna forced a smile. "Yes, I am."

She paused to kiss her mother's cheek and accept the reassuring hug her mother offered before she let Gavin usher her out the back door. They were silent as Gavin walked her to her car.

It was Anna who spoke first. "Honey, I'm so sorry. You were—"

Gavin pressed a finger against her soft, red-tinted lips. "You have no reason to apologize. I shouldn't have started something I couldn't finish."

"It wasn't your fault."

He shook his head. "We need to talk. I'll follow you back to your place."

After she nodded her agreement, he waited as she activated the keyless entry, then held the door for her. She slid behind the steering wheel. Gavin reached past her and secured her seat belt.

"Drive safely. I'll be right behind you." He locked and then closed her door before jogging to his own car.

Anna forced herself to concentrate on her driving rather than the horrible scene at her parents'. It was much worse than anything she could have imagined. Was it possible to be more embarrassed? Her father couldn't see that she wasn't his little girl anymore, while her brothers and her cousin were worse.

She wouldn't blame Gavin if he decided he didn't want to be involved with her. How could she? She might have to accept that he might no longer feel she was worth the effort. She bit her bottom lip to hold back a tremor. Nothing she could do or say could make up for what her family had just put him through.

She was still shaking from hurt, rage, and worry by the time she met Gavin in her driveway. Thank goodness she had her tears under control. Letting go like a leaky faucet couldn't take back what had already been said.

He was tight-lipped as they walked up to her front porch. She tensed even more as if she was waiting for the other shoe to fall. Nothing was said until they were inside the house with the door locked behind them. Gavin hung her jacket along with his in the small coat closet in her tiny foyer.

She was the one to admit, "I still can't believe it. You would think I was the same age as Wayne. How could they?"

Gavin went to her and just held her.

"I'm surprised you even want to hold me," she whispered against his shoulder.

"Let it go." He soothed a caressing hand down her back. "Besides, I can't think of anything I want more than to be right here with you."

Anna tilted her head back until she could look into his face. Despite the fact that the foyer was lit only by a single low-burning bulb, she was able to see his drawn features. Her family had put him through hell.

He didn't deserve to go from friend to enemy in a single evening. Nor did he deserve their anger and mistrust. All of it was her fault, and although she had seen it coming, she had been unable to stop it.

She lifted up on her tiptoes and kissed his cheek. Her voice was barely above a whisper when she said, "Wesley didn't mean all the things he said. He just let his anger get the better of him."

Gavin said gruffly, "It doesn't matter. Wes made his decision and I've made mine." His arms tightened around her.

Anna heard the pain in his voice and knew there was nothing she could say to erase it. "Maybe in a day or so, after he has had time to—"

"If I were you, I wouldn't put any cash on it." His sarcasm wasn't lost on her.

She sighed as she slowly entered the living room, stopping to turn on a Tiffany-style torchère lamp. "Too bad I didn't punch my big brother in his oversize mouth," she mumbled.

Why hadn't Wesley been on her side on this? If he had been, then surely she could have persuaded Ralph and Devin around to her way of thinking.

"Did you say something?" Gavin asked from just over her shoulder.

"Nothing important. Would you care for something?" Feeling more at ease in the role of hostess, she offered, "I could make some—"

"You don't have to entertain me, sweetheart."

"Sorry. What did they say to you after I left?"

"Believe me when I say you really don't want to know."

Her legs were so shaky that she sank down on the edge of the sofa, certain he was right. "Tell me anyway." She patted the cushion beside her.

"After Wes insisted on wedding bells, your dad at least, was a bit more reasonable. He acknowledged that we're consenting adults. But he let me know he's not prepared to sit quietly and let me take advantage of you. He'd rather see your feelings hurt now than have you be brokenhearted later."

Anna covered her face with her hands. Truly, she didn't want to hear more. Was it possible to feel any more embarrassed by all this? Somehow she doubted it.

"Sweetheart, are you okay?" he asked tenderly.

She dropped her hand and forced her chin up. "I have to be. This feels like something out of a very bad movie. At least this didn't spoil Kyle and Wayne's plans for a long weekend. They have been looking forward to it for weeks."

"Yes. You and your mom are right. Kyle would have never forgiven me if I had dragged him home with me." He reached over and squeezed her hand. "At least your mother seemed to be all right with us being involved."

Anna smiled. "Yes, she is. She knew something was going on with me. I told her earlier, while we were preparing dinner. Like you, she wasn't pleased by the secrecy, but she was willing to give us a chance."

She watched him push to his feet.

She whispered, "It's my fault. If I hadn't leaned toward you . . ."

He came back to her, dropping down beside her, and took her hands into his bigger one. "We both wanted that kiss. Don't beat yourself up about it. Anna, they were bound to find out about us. Sooner or later one of us was going to slip up. I can't tell you just how many times I've almost told Wes myself. The only thing that held me back was the promise I made to you."

He pressed a kiss into the warm center of her palm. "It's not like I didn't know how protective Wes is of you. It just never occurred to me that he'd believe I'd deliberately use you. The man I thought was my friend all these years evidently doesn't even know me." The bitterness in his voice was unmistakable.

"No, please, don't think that. You were angry, and so was Wesley. Once things settle down, the two of you will talk calmly."

"All that's needed to be said has been said. Tell me, do you agree with Wes? Do you think that I'm out to take advantage of you, to hurt you?"

"Absolutely not. I know better." She was pleased to see the relief in his dark eyes. There was so much more that needed to be said, only she didn't know how to say it without making him feel as if he was on the spot. "Gavin . . ."

She was silent so long that he prompted, "Anna, just say whatever you need to say."

"We've only been involved a few weeks, but I don't want you to think I'm trying to trap you into marriage." Her eyes filled with a mixture of concern and embarrassment.

He slid an arm around her shoulders, brushed a kiss against her temple. "Sweetheart, you don't have to defend yourself to me. I know this marriage thing wasn't your idea, but your family's."

She smiled in relief as she leaned her head against his shoulder, relishing their closeness.

He said close to her ear, "Your family is right about one thing." When she tilted her head back to see his face, he candidly admitted, "I want you . . . only you. I've been careful over the years to never hurt a woman the way my father hurt my mother. He'd promised her marriage to get her to sleep with him and when she became pregnant with me, he still didn't tell her the truth. Rather than marry her, he just disappeared from her life. He stayed away long enough to ensure that she would be desperate to see him again."

She moved a hand soothingly over his chest. "I understand."

"I don't want you thinking that someday I might change my mind and want to marry. That isn't about to happen. I won't do what my father did . . . I won't make promises I can't keep. I don't run away from my problems, nor do I throw money away. But that doesn't change the fact that I'm his son. There has to be a reason why I've never wanted to be involved in a serious relationship until now. I don't know. It's different this time . . . different because of you. I'm different with you."

Absently caressing her knuckles with a thumb, he whispered, "Anna, I care for you. And I don't want to hurt you, not ever. Would it be better if I walked away now?"

16

Her heart swelled with both fear of the unknown and longing as she slid her arms around his neck. "I appreciate your honesty. The last thing I need is empty promises. I've been running from my feelings for you for weeks now. I realized today that it doesn't matter if my family disapproves. Don't get me wrong. I'm not happy about their disapproval but it won't stop me. None of that changes how I feel about you. I want you, Gavin."

Anna didn't add that she wanted him so badly she was willing to take him any way she could get him. Gavin let out a heavy sign of relief an instant before their lips met in a long, sensual exchange.

"Oh Gavin," she whispered as she moistened suddenly dry lips. He responded with a heavy groan before he savored the sweet honey of her soft mouth. Anna arched her back, pressing her breasts into his deep chest, needing the hard pressure.

"So sweet," he murmured as he eased her back to fill his hands with her generous breasts. "Anna . . ." he whispered as he gently squeezed her softness before he worried her aching nipples with his thumbs. The hard peaks beaded as he stroked her through the layers of her sweater and bra.

She shivered from the pleasure. "Please . . ."

"What, sweetheart? Tell me what you need," he urged against her lips as he took yet another lengthy kiss.

She was breathless with yearning when he freed her mouth. He waited for her response. Anna blushed at the very idea of verbalizing her needs.

When she couldn't meet his gaze, he cradled her, whispering, "I want us to be lovers. No secrets, no desires unmet."

She bit her bottom lip before she confessed, "Every time you touch me, I want more. When you caressed my breasts, I didn't want you to stop."

"I don't want to stop," he said huskily as his lips warmed the scented hollow at the base of her throat. He released a throaty groan, then he kissed her, deeper than before. "Sweetheart, you have no idea how long I've craved your sweetness. The night you slept in my arms was the best and worst. The best because I could hold you, but the worst because I was too sick to make you mine." He kissed her before he asked, "Where do you need my touch? Or would you prefer my mouth?"

Anna buried her face between his neck and shoulder.

Despite the fact that her body shook from the power of his arousal, he needed to hear the words. "Anna . . . please. Do you want me the way I want you? Do you want me to make love to you?"

It took every ounce of courage she possessed to look into his eyes and say, "Yes, I want you to make love to me. I'm just not sure I can"—she swallowed the lump in her throat—"satisfy you. You've been involved with women like Natasha Baker. Beautiful women who are more experienced."

"You have nothing to be concerned about. With you it's different. I want you more than I've ever wanted any other woman. This isn't a contest. It's about the way you make me feel. You matter to me, Anna. If tonight isn't right for you, then we'll wait until it's right for both of us."

Rather than give in to her own doubts, she concentrated on how he made her feel. Anna brushed her mouth against his again and again. When he opened for her tongue, she slid inside and stroked his tongue with her own. Gavin moaned, deepening the kiss even more. She quivered with pleasure as he suckled. Gavin licked a path down her neck, sponging the warm hollow before moving down to the edge of her vee-neck sweater.

She pressed a hand against his chest. "Not like this."

"You've changed your mind?"

Quick to reassure him, she said, "No, I haven't, but I didn't imagine our first time would be like this. I wanted to look special for you."

He grinned. "Imagined it, huh?" Evidently he was pleased that she'd given some thought to the two of them together. He hastily reassured her, "You're beautiful just the way you are."

She kissed him tenderly. "No, I smell like turkey and the cream frosting I put on the cake. I envisioned a candlelit dinner and music. I'm being silly, aren't I?"

"Never that." He chuckled as he rose and walked over to the built-in shelves and her stack of CDs. He quickly made a selection and placed it in the compact player on a higher shelf. Smiling indulgently, he asked, "That's better. Now for the candles."

He grabbed an arrangement of taper candles he found on one side of the mirrored mantel and placed them in the center of the coffeetable. "Matches?"

Laughing, she shook her head. "There's a lighter in that

drawer." She pointed to the small desk tucked into the corner of the room.

"Great." Once he had lit the candles he glanced at her. "What else do we need?"

She couldn't stop smiling. "Wine. I'll get it."

"No, you stay right there. I'll find it." He headed for the kitchen.

Anna leaned back against the sofa cushion, hugging herself. She was nervous, but happy. Yet there was still something she hadn't told him. And she was starting to wonder if she should continue to keep it to herself. Gavin was back before she could decide. He carried a small tray of cheese and crackers, an opened bottle of wine, and two long-stemmed crystal glasses.

As he filled their glasses with a rich, fruity chardonnay, he said with a smile, "Not exactly dinner."

"It's wonderful. You're wonderful. Thank you."

He held out a glass of wine, but when she reached for it, he shook his head. "Not without a kiss."

She laughed as she rose and looped an arm around his neck. She teased his bottom lip with a flick of her tongue before she gave him a sweet kiss.

"We need to make a toast." He smiled down at her. "To us."

They clinked glasses. Anna hadn't taken more than a sip when Gavin took the glass away and pulled her into his arms. As they moved to the music, Anna rested her head on his shoulder.

When the soft soothing sounds of Natalie Cole's "Unforgettable" started playing, she whispered, "I love this song," as her lips brushed his throat.

"Sweet and sexy. Just like you." He pulled her closer, until her breasts were cushioned against his chest.

She trembled from the feel of his long length against her. He was all hard angles, unyielding muscle and heat. There was no doubting his arousal. He cradled her as he moved a muscular leg between her thighs, causing her to sway with him.

"How am I doing?"

"Very well." With her eyes closed she focused on the feel of him. She pressed her open mouth against his throat once more.

Gavin quivered, placing a finger beneath Anna's chin, angling her face up toward his. His kiss was hot, raw with need.

"Mmm," he sighed, as he deepened the kiss. He didn't stop until he had lifted her off her feet and her soft mound nestled his hard sex. "You feel so good . . . so right."

"Oh, honey . . ." she whispered throatily.

He trailed kisses down her throat before he placed her back on her feet, easing away just enough to blow out the candles. His big hands clasped her waist, and then he tossed her onto a powerful shoulder.

"Gavin!" she screeched, steadying herself by placing her splayed hands on his broad back.

He laughed as he walked down the short hallway toward the bedrooms.

"You have lost it."

"No doubt. But you drove me to it."

Once she was back on her feet, she teased him, "You call that romantic? One sip of wine and one turn around the living room? What about the cheese and crackers? I didn't get one bite."

"Hold on." He turned on his heels.

While he was gone, Anna didn't even try to suppress her joy as she turned on the bedside lamps.

He carried the tray and placed it on the nightstand. Anna started laughing all over again when he cut off a slice of cheese and offered it to her.

"What?" he quizzed, his eyes sparkling.

She was laughing too hard to answer.

He grinned. "Stop that, I'm being romantic here."

She laughed even harder before she was reduced to giggles.

Curving an arm around her waist, he mumbled, "Watch it. You're going to hurt my manly feelings."

She pressed her face against his shoulder, glad she had gotten the cheese down without choking. She stopped laughing when he licked the valley between her full breasts.

"Sweetheart, you have no idea how badly I need you. I've been walking around with a hard-on for weeks, thinking I shouldn't feel this way, but I couldn't help myself no matter how much I tried."

"Oh, Gavin." She pushed his sport coat off his shoulders and tossed it in the direction of the armchair before she ran her hands up and down the gray silk shirt that covered his back.

He pushed her cardigan down her arms as he kissed her again. "I really want it to be the way you imagined it would be. Tell me the rest, sweetheart."

She nodded. "I need a few minutes to get ready. Okay?"

He caressed the soft skin at her waist beneath her knit shell. "Ten minutes enough?"

"Yes."

She kissed him before hurrying into her walk-in closet. She emerged a few minutes later with a lacy black nightgown thrown over her arm.

"Just a quick shower, and I will be right back." She was a nervous wreck by the time she made it into the hall and closed the bathroom door behind her.

"I should have told him," she whispered aloud as she fumbled with the button at her waist. Her attempt to jerk down the zipper caused it to catch. "Hurry . . ." She wrestled with it. It took a few precious minutes before she managed to get it down far enough for her to wiggle out of the slacks.

"I'm a mess," she mumbled to herself as she yanked the shell over her head and then tackled the pantyhose, panties, and finally the bra. She used a covered elastic band she found on the vanity to gather her hair up into a ponytail.

Maybe she was wrong for not telling him but she hadn't because she didn't want him to know she'd lied. She couldn't bear it if he stopped caring about or wanting her. That was one risk she wasn't willing to take.

After turning on and adjusting the temperature of the shower spray, she climbed over the rim of the tub, closed the shower curtain, and reached for her favorite floral-scented shower gel and a bath puff. As she soaped her neck and shoulders, she concentrated on deep breathing, trying to calm her nerves. Self-absorbed, she didn't notice the door quietly opening and closing.

She jumped when she felt strong arms encircling her waist from behind and easing her back against a hair-roughened chest.

"Anna . . ." Gavin kissed her nape.

"You scared me," she announced, once she could speak, but she didn't turn to face him. With eyes closed, she leaned back against him.

"Get used to me being with you. I'd like to make a habit of showering with you, sweetheart." He moved his hands up and down her arms.

Enjoying the feel of the wide expanse of his chest, his taut midsection and hard stomach, she trembled when his heavy-muscled thighs pressed against her buttocks and the hard ridge of his penis flexed against her back.

"I stayed away as long as I could," he said as he rested a wet, widespread hand against her soft stomach. She sighed, wondering how much longer her legs could hold her upright. "Need any help scrubbing your back?"

Anna nodded, unable to get past the feel of being naked in his arms. His deep copper brown frame was as bare as her own mocha brown body. All the barriers were finally gone.

He took the shower gel and poured a generous portion into

his wide palm. When his hands were wet and sudsy, he began to massage the tight muscles in her neck and shoulders until she felt relaxed, almost boneless. And then he caressed from her elbows down the length of her arms and her closed hands until they rested open at her sides. She purred her enjoyment as his soapy hands massaged her back to the base of her spine. Her breath quickened as he moved his hands over and around the full curves of her buttocks.

His breath was uneven when he moved to cradle her generous breasts in each palm. He explored her softness, relishing the feel and texture of her smooth skin. She released a husky feminine moan as he rolled her elongated nipples between his fingers.

"Your breasts fill my hands as if you were made for me." He pressed a kiss against her nape.

Beyond speech, Anna closed her eyes. Yet, the ache deep inside was building. Her breath nearly stopped when he slid a long-fingered hand across her stomach and then into the thick curls covering her sex. Her lashes fluttered, and she sighed when he cupped and squeezed her mound rhythmically. She was a mass of tingling nerves endings by the time he parted her fleshy folds to caress her fully.

"Oh Gavin," she whimpered.

"Sweetheart"—he breathed heavily into her ear as he continued to stroke her—"you feel so good . . . so wet . . . so hot."

She leaned on him grateful for his supporting arm around her waist. Her legs nearly gave out all together when he moved to caress her ultra-sensitive clitoris.

"Gavin . . . hurry."

"No, baby. You're not ready for me . . . not yet."

She rested her head on his shoulder as the pleasure increased even more.

"Just relax and enjoy," he whispered as he gently pinched her taut nipple while worrying her moist core.

When Anna tried to turn in his arms, he held her fast. "I want to touch you."

"Not yet." Determined to concentrate on her and not himself, he ignored his manhood throbbing against her back. She whimpered when he circled her opening with a soapy finger, but when he slid that finger into her tight sheath, she cried his name and her entire body stiffened.

"Relax, I won't hurt you," he whispered as he eased in and out of her body. "Sweetheart . . . you're so tight."

Her whimpers rose as he stroked her, encouraging her to take a bit more. When he added another finger while increasing the friction she let out a breathless moan and her heartrate soared.

"Not . . . not this way."

"This way and every way. Sweetheart, close your eyes and let it happen."

She trembled as waves of pleasure washed over her. She let out a long moan when she climaxed.

"Yes . . . that's it."

After she quieted and the tremors eased, Anna turned and lifted her face to his.

He held her close. "Are you okay?"

"Yes, but I'm feeling selfish."

His voice was raspy when he confessed, "I like pleasuring you. It excites me to watch you come apart in my arms." He kissed her and then suckled her bottom lip while he moved his hands down her spine to her shapely hips. "You're so much woman and so damn sexy."

As she smoothed her hands over his shoulders, she was aware of his incredible heat and his manhood pressed against her stomach. Warm but cooling water rushed down her neck over her shoulders and down her spine. Gavin towered over her. Every inch of his frame touched hers. She knew she'd never felt smaller or more feminine than she did at that moment. She wanted to pleasure him as thoroughly as he'd pleasured her.

Placing kisses at the base of his copper brown throat, her lips and soft tongue lingered in the scented hollow and she kissed across his wide shoulders and the thick pad of muscles on his chest. She retrieved the shower gel. Once her hands were covered with suds, she moved them over his hard-ridged midsection and stomach. He winced when she touched a tender spot. Anna pulled back to study his heavy-lidded brown eyes. She leaned down to kiss the bruise she saw on the left side of his rib cage.

"You took a hard hit, didn't you?"

"Yeah, but I'll survive." He eased her back against him, his mouth hot and insistent as he took one tongue-rubbing kiss after another.

She was breathing heavily when she resumed her sensuous assault, moving her sudsy hands into the thicket of dark coarse hair surrounding his sex. Gavin moaned as if he were in pain when Anna moved past his shaft in order to soap the length of his feet and calves.

He didn't realize he'd been holding his breath until she soaped his inner thighs. He released a heavy moan as she cupped his testicles in her soft palms and gently caressed him. His entire body shook and his eyes were closed from the intense pleasure as she caressed the length of his erection from base to the crown. She jumped when his sex jerked in response to her attention.

"Did I do something wrong?"

He kissed her hungrily, greedily. "You did everything right."

"Show me the way you'd like to be touched."

He read the appeal in her pretty gray eyes. His strong legs

quivered so badly that he was forced to lock his knees. His kiss was hard and hungry before he nodded. He guided her soft hands around his sex, showing her how to give him the firm strokes he craved. It wasn't long before he begged her to stop.

He explained, "I've done without for so long that my control is limited. I don't want to disappoint either one of us."

She placed her arms around his neck and moved until her breasts were on his deep chest.

He kissed the tip of her nose, then asked, "Ready to get out? The water is cooling."

Trying to ignore the sudden flutter of nerves in her stomach, she nodded her head.

Gavin stepped around her and rinsed them off before he switched off the water and helped her out of the tub. She stood trembling on the thick, pink bath rug when he unfastened and dried her hair. She blushed as he took his time drying her before he wrapped the towel around her. Even though her cheeks were hot, she couldn't look away as he dried himself.

She slid her arms around his neck when he scooped her up and carried her into the bedroom. Her heart pounded with excitement and swelled with love when she saw the candles shimmering inside glass enclosures on the nightstands and the dresser, enfolding them in a warm glow. He'd also pulled back the comforter.

He allowed her body to slide down his until her feet sank into the carpet. He dropped his towel and sat down on the side of the bed before he pulled her between his thighs. Pressing soft kisses along her throat down to the swell of her breasts, he whispered her name.

Cradling her face in his wide palm he gave her no choice but to look into his dark, searching eyes. "What's wrong, sweetheart? You're trembling, and I suspect it's not with desire."

She dropped her lids. "I'm fine . . ."

"If you've changed your mind, all you have to do is tell me. I can wait. I won't push you into something you might regret later."

She kissed his forehead, his nose, his sharp cheekbones, and then lingered on his full, mustache-covered mouth. "I haven't changed my mind. I want to make love with you tonight."

Gavin growled low in his throat, tossing away Anna's towel and pulling her down with him onto the bed. The kisses were long, filled with need, causing her senses to reel. She stopped thinking altogether by the time he took her chocolate-brown nipple into his mouth. He laved the hard peak, enjoying her moans, and then sucked her nipple insistently. He took his time lavishing attention on first one breast before he eventually moved to the other one.

"So sweet," he crooned.

Pleasure raised goose pimples along her nerve endings, which seemed to pool in her feminine core. Gavin placed openmouthed kisses over her shoulders and down her arms. Then he lifted his head and looked into her dark gray eyes.

"Anna, you are so beautiful." He revealed his thoughts. "I can't tell you how many times I've fantasized about having you like this, with every delectable inch of you bare to my lips and mouth."

He cupped her damp mound and then slid down her body and settled between her parted thighs. He parted her soft folds, opening her to the hot flick of his tongue. Her senses went wild as sensation after white-hot sensation flared from deep inside. Her pleasure soared when he took her ultra-sensitive clitoris into his mouth to worry and then to suck. Anna was not prepared for the powerful heart-stopping release as she sobbed Gavin's name.

He was almost as breathless as she was when he moved up

beside her, smoothing a soothing hand down her spine. He squeezed the swells of her behind, burying his face in the scented place where her neck and shoulder joined.

"Gavin . . ." She wrapped her arms around his waist, holding on to him.

"You okay?" he murmured throatily.

"Better than okay."

Her kisses were filled with heat as she ran her hands down his chest. Pressing closer still, she rubbed her sex against one of his hard-muscled thighs, using the firm pressure to soothe the ache inside.

"I don't want you to worry about a thing." He pushed a lock of hair away from her face. "I have protection. I'll keep you safe."

Anna watched as he got up and picked up his discarded jacket. Inside his wallet he pulled out several foil packets. Her eyes had gone wide at the size of his engorged manhood. There was nothing small about him. Could she accommodate him?

He dropped the condoms on the nightstand. When he settled beside her, she reached out a hand to caress his chest. When she touched his stomach he stilled and held on to her hand.

"Baby, I'm too far gone for that," he confessed as he tore open a condom and then expertly sheathed himself.

Gavin took his time kissing Anna as he smoothed a hand along her spine while he settled between her parted thighs. He watched her reaction as he rubbed the crown of his sex between her moist fleshy folds. She stiffened, her eyes were tightly closed as if she dreaded what was to come. He dropped his head to lave her aching nipple before he suckled as he caressed her. He didn't stop until she was breathless with yearning, open to his slow penetration.

He kissed her lids, whispering, "Don't close me out. Let me see your eyes as I make you mine and I become yours. That's what you want, isn't it?"

"Oh yes . . ."

Bracing his upper body on his arms, he moved forward, careful not to rush her. She was incredibly tight. He forced himself to go slow, each new thrust taking a bit more while perspiration drenched his upper body. His strokes were shallow as he gave her time to adjust to his size.

"Anna?" He groaned in disbelief when he met resistance. His heart pounded and his breath was ragged as he accepted the indisputable proof that she'd never been with a man.

Why? Why hadn't she told him? He wanted to shout his frustration. His big body shuddered from her sweet heat. He knew he should stop, but how could he? How, when his entire body was one huge ache of unrelenting need?

He buried his face against her throat as he struggled for control. Unfortunately, Anna chose that moment to shift beneath him and shattered what little control he had left. With a harsh groan Gavin pushed forward, and she cried out at the sharp pain, clenching his shoulders. He didn't stop until he was deep inside of her.

"I'm sorry . . ." he whispered into her ear, tightening his hold around her. Panting for breath and fighting for some measure of control, he forced himself to lie still.

He was still for so long that she asked, "Is that it?" Her disappointment was evident.

Gavin chuckled, but it was her incomparable moist sheath that sent him over the edge. He withdrew and then surged back inside . . . once, twice, three times. After the fourth stroke, Anna moaned her pleasure. She moved with him, matching his rhythmic strokes. He moaned as he quickened the pace, intensifying their enjoyment. He didn't ease even when they were both drenched in perspiration and she was close to completion.

"Anna . . ." Gavin panted when she tightened her inner muscles, milking him. Having no idea how much longer he could last, he slid a hand between their bodies to caress her clitoris. She cried out as she was hurled toward a mind-numbing release. He held on to her until she collapsed against him, and then he shouted as he experienced his own earth-shattering climax. They clung to each other until he realized he must be crushing her and rolled with her onto his back. Her head rested on her chest.

He moved a soothing hand over her hair. "I'm sorry I hurt you. Are you okay?"

"I've never been better." She smiled, kissing his throat. "It was like the Fourth of July, sizzling heat and sparks going off inside me. I can't put it into words."

He chuckled before he sobered. "I wanted to pull out when I realized that you were a virgin, but I couldn't stop. Anna, why? Tell me why you let me think you'd been with another man."

She tried to tuck her face beneath his chin, but Gavin wasn't having it. He propped one arm behind his head and turned, in order to see her clearly. His other arm was anchored around her waist.

"Anna?"

"I couldn't tell you."

"We've known each other close to twelve years. I heard about the guys you dated in college. I've heard about the one your friend Janet tried to fix you up with."

"So I dated. So what? That doesn't mean there has been a man who made me care enough to want to share my body with him."

"But . . ."

"No buts. Why are you questioning me?"

"You didn't tell me. I took no pleasure in hurting you." He sighed, then asked "Why me?"

"I'm attracted to you in a way I've never been before to any other man. I've wanted you to make love to me for a while."

He searched her eyes before he repeated, "Why didn't you tell me? Anna, I hurt you. I could have found a way to make it less painful."

"Forget the pain. I'm fine." She placed a kiss in the center of his chin. "Why are you so upset? Would you have preferred I slept with some other man?"

"Hell no. I didn't realize until now that I'm selfish enough to want to be first. What I don't like are secrets. I wish you had told me."

She glanced away from him. "I wanted to tell you but I was afraid you wouldn't want me if you knew. I wasn't willing to take the risk. Are you sorry we made love?"

"Absolutely not." He kissed her. "You're so incredible. I hope you don't regret this decision." He moved a possessive hand under her hair, messaging her nape.

"Never." She rained kisses against the base of his throat, her soft hand moving over his chest. She lay with her head on his chest, recalling the worry and uncertainty she'd suffered. She was thrilled to be proven wrong.

"You are awfully quiet."

"Just thinking."

"Care to share?" he persisted.

She fingered his flat nipple and felt him tremble. "You're sensitive there, aren't you."

"Yeah. Are you changing the subject?"

"No, but I'm realizing that I have so much to learn."

"About making love?"

Although embarrassed but nonetheless needing to know, she made herself ask, "I want to satisfy you. Did I?"

He quirked a brow. "Very much so. You have doubts?"

"A few . . ." she confessed. "Just because you're experienced and I'm not doesn't mean I want to disappoint you."

"There was never a chance of that, sweetheart. I wanted you too badly."

"I can still feel you. You're—" She stopped abruptly.

Gavin laughed throatily, giving her a long kiss. "Just because I'm hard does not mean you didn't take care of my needs. As I told you before it has been a long time for me."

"Why?"

He said candidly, "I've lost my appetite for casual sex. It has to mean something. I got used to being without until you came to work for me."

"I'm flattered." She began caressing the dense hair below his flat stomach. "Let me . . ."

He shook his head. "Not tonight. I don't want you sore."

"Are you sure?"

"Very."

She rested against him, but he was quiet for so long she said, "A penny?"

"A quarter is more like it. I was thinking about something Wesley said."

"Please don't." She snuggled even closer, her arm tightened around his waist and her eyes closed. "At least not tonight."

After a time Gavin said, "Honey, I have been—" He stopped when he realized she'd fallen asleep.

17

Anna woke to the sweetest ache, causing shivers to race up and down her spine. Her breathing was rapid and uneven. She sighed from the pleasure as Gavin gently laved her nipple. She was whimpering by the time he took it into the heat of his mouth to suck. When he switched to the other peak, she ached all over, but the burning heat centered in her womb.

"Gavin . . ." was all she could get out as her cries escalated. He didn't stop until she climaxed.

"What a way to wake up." She laughed around another deep sigh.

"So sweet," he soothed as his large hand covered her damp mound and squeezed gently. He said, "I've been aching for you from the moment I opened my eyes," an instant before he covered her mouth with his. When the kiss ended they were both struggling to get enough air into their lungs.

He slid a finger between her feminine folds as she opened

for him. He teased her with gentle caresses rather than the firmer strokes she craved. Moaning, Anna slid her tongue into the corner of his lips before laving his bottom lip and then suckling it, causing a groan from deep in his throat.

They both sighed when she rubbed her breasts into his chest. He deepened the kiss as she ran her hands across his taut stomach. Her soft hands encircling his heavy shaft had him releasing an even huskier groan. He clearly wanted her as desperately as her wet core declared her desires for him. Yet he made no effort to join their bodies.

She urged, "Now . . . I want you now," as she fondled the wide crown of his sex.

Gavin clasped her hands in one of his before he began caressing her clitoris repeatedly.

"Not this way," she barely managed to get out as she arched her back and her lids closed at the intensity of his caress.

"What way?" he asked, as if he didn't know he was driving her out of her mind.

She nipped his lobe, letting him know she didn't appreciate his teasing. The soft wash of her tongue warmed the base of his throat before she moved over his chest to linger on one of his hard little nipples.

"Anna . . ."

She smiled before she moved to his other nipple and took it into her mouth to suckle.

"That's not fair," he said, an instant before he locked an arm around her waist and pulled her up his length until he could reach her kiss-swollen mouth. His kiss was urgent . . . demanding.

When she broke the seal of their mouths, she said, "Fair? You call waking me like you did fair?"

He chuckled and then moaned while nestling the blunt crest of his penis between her plump folds. Anna bit her bottom lip as he moved against her . . . teasing . . . not penetrating. Her breathing was quick and uneven as she opened her thighs even more.

Gavin growled low in his throat as he eased only the crown of his sex into her sizzling hot heat. They both cried out when he completely filled her. She sighed as she wrapped her legs and arms around him.

She was clear-headed enough to ask a single question. "Are you wearing . . ."

"Condom?" he finished for her. "Yeah . . ."

He remained still, giving her time to adjust to his size, his open mouth against her throat. When he slowly pulled back, she moaned a protest.

"No . . ."

"Yes . . ." he said an instant before he plunged back into her tight sheath, only to repeat the process, again and again.

Anna moaned her approval. Her sighs increased into whimpers of unbelievable pleasure.

"You fit me like a velvet-lined glove," he whispered as he hungrily kissed her.

"Oh . . . oh . . . oh . . ." was the only coherent sound she could manage.

"Are you close, sweetheart?" he said, gritting his teeth against his own spiraling pleasure.

Panting, she tightened around him, causing them to both gasp aloud.

"Tell me . . ." he rasped, increasing his pace.

"Yes-s-s-s-s . . ." she screamed as she climaxed in a rush of exquisite pleasure.

Gavin cradled her until she quieted. They enjoyed a tongue-stroking kiss. Pushing her hair away from her damp face, he asked, "You okay?

"Mmm."

Aware of his rock-hard shaft still very much a part of her,

she watched his face as she began rhythmically tightening her inner muscles around him. Gavin's breathing quickened, and he began giving her the hard, endless strokes that soon had her gasping again.

"Anna . . ." he breathed into her mouth.

When she began moving with him, he lifted her legs until they rested on his forearms, opening her even more to his deep penetration.

He panted. "Tell me if it's too much . . . if you're too sore."

Anna shook her head. She was beyond speech, all she could focus on was the way he felt and the shattering pleasure starting all over again. Dropping his head, he took another kiss. And then he lowered his head to lave her hardening nipple before he sucked deeply. She called out his name.

Gavin freed her nipple long enough to say, "Come with me . . . baby." Then he turned his attention to the other aching breast.

Anna clung to him as she squeezed his firm buttocks and arched her back to meet his every thrust. Sliding a long-fingered hand between their bodies, he rubbed her clitoris. Unable to hold even a portion of herself back, she shattered into yet another mind-blowing orgasm. Soon Gavin's large body convulsed along with hers as he reached his own climax. They clung to each other as their heart rates gradually slowed and the tremors diminished. He rubbed her cottony soft hair and held her close to his heart.

Gavin smiled at her. "Now that's the way to start the morning." He gave her a tender kiss, then chuckled when she blushed. "Be right back," he said before disappearing into the bathroom down the hall.

Anna stretched her arms over her head while listening to the sound of the toilet flush and water being turned on. He returned and scooped her up as if she weighed next to nothing.

"What are you doing?" She quickly wrapped her arms around his neck for balance.

He grinned down at her as he took her into the bathroom with him. "Thought a hot soak in the tub would take care of that soreness." He put her down beside the tub.

Embarrassed to be standing nude in front of him, she insisted, "What I need is some privacy."

"Oh." He brushed a kiss over her temple. "I'll put the coffee on. You've got five minutes." He left whistling.

Anna was still blushing by the time he returned, but at least she had time to use the bathroom and brush her teeth. Gavin joined her in the tub. It was a tight squeeze but they managed with her back to his front, his long legs on either side of her hips.

She laughed when his stomach growled. "I know what that means."

"I have what I want." He tightened his arms around her. "Next time we do this, let's use my tub. It's bigger."

Just then, the telephone rang.

"Mine or yours?"

"Either way, one of us has to get it." She slid forward so she could rise. Gavin steadied her with his hands around her waist. Anna quickly wrapped a towel around her and raced for her room. It was her bedside extension.

"Hello?"

"Are you okay?" Wesley asked.

"Why wouldn't I be?" Her voice filled with anger.

"After last night, you can ask me that?" her brother said impatiently. "Sis, I'm calling to make sure you're all right."

Gavin pressed a kiss against her nape, causing her to jump. She quickly said, "Look, I have to go."

"He's there with you, isn't he?"

"That's not your business, big brother. Goodbye." She sighed as she replaced the receiver.

Gavin's mouth was pulled taut with tension. "Wesley?"

"Yes."

Gavin cupped her bare shoulders, easing her against his chest. "What did he say?"

"Nothing that matters."

"If it upset you, then it matters."

"It's nothing, really." She tried to dismiss it until she turned to look up at the stubbornly set jaw. Reluctantly she said, "He asked if you were here. As you heard, I didn't give him an answer."

Gavin swore. "He's like a dog with a bone, and he's not about to drop it. You know that as well as I do."

"Wes can be stubborn."

"More like muleheaded. I don't like coming between you and your family. I know how close you Prescotts are."

"You're not the problem." She reached up and encircled his neck. "Can't we forget about this? Just enjoy being together?"

He brushed a kiss onto her kiss-swollen lips. "Have something in mind?"

"I don't know, but I am available. I don't have to work the rest of the weekend. I have a very understanding boss."

Gavin laughed. "Mmm, I like the sound of that. What do you say we spend a few days away from everyone and everything? I know of a great resort in Florida. It's a place to relax and get away from it all."

Her eyes sparkled with excitement. "You have the time?"

"Yeah. We don't have a game on Sunday. No practice until Monday. Kyle is occupied for a few days with all the things he and Wayne have to do. What do you say?"

"Yes." She laughed and kissed him.

"Good." He kissed her back. "Then, I'd better get dressed and get busy. I'll pick you up in a couple of hours. Okay?"

"You think you'll be able to arrange for reservations and a flight that quickly?"

"No problem. Pack a bathing suit and absolutely no nightgowns."

She laughed and smiled dreamily as she watched him dress. "Are you sure my boss won't mind?"

With a wide grin, he said, "I don't think you have a thing to worry about." He placed a lingering kiss on her soft mouth. "See you soon."

She smiled as she walked to the door with him. A few days away with the man she loved was a dream come true. There was no longer any doubt in her mind that she loved Gavin Mathis with all her heart.

By four that same afternoon they were on a plane headed south, leaving the gloomy forecast of possible snow showers behind. Anna had changed into black slacks and a black and white pinstripe blouse. A black cardigan sweater was tied loosely over her shoulders, while Gavin wore slim-fitting jeans and a navy silk pullover sweater.

He was holding her hand, when he said close to her ear, "Happy?"

She smiled at him, "Absolutely. How about you?"

He gave her hand a gentle squeeze. "Without a doubt." He used a long forefinger to lift her face toward his. The kiss was sweet, but brief and filled with promise.

She was used to fans coming up to one of her brothers for an autograph or to talk football. It didn't bother her that Gavin had been stopped in the airport and later on the plane. What bothered her was the beautiful flight attendant who couldn't seem to take her eyes off Gavin.

Anna needed no reminders that there were plenty of women willing to do just about anything to take her place at his side. After all, Gavin was a professional football player. Many saw only that and were more interested in sharing his income than in getting to know the man himself.

She knew she had nothing to complain about. He'd given her his undivided attention. He even accepted her inexperience without being angry with her for keeping secrets. There was no doubt in her mind that he was where he wanted to be. Nonetheless, she couldn't forget that they wanted two different things from life. She couldn't forget that what they had was for the present. It had to be enough. She wasn't about to let a little-girl fantasy of happy-ever-after diminish what they had. Before she'd left home she'd made a promise to herself that she would concentrate on nothing more than enjoying the time they had together.

"More champagne?" the flight attendant asked, smiling at Gavin.

Anna didn't even look up from the fashion magazine in her lap.

Glancing up from the financial page of the newspaper, he said, "Not for me. Anna?"

"No, thanks."

Once they were alone he asked, "You're not worrying, are you? Remember we agreed to focus on each other."

Noting the concern that creased his brow, she reassured him, "I'm looking forward not backward."

"Good." He pressed a kiss into the center of her palm.

The weather was still warm and balmy, even though it was late afternoon when they touched down at the Orlando airport. Gavin had arranged for a limousine.

"I could get used to this." Anna laughed, leaning back against the suede-covered seats.

"Please do. I like seeing that sparkle in your pretty eyes." His arm was around her shoulders. Their heavy coats were on the seat across from them.

She relaxed and enjoyed the passing scenery while Gavin pointed out the sights as they left the city behind. The Gladwin was a private resort, more than sixty miles south of the popular tourist destinations.

Their car turned off the road onto a tree-lined drive. They continued on past the deep blue lake surrounded by picturesque cottages. They stopped in front of the sparkling glass-fronted, two-story, wooden Gladwin Lodge that housed two four-star restaurants, fully equipped gym, health spa, and a variety of exclusive boutiques and shops. The resort's amenities include a golf course and tennis courts.

"It's lovely, just like a postcard," she exclaimed.

"More important, the Gladwins respect their guests' need for privacy, which is important, considering the number of celebrities who come here to relax and enjoy themselves, out of the limelight. Whenever I can string a couple of days together, I come here to relax and play golf. They have a first-class course on the far side of the lake."

"Sounds wonderful."

Gavin brushed her lips with his before he stepped out onto the gravel-covered drive and then held a hand out to her. Anna looked around with interest as they walked hand-in-hand up the wooden steps to the lodge.

"Good evening, Mr. Mathis. Welcome back to Gladwin Lodge." The manager stepped forward with a wide smile.

"Good evening, Mason."

The two men shook hands before Gavin introduced Anna. John Mason ushered them over to an elegant desk and to the two tapestry chairs in front. Gavin signed the register and was given two keys to cottage number twenty-five.

When they were outside again, Gavin asked, "Would you like to stretch your legs? We can walk over to our cottage. It's not far."

Anna slipped her hand into his. "I'd like that. It will give me a chance to look around."

Gavin sent the driver ahead with their luggage to follow the winding road behind the cottages. They took the paved pathway between the cottages and the lake that was dotted with boats. Anna could see where several larger boats were anchored at the distant pier. Even though it was early evening, the outdoor lamps that lined the pathway had been lit. While she enjoyed the view, he enjoyed watching her.

"What do you think?"

"It's beautiful, warm, lush, and green. Nothing like the snow they were predicting when we left home."

Anna frowned. She didn't want to think about the problems waiting for them back in Detroit. And she certainly didn't want Gavin remembering that it was his interest in her that might very well have lost his best friend.

She tilted her head. "I can't believe that you didn't bring your golf clubs."

He chuckled. "Golf is the last thing on my mind." Wrapping an arm around her waist, he said, "You are much more appealing. Certainly more beautiful."

"Thank you." She smiled.

"I like the area so much that I'm considering buying property down here."

"Really? I imagine the sunsets are breathtaking."

"They are." He ran a hand up and down her silk-covered arm. "There's our cottage."

The chauffeur was leaning against the car, waiting for them.

"Oh Gavin. It's charming."

He grinned. "Wait until you see the inside." He asked the driver to place their things on the front stoop and tipped him. He unlocked their cottage and brought the luggage in himself.

The cottage was small, painted in bright pastel blue. They stepped into a large combination living/dining room. The compact kitchen was off to one side. Anna walked ahead into the beautifully appointed bedroom, also done in shades of blue. The bed was a California king; a small fireplace was directly in front of the bed, but the grate was filled with pillar candles. Two armchairs with ottomans were placed near the floor-to-ceiling patio doors. There was a connecting bathroom tiled in blue with cream fixtures and a spa-size whirlpool tub, plus a roomy, clear-glass shower stall.

"We have a patio," she said, walking over to the glass doors. "Honey, it overlooks the lake. Come and see."

He came up to stand behind her, sliding his arms around her waist. "Like it?"

"Mmm." She turned toward him, gliding her hands up to his shoulders and around his neck. "I am glad we came. After what happened yesterday . . ."

He stopped her with a kiss. "Remember our promise not to let what happened yesterday intrude on our time here. This trip is for us."

"What is happening between us?"

"I have no idea. But I want to hold on to it and you for as long as I can."

Unable to look away from his dark eyes, she wasn't sure what she expected him to say. It was more than enough to soothe her worries. All that mattered was the happiness they shared at this moment. She stretched up to press her mouth against his. The kiss was velvety soft, but edged with desire. One brush of his tongue and she was pressing her soft curves against his long, hard body.

As Gavin deepened the kiss, Anna moved soft hands over his chest, then down to his trim waist, yet she didn't stop there. She caressed the distinctive bulge in his jeans. He covered her hand with his, holding it still.

When she lifted questioning eyes to his, he said, "Let's not start something we can't finish."

"But why? You didn't bring protection?"

"Absolutely." He grinned. "What about dinner?"

"I can wait. You don't have to." She pressed her lips against his before whispering, "I want to give you the same pleasure that you have given me time and time again."

Gavin let go of her hands. She carefully unzipped his jeans and released the button at his waist. He let out a husky groan from deep in his throat as Anna slid a soft hand beneath the waistband of his silk briefs, moving up and down the throbbing length of his shaft. His hands were not idle. He opened her blouse and unhooked her lacy bra. He covered her full breasts, filling his hands with her sweet bounty. He used a forefinger to rub her stiff nipple.

"No more," he said as he lowered his head and took a soft breast into his hungry mouth, while trying to control the searing heat as a result of her touch.

"I want to hear you scream with pleasure as you reach a climax," he said, an instant before he began sucking her nipple in earnest. Anna whimpered as she struggled to remain upright. He worried the tight peak with his teeth.

"I can't . . ." she managed to say, before her knees gave out on her.

Gavin caught her before she fell, lifting her high against his chest, but he didn't stop enjoying each breast.

"I'm going to . . ." was all she got out before she convulsed in his arms as she climaxed.

He laid her down on the bed and went to work on removing her clothes.

Caressing his cheek, she asked somewhat breathlessly, "What are you grinning about?"

His eyes smoldered with desire as he undressed. "I love to watch you come. Your body is so sweet and ripe. Do it for me again. Only this time, I want to be inside you."

Before she could respond, he sat down on the end of the bed and began kissing and caressing the soles of her feet, to her calves. She sighed when he kissed her thighs, licking her sensitive skin. When he reached her mound, he cupped and squeezed her. After parting her slick folds, he was pleased to find her ready for him.

His eyes never left hers as he reached for the box of condoms he'd placed on the nightstand. She took the foil packet from him and opened it. He moaned as she caressed the broad crown of his sex. Sitting up, she pressed her lips to his chest and then licked each flat nipple in turn. His heart pounded as she placed her lips against his, taking his bottom lip into her mouth to suckle.

She carefully sheathed his penis in latex before he covered her body with his. He kissed her soft mouth over and over again, one sizzling hot exchange after another.

"I can't get enough of you. I want you again and again," he whispered quietly.

Anna released a soft sigh as he shifted between her thighs. He moved against her softness and slowly entered her.

He gritted his teeth against her exquisite heat. "Oh yes, baby. You feel so good, wet, hot, and incredibly tight. Am I hurting you, sweetheart?"

"No . . ." She wrapped her long legs around his waist.

He held himself perfectly still, giving her time to adjust to his size. She ran a caressing hand over his wide chest, smoothing over hard muscles, and then worried his small taut nipples. Gavin growled before he dropped his head and licked a swollen nipple. Anna whimpered her enjoyment as she tightened her inner muscles.

Soon Gavin was giving her long, hard strokes as he pulled out and then plunged back again. He felt as if he were going up in flames as he cupped her soft behind. They moved in a dance as old as time. She called out as she climaxed first, and he quickly followed as numbing pleasure rushed over them both.

They held on to each other. Finally he shifted onto his

back, freeing her of his weight. Placing a tender kiss on her lips, he pulled her onto his chest.

Anna yawned tiredly as she nestled into his arms.

"You're going to sleep on me?" he crooned.

"It's a strong possibility."

He chuckled as he kissed the side of her throat. Playing with a lock of her hair, he asked, "Want to share a shower?"

"I'd rather eat." She laughed when her stomach rumbled.

"Would you rather go out to dinner or eat sandwiches here?"

"Eat here. Is there food or do we have to call room service?"

"The fridge is fully stocked." He pressed a soft kiss before he went into the bathroom.

When he returned he was wearing a bathrobe with the resort logo on the pocket and carrying a damp washcloth.

"This might help the soreness." He sat beside her on the bed and placed the warm cloth between her legs. "Better?"

"Yes." She sighed, even as she blushed.

"Still sore?"

"Just a little." She couldn't meet his gaze.

Gavin leaned over and kissed her tenderly. "Sweetheart, don't be embarrassed. We're lovers. I want to share everything with you. There should be nothing we can't talk to each other about."

Meeting his gaze, she said, "I want that too."

He pressed a kiss against the enticing mole on the side of her throat. "That's my girl. Ten minutes, or I eat without you."

"You'll wait," she tossed back.

Anna was smiling as she took her toiletry bag into the bathroom and took a shower. As she looked into the mirror, arranging her hair, she noticed that the insides of her lips were tender. She found a small tin of ointment and applied it to her mouth. They weren't swollen from his kisses but from her biting down hard to keep herself from sobbing out her love for him as she climaxed.

She'd been overwhelmed by the sheer intensity of the emotion. She couldn't help wondering if she had been lucky that time. Would she be forced to do the same the next time they made love? She truly hoped not.

She'd never felt this way before and had no idea how to contain her feelings. It happened when her emotions took flight, and she stopped thinking all together. Surely it wouldn't happen again? She couldn't tell him. She didn't want him feeling guilty because he didn't feel the same. Just being together was enough for her. Wasn't it?

18

Gavin found the makings for sandwiches in the refrigerator. When he picked up the knife to slice the homemade loaf of whole-wheat bread, he realized that his hands weren't steady.

While he had been in the bathroom washing up he explained away the weakness in his limbs to sex. Sex was not a big enough word to encompass what they'd shared. The mind-blowing release shattered all preconceived notions he held about intercourse.

He'd never experienced anything even close to what they'd shared. It hadn't happened just once but every single time he was inside Anna. She fit him as if she had been created to pleasure him . . . only him. What in the hell was happening here? More to the point, what was he supposed to do about it?

Yes, he cared deeply for her. Their relationship had already cost him something he valued very much—his friendship with Wesley. Gavin frowned as he assembled the sandwiches.

How could Wesley believe that what was going on between him and Anna was only sex? How could Wesley believe, even for an instant, that he would use her for his own pleasure? What hurt the most was that Wesley wouldn't listen to what he had to say, let alone give him the benefit of the doubt. Wesley's mind had been made up.

Gavin didn't need Anna's brother to tell him that she was one of a kind. She was a wonderful, caring person, and he intended to treat her with care and respect. In the short time they'd been together, she'd made him happy. No, Wesley was more than wrong about them. What her family needed to do was stay the hell out of their relationship.

"Doesn't look like you need any help," Anna said as she walked into the kitchen area.

Glancing over his shoulder at her, he said playfully, "What? You think you're the only one who knows her way around the kitchen?"

She laughed when he put a pickle spear into her mouth for a bite. Dropping down onto one of the dining chairs at the small table, she finished chewing before she said, "I never said that. But I have seen your handiwork. If I were you, I wouldn't quit my day job."

He grinned as he opened a bag of potato chips and dumped them into a serving bowl. He placed it and the platter of sandwiches in the center of the table. He carried a cold beer in one hand and a glass of fruit punch in the other as he settled beside her.

"Looks good. Did you put any mustard on it?"

He wrinkled his nose. "Whoever heard of a ham and cheese sandwich with mustard? You're supposed to use mayo." Yet he grabbed the small jar from the well-stocked cupboard.

"Mmm," she said, biting into a corner of her sandwich. "You were lost in thought when I came in. Care to share?"

"Nothing important." He chewed the chip she stuck into his mouth. "What? You think I look hungry?" he asked as he polished off his sandwich.

She was smiling when she said, "Oh yeah. This is good."

"Don't sound so surprised," he admonished as he offered her a part of his second sandwich.

She only giggled as she took a bite. When she leaned over to dab at the mayo in the corner of his mouth with her napkin, he grabbed her hand and pulled her down onto his lap.

"I thought you were hungry."

"Mmm." He reached under her robe to caress her breasts. He placed a lingering kiss between the full swells. "I am . . . for you."

He made slow, leisurely love to her. There was nothing rushed about their coupling . . . sheer pleasure was all that seemed to matter.

Gavin sank down on the bed beside Anna. He leaned down to press soft kisses on her cheeks, forehead, then her lips.

Slowly opening her eyes, she said groggily, "What time is it?"

"After ten, sleepy head." He gave her yet another good morning kiss, this one long and sweet.

"You're kidding, aren't you?" She sat up suddenly, then blushed when the sheet slid down to her waist, baring her breasts. She yanked it over her chest, tucking it under her arms.

He grinned, his eyes sparkling with appreciation. "The sun has been up for hours."

"Why did you let me sleep so late?" Water beaded on his bare chest and shoulders and a towel was slung over his neck. "What have you been up to?"

"Besides watching you sleep?" He chuckled as she made a face at him. "I've been up since seven. Went for a run around the lake."

She pressed her face against the place where his neck and shoulder joined. "You smell like soap." Rubbing a hand over his cheek, she smiled. "Clean shaven and fresh. You're still wet." She tucked a lock of hair behind her ear. "I must look a mess."

"More like sexy and sleepy." He reached down to the bench at the end of the bed and handed her a silk robe. "Come on, baby. Get up. I've made plans for the day."

She blushed again when she pushed her arms into the silk sleeves and tied the belt tightly around her waist. "What kind of plans?"

"I'll tell you after you're dressed."

She gave him a hug, kissing his chin before she backed away. "Why don't you put the coffee on? You can make coffee, can't you?" she teased.

"So little faith." He shook his head.

"With good reason," she tossed back as she disappeared into the bathroom.

Gavin called after her. "Put on your bathing suit, okay?" His lips quirked upward at the corners.

"What do you have in mind?" Her brown eyes sparkled with curiosity.

"I'll tell you after breakfast."

"Be that way."

The mirrored wall was still covered with the steam from Gavin's shower. She stared longingly at the large tub, but shook her head knowing if she indulged, it would be close to an hour before she'd finished.

After a shower, she dressed in a pink tankini, a pair of knee-length black shorts, and low-heeled sandals. She put her hair up into a ponytail. A touch of lip gloss and gold stud earrings, and she was ready. The table was set with the resort's white- and navy-rimmed signature china.

"Smells good," she said dropping into the chair he held for her.

He was pleased with himself. He'd warmed a half-dozen blueberry muffins, courtesy of the lodge's kitchen, and made a pot of strong black coffee. "Not exactly up to your standards, but it will do in a pinch."

"Mmm," she teased. "I'd better keep you around."

He laughed. "I have my moments. No need to ask how well you slept."

"So . . . tell me."

"What?"

"You know what, Gavin Mathis."

He grinned boyishly as he sipped from a glass of orange juice. "You just have to wait and see." He roared with laughter when she stuck her tongue out at him. "Watch it. I might see that as an invitation. Then we certainly wouldn't get out the door."

Anna tossed her head, taking a sip of coffee. "How much longer are you planning to keep this secret that involves the lake?"

"Not much longer." Reaching out to toy with her fingers, he noticed a small bruise at the base of her throat. "Did I do that?" When she lifted a questioning, perfectly arched brow, he gently touched the mark on her pretty brown skin.

"It's nothing."

Sober, he said, "I'm sorry. I hadn't planned on leaving marks. Your skin is unbelievably soft and delicate." He stroked her hand where it rested on the table. "And I don't like the thought of another man touching you. Does it hurt?"

She blinked at the rapid change of topic. "No, it doesn't hurt. What made you think of—"

He shook his head. "Forget I said it." He rose to place his mug and empty plate in the sink.

She followed to where he lounged against the sink. After placing her mug and plate in the sink, she lifted her arms to lock them around his neck.

"I have no idea where this 'other man' stuff came from, but you, Mr. Mathis, are the only man who keeps me purring."

He relaxed against her, and then placed a lingering kiss on her gloss-covered mouth. "Ready?"

"Where are we going?"

"To the other side of the lake for a swim and picnic." He brushed his lips over the mark on her throat.

"I'll be ready in a few minutes." She headed back to the bedroom.

"Okay, I'll wait outside."

"Men." She shook her head as she went into the bathroom. After collecting towels, sunscreen, and a lipstick, she put it all in an oversize tote bag and placed a wide-brimmed hat on her head.

She found him in the drive, seated behind the wheel of an open Jeep. She tossed the bag into the backseat before she climbed in. He made one stop at the lodge to pick up the picnic basket and they were soon on their way. They took the scenic route to the other side of the lake. He parked on the grassy hill and they walked hand-in-hand down to a somewhat secluded sandy beach.

Anna spread a blanket while Gavin pulled off the short-sleeved chambray shirt he wore over his swim trunks. She forced her eyes away from the long, muscular body, searched for the sunscreen and passed it to him. She watched as he covered his legs and arms. He handed her the lotion to do his back and chest.

Once his dark skin glistened in the sun, he smiled up at her. "Your turn. Need any help?" His eyes twinkled with mischief.

"I think I can manage." She unzipped her shorts and stepped out of them.

"Pretty," he said, huskily, as he noted the two-piece suit that lovingly clung to her curves.

The thin-strapped top with built-in bra stopped at her belly button, and the bottom was modestly cut at the hip. He couldn't look away from the expanse of generous curves and creamy brown skin as she sank onto the blanket. She coated her throat and upper part of her chest before he took the sunscreen to warm it in his cupped hands and spread it on her arms and legs. He placed a kiss on her nape when he finished with her back.

"I like that suit, or rather, I like you in it."

Despite all that they'd shared, she blushed as she thanked him.

Pointing toward the raised swim platform in the lake, he grinned. "Race you."

Her eyes were twinkling when she quickly agreed.

"Want a head start?" he offered.

"I wouldn't like to take advantage," she said with a straight face.

Grabbing a twig, he drew a line in the sand. Once they stood side by side, she shouted, "Go!"

They took off toward the water's edge. He hit the water first and began an easy breaststroke across the lake. He was about halfway to the platform when he glanced over his shoulder to check if she was gaining on him, but he didn't see her. Gavin stopped and turned toward the shore to see Anna propped up on an up-raised arm, lounging on the blanket, hat perched saucily on her head. She waved at him.

He was laughing so hard he nearly swallowed a mouthful of water as he started back. He wasn't even winded when he stood over her dripping water, hand on a lean hip.

"What are you doing?"

"Relaxing." She tried to say it with a straight face, but ruined it by laughing up at him.

"What happened to our race?"

"Surely you don't expect me to get my suit wet. I thought you liked it."

Shaking his head, he grinned. "What I like is you in it."

He squatted down beside her and scooped her up, then tossed her over one broad shoulder.

She screeched as her hat plopped down on the blanket. "Oh no, you don't," she yelled at him, as he raced into the water.

He was in water up to his waist before he tossed her in. When she came up for air, he teased, "Aw, honey. Your suit is wet."

"You are so wrong." Wiping the water out of her eyes, Anna did her best to glare at him, but she was laughing too hard. Moving toward him as he backed up into deeper water, she warned, "I'm going to get you for this."

"You have to catch me first," he said from over his shoulder.

Gavin reached the platform a few strokes ahead of Anna. They were both breathing hard. She lay on her back. When he leaned over her, she pressed both hands against his chest.

"Oh no, you don't. I'm still mad at you." Her eyes told their own story, they were sparkling.

"Aw . . . sweetheart, don't be that way."

He placed tender kisses along the inside of her arm to her elbow, lingering there before he continued on up to the slope of her shoulder and nestled at her throat.

By this time, she was lifting her arms to his neck and parting her lips for him. "One little kiss."

He took that one, then he whispered huskily, "Another?"

She pushed against his chest. "We're not alone."

It was then that he noticed a group of women headed their way. He swore beneath his breath, then laughed when his stomach growled.

"One of us is ready for lunch."

"A few muffins are hardly enough to put a dent in my appetite." He caressed her cheek. "Want a ride back?"

"No, thanks. I think I will float on my back."

The swim back was leisurely. They toweled off before they moved beneath a shade tree to share the basket, filled with grilled chicken breast on tossed salad greens, slices of Brie, blue cheese salad dressing, and a fragrant French bread. There was a bottle of chardonnay and fresh fruit. They were both holding their stomachs by the time they finished.

"That was fabulous." She leaned back against the tree.

He lounged beside her, his head on her lap. "This is the life. I could get used to this."

"You won't get an argument out of me." She stroked his brow, enjoying the firm lines of his muscled body stretched out beside her. "Tell me something. Why did you decide to go to Michigan State? I bet you received an offer from Ohio State."

Gavin, like his brother, had been born in Dayton, Ohio.

"Yeah, I did. But my mother thought I'd get a better education there. She made sure I knew that an athletic scholarship was only a means to an end. It was my chance for a degree in business and finance."

"She sounds like a wonderful woman. Is that why you named the foundation after her?"

"Mmm. She valued education and regretted that she never went to college. But she was determined to make sure I took full advantage of the opportunities I had. I thought naming the foundation for her and helping those who needed a break would be a perfect way for me to honor her memory."

"You're absolutely right. I'm sorry I never had a chance to meet her," she said softly.

He nodded. "Me too. Like all the other fellows back then I was tempted by the offers that came my way during my sophomore and junior years, but I knew what I had to do. By the time Wes and I finished and had our degrees, we knew what was important."

"How did you handle all the women that came your way?"

He grinned. "That was a long time ago. You live and learn."

Anna had no difficulty recalling that while her family had been at Wesley and Gavin's graduation, Gavin's father hadn't bothered to come.

She remarked dryly. "The women are still coming." She referred to the two attractive women who were sunbathing a few yards away. They hadn't taken their eyes off Gavin since he came out of the water. Not that she was surprised. All she had to do was remember the very lovely Natasha or the flight attendant on the plane. There was no shortage of beautiful women ready to appreciate all his finer points.

Gavin cupped her nape, bringing her face down toward his. "Why are you bothered by them?"

"Shouldn't I be?" She wanted to look away from his dark gaze.

"Absolutely not. Sweetheart, I'm where I want to be." He urged her down until they shared a lingering kiss. He traced the generous lines of her lips with a fingertip. "How about you?"

She sighed softly. "Me too."

"I'm glad to hear it," he murmured, then said, "If we were alone, I'd show you how much I want you . . . only you, Anna."

"Here?"

"Oh yeah. Aren't you getting sleepy after that big lunch?"

Anna smiled as she looked into the heat of his gaze. His eyes slowly moved over her bustline, down to her waist. Turning his head toward her tiny strip of bare midriff, he flicked his tongue across it, causing flames of desire to shoot over her breasts and down into her feminine core.

She let out a soft moan. "Why do I have a feeling that sleep isn't what you have in mind?"

"You're right about that."

His mouth was hot and hungry as he helped himself to yet another kiss. When she lifted heavy lids, her breathing was as uneven as his.

"We can't," she whispered, wanting nothing more than to rub the aching tips of her breasts against the hard pad of his chest. "At least not here."

"Hmm." He repeated the kiss, his tongue briefly caressing hers.

"Stop . . ." She forced herself to pull back. Her cheeks were hot with embarrassment. "Let's get out of here."

She didn't hear a complaint from him as he helped her collect and repack their things. He held the basket in front of him until they reached the jeep. He didn't waste any time getting back to the cottage. The only stop he made was to drop off the basket.

They were out of breath by the time they closed the cottage door behind them. Gavin pulled her close for a series of sizzling hot kisses. She sighed her enjoyment, running her hands all over his shoulders and his chest. When she slid her hand inside the waistband of his trunks he released a throaty moan, helping her by pushing them off his lean hips.

Anna was the one who pulled back to rain kisses from the base of his throat, down his chest, lingering at his navel. When she pressed a series of kisses in the thick curls surrounding his sex, he let out a gasp. Gavin's hands remained at his side but they were clenched, his face taut with need.

He groaned her name when she cupped the heavy sacs below his erection and squeezed gently before she placed a series of wet kisses along the entire length of his throbbing shaft. When she reached the broad crown, she opened her mouth to take him into her mouth to lave and then suckle. He moaned from the intensity of his pleasure before he pulled her up against his chest as he struggled to catch his breath.

"Let me pleasure you the way you pleasure me."

Gavin shook his head, still fighting to regain his control. "Another caress from your sweet mouth, and it would have been all over for me, sweetheart. When I come, I want to be deep inside you."

Before Anna could protest, he had stripped her and pulled her down onto the thick rug covering the tile flooring. Gavin started at her pretty toes, kissing along her soft frame. When he parted her thighs, he caressed her feminine core with his tongue. Anna, cradling his head, begged him to stop. He ignored her pleas, tonguing her until she reached an intense release. Before she could catch her breath, he rose to his feet.

She gasped. "Where are you going?"

He mouthed the word "protection" before he disappeared into the bedroom. When he returned he was wearing a condom. Her arms and legs were open, welcoming him. He didn't hesitate, but dropped down to join his body with hers. She let out an appreciative moan when he filled her to the point of bursting. And then she gasped in surprise when he rolled with her until she was the one on top, straddling his hips.

Even though her eyes were filled with questions, Gavin cupped her hips as he showed her how to move to pleasure them both. And the pleasure came in a pulsating rush until neither one of them could hold even a portion of themselves back. They reached the ultimate pinnacle together, shattering from the sheer joy as they climaxed as one.

It was Anna who recovered first. Pressing her lips against his, she barely got out, "Is it always like this?"

19

"No. It has never been this good with anyone but you. Only with you . . . Anna."

Surprisingly, it was the simple truth. She was the only one who made him lose control, lose touch with everything around him by the way she made him feel.

Overwhelmed with emotions, she nestled against his chest and wrapped her arms around his neck, burying her face against the base of his throat as she blinked away tears.

Gavin held her tight, never wanting to let her go. Eventually the hardness of the floor forced him to move.

"Bed or bath?" he murmured near her ear.

"Bath."

They walked hand-in-hand into the bathroom and filled the spa-size deep tub before settling back. Gavin's hands slipped into the warm water to move between her legs, parting her soft folds to find that she was hotter than the water surrounding them.

"Gavin . . ." She trembled as he circled her clitoris. He soon had her throwing back her head, her entire body stiffened as she moaned, "You are driving me crazy."

"I can't help it," he said, sucking her earlobe.

Each sweep of his tongue sent shivers up and down her spine. She was panting as she moved her hips against his erection. She was a heartbeat away from another climax when she tried to turn, to face him. He held her fast as he gently squeezed a breast, toying with her nipple with his thumb while applying pressure against her feminine core.

"No . . ." She shook her head. "Not like this."

"Yes, like this," he said into her ear as he increased the friction.

"What about you?" she barely managed to get out.

"It's all about pleasuring you." He didn't stop until she cried out her release.

Exhausted, she didn't offer a protest when he dried them both off, then carried her to bed. Her lids were closed when she felt the warm wash of his tongue on the inside of a thigh. Her lids fluttered as she moaned, her traitorous body opening to accommodate him.

She had barely said his name when she felt the heat of his tongue against her mound. He loved her until she cried out his name as she climaxed. He didn't move until she quieted. He settled behind her, an arm curled around her waist.

"Sleep," he soothed, stroking her hair. "I'll wake you in plenty of time to dress for dinner."

He was careful to keep his arousal away from her softness. She would be sore if he took her again so soon. He had always had a strong sexual drive, but had learned early how to control it.

Over the years he had managed not to let any woman get too close, never sure if the true attraction was him or his income. He'd grown quite adept at protecting himself against heartache. With Anna, it was different. She didn't need his income. She was doing well financially on her own. Even if she needed money, it wasn't a problem for her, not with three wealthy men in her family.

Since they'd become lovers, all he could think about was her. He couldn't get close enough. He couldn't recall ever wanting a woman more. He enjoyed pleasuring her . . . hearing his name on her lips when she came apart in his arms.

Somehow, Anna's sweet and open responses had demolished every single barrier he'd used for so long to protect himself. He genuinely wanted her happiness, even more than his own. His need to protect her was firmly in place. Frankly, he wasn't looking forward to leaving her at her door on Sunday night. He didn't want what they shared to end. He'd quickly grown used to having her beside him in bed. Although this relentless need scared him, he couldn't pull back.

Gavin had called to check on Kyle before they'd gone out to dinner. Other than a quick hello, Anna hadn't asked her mother one question about her infuriating male relatives.

It was much later when they walked back to their cottage hand-in-hand after sharing a candlelit dinner at the lodge's Gladwin Room. The seafood restaurant had served fabulous food.

"It's a beautiful night," she said as the warm, balmy breeze caressed her bare shoulders. "I don't want to go home tomorrow. Do we have to?"

"I am afraid so," he said as he pressed a kiss into the center of her palms.

"You don't sound eager to get back to the real world either."

"I'm not." He stopped, cupped her shoulders to turn her to

face him in the deepening shadows. "Just being able to spend a few days alone with you means so much to me."

Sliding an arm around his waist, she whispered, "I feel the same way."

Gavin held her tight for a long moment before they resumed their walk. After a time, he said, "We're going to have to do this again."

"Not for a while. Since the team will be in the playoffs, you won't have time for anything but football."

"True." He was thoughtful before he said, "We need to talk."

"Nope. You can't get serious on me. There will be time enough for that when we get back."

"Okay." He smiled. "We've had a wonderful dinner and danced under the stars. We have what is left of this beautiful night to enjoy."

"Our last night in paradise." She sighed. "What do you have in mind for the rest of the evening?"

He grinned. "That, sweetheart, depends on what you'd like to do."

She smiled. "We've put a week's worth of vacationing into two short days."

"How about continuing this walk over to the pier?"

"I like the idea, as long as it's slow and leisurely . . . something you know nothing about with those long legs," she teased, thinking of the records he'd broken and set on the football field.

They walked, enjoying a comfortable silence.

It was Gavin who said, "We're going to have to come back when we have more time. We could bring the boys over on one of their school vacations."

She laughed. "You're missing your golf clubs, huh?"

He chuckled, shaking his head, "No, I'm not." He pulled her into his arms and kissed her soundly. "I've enjoyed every minute we've had together, but I admit I was thinking about my brother. Wondering if he has ever been on vacation. I doubt George has ever taken him anywhere. As for his mother . . ." He shook his head. "When I think about it, there is still a lot I don't know about him."

Anna reached up to unknot his tie and undo the top buttons of his silk shirt. She placed a tender kiss at the base of his throat. "Your mother did all right by you, Gavin Mathis. You're a good man."

His voice was suddenly gruff with emotion. "Thank you." Caressing her cheek, he admitted, "She would have liked you and would have appreciated the care you've given Kyle these past few months, as I do."

"Thank you." She had to blink away tears. It was the nicest thing he could have said to her. They stood on the pier, gazing out at the water.

"I have something for you."

"Really?" She smiled.

"Oh yeah, a little something to help you remember this trip." He reached into his jacket to the inside pocket and brought out a long slender jeweler's box.

"Honey, you didn't have to do this."

"I wanted to. I just hope you like it." He flipped up the lid. Inside was a gold bracelet with a heart-shaped diamond charm. "When did you go shopping?"

"While you were sleeping this morning. Do you like it?"

"Oh yes. It's lovely." She held out an arm.

Laughing, Gavin shook his head and dropped down on one knee to fasten the bracelet around her ankle. Anna giggled, admiring her ankle, glad she hadn't worn hose. When he rose she wrapped her arm around his neck and stretched up to him. They exchanged a warm kiss.

He groaned when she moved her tongue over his. He warned, "Don't start something you don't plan on finishing.

Moving against his rock-hard shaft, she whispered, "Wouldn't dream of it."

One kiss wasn't nearly enough for either of them. His voice was deeper than usual when he asked, "Ready to turn back?"

She nodded. "Whenever I wear the bracelet, I'll remember this night. Thank you."

"You're welcome." His fingers were laced with hers the entire way back to their cottage. Once they were inside, Anna hugged him, not wanting the night to end.

"Why don't you light the candles while I shower and change into something pretty?"

"I like the sound of that."

She emerged in a midnight blue silk nightgown with deep side slits that showed off her generous curves and her long shapely legs. The bed was turned down and the candles were lit. Gavin's clothes were on the chair. Wearing only a white robe, he came up to her and placed a kiss against her throat.

"You smell good but look even better. Give me a few minutes to shower."

"Take your time. I'm not going anywhere."

She curled up on the bed to wait. When she woke the room was dark and she was alone. A single glance at the illuminated clock confirmed it was nearly two in the morning. Upset with herself for ruining their last night, she got up and pulled on the matching lace robe. She found him seated on the patio, his pajama-covered legs propped up on the railing as he stared out at the lake. His chest was covered by his robe.

"Honey . . . I'm so sorry. I didn't mean to—"

"Shush." He took her hand, urging her onto his lap. "You have no reason to apologize, sweetheart. You were sleeping so soundly, I didn't have the heart to wake you."

Cradling his cheek, she insisted, "But it's our last night here. I ruined it."

He brushed her soft mouth with his. "Stop. You haven't gotten much sleep in the last few days, thanks to me." He chuckled at her blush.

"Couldn't sleep?" She rested her head on his shoulder.

"I couldn't turn my brain off."

"Want to talk about it?"

"Yeah." Gavin kissed her brow. "I've been thinking about the two of us. We'll be back to the real world once that plane touches down at Metro tomorrow afternoon."

"You're talking about my family, aren't you?"

"I'm talking about the two of us. I have something to ask you. And I don't want you to answer me until you've given it some thought. Okay?"

Her heart picked up a beat, but she nodded her agreement. "Tell me."

"I don't want things to go back to the way it was, with you living at your place and me in mine."

"I'm at your place most of the day."

"It's not enough for me. Truth be told, I want you sleeping beside me every night. But because of Kyle, I know that's not possible." He paused before he said, "Our time alone will be limited, unless you move into the guest cottage."

"Kyle isn't a baby. He's going to notice that something is going on between us."

"I know. This way we can spend more time together. When we need privacy we can have it."

She studied his face, thoughtful for a moment. She could see how much this meant to him. His offer wasn't exactly what she longed for. Although she was disappointed, she wasn't crushed . . . not as she'd be if she was forced to do without him.

She was silent for so long that he confessed, "I know I'm being selfish, and I know I'm asking a lot. Sweetheart, I don't want what we've shared to end because I'm busy finishing the season or because of the situation with Kyle."

Anna buried her face into the place where his shoulder joined his neck, inhaled his scent. He smelled like soap, his favorite citrus aftershave, and his own natural scent . . . all very heady. There were things she needed to say but didn't dare tell him.

She wasn't ready to share her feelings for him, nor was he ready to hear them. Their relationship was too new. She also didn't want to even think of her family's reaction. They didn't want her dating him. They would consider her moving into his guest cottage no different from living with him.

Anna took a deep breath before she confessed, "I want to be with you just as much as you want me there."

"Then please just think about it. Okay?"

"I will." Moving off his lap, she urged, "Let's go to bed. We have the morning together before we have to leave for the airport."

He didn't protest. They went to bed together, and despite the late hour he made love to her. It was while they were in the limousine on their way to the airport that she told him she would move into his guest cottage.

Gavin was silent on the ride into Detroit to her place. Was he regretting the loss of his long-standing friendship with her brother? Was he blaming her as she was blaming herself? Were the problems they'd avoided discussing the past few days back with a vengeance?

It was not until the limousine stopped at her driveway that Anna asked, "What is it? You've been awfully quiet since we landed."

"Just thinking," he said as he climbed out of the limousine and held out a hand to her. Once she was standing on the gravel drive beside him, he took her luggage from the chauffeur and walked with her to the small front porch.

She quickly unlocked both the storm and screen doors and turned off the alarm. He took her luggage into her bedroom. When he returned, she'd turned up the heat and switched on the lamps. She was feeling uneasy when he just looked at her.

"What?"

"Need anything before I take off?"

She forced herself to ask, "Why are you in such a hurry to leave? Has something changed between us while I wasn't paying attention?"

He studied the concern she didn't bother to hide on her soft brown features. "Not a thing." He wrapped his arms around her waist. "I don't want to leave you at all, but I have to go pick up Kyle. He and I need to talk. I don't want what happened with your family or what's between us to affect him. He's had enough to deal with."

Nodding her understanding, she revealed, "For a few moments I was wondering if you were regretting what happened between us. If you blamed me for—"

He interrupted, "Where did that come from?"

She leaned against him, her arms going around his neck. "You had a terrible argument with the two men you love and trust, that's where it came from. It has been hard on you. And I'm feeling responsible."

"Don't." He put a finger under her chin, tilting it up until he could look into her troubled eyes. "I hate that you're blaming yourself. You're not responsible for what came out of the Prescott men's mouths. We've been back in the city a little over an hour, and it's starting all over again." He leaned down to brush her mouth with his. "We'll work it out . . . somehow."

Resting her cheek against his chest, she wished that it

wasn't her family making such a fuss and trying to come between them.

"Sweetheart, I have to go."

"I know." Anna forced a smile. "Would you like me to go with you to my folks?"

"No need. I'd like you to relax and then pack." Gavin reached into his pocket and pulled out a single key. He placed it in the center of her palm, closing her fingers around it. "It's to the cottage." He pressed another kiss against her lips, this one filled with need. "I'll call you later tonight. I'm sorry, but I have to wait until tomorrow to see you."

"Are you sure this is what you want?"

"You talking about your moving in?"

"Yes."

"I don't have second thoughts. Do you?" His body suddenly went tight, a frown creasing his forehead.

"None. I want to be with you as much as we can manage it."

"Good. It's what I want also. Maybe I can stop back in a few hours and take over whatever you have ready to go."

She smiled. "I'd like that. I've gotten used to your goodnight kisses."

"I've gotten used to sleeping with you beside me." He stepped back. "Later."

"Yes . . . later." She walked with him to the door. She waited until he waved from the limousine before she closed and locked the door.

She went into the kitchen to put the kettle on to boil before she dialed her parents' number.

"Prescott residence."

"Hi, kiddo. You and Kyle have a good weekend?"

"Hey, sis. Yeah." Wayne's voice was filled with enthusiasm. Anna listened as he rattled off all they had done in the last few days.

"Hold on. Mom wants to talk to you."

"Okay." She poured boiling water into a ceramic teapot with loose tea leaves. Using a small strainer, she poured the tea into her mug.

"Hi, honey. How was your trip?" her mother asked.

Anna smiled at the sound of her mother's caring voice. "Wonderful. How was Sunday dinner?"

"Well, we missed having you with us. Conversation was a bit strained."

"I can imagine. Did Wesley and Kelli drop by?"

"Yes. They wanted to spend time with Devin before he left."

"Oh no. Gavin is on his way over to pick up Kyle."

"Calm down, precious. Wesley and Ralph took Devin to the airport. Only your father and the boys are here."

She let out a breath she didn't realize she was holding. "I just don't want them to get into another argument."

"Neither do I. Kyle is packed. He and Wayne are playing pool in the den. And your dad is asleep in front of the television in the family room."

"Mama, it may get worse before it gets better," Anna warned her. "I've decided to move into Gavin's guest cottage."

"Anna, aren't you two rushing things a bit?"

"Perhaps. We want to be together as much as we can."

"Are you sure about this?"

"The only thing I'm sure about is that I love him," she admitted softly. "And I want to be with him very much."

"I'm not thrilled with this decision. I think you're going too fast, but I trust you to do what is best for you. Honey, I want you to know that even though your dad's going to have a cow when he hears, we both love you."

"Thank you, Mom. I love you both too. I'll talk to you tomorrow. Bye."

20

Anna moved into the luxuriously appointed guest cottage on Monday. True to his word, Gavin had stopped by to pick up several pieces of her luggage.

Anna couldn't shake the feeling that something was very wrong, no matter how many times he denied it. Her being near him hadn't quite brought the emotional connection she craved. Even though she now slept only a few yards away from him, they hadn't managed to have any more private time together. Perhaps it was because Gavin was clearly troubled, yet he wouldn't talk about it. She suspected it was the estrangement between him and her brother that weighed heavy on his heart.

She wasn't the only one who noticed the change in him. Just the other morning Gretchen had asked Anna what was wrong between Gavin and Wesley. The two men jointly owned a thriving sporting goods business and normally talked during the day. Suddenly the only communication between them was through their personal assistants.

Anna had placated Gretchen, assuring her that Gavin and Wesley were going through a rough patch but she hoped it would eventually work itself out. However, she knew that was perhaps wishful thinking on her part.

There wasn't a doubt that she felt responsible. She had come between the two, and she hated it. She wondered what she could do, if anything, to resolve the problem. She'd talk to Wesley privately, if she believed it would help. But Anna knew her oldest brother well.

Once Wesley made up his mind about something, it was nearly impossible to get him to change it. He was a family man who believed in protecting his own. The fact that she didn't want or need his protection didn't enter the equation. Wesley believed he was doing what was best for her. It didn't matter that both she and Gavin were hurt by his decision. Or that she was old enough to decide what was best for herself.

Jack Hansom, the Detroit head coach, let out a round of expletives in Gavin's and Wesley's faces. "In my office! Now!"

Sporting bruises on their faces, the two men avoided looking at each other as they followed the older man off the practice field and into his office.

Hansom closed the door behind them before going on the offensive. "I don't know what the hell has been going on between you two this week, but I know damn well this has got to stop, now. Today out on that field, it got out of hand. You two aren't here to take out your anger on each other. We don't have time for this kind of crap."

He paused long enough to catch his breath before he yelled, "I certainly don't need my two best men knocking each other around on the practice field. I don't know what in the hell set you two off, but one thing I do know, you two had damn well better work it out. Nothing and I mean nothing is going to come before what we have to do at game time on Sunday. Work it out!" He slammed the door on his way out.

Wesley broke the palpable silence in the room. "It's not my fault you can't hang on to the damn football."

"Not your fault? If you hit the stupid-ass mark once in a while, we wouldn't be in here now. You came after me, Prescott. We can't afford for you to ditch the game like you did at practice today."

"Ditch the game? You're out of your damn mind. If you could keep your mind on what you're supposed to be doing—"

Gavin swore heatedly. "We both know what's got your nose bent out of shape. And it doesn't have a damn thing to do with what happened out there on the field. This is about me and Anna."

"You're damn right. You had no right to put your hands on her in the first place. You knew she was off limits. It's not like the Motor City isn't full of attractive women ready to take care of that itch in your jockeys."

"Is that what you think this is about? Sex?" Gavin tossed his helmet into an empty chair and then ran a hand over his close-cut natural.

The two glared at each other. Even though Wesley was two inches shorter than the other man, he faced him toe-to-toe. "Hell. Tell me something I don't know."

"You don't know jack about this. Anna and I care about each other. We have for some time."

"Just tell me one damn thing, Mathis. Why in the hell didn't you try to fight it?"

"You think I wanted this? You think I didn't try everything I could think of to stay away from her?" Gavin shouted.

"Yeah. That's exactly what I think," Wesley shouted back.

"You're wrong. The attraction between us just happened. It certainly wasn't planned."

Wesley just glared at the man he had considered his best friend for nearly twelve years. "What you did was take advantage of her feelings for you."

"That's what you want to believe." Gavin sighed tiredly. "You might as well hear it from me first."

"Hear what?" Wesley glared at him suspiciously.

"I've asked Anna to move in with me but because of Kyle we decided it would be better if she stayed in the guest cottage. She moved in on Monday."

Wesley felt so betrayed and disappointed that his face had tightened with rage while his hands opened and closed. "She isn't one of the groupies you usually screw around with. This is my baby sister we're talking about, damn it!"

"You know as well as I do that I've never gotten into the groupie thing." Gavin was so angry he was shaking. "You're busy trying to turn something that's special into something ugly. You aren't just doing me a disservice, but more importantly, you're hurting Anna. She has always looked up to you."

"You're the one hurting my family. I'll be damned, before I will let you get away with it. Some day soon, Anna is going to wake up and realize you are using her. She's pretty and available, which is all you're about."

Determined to hide his hurt feelings behind a pointed glare, Gavin stared at his long-time friend as if he didn't recognize him. Gavin had loved Wesley Prescott like a brother for so many years, but he now realized that he didn't know him at all. Wesley had never really believed in him, because if he had, he would know beyond a doubt that Gavin wasn't capable of deliberately using any woman, especially not someone he treasured as he did Anna.

Gavin's face was hard and his eyes were cold when he warned, "You just make damn certain that what's going on between the two of us stays between us and not out on that damn field." He grabbed his helmet and walked out.

Gavin was still brooding by the time he picked Kyle up from school.

"Hey," his brother said as he got into the front seat, fastening his seat belt.

"Hey, Gavin." Wayne grinned as he climbed into the backseat of the Navigator.

"Hey yourselves. How was your day?" Gavin checked behind him before he pulled out into traffic.

"Good. What happened to you? You look like you ran into a wall."

"Nothing unusual. Just a rough practice session." Not about to go into the details, he quickly changed the subject, "How you doing, Wayne? Keeping those grades up?"

"Cool." Wayne answered. "No problems."

"Kyle? How were your classes?"

"Everything is cool," he said before he plunged right in to say, "I talked to a few of the kids in the band and they told me that Mr. Cummings gives private lessons on Tuesday and Thursday nights after school." Kyle eyed his older brother hopefully.

Gavin glanced at him before saying, "Are you sure that is what you want to do? Taking trumpet lessons calls for a commitment on your part. There will be practice every day and then later, band tryouts. Just because you take these lessons doesn't automatically mean you are in the band."

"I know, but I really want to do this. If I practice, I might become good enough to make the band next year. Mr. Cummings might be willing to give me private lessons."

"That will be great. You can do it, if you put your mind to it," Wayne encouraged.

"Wayne is right. But you have to be willing to put the effort it takes into learning an instrument."

"I'm serious about this," Kyle insisted. "Do you think he'll be willing to teach me?"

"If not, we can find someone who will." Gavin shrugged. "But I want you to be sure. I'd like you to really give it some thought before you decide."

"If it costs too much, I've been saving my allowance. I can help pay for the lessons." Kyle looked genuinely worried.

Gavin shook his head. "It isn't the money. I'll spring for the instrument as long as you take the time necessary to practice every day, as well as keep your grades up. Your school-work comes first."

"It won't be a problem. I promise. I won't let my grades slip. In fact, I'll study harder. Just wait and see."

"Okay, but the minute one of your grades starts to go down or you forget to practice or do your chores around the house, I'm taking the thing back. Understand?"

"Yeah," Kyle said with a wide grin. "Thanks, bro."

Gavin smiled. "No problem." He was pleased by his brother's progress in just a few short weeks. His grades were coming up and his attitude had undergone a huge change once Kyle realized that Gavin wanted him to stay.

"Can you and Wayne stay out of trouble tonight while Anna and I are at the charity dinner?"

"Yeah. We're not little kids." He looked offended. "Besides, Mrs. Tillman will be around if we need something. I don't know why you think we need a baby-sitter."

Wayne felt the need to add his opinion. "That's right. We know how to take care of ourselves."

Gavin hid a smile. "She's just keeping an eye on things, not baby-sitting. But we might not be back until late. I want both of you in bed by midnight. Got that?"

"Tomorrow is Saturday," Kyle complained.

"I know. But I thought you fellows would like to go horseback riding with me in the morning. Kyle, remember I told you about the horse farm in Rochester."

"Yeah!" Both boys cheered.

"Well, there is a trade-off. That means not giving Mrs. Tillman any problems, and both of you in bed with lights out before I get home."

"Got it," Wayne and Kyle agreed with enthusiasm.

After stopping off at Wayne's place to pick up his overnight case, they headed to Gavin's. When he parked beside Anna's car in the garage, the boys were busy planning their evening. They were still at it when they trooped into the kitchen.

"Hey, sis," Wayne grinned at his sister.

"Hey, Anna," That came from Kyle. He'd barely taken off his coat and backpack before he headed for the snack area where she kept cool drinks and fresh fruit in a refrigerator drawer.

Anna smiled up at Gavin over the boys' heads. "No one gets fed unless I get some love." Wearing a bib apron, she'd been rolling out pizza dough.

Both boys complained as they gave her hugs. "You fellows go wash up before you touch any food."

Gavin leaned back against the counter as he waited until they were alone. He placed a soft kiss on her lips. "Is Mrs. Tillman here?"

"Not, but she will be at five. Can I make you something to hold you over until dinner? Sandwich?"

"Naw, I'm not hungry."

She put the layers of pizza dough between parchment paper into the refrigerator. The fixings were all ready and waiting in covered bowls.

"Hard day?" Her eyes were soft as she studied him, noting the bruises on his face and on his knuckles.

"Yeah. I'll tell you about it later."

"All right. Can you keep your eye on the boys while I go get ready?"

"Sure." He glanced at the desk. "Get any work done today?"

"A little. I tested a new recipe for the book."

"Is that what the boys are having tonight?"

"No. They're going to make their own pizza. And there are salad, snacks and chocolate chip cookies."

"Did I hear chocolate chip?" Kyle said with a grin.

"You did. You can have one before dinner." She smiled as she smoothed his collar. "How was your day? How did you do on that science paper?"

"Don't know yet. She didn't give them back." He went on to tell her about his music lessons.

"Good. That means you're going to take time with this?"

"Yeah." He grinned.

"Good." She gave him a quick hug.

Wayne asked, "Do I smell cookies?"

"You do." Anna laughed as she went back to preparing a huge salad. "Only one before dinner."

Gavin leaned back and watched as she worked all the while talking to her brother about his day.

"Can we make the pizzas now?" Wayne wanted to know.

"Not until Mrs. Tillman gets here. Why don't you guys do your homework, get it out of the way?"

They grumbled but finally agreed and headed off to Kyle's room to put their things away.

"No horsing around," Gavin called.

"You sure you don't want something before I take off for my hair appointment?"

He shook his head as he walked over to pull her into his arms. "All I need is a little more of your sweet sugar." His lips covered hers as he held her against his chest before burying his face into the side of her soft throat.

Anna pressed a kiss on his unshaven jaw when he lifted his head. "I missed you today."

"Me too."

"Did something happen today to upset you?"

He kissed her hard. "We'll talk later. Why don't you get going?"

"Okay." She gave him a squeeze around his waist before she moved back. "See you later."

"Seven."

"I'll be ready." She waved before she hurried out.

After a quick trip to the beauty salon, Anna soaked in her favorite rose-scented bath oil. She creamed her skin with the same scented lotion before she put on a dark blue strapless bra and lace thong panties and then slipped on sheer, navy thigh-high silk stockings topped by a wide band of elastic lace to hold them in place.

She was smiling as she put on her makeup, added a bit of crimson-tinted blush, a touch of smoky brown eye shadow, and crimson lipstick and a sheer gloss. She put on black pearl earrings and a black pearl pendant. Her black locks were pinned up in an elaborate chignon.

As she smoothed the strapless, floor-length midnight blue silk-jacquard dress over her hips, she heard the knock on the outside door. After a quick dab of perfume behind each ear and the backs of her knees, she was ready.

"Coming," she called as she hurried out of the beautifully appointed bedroom to the door. She appreciated that Gavin always knocked, even though he had a key.

"Hi, honey. You're look awfully handsome," she said with a smile, giving him the once-over.

Gavin was dressed in a midnight blue, custom-made tuxedo, so dark in color it looked black. His snow white silk shirt was lined with a single row of tiny sapphire studs; a white silk cumberbund encircled his waist, and he wore a white silk necktie.

He grinned as his dark eyes slowly moved over her shapely length. He took her into his arms for a tender hug before he kissed her forehead.

"You're absolutely beautiful," he said close to her ear. "I don't dare kiss you for fear of ruining your makeup. You smell even better."

"Thank you." She caressed his clean-shaven cheek, inhaling his clean male scent. "I'm almost ready." She handed him her ankle bracelet. "Please?"

Gavin squatted down, while she rested her hand on his shoulder. He caressed her ankle before he fastened her bracelet. Before he rose, he left a lingering kiss against her ankle.

"Be right back. I'll get my coat."

He held on to her elbow. "I have something for you." He slid a velvet-covered box from his pocket. Popping the lid open, he said, "For you. Will it go with your dress?"

Anna gasped, a hand covering her mouth. "Diamonds go with everything."

Tucked inside a satin lined box was a pendant. The cushion-cut two-carat diamond, surrounded by a row of small round pink diamonds, was set in platinum. Beside the necklace was a pair of matching lever-back earrings, also set in platinum.

She was silent so long, he asked, "Do you like them? Will you wear them tonight?"

"Oh, Gavin. They're beautiful. I just didn't expect anything like this. They are so costly. I'm not sure I can accept."

He frowned. "Why not? When I saw them, I knew they would look lovely against your dark skin.

"But . . ." She just stared at him.

"No buts. I want you to have them. Please don't say no."

"I don't want you to think that I'm here because I want things from you."

"Oh, baby. I'd never think that. I know you, remember?"

She nodded.

"Please accept them."

She searched his eyes, evidently satisfied by what she saw, and she nodded. She threw her arms around his neck and brushed his lips with hers. "Thank you." Then she laughed. "I've gotten lipstick on you." She wiped it away with her fingers. "Be right back."

He groaned in protest, preferring to keep her right where she was.

"I won't be long." In her bedroom she removed her pearl jewelry and replaced it with the earrings and pendant he'd given her. She took time to repair her lipstick.

Gavin helped her into a navy velvet evening coat. She covered her hair with a sheer silk scarf. They followed the lit walkway that had been cleared of ice and snow, to the side entrance where a dark gray limousine waited.

Once they were comfortably seated in the backseat, he warned that more than likely her parents, Wesley and Kelli, and Ralph would be there.

Anna nodded as she tightened her hands on the tiny navy beaded purse in her lap. "Mama mentioned they were planning to come. It's not a problem. Besides, I need to talk to my hardheaded brother, anyway. I won't let him get away with treating me like a child. Someone has to set him straight."

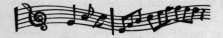

21

Gavin took one of her hands in his. "You're a little late. All that needed to be said has already been said today." His eyes were on the passing scenery as the car headed south toward Jefferson Avenue.

"So that's what's been bothering you."

He nodded. "Wes and I had a disagreement on the field. It was stupid, but it happened. Neither one of us was setting much of an example for the younger guys. Need I say how put out Coach was?"

Anna placed a comforting hand on his muscled thigh, giving it a gentle squeeze. Blinking back tears, she whispered, "I'm sorry, honey. I know how much it hurts. You and Wes have been close for too many years. My feelings for you shouldn't affect your friendship."

"Don't," he said quietly, pressing a kiss on her cheek. "I

don't want you blaming yourself. It isn't your fault. Wes has made his choice, and I have made mine. We both have to move on."

Anna bit the tender inside of her lip to hold back the tears. No matter what he said, her heart was heavy because she had come between them. And both men had been impacted negatively by this, and hurt because of it. There had to be something she could do or say to ease the situation. There just had to be.

She certainly wasn't pleased by the rift in her family, but she couldn't help whom she loved. And she wasn't about to give Gavin up because of her family's disapproval.

The fund-raiser was being held at the Omni Detroit Hotel at River Place in the quaint River Town area. The prominent sports figures as well as community leaders had received invitations. The one-thousand-dollar-a-plate affair would generate much-needed revenue for the upcoming sports camps planned for inner city youngsters involved in both the Boys and Girls Clubs and the community centers in the city.

As soon as Gavin and Anna neared the Riverfront Pavilion Room they were greeted by some of the Lions team members and their wives. There were athletes from all Detroit-area sports teams, including the Tigers, Red Wings, Pistons, and Shocks.

Mayor Kilpatrick and city council members were present, as well as representatives from Ford, GM, and Chrysler motor companies. The business community was also represented by leaders such as Charles Randol and his wife Diane, as well as prominent attorney Quinn Montgomery and his wife Heather. Dexter Washington, who headed the Malcolm X Community Center, and his wife, Anthia, were seen moving through the crowd.

After they had checked their coats, Anna and Gavin con-

tinuously stopped and exchanged greetings. The cocktail
hour was in full swing as they slowly made their way to their
assigned table.

Anna spotted her family across the crowded table. She
slipped her hand into Gavin's and was frankly relieved that
they wouldn't be sharing a table. Before Gavin could go and
collect their drinks she whispered into his ear that she was
going over to say hello to her family.

"Would you like me to go with you?" Gavin asked as he
held her chair.

"No, but thanks for the offer. Be right back." She threaded
her way through the crowded room. "Good evening," Anna
said as she stopped behind her mother's chair.

"Hi, honey," Donna said as Anna hugged her. "You look
beautiful."

"Thanks, Mama. So do you," Anna smiled and then turned
to her father, who like the other men at the table was on his
feet. "Daddy." She pressed a quick kiss to his lean brown
cheek.

"Your mother is right. You're beautiful," he said quietly.

"Thank you," she said as she moved out of his arms.

She ignored Wesley's hurt look when she spoke to him but
didn't offer him a hug. She did hug Kelli and said, "You look
wonderful. Love that dress."

"You are the one," Kelli whispered as she squeezed her
hand reassuringly. "You okay?"

"I'm trying," Anna whispered back. When she turned, she
suddenly recognized the man Ralph was in conversation
with, an old teammate from Ralph's basketball days at University of Detroit. "Scott, is that you?"

Scott Hendricks, tall, dark, and handsome NBA player,
grinned down at her. "Anna, how are you?" He gave her a
hug. "You're looking good, girl."

"Thank you. How have you been? I haven't seen you in years. How's your sister Taylor and her husband, Donald?"

"Doing well. They have a new baby. In fact, they have two kids. And they're considering moving back to the area now that Donald has retired from the NBA."

"That's wonderful. It was good seeing you. Give your family my best." To her cousin, she said, "Ralph, please introduce me to your date."

The look Anna gave Ralph warned him not to even try hugging her. After the introductions were made, she excused herself and returned to her own table.

Gavin was standing beside their table talking to Dexter Washington when she approached. She overheard Dexter say, "Whatever is going on between you and Prescott, I hope you two get it straightened out soon. The boys at the community center need the both of you to give that football camp this spring. You two can't let us down."

Gavin saw her first and slid an arm around her waist. "Anna, you remember Dexter Washington, don't you?"

"Yes, of course. How are you, Mr. Washington?"

"I'm well, thanks. Talk to this guy for me. Maybe you can convince him to do our football clinic again this year."

"I will." Anna smiled. "Give my best to your wife."

"I will. Bye."

Gavin asked curiously, "How do you know Anthia Washington?"

"She and my mother are on some of the same charity committees."

He whispered close to her ear, "How did it go? You okay, sweetheart?" When she didn't respond quickly enough, he repeated, "Anna?"

"I'm fine." She swallowed the lump in her throat.

He nodded as he held her chair for her.

Anna sat with her hands resting in her lap as she concentrated on not crying. It was an impossible situation.

There were no speeches and everyone seemed relaxed as they began to serve the meal. The women managed to keep the men off their favorite subject, football. From soup to salad the meal was fabulous, and the prime rib and lobster entrée was a hit.

"You don't care for your lobster?" Gavin noted the way she picked at the food.

Determined not to cause him any more concern, Anna smiled. "Everything is fine. Relax and enjoy yourself."

He wasn't convinced but he didn't make a fuss. Anna was relieved when the table was finally cleared. The band began warming up in the front of the room as they prepared for the dancing to come.

Anna smiled when Donna and Kelli came over. They greeted Gavin and then invited Anna to go with them to the ladies' room. Once the three of them were inside the crowded room, they moved past the line to the stalls and stopped in front of the mirrors.

Donna was the first to ask, "Are you all right? You looked upset at the table."

"I'm fine now, but I have to admit I was feeling a little weepy. I hate being estranged from my family."

Donna put a comforting arm around her daughter's waist and gave her a hug. "You are still very much a part of this family. We all love you."

"I know, Mama. It's so hard. I didn't want to speak to my own father, brother and cousin. I wanted to knock all three of their heads together for being so stubborn."

Kelli whispered, "Well, you got to Wesley. He was very upset and so was Ralph that you didn't do more than speak to them. And I don't blame you. They both had it coming."

Kelli's dress was pale green and complemented her pale

brown complexion nicely. "My husband has been acting like a wounded bear since Thanksgiving. But it got worse after that fistfight he had with Gavin at practice."

"Fistfight?" Donna and Anna said in disbelief at the same time.

"I thought they just had an argument." Anna was genuinely shocked.

"They were going at each other until the guys pulled them apart. It got real ugly."

"This has gone too far," Donna whispered in outrage. "Those two have been best friends for nearly twelve years."

"You're right. It makes no sense." Anna added, "But neither does treating me like a little girl."

Kelli smoothed a hand over Anna's arm. "It's going to work itself out. It just has to."

"I hope you're right. But it doesn't feel that way now. Should I come by for dinner on Sunday as if nothing happened? I don't want to get into another argument, especially with Daddy."

"Whether you argue with your father or not, I am expecting you to come with Kyle just like always." Donna looked into her eyes. "I've tried time and time again to change your father's mind. It hasn't helped. But we are still your family and nothing will change that. Is that clear?"

Anna recognized that tone of voice. "Yes, Mama," she didn't need to be told it would break her mother's heart if she deliberately stayed away.

"Ready?" Kelli asked.

The other women nodded. They parted company at the entrance to the ballroom. The band had been set up on a small stage and was playing full blast. When Gavin spotted her he smiled. He'd been standing near their table, talking to one of his teammates. He excused himself and approached her.

"You know we can leave any time you're ready." He rested his arm around her waist.

Smiling up at him, she said, "There is no need."

"Let's dance." He slipped her tiny beaded purse into his pocket and escorted her to the already crowded dance floor.

He let out a sigh once he had her in his arms. "I've been wanting to hold you like this all evening." He kissed her temple, saying, "Sweetheart, I know how hard this is on you. I'm so sorry to have placed you in the middle of it."

"You haven't. It's not your doing. The muleheaded men in my family started this, not you."

Since they were both tall their bodies fit perfectly. This past week had been so hectic, and they hadn't spent nearly enough time together.

"Let's concentrate on enjoying each other." In a rough whisper, he admitted, "I missed you this week. I especially miss sleeping the entire night in your arms, like we did while in Florida."

"We had such a good time. Did I thank you for the trip?" she teased.

He grinned. "You know you did. And you're more than welcome to thank me again, later tonight."

They were laughing when Gavin was tapped on his shoulder. He glanced back to find Wesley standing there. A muscle tightened his cheek, but Gavin didn't say a word, just handed Anna off to her oldest brother.

As Wesley looked down at her, his mouth was taut with tension. "Sis . . ."

"Just say what you came to say," she said frostily.

Wesley looked as if he wanted to shake some sense into her when he said, "What's going on with you? Why can't you see that a man like Gavin can never make you happy?"

"A man like what?" she hissed, and then took a slow calming breath, before she went on to say, "For a moment there you forgot something, didn't you, Wesley? Evidently I'm not the only one who has poor judgment, since Gavin has been your friend and business partner for years. Are you so angry about my relationship with him that you're willing to put your business in jeopardy?"

"To hell with the business. This is about family. I love you. I want you happy," he nearly snarled.

Anna struggled for a calm she was far from feeling. Despite everything that had happened, Wesley was her big brother who had always been there for her. And she loved him dearly.

She also knew he was the one person who could ease the tension in the family. If she could reach him, then the others were bound to come around. She couldn't just walk off in a huff. She had to make him understand that Gavin was her choice, and he had to respect her decision.

She didn't like what the angry words spoken on Thanksgiving had done to their close-knit family. The estrangement was hard on all of them, but especially her mother.

"Wesley, if you would only try to respect my right to make my own choices." She paused before she said, "Gavin is important to me. If we didn't care for each other, we wouldn't—"

He broke in, saying. "Women have always found him attractive, even back at State. There has never been a shortage of them willing to do just about anything they could to get him. I don't want you to be another one on a very long list."

"He isn't a saint, I know that. But neither am I. Aren't you forgetting that I am old enough and smart enough to make my own decisions? If I'm wrong, the only one who will be affected will be me."

They danced in silence for a few moments, then he asked, "Why are you putting yourself in this position? Can't you see that you're setting yourself up for a hard fall? You're practically living with the man."

"I never tried to run your life, why are you trying to run mine?"

Wesley wasn't even close to backing down. "Mama and Dad taught you to have more respect for yourself. You weren't raised to think so little of yourself. Why can't you see? Yes, he wants you now, but he won't ever marry you. Believe me, I know what I'm talking about."

Anna glared up at him. Suddenly she stopped all pretense of dancing. "I know how Gavin feels about marriage. It's fine with me. Why am I even telling you this? You're so stubborn you'd rather lose a friend than admit you could be wrong. You can't even give me the respect I deserve as a woman who was raised by two very caring parents . . . your parents. Fine. For all our sakes, I suggest you stay away from Gavin and me." With that, she walked off the dance floor. Her anger hadn't cooled one little bit when she saw Gavin talking to Natasha Baker.

Natasha looked gorgeous in a black sequined gown that hugged her curves. Judging by the way the woman hung on Gavin's arm, and the scowl on his face, things weren't going well.

Already upset, Anna wasn't up to more unpleasantness, even though Natasha evidently had no qualms about going after what she wanted. Anna had about as much as she was willing to take for one evening.

Gavin smiled when he saw Anna. He pulled her against his side, wrapping an arm around her shoulders. "You remember, Natasha, don't you, sweetheart?"

"Yes." Anna couldn't help noting the way the other woman didn't bother to hide her feelings. The look she gave Anna was openly hostile. "Natasha. What a lovely dress."

"Thanks." She didn't return the compliment. "Enjoying your evening?"

The cold look in the other woman's eyes told Anna that

Natasha wasn't thrilled by the change in Gavin and Anna's relationship.

Gavin said, "Please excuse us, Natasha. Anna, I believe this is our dance," before he led her back out onto the dance floor.

Only when she was in his arms, held close to his powerful body, did Anna begin to relax. They held on to each other, enjoying the slow beat of the romantic melody.

"I want you to know that there is nothing going on between Natasha and me. There hasn't been—"

Anna pressed her fingertips against his lips. "Don't. There is no need. If you wanted to be with her, you would be."

He smiled, easing her even more deeply against his chest. When the song ended, they reluctantly moved apart. Gavin was not thrilled when one of Anna's former bachelor clients, Brad McAdams, stopped them.

"My turn." Brad grinned at Anna. "May I have this dance, pretty lady?"

"Aw, man, can't you see we're busy," Gavin complained.

Brad laughed, taking her hand and leading her back out onto the floor. Gavin knew better than to make an issue of it. He was forced to watch from the sidelines as Anna danced with Brad and then several of his other teammates and her former clients. A few of the guys came up and teased him about her popularity. He managed to hold on to his temper—just barely.

It was approaching midnight when Anna told Gavin she was ready to leave. He wasn't about to protest. The entire evening had turned out to be nothing short of a strain on both of them.

They were enclosed in the back of the limousine when he surprised her by acknowledging, "I didn't enjoy seeing you in other men's arms." When she started to interrupt him, he said, "Please, let me get this said." At her nod, he went on. "I've never considered myself to be the jealous type. If I'm with a woman who wants to be with someone else, it's fine with me.

He stroked her soft cheek before he admitted, "With you it's different. We're a couple, and I want everyone to know you are off-limits. And it's not that I want to wrap you up in cotton wool or anything. Because you are precious to me, I don't intend to share you either."

She pressed a kiss into the center of his wide palm. "I understand. I feel the same way about you. Honey, I want you to know you have nothing to worry about. I am also where I want to be."

He kissed her tenderly, easing her close against his side. She rested her cheek on his shoulder. He said quietly, "I can only imagine how difficult it was for you not being at your family's table. I just want you to know how appreciative I am that you chose to be with me. It means a lot to me, Anna."

Anna bit her lips to keep from crying. Instead she pressed her lips against his. "Thank you."

They spent what was left of the ride in a comfortable silence.

It wasn't until the outside gates swung closed behind them that he assessed dryly, "A night in hell would have been more fun."

"No doubt about that," she said around a long sigh.

"What did he say?"

He didn't explain whom he was referring to but he didn't need to because she knew he was talking about her brother. She shook her head. "You don't want to hear it, and I don't want to rehash it, at least not tonight."

The car eased to a stop in the wide circular drive at the front entrance. Gavin didn't wait for the chauffeur but stepped onto the pavement and held his hand out for her. After he tipped the driver, they walked hand-in-hand up to the front door, and he unlocked it.

The house was quiet. They headed toward the staircase. Ascending them together, he said with a smile, "Wonder how much trouble the boys gave Mrs. Tillman."

She playfully gasped. "Surely, you're not implying that our brothers are anything but angels?"

"How much are you willing to bet that they only turned off the lights when they heard the car pull up in the drive?"

She laughed. "You're probably right."

"All's quiet. That's a good sign." He lowered his voice to a whisper.

The guest bedroom door across from Kyle's room was closed with no light showing from beneath it. Gavin put a finger to his lips as he quietly opened his brother's door.

Wayne was asleep on the top bunk buried underneath the blankets, while Kyle was asleep on the futon. He'd pushed off his blankets onto the carpet. The television was still blaring in the background.

Anna covered Kyle while Gavin switched off the set, sending the room into darkness except for the night light in the connecting bathroom. They tiptoed out, closing the door quietly behind them. With a grin, Gavin took her hand, pulled her to the end of the hall and into his rooms.

"What are you doing?" She smiled, as she slid her arms up to encircle his neck.

"You know exactly what I'm doing." His voice was husky with need as he nestled her cheek.

Stepping back after only one kiss, she shook her head. "There is no point in starting something we can't finish . . . at least not here."

"Oh, I can finish it," he assured her as he followed her retreating steps.

"Glad to hear it." She giggled as she dashed out his door and down the hallway to the stairs.

Striving to be quiet Gavin hurried after her. Their footsteps were cushioned by lush carpet.

"You're too slow," she teased.

At the bottom of the stairs, he grabbed her around the waist, lifting her off her feet.

"If you toss me over your shoulder, I promise you that you will be sleeping alone tonight."

"Aw, baby, don't be that way. I can move faster than you can, especially in those heels," he cajoled as he placed her back on her feet.

"I'm not a football, Mathis. I got enough of being tossed around when I was a kid."

"Yes, sweetheart," he answered meekly.

They went out the side door and Gavin locked it behind them.

"Got your key?"

"Don't need one." She smiled up at him. "You have yours."

"Are you sure you don't need a lift?"

She didn't bother to comment. Her arm was linked through his as they followed the walkway to where it branched off to the right. The exterior light lit the way. The cottage was built out of the same pale stone as the house.

Gavin opened the door. With his hand on the back of her waist, he urged her inside. The drapes had been closed, but she'd left a lamp on in the sitting area of the oversize room. He removed her evening coat and the silk shawl draped over her shoulders, tossing them onto the deep cushioned sofa, along with his own coat and suit jacket.

Anna requested softly, "Unhook me . . . please."

Her breath momentarily caught in her throat as he not only unhooked but also unzipped the dress. He soon had it sliding down her hips and onto the carpet. She made no move to cover herself, but stood in nothing more than lace-edged silk stockings, a pair of lacy thong panties, and a strapless bra.

Gavin released a small gasp, his dark gaze slowly traveling from where her long locks were elegantly pinned on her head, to the creamy brown graceful lines of her neck, over smooth shoulders, full breasts, and shapely hips, down to incredibly long legs, a gold bracelet around her ankle, and feet with crimson-painted toenails inside high backless heels.

"See something you like?" she asked breathlessly.

22

"**O**h yes. You are so beautiful." His voice had dropped even deeper than his normal baritone. He cupped her elbows, pulling her against him as he kissed the side of her throat. His arms slid to encircle her waist for a gentle squeeze. "You always smell wonderful." Then he took a step back.

She watched him practically tear his tie from his throat and then remove the studs from his dress shirt. He dropped them into his pocket before he flung the shirt along with the cumberbund onto the chair. He stepped out of his shoes and pulled off silk socks. She caught her breath when he unfastened his trousers and unzipped them. She couldn't look away as he pushed them, along with silk briefs, down his long, muscled legs.

Devouring him with hungry eyes, she watched as he approached her with his thick shaft jutting toward her.

"Let me." He licked the skin at the base of her throat as he turned her and unclasped the bra, letting it fall to the carpet.

He slipped a large finger on either side of the lace-covered panties and eased them down, then off. His hands rested on her waist as he pressed against her. He groaned huskily.

She shivered when his open mouth slowly journeyed along her back to the base of her spine, then over the curve of each hip. He didn't stop there, but dropped to a knee and continued down the back of one silk-covered leg before he slowly gave the same caress along the opposite leg. She cried out his name at the tiny love bites he gave her along the way. If she hadn't had a hand braced on his shoulder she would have fallen.

"Gavin . . ."

He rose and faced her. "I want you, Anna mine." His lips covered hers.

She clung to him, standing in nothing more than her hose and jewelry. His mouth was sizzling hot and demanding as he pushed into her mouth to stroke her tongue with his.

"I've been thinking about little else all evening but having you to myself. No interruptions . . . no one but you and me."

She sighed as he pressed her breasts into his chest. She rubbed the sensitive tips against him, needing the friction and his heat.

"Hurry . . ." she moaned before she ran kisses over his chest to his nipples and then tongued them.

He shivered at the sweetness of the caress. "No, there is no need to rush." He surprised her when he asked, "Where did you get those panties?"

"So you do like them," she crooned before she licked his throat.

He chuckled throatily, "I was ready to remove them with my teeth. If I had known you had those on under that dress we would have left hours earlier."

"I'll buy a pair in every color of the rainbow."

"Good idea. If I have anything to do with it you won't be wearing them long."

Gavin easily swung her off her feet and lifted her until he could enjoy her breasts without straining his neck. He took an engorged nipple into his mouth to leisurely lave and then to suckle. He didn't stop until she begged him to hurry. Still he took his time before he moved to the other breast to give it the same breath-stealing treatment. She was so close to climaxing that she urgently whispered into his ear that she wanted him . . . inside her . . . now.

Anna threw her hands around his neck before sharing a deep and lengthy kiss. They barely made it into the bedroom. She was the one who took the condom from the supply he'd left in the nightstand. She pressed a kiss along his upper torso before she rolled the condom into place, giving him a sweet caress.

She was beyond thought by the time he parted her feminine folds and found her moist, ready for him.

"Now . . ." she insisted.

"I like you like this . . . hot for me," he said as he pressed forward, guiding his shaft into her incredible heat. It wasn't long before they were both climaxing as one, clinging to each other as they shuddered from the intensity of their release.

Gavin groaned heavily, burying his face against her throat as he held her close to his heart. Anna's eyes were filled with tears and her lips sore from biting them to keep from declaring her love as she struggled to compose herself. It wasn't until after they shared a hot shower that they both fell into a contented sleep.

Sunday dinner at the Prescotts' proved to be unusually tense for everyone. For the first time in memory, Anna was relieved that Wesley was on the road and couldn't join the family. The strain that had begun on Thanksgiving Day hadn't lessened as much as she'd hoped. Nothing had been said about her relationship with Gavin or their new living arrangement but she sensed her father's disapproval.

It wasn't until after the kitchen was clean while the ladies were planning the upcoming Christmas menu that Anna learned just how bad things were.

"I can't believe I'm admitting this, but for once, I'm glad my husband missed dinner." Kelli admitted, "I have had about as much as I can take of his attitude when it comes to you and Gavin. I tried, Anna, but I just can't talk any sense into him. He refuses to see you as an adult capable of making your own decisions."

"Oh Kelli. I don't want you two arguing about me." Anna's concern was evident.

"I don't see why not. Someone has to try and knock some sense into his hard head. I hate to say this, Donna, but talk about stubborn. Once the Prescott men make up their minds, there is nothing that anyone can say to change it."

"I agree." Donna sighed tiredly. "I've been working on your dad, Anna, as well as Devin and Ralph for over a week, and it's not doing much good. Nothing I say seems to be making any difference. Before this, I never believed that anything or anyone could come between our family. This has proven me wrong."

"What are you saying?" Even before she asked the question, Anna knew she wasn't going to like the answer. "We're still family."

"Precious, I don't like being the one to tell you this."

At her mother's hesitation, Anna persisted, "Please, whatever it is, go ahead and say it. You're scaring me."

Taking her daughter's hands into her own, Donna confessed, "Your older brothers and cousin don't think Gavin should be invited to our family's Christmas dinner."

"What?" Anna jumped up. Her eyes were wide with disbelief.

Kelli added unhappily, "It's true. Wes told me that he would rather stay home than share a meal with Gavin."

"So it's been decided? Gavin isn't invited to the family's holiday dinner? A dinner he hasn't missed in over twelve years?" Anna's voice rose with her indignation. "I should have expected it. I don't know why I'm even surprised."

"I'm sorry, baby, but your dad is going along with them," Donna confirmed.

"This is just plain wrong," Anna said furiously. She moved restlessly around the room, before she stopped suddenly. She said quietly, "I think I should go."

"No honey, please."

"Mama, how can I stay? I refuse to go in there and get into another shouting match with Daddy and Ralph."

"This is still your home." Donna was nearly wringing her hands.

"Mama, would you please tell the muleheaded male members of this family that this isn't fine with me." Her eyes were bright with tears as she said, "Kyle and I will be spending the holiday at Gavin's."

"No." Donna was upset.

"It's no less than I expected," Kelli said sadly, wiping at her own tears. "Wes wouldn't let anyone else run his life for him. Why should he think you would stand back and let him and his cohorts run your life for you?"

Anna was shaking when she went to get Kyle. She didn't so much as glance into the family room where Ralph and her father were watching football.

Donna pulled her aside before she and Kyle could leave. "Honey, you can't leave this way."

Anna gave her mother a hug. "I think it would be best. Besides, I'm too upset to even speak to them right now."

Donna kept her voice down so the boys would not overhear her before she said tightly, "I'm not about to sit back and let my family splinter this way. You're my child, just as much as your father's. I expect you, Kyle, and Gavin here for the Christmas dinner."

Anna kissed her mother, running a soothing hand over her slender shoulders. "It's going to be all right. No one wants to repeat Thanksgiving Day. I have to go now. Kyle's waiting."

"I'm not having it," Donna said, blinking back tears.

Placing a kiss on her cheek, Anna whispered, "Try not to worry. It will all work itself out."

Ushering Kyle ahead of her, Anna left with a heavy heart. Despite her words to her mother, she knew it was for the best. If Gavin wasn't welcome, then neither were she and Kyle.

She blinked back tears, letting the cool night air soothe her hot cheeks as she got in the car. She didn't want Kyle upset by all this. He was just starting to relax and act like a typical male teen.

"Are you going to tell me what's going on? Or are you going to pretend that everything is just fine, like Gavin and the other adults?" Kyle said.

Anna took her eyes off the road for a long moment. It was Kyle's shout that warned her that another driver had cut in front of her. She hit the brakes and barely missed hitting the car.

"Sorry," she said, letting out a deep breath. "Are you okay?"

"Yeah. Anna, I'm not a little kid. Wayne heard your folks talking. This is about Gavin being your boyfriend, and your two older brothers not liking it. Right?"

"Yes, my cousin and brothers are trying to treat me like a little girl because I'm the youngest." She eased the car to a stop at the red light.

"You like Gavin, huh?"

"Yes, I do. Do you mind?"

Kyle seemed stunned for a moment as if he didn't expect her to care what he thought, let alone ask his opinion. "No. Why should I? All that counts is that you like my brother and he likes you. Besides, you've always been fair with me."

"Thanks, Kyle." Anna smiled as the traffic light changed.

"That's why you moved to the guest cottage, isn't it?"

"Yes," she reluctantly admitted, hoping he didn't notice her momentary hesitation.

She would also like to keep the conversation away from intimate matters. She wanted to be honest but he was only fifteen. Teens were much more sexually aware than she had been at their age. Nonetheless, the details of her and Gavin's relationship must remain between the two of them.

"That's what I thought." The boy was thoughtful for a few moments before he asked, "This problem between your family and Gavin, does that have anything to do with me and Wayne?"

"I don't understand."

"We've been friends for a while." Kyle drummed his fingers on the dashboard. "You think your folks will still let him hang out with me?"

Anna reached over and squeezed his arm. "Absolutely. This has nothing to do with you and Wayne. This is really about my cousin and my brothers acting stupid."

Kyle laughed. "I'm sorry that Gavin and Wesley aren't friends anymore."

"So am I. Make me a promise that you won't grow up to be as muleheaded as your brother and mine."

Kyle hooted with laughter. "Deal."

After a time, Kyle surprised her when he asked, "Can I ask you something? Something you won't tell Wayne?"

"Of course, if that's what you want. Sounds serious."

"Naw. Wayne really likes this girl in our English class, Marcy Gordon. She's kind of cute. She is always smiling at him, pretending she really likes him."

"Pretending?"

"Yeah. As soon as his back is turned she is grinning in my face. What's up with that? She knows Wayne and I are buddies!"

"That could be a problem, especially if you also like her."

"Hey, I think she's cute. But who needs a girl who plays one friend against the other. Acts like a hoochie, if you ask me."

Anna couldn't hold back the giggle. "That bad, huh?"

He nodded. "Do you think I should tell Wayne? I don't want him thinking I'm going after her."

"I think you should tell him. At least then he'll know what's going on."

"Yeah. I thought that too. I don't want him mad at me."

"He won't be. He might even be glad that you were honest with him."

"I hope you're right."

Anna and Kyle had started decorating the house for the holidays. Gavin had helped them decorate the seven-foot Christmas tree in the foyer with gold and red satin balls and the smaller one in the living room in silver.

When they got in, Kyle and Anna finished putting spiraling Christmas lights down the main staircase banister and placing the poinsettias on the tables in the hall and all the rooms on the main floor.

Then they relaxed in front of the television in the media room. Sharing a bowl of popcorn, they were watching a marathon of reruns of *The Jeffersons* on cable when Gavin called from the airport. He hoped to be home around ten-thirty.

Kyle asked if he could stay up until his brother came in

and Anna reluctantly agreed, in exchange for the promise that he be in bed no later than eleven and not complain about getting up for school the next morning.

At the sound of the buzzer, Kyle dashed out of the room, calling from over his shoulder that he'd get it.

"Wait a minute," Anna said, catching up with him in the foyer, knowing it couldn't be Gavin. "Who is it?"

He looked stunned when he turned to her. "My father."

"What?" Shocked, she asked, "You saw him on the monitor?"

"Yes. It's him, all right. He was in a cab." Kyle suddenly looked like a frightened little boy. "I shouldn't have let him in."

Squeezing his hand, she said, "No, you made the right choice. No matter what he has done, he's still your father. Don't worry. Gavin will be here soon." She wanted Gavin to hurry because she had no clue as to how he wanted to handle this situation. "If you don't want to talk to him tonight, you can go on up to your room. I'll tell him that you've gone to bed."

Kyle shook his head, jutting out his chin and looking for all the world like his older brother.

"No. I'll face him. Besides, I did nothing wrong. I wasn't the one who walked away."

"You're absolutely right. You have nothing to apologize for. Just remember, Gavin and I love you. You're not alone."

He nodded just before the doorbell chimed.

"I'll get it." Anna went to the oak door with Kyle a few steps behind her. "May I help you?" she said, studying the tall, thin man waiting on the other side of the locked wrought-iron and glass storm door.

"I'm George Reynolds. That young player behind you is my son. May I come in? It's cold out here."

The ground was littered with a fresh blanket of snow.

"Sorry." She was caught in a gush of cold air once she unlocked and swung the storm door open. "Come in."

She shivered, uncertain if it was from the cold night or the load of problems this man undoubtedly would bring along with him.

George was grinning like a long-lost friend as he brought a large suitcase inside. Closing the doors, he offered his hand. "And you are?"

"Anna Prescott. I'm a friend of Gavin's as well as the chef." She watched as he approached Kyle.

"Well, well, son. You must have shot up a couple of inches in only a few months." George beamed as he slapped Kyle on the back.

Judging by Kyle's reaction, the defenses that she hadn't seen in weeks were firmly in place.

"Good to see you, kid." Turning back to Anna, George asked, "Where is Gavin?"

"He's on his way home. He shouldn't be long. He had an out-of-town game." She forced a smile. "May I take your coat?"

"Sure can." George smiled as he shrugged out of the leather jacket.

Although George's dark face was lined from years of neglect, his hair had touches of gray at the temples, and he was several inches shorter than Gavin, there was no doubt that both of his sons had gotten their good looks from him.

After she'd hung his coat in the hall closet, she said to Kyle, "Please show your father into the living room while I go put on some coffee."

Gavin released a groan as he eased his bruised and tired body from the Navigator. Despite his sore ribs and scrapes down his left side and shoulder, Gavin's heart quickened with anticipation. He hadn't seen his woman in days.

They hadn't made love in over a week. And he was damn tired of sleeping alone. Everything seemed to be working against them. He wasn't comfortable leaving Kyle in the house all night long. He only allowed himself a few hours with her, before he went back to his own empty bed.

She hadn't said it, but he wasn't a fool. He knew she wanted more than what he could comfortably give. What he was, was a selfish bastard . . . too concerned with his own needs to let her go. His feelings for her grew with each new day, and they scared him. Yet he was not about to walk away. How could he when she had made the house that had been too large for him into a home. He liked coming back, knowing she would be there.

Shifting his garment bag to his other hand, he let himself into the side door. What he needed was an hour in the hot whirlpool tub and a few hours in Anna's arms. He dropped the bag on the bench near the door before walking into the brightly lit kitchen.

"Hey. Where is everyone?" He called.

"Gavin!" Kyle raced into the room, Anna right on his heels. "You okay?"

"Yeah." Gavin shrugged, looping an arm around his brother's neck, giving him an affectionate squeeze. "Just a little banged up." He smiled at Anna while his eyes stroked her sweet frame. He reached out an arm to her. She came to him, wrapping her arms around his waist for a hug.

"We're glad you're home," Kyle confessed.

His gaze went from Anna's worried face to his brother's scowl. "What's going on?" He barely got the question out when he looked up to see his father enter the room.

"Hello, son. Tough game?"

23

"I just got in. It's good to see you." Then he quickly amended, "Both of my sons. I came for the Christmas holidays."

"Hell no," Kyle shouted. "You're here to take me away. If you think I'm going anywhere with you, you're wrong." His dark eyes filled with tears.

Gavin placed a hand on the boy's shoulder in an effort to soothe him. He said quietly, so as not to be overheard, "Calm down. Don't let him rile you." To George, he said, "Why now? Feeling paternal all of a sudden?"

George said confidently, "It was wrong of me to leave Kyle without asking, but I knew you would do right by him." He couldn't meet Gavin's challenging gaze.

"Stop talking about me as if I'm not standing right here." Kyle dashed away angry tears.

Anna interrupted, saying, "Kyle, it's past your bedtime.

Gavin, I'm sure you're hungry. Why don't you and your father go into the living room. I'll bring in some sandwiches."

"I can't go to bed now." Kyle's voice was touched with anxiety.

"Yes, you can," she said softly. "You have school in the morning. Nothing is being decided tonight."

"Anna's right," Gavin interjected. "You go on up and get ready for bed. I'll be up to talk to you a little later."

Kyle wasn't pleased, but mumbled a hasty good night before taking off for his bedroom.

George said to Gavin, "Glad to hear you've got him in school."

"Like you give a damn. Where the hell have you been? And what do you mean, walking out without a word to anyone?" Gavin demanded.

Anna's hands were shaking as she began preparing the sandwiches.

"Look, I know that was wrong, but I had some business I had to take care of."

"Business?" Gavin laughed without a trace of humor. "More like whoever you owed money was looking for your sorry ass."

"Gavin," Anna gasped.

"Sorry." He ran a hand over his hair, impatient with his runaway temper.

She asked, "Is there a reason this has to be settled tonight? Your father is going to be here until the holidays. You're just getting in, and we're all tired."

"None," Gavin agreed, striving for a calm he didn't feel. Turning to his father, he said, "Where is your luggage? I'll show you to your room."

"In the front hall. I'll get it."

Anna waited until they were alone and whispered, "You don't think he's here to take Kyle, do you?"

"No. It's not going to happen. No matter what he does, Kyle stays with me. I made him a promise, and I am not going back on my word."

Her relief was in her smile. "I think Kyle needs to hear that from you. He was very upset when he recognized who was at the front gate."

"I'll talk to him." He cradled her for a few moments before he said, "Sweetheart, I apologize for putting you to so much trouble, but I've lost my appetite."

"It's no trouble. I can easily wrap the sandwiches and save them for tomorrow." She laughed. "Someone around here will eat them."

He whispered into her ear. "Will you wait up for me?"

"Are you sure that's what you want? Honey, even I can see that you're exhausted."

"I'm sure." After going up on tiptoe to brush her mouth against his, she gave him a little push. "Go on. Your father is waiting for you."

"I won't be long."

"Don't rush on my account. Kyle needs you."

Gavin retrieved his own bag before taking his father up to the guest room at the top of the stairs. After a brief good night, he stopped in his own room to drop off his bag, then knocked on his brother's door.

"Come in."

Gavin walked in, closing the door behind him. Kyle was in bed, but as Gavin expected, he was wide awake. Judging by the anxious look on his face, Anna was right. Kyle needed to know his plans.

"Well?"

"George is staying for the holidays. I put him in the room at the top of the stairs."

There were angry tears in his eyes when Kyle asked, "Are you going to let him take me when he leaves?"

"No. The only way you're going with him is if you decide you want to leave."

Kyle pleaded, "You mean it?"

"Of course I mean it. You and I are family. If George wants to stay, he's welcome. But that doesn't change things between us."

"Thanks." Kyle launched himself at his brother.

Gavin gave him a reassuring hug. "There is nothing to thank me for. You're my brother and I love you. Now you get in that bed. You still have school tomorrow."

"Okay," Kyle said with a grin. "I love you too."

Anna was creaming her skin with perfumed body lotion when she heard the knock on the outside door. "It's open," she called as she slipped a pink nightgown over her head.

"Hi." Gavin's big body nearly filled the bedroom door as he watched her.

"Hi yourself." She smiled as she walked over to him and touched his lips with her own. "Did you talk to Kyle? Is he okay?"

He nodded as he encircled her waist. He pulled the clasp from her hair and smoothed it out over her shoulders. "He's better. I promised him I wouldn't let George take him away."

"Have you ever considered you and your brother are wrong about your father? Maybe he only came for the holidays, like he said."

"Maybe. The problem is, I can't trust him. If he decides he wants to take Kyle with him I can't let that happen. George Reynolds doesn't know a damn thing about raising a kid. Look how he walked out on Kyle without a word of explanation to anyone. He's unfit to be anyone's parent."

Anna was worried. Kyle had gone through so many adjustments these past few months. He was just beginning to act like the carefree teenager that he should be rather than the bitter angry boy that George had left behind last September.

"How will you be able to stop him? He is Kyle's sole remaining parent."

"I have temporary guardianship for now." He sighed tiredly. "I'll find a way. My lawyer will be here in the morning and will help sort it all out. If necessary, I'm prepared to take him to court. Kyle is finally happy and feels secure here. I won't let our father jeopardize that."

She reached up to caress his unshaven cheek. "You look tired, honey."

"I am. Let's go to bed."

"What about your father? Should you leave him in the house alone with Kyle?"

"He's not going anywhere. He's probably broke. I bet that's what brought him here." His hands went to his shirt.

"Let me." Anna unbuttoned his chambray shirt. "Are you okay? You're leaning awfully heavily on that door."

"Don't make a fuss. I'm okay, sweetheart." He eased forward until her breasts rested on his chest. When she tried to step back, he grumbled, "Where are you going?"

"You're not okay. Honey, you took a hard hit tonight. I want to see your side." She gingerly eased the shirt off his shoulder and down his arms. "Oh no."

"It just a scrape."

"A scrape? Your whole left side is bruised from your shoulder to your waist. Why do you play this crazy game? You could have ended up in a wheelchair."

"Don't." He gave her a tender squeeze. "I'm fine. Come on, let's go to bed. All I could think about on the trip back was being able to hold you in my arms."

"I don't like seeing you all banged up. But I know it's what you want to do." With her arm around his waist, she walked with him over to the bed. Her hands weren't as steady as she would've liked as she unsnapped and unzipped his jeans. After he sat down on the edge of the bed, she helped him out of his sneakers and socks before she eased the jeans down his legs.

"Okay?" she asked as she covered him.

"Yeah," he said with his eyes closed.

She went around the opposite side of the bed, turned off the lamp, and was careful not to bump him as she slipped into bed.

"You're too far away," he complained as he reached out to her and eased her against him, her back to his front. "That's better." He draped her hair over one shoulder and pressed a kiss against her nape.

He said quietly, "I don't trust him."

"I know. I missed you," she whispered.

Tightening his arm around her, he murmured, "I missed you too."

She turned until she faced him. "Does it hurt?" She referred to his injury.

"Stop worrying. I'm fine. I noticed that you and Kyle finished decorating the house. It looks nice. Did you go over to your folks for dinner?"

"Yes."

"How did it go?"

"Okay."

He caressed her cheek. "You don't sound like it went okay. What happened? Did your father give you a hard time about our living arrangements?"

"Not exactly. Dad isn't pleased, but my folks aren't the problem." She hesitated as if trying to figure out how to say what needed to be said. Finally she confessed, "My cousin and brothers have convinced Dad not to invite you to the family Christmas dinner."

"Why doesn't that surprise me?" His voice was tinged with bitterness.

Anna heard his disappointment and she also heard his hurt. Close to tears, she insisted, "I'm sorry, honey. You've done nothing to warrant such callousness."

His laughter held no humor, recalling the harsh words between himself and Wesley. "I'm sleeping with their baby sister. At least they didn't blackball Kyle, did they?"

"No, but I want you to know I'm not having it. If you aren't welcome, neither am I." Her voice was brimming with emotion.

"You can't mean that, Anna. You're a Prescott."

"I'm also a grown woman living my own life the way I see fit."

Gavin leaned over her until he could search her beautiful but troubled eyes. "You don't have to do that. You and Kyle can go without me."

"Absolutely not." Her chin jutted to a stubborn angle.

"I mean it, Anna. I don't want you to stay away from your family on Christmas or any day because of me. I've spent holidays without family. You haven't. Besides, your entire family will be hurt if you aren't at that dinner, especially your mother."

"I know," she said, rubbing her cheek against his chest. "I've made up my mind. If you aren't welcome, then neither am I."

"No, Anna."

"What's the big deal? I can fix a wonderful dinner here for all of us. We'll start our own holiday tradition."

"You'd do that for me?"

"That and so much more," she whispered the gentle promise.

They shared a lingering kiss. "I don't know what I've done

to deserve you, sweet Anna, but I'm planning to hang on to you for a long, long time."

She gave him another kiss. "Shouldn't you sleep in your own bed tonight? What if I bump you?"

"I'm where I want to be. Besides, I'll leave before anyone gets up."

She nodded before she switched topics, "So you think all your father wants is money?"

"He won't get it. When he left the last time, I swore I'd never give him another dime."

Anna decided to keep her fears to herself. She wouldn't put anything past George Reynolds. She sighed tiredly, relaxing against him. She began smoothing her hand over his arm and his uninjured shoulder. Like Gavin, she'd already made up her mind. She wasn't going to let anything come between them . . . not even her family.

"Anna, somehow we'll work this out. I don't want you to spend the day away from your family." He pressed a kiss against her temple. "We can always divide the day . . . spend the morning here, and then you and Kyle spend the rest of the day with your family. Later that night, you and I can be together."

Anna turned her head, kissing his throat. "Thank you. I appreciate your wanting to help. Only this is something you can't fix. Can we talk about something else?"

"Sweetheart . . ."

"No, Gavin. I don't want to talk about this anymore, at least not tonight. All I want is to enjoy being in this bed with you." She snuggled closer.

"Okay." He lay awake listening to her even breathing. As far as he was concerned, the matter was far from settled.

*   *   *

They were having breakfast the next morning when George joined them. Kyle and Gavin exchanged a look before Gavin spoke to his father. "Good morning."

Anna said, "I will get another plate. Hope you like French toast, eggs, and turkey sausages."

"Coffee?" Gavin rose to get a mug.

"Yes. Thanks. You all are up early." George looked from one to the other.

Gavin said, returning with the hot drink, "Kyle has school. I have practice, and Anna has her work. She's writing a cookbook, aren't you, sweetheart?"

She smiled. "That's right. It's a family cookbook, dating back to my female ancestors on my mother's side. I have the journals—" She stopped when she realized George wasn't bothering to even pretend that he was interested. She set a full plate in front of him. She often kept food warming on the stove in case one of the staff had missed breakfast.

"Morning." Gretchen came in with a ready smile.

"Good morning." Anna breathed a sigh of relief. The conversation had nearly come to a halt. Kyle wasn't trying. He'd closed up the moment his father had entered the kitchen.

"Hey," Gavin said as he took his plate and utensils to the sink. "How was your weekend?"

"Not long enough." She looked expectantly at Gavin.

"Oh. Gretchen Hamilton, my father, George Reynolds. Gretchen is my executive assistant and works out of the home office."

"Hello." Gretchen momentarily lost her smile but quickly recovered. She went over to shake hands. "It's good to meet you. I've heard a lot about you."

"None of it good, I'll bet." George laughed as if he'd told a joke.

Anna quickly said, "Gretchen, would you care for breakfast?"

"I'll get it. I only want coffee and toast." She came around the island and got both. "Gavin, do you have a moment? The principal from Kettering High School called and asked if you can talk at their career day in April. I have the date written down, and I also have some checks I need you to sign."

He nodded. "I'll be right in."

Gretchen asked, "Anna, did Vanessa call?"

"Yes, she will be in, but she is running late."

"Thanks. What would we do without you?" Not expecting an answer, Gretchen said, "Kyle, I bet you're excited. Only a few days more before Christmas break. You have a good day in school," before she disappeared down the hall with coffee in one hand and her briefcase in the other.

Gavin refilled his own coffee mug before he excused himself and followed his assistant.

"Are you okay?" Anna asked Kyle, after noting his nearly full plate. She placed a hand on his forehead.

"I'm fine. Just not hungry. I forgot my science book in my room. Be right back." He hurried out of the room.

"Would you care for something else, Mr. Reynolds?" she asked, lifting her mug to her mouth.

"No. I'm fine." He smiled.

Anna saw traces of Gavin and Kyle in his smile. He had apparently been a handsome man in his younger years. Unfortunately, he wasn't aging well. The lines around his eyes and mouth were pronounced, and his skin didn't glow with good health. Anna suspected liquor and hard living had taken their toll on him. Yet it was still evident why women were swayed by his easy charm.

"Something going on between you and Gavin?"

"Beg your pardon?" Anna blinked in surprise.

"He's interested in you."

"Mr. Reynolds, my relationship with Gavin is private. As for Kyle, he's the one who has had a difficult adjustment."

"That's why I'm back. Hey, do you think Gavin will let me use one of his cars while I'm here?"

Anna, who'd been collecting plates, hesitated. "A car?"

"I need wheels while I'm here. There are at least four cars in that garage. He can't drive every one of them."

"You'd better talk to Gavin about—"

"Talk to me about what?"

"I need wheels while I'm here, son. How about I borrow one of your cars?" George asked without any hesitation. "What do you need with so many cars?"

Anna was surprised when he answered, "As you know, I don't believe in throwing money away. The Navigator, I bought. The Ford was given to me as a signing bonus. The Town Car was a gift for shooting a commercial for the company. The compact belongs to Anna. Now answer my question for me. Where are you headed?"

"Casino in Windsor."

Anna saw Gavin's mouth tighten before he went over to the locked steel case mounted on the wall near the side door. Unlocking it, he took out a set of keys. He tossed them to his father. "Dark blue Town Car. The tank should be full. Excuse me, I better get Kyle moving."

George rose. "Thanks for the meal, pretty lady. Bye." He grabbed his coat and was out the door before Anna could respond.

She shook her head. He hadn't bothered to say even a few words to Kyle and then had left without telling the boy goodbye.

Gavin returned with Kyle. They were ready to go. Gavin paused to give her a quick kiss on her cheek before he ushered Kyle out the door. As Anna called goodbye, she couldn't help being concerned about Kyle. His father's return was putting a strain on all of them, but especially Kyle.

"Something smells good," Mrs. Tillman said as she paused in the kitchen doorway.

Anna smiled as she took a roasting pan out of the oven. "Stuffed chicken thighs and legs. It's a recipe handed down from my great-great grandmother Rhea-Ellen. According to her journal, my great-grandfather, who was from Trinidad, often enjoyed the dish."

"It smells wonderful. What's in it?"

"After taking out the bone I stuffed the cavity with a mixture of water chestnuts, garlic, soy sauce, scallions, vinegar, chives, and celery. Would you like a sample?"

"I don't want to eat up Kyle and Mr. Mathis's dinner." Mrs. Tillman came over to look over Anna's shoulder. "What are you serving with it?"

"Rice, steamed vegetable medley, and a salad. It's not a problem to fix a plate for you, Mrs. Tillman. This is my third try. You can tell me if I have too much or not enough spices."

"Okay. But I have to take it with me, darling. I'm meeting a friend for a movie. I have to get home and change. Please, tell Mr. Mathis that I will start in the upstairs linen closet tomorrow." She went to get her coat and purse.

"I will. The house always looks wonderful, Mrs. Tillman. We couldn't get along without you. I know Gavin appreciates your work," Anna said as she wrapped several pieces of stuffed chicken into a foil packet. "Would you like to take a slice of sweet potato pie with you? I made three."

"I'd love it." Mrs. Tillman laughed. "Good heavens, I must have gained eight pounds since you've been here. You're always making something I can't resist. Pretty soon I won't be able to fit through the door."

Anna laughed along with her. "I'm so glad you enjoy my cooking."

"Is Gretchen gone for the day?"

"Yes, she had a dental appointment this afternoon. Vanessa left a little while ago."

Just then the buzzer at the front gate sounded. "Wonder who that is?" Anna handed over the slice of pie she'd placed in a plastic container before she wiped her hands on a paper towel and unfastened her apron.

"Perhaps Mr. Reynolds is back?"

"No. He's using one of the cars and has the code number. I'd better get that," she said from over her shoulder. "Enjoy your evening."

"See you in the morning," Mrs. Tillman said, "And Anna, thank you."

Anna was surprised to see her father's face in the monitor. "Daddy? Just a minute, please." She pressed the button to open the electronic gates. She still hadn't figured out why he'd come by when he walked in the front door.

"Hi." Anna waited for him. She kissed his cheek, accepting his warm hug. "This is a surprise. Come in." She reached for his heavy suede jacket and hung it in the closet.

"I know you're wondering why I'm here," Lester said as he followed her down the hallway into a small and cozy family room.

"I am curious. Are you here to see me or Gavin?" she asked, motioning him into an armchair.

"Both. Is he in?"

"Not yet. Gavin and Kyle should be home soon. Can I get you anything?"

"No thanks, precious." Lester reached out and took her hand into his. "I came because I thought you and I needed to talk." He hesitated before he said, "Your mother and I aren't pleased by your living arrangements."

24

Anna lifted her chin. "I know, but—"

"No buts. You're a wonderful daughter, never giving your mother or me a moment of trouble. We're proud of you, precious. And you know we love you very much. But we raised you to be able to stand on your own two feet, not wait for some guy to take care of you. Married folks take care of each other."

She took a deep breath before she said, "Gavin isn't supporting me. Yes, I'm staying in the guest cottage, but I have responsibilities that have nothing to do with our relationship. And yes, I work for him, and he pays me a salary . . ."

"I know all that. That's not what I'm talking about. I'm talking about what is right for you. I know you love him, baby girl, but evidently that love is onesided or he'd ask you to marry him, not live with him."

Unable to remain seated a moment longer, Anna jumped

to her feet. She went over to the French doors, only to stare out at the snow-covered lawn. Eventually she turned to face her father. "I can't live the life you want for me. And you're right. I am in love with Gavin. If that weren't the case, I wouldn't be living here." She paused before she went on to say, "You are wrong. I'm happy with the way things are. He treats me well and cares for me."

"Are you telling me you don't want to be his wife?" Lester persisted. "Are you?"

"No, I'm not. But marriage isn't everything. I'm happy, Daddy. Why can't you and Mama accept that, and be happy for me?"

"We're your parents and quite naturally want only the best for you." He sighed wearily, shifting in his chair. "That's not the reason I came. Your mother and I are upset that you aren't planning to spend Christmas Day with the family."

"I'd like nothing more than to spend the holiday with my family, Gavin, and Kyle. Thanks to my brothers and cousin, that's not going to happen. I'm sure—" Anna stopped because she thought she heard the side door open. "Excuse me for a moment."

She went into the kitchen. "Hi." She smiled at Gavin and Kyle loaded down with packages. "What's all this?"

Kyle grinned boyishly. "Christmas gifts. We stopped by the mall on the way home. On Saturday we're going snowmobiling. Want to come?"

"Sounds like fun." Anna said to Gavin, "My father is here. He's in the family room."

"Everything okay?" Gavin asked quietly.

She nodded, forcing a smile. "Kyle, why don't you go in and say hello, before you take those things upstairs. Then, you can get a start on your homework."

"Okay." Even though he was loaded down with shopping

bags, he managed to grab a bottle of juice and a piece of fruit before he left.

"How'd it go, sweetheart?" Gavin asked softly.

"He's upset. I have to get back."

He brushed his mouth against hers. "I'm going with you."

"I'd rather you didn't."

"We're in this together. Right?"

"Right."

Gavin was right behind her, his hand at the back of her waist. She stopped suddenly, placing her hand against his chest.

"Please try not to get upset."

He nodded before they entered the family room together.

"Lester." Gavin held out his hand to the man he'd loved and respected like a father.

"Gavin." He stood and shook the younger man's hand. Both men were tall but Gavin topped her father by three inches.

Kyle stood up. "I've got homework, Coach. Are you staying for dinner?"

Lester smiled. "Not this time. It was good seeing you."

Gavin waited until Lester sat down and Anna sat in the armchair she had vacated earlier, before he took the chair on the other side of her. "What brought you out on such a snowy afternoon?"

"Considering what happened on Thanksgiving, I thought it would be best if we talked."

Gavin admitted, "Anna and I never meant to cause problems in your family. We care about each other and want to be together."

"If you cared, truly cared for my daughter, you'd give her your name, rather than ask her to live with you." A muscle jumped in Lester's jaw.

"Daddy, how could you?" Anna gasped, close to tears.

"It's how I feel, little girl. Nothing is going to keep me from caring for my own. I'd be less than a man if I didn't do what is right."

Gavin reached out and took her hand before he said candidly, "I know you don't agree with the way we've chosen to live."

"You're right about that, but that's only part of the reason why I'm here." Lester paused and then said, "Anna is an important part of this family. And I for one will not keep my mouth shut while you plan to stay away from us on Christmas Day."

"It wasn't my idea," she said impatiently.

"It's upsetting your mother, and I won't have that."

"I didn't start it, Daddy. You, my brothers, and cousin started this fight on Thanksgiving. Why? Because they saw us kissing."

"We were upset, Anna. The boys were taught to look out for you, always. I won't apologize for that."

Anna had had enough. "Daddy, why did you come? Just to start another argument?"

"No. I came because I want you and Gavin to spend Christmas Day with the family."

"You do?" Anna exchanged a quick glance with Gavin before she returned her attention to her father.

"Yes, I would like both of you and Kyle to come."

"I don't know." She was thoughtful for a moment. "It won't work. It's bound to lead to another shouting match, and that will upset everyone all over again. Wesley, Devin, and Ralph aren't going to keep quiet."

"Let me worry about them. You three just come."

"Gavin?"

"It's up to you, sweetheart. Besides, my father has come for the holidays. I wouldn't want to impose."

"He's invited," Lester offered, rising to his feet. "I've got to get home, before your mother gets worried. Think about it. We're family and family may disagree, but we love each other regardless."

"I'll see you out," Gavin said.

Anna went over and kissed her father's cheek. "Thanks, Daddy."

"I love you, precious." He kissed her.

"I love you too. Give Mama my love."

"Will do."

Once Lester had retrieved his coat, Gavin walked him out. They were on the front walkway when Lester said, "I expect you to take good care of my girl."

"I will," Gavin promised.

Lester hesitated a few moments before he said, "Even though we disagree on your living arrangement, I want you to know that I'm proud of the way you've handled the situation with Kyle."

Gavin swallowed the lump of emotion lodged in his throat. "Thank you. That means a lot."

"Any idea what your father's up to this time?"

"Money, what else? He was here less than twelve hours and has spent more time in the casinos than he has with any of us."

"He can't control it, son." Lester put a hand on Gavin's shoulder. "What about Kyle? Is your father going to try to take him when he leaves?"

"I don't know his plans but Kyle stays here with me. This is his home."

Lester nodded his approval. "A man always takes care of his own." He went on to say, "If you offered to marry my Anna, you wouldn't get an argument out of me or the boys."

Gavin stiffened. "Anna and I don't need the formality. We're already a couple."

"If Anna let you believe that, then you don't know her as well as you think you do." Lester got in his car and drove away.

Anna's anxious eyes followed Gavin all through dinner. It wasn't until Kyle had gone off to bed that they had an opportunity to talk privately. She was curled up on one end of the leather sofa in the family room, reading one of her grandmother's journals, when Gavin came in, carrying a huge bowl of freshly made hot buttered popcorn.

"Want some?" He placed the bowl on the coffee table and settled himself beside her.

She smiled but shook her head.

Playing with a lock of her cottony soft hair, he asked, "What's bothering you? You haven't said more than a few words all evening."

"You heard what my father said about us."

"He said nothing that we haven't already discussed. We knew your parents weren't in favor of their daughter living with any man without benefit of marriage. Why are you letting this bother you so much?"

"How can you ask me that?" She put the journal facedown on the end table. "My father told you that you should marry me and why."

"Are you saying that you want to get married?"

"I never said that."

"You know how I feel about marriage. Is that the problem?"

"There is no problem," she insisted, yet she couldn't meet his gaze.

"Oh, there's a problem but you're just not telling me what it is." He sat forward, his forearms braced on his knees.

She looked away, suddenly realizing how exhausted she was. She'd been so careful to keep her feelings hidden. Each day it was a little more difficult to keep quiet. Nothing she could do or say would change that.

Regardless of his deep regard for her, Gavin couldn't make himself love her. She wanted his babies and his name. She wanted to belong to him, and for him to belong to her. That was her dream, not his. She also didn't want him to feel guilty because of it.

Gavin was not a callous man. He could never accept that by being with her without a commitment, he was hurting her slowly by painful degrees.

Her father certainly didn't have any trouble figuring out that she was in love with Gavin. His protective instincts had taken over. She still hadn't gotten over the fact that her father had told Gavin straight out that he should marry her.

"Anna?"

"What do you want me to say?"

"I wish I knew." He laced his fingers through hers, and with a slight tug he pulled her up and into his lap. He held her, his face buried in her sweet fragrant hair.

"Anna, I want you happy. I don't want to ever hurt you in any way. You would tell me if you were hurting, wouldn't you?"

She caressed his strong jaw. "Gavin, how could you be hurting me? I am where I want to be."

"Are you sure?" He studied her face.

Anna encircled his neck with her arms while she lifted her face to kiss him.

His breathing changed suddenly. It was now as rapid and uneven as hers. "Are you?"

"Gavin . . ." She kissed him again and again.

Gavin groaned, deepening the kisses. Soon his tongue was enjoying the honeyed depth of her mouth. His hands had just slid beneath her top to smooth over the skin at the back of her waist, when he heard his father's voice.

"Sorry, son," George said as he backed out of the room.

Reluctantly he released her. "Come on in." He whispered in her ear, "Can we finish this later?"

She nodded, her cheeks instantly hot with embarrassment. She said, "Excuse me, I'll make some hot chocolate," before she hurried out.

George said, "Don't leave on my account."

"I'm not." Anna's legs were unsteady as she walked toward the kitchen. The only thing clear in her mind was that if she wanted what they shared to last, she had no other option but to keep her feelings to herself.

Gavin looked at his father suspiciously. George was grinning from ear to ear.

"Have a seat." Gavin motioned to one of the leather recliners. "Where have you been all day?"

"Making a bundle." George beamed as he dropped into the lounger, taking two big cigars out of his inside jacket pocket. He tossed one to Gavin.

Gavin raised a brow but caught the cigar. "I'll believe it when I see it."

Grinning, George reached in his pocket and pulled out a check for twenty-five thousand dollars made out to him.

Gavin glanced at the name of the Windsor casino. "Wow. Congratulations."

"I told you. It's more than even you can laugh at, Mr. Multimillionaire," George boasted as he puffed, trying to light the cigar. He laughed deeply. "I should tell your lady to break out the Dom Perignon. I have to hand it to you. Anna's a looker, and you got her right where you want her." He laughed heartily. "She cooks in your kitchen and sleeps in your bed. Like father, like son."

Gavin surged to his feet. Jabbing a finger into his father's chest he snarled, "You watch what you say about her. You don't know a damn thing about Anna's job or our relationship."

"What's to know?" Even though George had pushed to his feet, he was forced to look up at his son. "She's staying in your guest house. I'm not stupid. I got eyes. Something is going on besides cooking."

"And how is that any of your business, George?"

George raised his hands, palms up. "Calm down, son. I'm sorry. I didn't mean anything by it. Anna is a lovely woman."

"Yeah, she is." Gavin frowned, backing off. He paced the room, giving himself time to cool down. "Tell me about the money. How did you win it? Playing the slots?"

"Won it playing twenty-one, the rich man's game. I got enough to pay you back the money you've shelled out on the kid's clothes and such."

"You don't owe me a thing. Anything I did for Kyle is because he's my brother, and I love him."

"I insist." George beamed, swirling the lit cigar in his mouth.

"Here we go, three mugs of hot chocolate." Anna carried in the small tray. "And a little extra chocolate decadence," she said as she resumed her seat, referring to the super-size chocolate chip and macadamia nut cookies she brought along.

"None for me. I'd rather have some of my son's cognac. Got any Hennessy, son?"

"Sure." It took all he had not to cringe each time the man called him son. It was a relationship he took no pride in. He hated that "like father like son" comparison, but the comment about Anna had gotten to him, big time. Going after his father with his fists would further complicate a complicated situation, and he knew it.

Gavin walked over to the armoire. Behind the double doors was a fully stocked bar. He picked up a crystal decanter and poured the dark liquid into a crystal tumbler and then passed his father the drink.

"You're not joining me?" George puffed contentedly on his cigar. "This is a celebration."

Gavin shook his head. "Hot chocolate is fine." He handed Anna one of the mugs and took the other. "Mmm," he sighed, taking a big bite of one of the cookies.

"What are you celebrating?" Anna asked George, forcing a smile. "Someone win the lottery?"

George laughed. "What do you think of that?" He proudly displayed the check.

"Really." Amazed, she looked from one man to the other.

"He won big at the Windsor casino," Gavin explained.

"Congratulations," she offered, lifting her cup toward him and taking a sip.

George nodded, taking a deep swallow of his drink.

Anna smiled. "Don't spend it all in one place."

George leaned back in his chair, propping his feet on the ottoman. "I tried to pay my son back all the cash he laid out on the kid. He won't take a dime."

Gavin decided against mentioning the money he'd lent his father over the years. There was no doubt it would eat up the check and then some. He had given the man nearly half a million, enough for him to have started his own business in any field he chose.

Gavin said, "Anna's right. This is your chance to make a fresh start. If you're interested in making a good investment, I can help you. I've learned not only how to make money, but how to make it work for me. That's the key."

George grinned. "Thanks, son. But I have some ideas about that my own damn self."

Anna glanced at Gavin. "I think I will say good night."

Gavin was a few steps behind her when she started down the hallway. He caught her around the waist and dropped his head close to hers. "What's your hurry?"

She whispered, "You should talk to him. Maybe you can talk some sense into him." Even though she carried a mug in each hand, she leaned back enough to brush her lips over his jaw. "Will I see you later?"

He whispered back, "Count on it. I'll try not to make it too late."

"Take your time. If I'm asleep . . . wake me."

"I will." He gave her a gentle squeeze and released her.

Gavin took a couple of deep, fortifying breaths before he went back into the family room. He'd spoken to his lawyer earlier and had been careful not to antagonize the other man. That was until he'd lost his temper. If he wanted to keep Kyle with him he needed George's cooperation.

"Interested in hitting a few nightclubs with me tonight?" George grinned, sipping from his drink. "Father and son checking out the ladies?"

Gavin swallowed the abrupt refusal. "Not tonight. About your winnings, if you invest wisely, you can double, maybe triple it. The market is fluctuating right now, but there are still—"

"You're talking about the stock market? Hell no. I plan to double it, only my way. Wait and see." George walked over to the armoire to refill his glass. When he was resettled in the armchair, he switched on the television, flipping until he found a sports channel. "I got some money on this one," he said, referring to the college football game under way. "You want in?"

"No thanks." Gavin reached over to finish off the cookies. His gaze, like his father's, was on the screen for a time. Eventually he said, "Don't you think it's time you told me why you're here? We both know it doesn't have a thing to do with the holidays. If it's not money, what is it?"

The other man's forehead creased in a frown. "Just wanted to check in to see how the kid was getting along. I know I shouldn't have just disappeared like I did. But I was in a bind. I needed money, and I needed it fast."

"What was the hurry?"

George was silent for a moment as if he were weighing his response. "I owed money to a shark. And he wasn't takin' no for an answer."

The game forgotten, Gavin demanded, "Shark? As in loan shark?"

"Yeah, but I handled my business. I didn't want the kid mixed up in that kinda trouble."

"Damn straight. How did you get yourself in that kind of trouble?"

"Ran into a bad streak in Vegas. Hell, it happens to everyone."

"No, it doesn't. Have you paid off this guy?"

"I appreciate your concern, but it's over. I took care of it."

"You better have." Gavin scowled. "From what I can see, the problem is how you make your living . . . gambling."

George grinned as if Gavin had paid him a compliment. "I'm good, son. I know what I'm doing."

"It seems to me it's only a matter of time until you lose it all again. Besides, what kind of life would that be for Kyle? Do you still have a place in Dayton? From what Kyle told me, you had him on the move until you brought him here. What kind of life is that for a child?"

George squirmed, apparently uncomfortable with the conversation. "I admit he's been better off with you, for now. But once I get my own place, that's going to end. I have enough to do that now."

"I see. Where exactly are you going to get this place?"

"Don't know yet. But when I do, I can take the kid off your hands. Maybe I will look around here. You guys have some fine casinos in Michigan."

Too damn many, Gavin thought, but kept it to himself. He frowned into his empty mug.

"Kyle is settled here. He wants to finish high school in Detroit. And I want him with me."

George took his gaze off the television for a moment. His eyes were glossy. "That's bound to put a hell of a crimp in your style, son. Hell, I'm surprised you don't have women coming out of the woodwork. A man in your position can have any woman he wants." He laughed heartily. "Hell, if it were me, I'd be in a different honey's bed each night."

Gavin lifted a brow. "That's kind of risky, especially in this day and age."

"Hell no. It makes perfect sense to me," the older man said as he drained his glass.

Gavin knew he shouldn't ask, but he had to know. "Have you ever genuinely cared about a woman?"

"What makes you ask that?" George looked at him from over his shoulder as he refilled his empty glass again. He didn't bother to wait for an answer but went on to say, "Sure, I have. I loved your mama and Kyle's. I don't have kids with just anyone." He looked offended.

Gavin had serious doubts as to whether the man knew the meaning of the word, "love," judging by the way he'd mistreated, his mother, Eloise, over the years. He took a series of calming breaths. He had to remind himself, yet again, that getting into an argument with his father now wasn't wise.

He couldn't stop himself from adding, "For all you know, you could have a string of bastards around the country."

George roared with laughter before he raised his glass to take a long sip. "Never know."

Gavin had had about as much as he could stomach for one night. Picking up the tray, he rose to his feet. "I'll leave you to it. Night."

He made a stop in the kitchen before he headed back toward the stairs. He was swearing beneath his breath as he took the stairs two at a time. "Selfish bastard."

He knocked on Kyle's door and when there was no answer, he quietly let himself inside. Kyle was sprawled on the top bunk, and the television as usual was still on. Gavin turned off the set and pulled the comforter over his brother before he left.

Mumbling to himself as he headed down the hall to his own rooms, "Kyle is a good kid. He deserves a chance," Gavin promised himself that he would find a way to keep his brother with him.

After shaving and taking a shower, he changed into a clean but threadbare pair of jeans and an old Michigan State sweatshirt. He slipped his bare feet into loafers.

Pausing to peer inside the family room, Gavin found George in the same spot, only he was snoring with the television still on. Gavin was deep in thought when he grabbed a jacket and went out the side door. In less than a couple of minutes, he knocked on Anna's door. When she didn't answer after a time, he slid his key into the lock and let himself inside.

The sitting room was lit by a single lamp. The bedroom doorway was open and music played softly from the CD player. He smiled when he recognized Natalie Cole's "Unforgettable."

On the bed, the down comforter and top flannel sheet had been folded back, the pillows were stacked double, and the bed was empty. The only light in the room came from a lit pillar candle inside a crystal vase on the dresser. He knocked softly on the open bathroom door.

"Hey, sweetheart. May I come in?" "

"Hi" she said, from where she rested in the spa-size whirlpool tub. Rose-scented foam swirled around her.

"You look comfortable." He smiled.

"I was just getting out." Her eyes were downcast.

"Don't rush on my account." He sat down on the lid of the commode. "Would you like me to scrub your back?" He followed the lines of her soft shoulders to the graceful lines of her throat.

"Not tonight. Would you please hand me that towel you're sitting on?"

Gavin smiled, rising. He shook out the ivory bath sheet and held it out for her.

"Did you have that talk with your father?"

"Sort of. Do you mind if we don't talk about that sorry excuse for a man for one night."

As Anna rose, Gavin envied the bubbles that slid down her generous curves. He inhaled the perfumed bath oil she preferred as he held out his hand to steady her as she stepped out. She presented her beautiful back to him, and he wrapped the thick bath sheet around her. He rested his hands on her stomach. He held her for a moment and inhaled her woman's fragrance while he relished the feel of her soft bottom against his arousal.

"You look and smell wonderful." He pressed his lips against her brown nape. "If I'd come a few moments earlier, I could have joined you." Her black locks were pinned on top of her head.

"Mmm," she murmured before she moved to the mirrored counter. "I'll be out in a moment."

Frowning, he followed her and turned her around to face him. "Is something bothering you, sweetheart?"

"No. Why would you ask?"

He smoothed a caressing finger down her cheek. "You tell me. You haven't looked me in the eye since I walked in this room. And your eyes are red. Have you been crying?"

25

She hastily explained. "I got soap in my eyes."

"Are you sure that's all it is?"

She nodded but couldn't meet his questioning gaze.

"If something else is bothering you, let's get it out in the open."

"Nothing is bothering me. It's been a very long day. Let me finish up in here, and I'll be out in a few minutes."

Gavin kissed her cheek. "Okay." He held her, burying his face against her fragrant neck. "If you're too tired to make love, I'm cool with it. It's enough for me just to hold you."

He meant every word. The unvarnished truth was, he'd rather hold her all night long, every night, than have sex with anyone else. He hadn't been tempted by another woman since the first time he'd tasted her sweet lips. Drop-dead gorgeous no longer held the appeal it once had. Anna took care of all his needs and kept him hungry for more of the same.

She gave him a little push. "I'll be right out."

Gavin lingered and then took a step back, not fully convinced that something wasn't wrong. What could he say or do to make things better? He slowly turned and then went back into the bedroom. He wandered over to the French doors that opened onto the garden, a garden buried under several layers of snow.

Something wasn't right with her, he could feel it. Yet, she preferred to keep it to herself. Why? There was no doubt that her father's visit had upset her. Suddenly she was keeping secrets. It was not like her. Furthermore, he didn't like it one little bit.

If she was upset he wanted to know about it. He had to find out if this discord had something to do with her family, or if it was due to dissatisfaction with their relationship. Maybe it had just been a very long day and he was seeing problems where there were none.

Since his father had put in an appearance, Gavin couldn't honestly say he'd been attentive. Maybe she was feeling neglected. They hadn't made love since the week before this last road trip. Was that—

"You're not ready for bed." She walked in, wearing an ivory silk nightgown that barely covered her shapely behind, leaving her long and beautiful legs deliciously bare.

Gavin's mouth went dry as he moved to her side of the bed. He caressed her cheek, running a finger down to the hollow at the base of her throat.

"Would you tell me if something was bothering you?"

Throwing her arms around his neck, she caressed his nape. "I don't like that worried look on your face. Let me see if I can do something about changing it." Pressing her open mouth to his, she slipped her tongue inside to savor the taste and feel of him.

Gavin groaned, deepening the kiss even more. He murmured a husky protest when she moved back, breaking the seal of their lips.

"You, Mr. Mathis, are wearing too many clothes." She began tugging his sweatshirt up and over his head. She kissed his neck, lingering at his collarbone. She tongued the hollow, inhaling his clean male scent.

"Oh, baby . . ." he moaned, his hands resting on her hips. He caressed and squeezed her softness. When she licked his hard flat nipple, he let out a husky groan. "I thought . . ."

She kissed him repeatedly and then unsnapped his jeans. Her caressing hand moved over his hard concave stomach, then stroked over the prominent ridge of his sex. There was no mistaking his need. He hardened even more as she stroked him through the layers of his silk briefs and jeans. He groaned heavily.

"Thought what?" she crooned as she carefully unzipped and pushed the heavy denim over his tight buttocks and down his legs.

"I thought we decided you were too tired tonight," he managed to get out in a rush of air. His pulse hammered in his veins as the rushing of blood caused his penis to harden even more, his testicles to tighten with need.

"You thought wrong." Anna licked her way down his chest to his navel. Her tongue journeyed over hard muscle. She hesitated only a moment to gauge his reaction before she pressed hot kisses through the thick, coarse hair surrounding his sex while gently cupping him.

Gavin called out her name when she licked the entire length of his shaft, from the thick base to the heavy crown. He didn't believe he could get any harder or longer until she took the crest into her mouth. He released a rough shout of pleasure.

Anna caressed his firm buttocks as she leisurely laved him before she tongued the ultra-sensitive peak. Gavin, doubting his control, lifted her up and against his chest. Panting, he simply held her close.

"If you're trying to drive me out of my mind with pleasure"—his voice was hoarse as he kissed her hungrily—"you succeeded."

"I wanted to give you the same kind of pleasure you've given me," she confessed.

"You did that and more."

"Let me finish what I started."

"I can't . . . I need to be inside you."

They came down on the bed together, she on top of him. His hands moved to the hem of her gown and didn't stop until her body was bare and ready to receive his tongue-stroking kisses. When he left her lips, he journeyed along her neck to linger in the sweet valley between her breasts.

He laved her breasts before he worried her nipples. He didn't stop until they stood up, aching for more. He took a hard peak into the warmth of his mouth to suck. Her moans intensified as he slowly enjoyed her. She wasn't given a chance to collect her scattered wits before he turned to the other ultra-sensitive nipple. He didn't ease the exquisite torment until she begged him to take her.

Gavin rolled with her until she faced away from him. He began covering her entire back with his openmouthed kisses, following the line of her spine to the flare of her buttocks. He used his teeth to tantalize her lush hips, and then shifted until he could lick down the length of her legs from inner thighs to shapely calves, all the way down to the soles of her feet.

"No," she protested when he moved away.

"Give me a moment, baby," he urged as he reached to open the nightstand drawer. He retrieved a foil packet.

"Hurry . . ." she whimpered, but sighed when he settled on his back and lifted her to straddle his hips. He parted her softness, stroking her. The sizzling hot caress had them both releasing impatient groans.

"You're wet . . . ready for me, aren't you, baby?" Gavin teased her with the crest of his sex.

"Oh . . . yes. Gavin, now. I need you."

Slowly, carefully he pushed forward as Anna cried out his name. With his dark eyes closed, Gavin, breathing deeply, struggled to maintain a measure of control. He was so close . . . to losing it.

When she arched her back, he surged forward, unable to deny either one of them. Her breath quickened as she began to move against him. He moaned, wrapping an arm around her waist and bringing her down until her breasts were cushioned against his chest.

"Yes . . . yes," she urged as he began to move beneath her. She tightened her inner muscles around him, causing him to groan harshly.

He cradled her hips, slowing her movements. He insisted huskily, "Slow and easy."

"No . . ." she whispered into his ear. "I want you now . . . now." Her damp sheath caused him to give her more of his steel-hard length.

All too soon it was he insisting through tightly clenched teeth, "Come with me, sweetheart. Now."

He moved to cup her breasts, squeezing them tenderly. He tugged her nipples as he filled her, then pulled back, only to fill her yet again. With her mouth against his throat, she sobbed as she reached a shattering climax. Her release triggered his. He couldn't hold back, not an instant longer, and convulsed as the sheer force of his release overwhelmed him.

Gavin held Anna against his heart, smoothing a hand down her back.

"What did you say?" he asked suddenly.

Her entire body stiffened.

He kissed her cheek. "When you climaxed, sweetheart. Your mouth was pressed against my throat. Tell me again."

She hid her face between the place where his throat and neck joined. "You are an incredible lover. It was good . . . so good."

"Mmm," he sighed. "Yes, it was."

He held on to her even after she fell asleep. For a moment he'd thought she'd said she loved him. Evidently he'd been wrong.

"Is something wrong, Anna?" Janet said quietly.

The two of them were in Anna's kitchen working on a recipe. The smell of hams baking in the oven and chickens turning on rotisseries filled the sunny kitchen while Krista filled pie tins lined up on the counter with apples and Lori prepared the side dishes at the center island.

"No. I just can't get this recipe together. Both you and Krista have gone over it. I can't figure out why it hasn't come together." Anna's eyes suddenly filled. "At the rate I'm going, I'll never get this cookbook even close to being finished. How can I approach a publisher unless I finish it?" She hastily wiped away the tears.

Janet whispered, "This isn't about the cookbook. We've been friends and business partners too long for me not to know something is wrong. Talk to me."

Embarrassed, Anna shook her head. "Neither one of us has time for this. I shouldn't have come. You have meals to get out and I have a dinner to cook for tonight."

"Come on, let's go into the living room." Janet didn't wait for an answer but led the way.

Once they were seated side by side, Janet ordered, "Talk."

Anna quietly revealed, "I'm not sure I can even tell you about it. It hurts too much."

"This has something to do with that gorgeous man of yours, doesn't it?"

Anna threw up her hands helplessly. "All I know is that my life is a mess, and I can't stop crying. A few nights ago Gavin asked if I'd been crying and I lied to him. Janet, I lied. I told him I'd gotten soap in my eyes."

"This sounds serious. It's not like you to even tell a white lie."

"I love him, but I don't want him to know," Anna reluctantly whispered, "Every time we make love I have to practically bite my tongue off to keep from telling him how I feel."

"Maybe it's time you told him. Doesn't he have a right to know?"

"No. Gavin's a very special man. Letting him know how I feel will only make him feel guilty."

"Guilty? But why?"

"He already feels badly because our relationship has caused such a rift in my family. He doesn't need this too."

"Your stubborn menfolks started this mess, not you or Gavin. Whichever way you and Gavin choose to conduct your lives is no one else's concern. I still can't get over that Thanksgiving fiasco."

"Me neither, but that doesn't change how Gavin feels or for that matter how I feel." Anna pressed a hand over her heart. "I can't forget that Gavin lost his best friend because of me."

"Not because of you," Janet insisted. "Gavin lost his friend because Wesley is plain stubborn. How does Kelli feel about all this?"

"About the same as my mother and I do. Oh, Janet. It's such a mess." She jumped to her feet and began restlessly moving around the room. "What am I going to do?"

"Tell Gavin the truth. If you don't tell him, sooner or later he's going to figure out how upset you are by all this."

"Janet, I can't. Things were bad enough that Wes, Ralph, and Devin decided that they didn't want Gavin at our family Christmas dinner." She threw her hands up. "The man has been included in all our family gatherings since I was a teenager."

"That's not right."

"Absolutely not. I was so upset that I decided if Gavin isn't welcome, then neither am I."

"Oh, I bet your parents didn't appreciate that."

"You got that right. As far as I'm concerned, it can't be helped." Anna paused, then said, "Mama isn't having it. She told my dad to fix it. So he came by to talk to me and Gavin. Daddy told Gavin that he was welcome. My parents want us all to be together on Christmas."

"I always liked your dad." Janet smiled.

"He's a good man. If only it had stopped there." Anna covered her face. "I have never been more embarrassed. Daddy didn't bite his tongue. He came right out with it. He doesn't like our living arrangement and believes that if Gavin wants me he should marry me."

"Honey, your dad is an old-fashioned kind of guy. Accept it."

"Daddy practically came out and insisted that Gavin marry me or leave me alone."

Janet shook her head. "You've had a tough week."

"You don't know the half of it. Out of the blue Gavin's father showed up. Poor Kyle is scared that he's going to take him with him when he leaves."

"You've got to be kidding."

"I wish I was. Gavin has enough to deal with without me adding more problems by telling him that I'm in love with him. Believe me, this isn't the right time for a confession."

"Anna, how long do you honestly think you're going to be able to keep it from him?"

"I don't know." She sighed. "Gavin cares for me. It's enough. I don't want him to ask me to marry him because he feels guilty."

Janet wondered aloud, "Do you think he would?"

"No, but that doesn't change the fact that my father has been more of an influence on him than George Reynolds has. Or that he believes marriage is not for him. I have no choice but to accept that. He has been honest with me from the first. The problem is mine, not his."

Janet didn't look convinced but she reassured, "Gavin cares for you. And for now I think you should concentrate on nothing more than being happy. I say forget your family and his father. Just enjoy being together."

Anna gave her a hug. "Thank you. I feel so much better. Maybe all I needed was to talk about it, get it out."

"You're welcome. This will be your first Christmas as a couple. Romantic dinner, late at night. Sounds good to me."

"Sounds ideal. Even though my mother will be very upset if I don't show my face on Christmas, she will be even more upset if my brothers and cousin get into another fight with Gavin."

"I don't envy you having to tell your mother."

"I know. We're going Christmas shopping on Friday. I'll tell her then."

George came in with a heavy scowl on his face later that evening. Kyle was cleaning the kitchen, while Gavin and Anna were still at the table enjoying a cup of coffee.

"Would you care for some dinner?" Anna asked.

"Hell no. What I need is a damn drink."

Anna and Gavin exchanged a look.

"I don't know what's wrong but I know you have no right to swear at Anna," Gavin snapped.

George sent Anna an impatient look, yet offered a hasty apology and headed down the hall.

"What's with him?" Kyle went back to filling the dishwasher.

"I don't have a clue. But I suppose I'd better go find out."

Kyle caught his brother's arm. "You don't think he's changed his mind about signing, do you?"

"No, bro. My guess is he's lost at the casino." Gavin said to Anna, "Great dinner, sweetheart," before he left and, disappeared down the central hallway.

He found George in the living room, helping himself to Gavin's stock of Scotch. "What set you off?" Gavin leaned a shoulder against the door jam.

After swearing long and hard, George drained his glass. "Nothing to talk about. It's all gone."

"What's all gone?"

"Twenty-five grand, that's what."

"You lost it all?" Gavin said incredulously. "How? What, you didn't have sense enough to stop when you saw your luck was changing?"

"It's gone," was all George said as he refilled his glass.

Gavin straightened, swallowing down the "I told you so" retort rising in his throat. "Drinking yourself into a stupor isn't going to change anything."

"It's easy for you to say. Look at all this. Everywhere I look shouts money with capital letters."

"You think someone handed it to me? Is that what you think?" Gavin shook his head in disbelief. "You feel so sorry for yourself that you forgot were I came from." His laughter held not even a sliver of humor. "You were there, man, when it all began for me. I am not the issue here. You are. What are you going to do?"

"How in the hell should I know?" George yelled, flinging the costly crystal glass into the fireplace. "I don't even have enough money to buy the kid a stinking Christmas gift. If there hadn't been gas in the car, I wouldn't have made it back here."

"If you want someone to feel sorry for you, keep looking. You have no one to blame but yourself."

"You think I don't know that?" George filled a new glass before he sat down on the sectional sofa. "Join me, I hate to drink alone."

Gavin snapped. "You toss another glass into that fireplace and I promise you, you're going next."

"What do you want from me?"

"One thing. I want you to sign over your parental rights to Kyle over to me. I don't want Kyle to go through what I went through. I want him to grow up knowing that if his father doesn't care about him, it's okay, because his older brother does."

George slowly put his glass down on the coffee table. He was smiling when he said, "Okay, but it will cost you."

Gavin glared at the man who fathered him for a long, tension-packed moment. "Cost me? What are you resurrecting? Slavery?"

"Very funny." George leaned back, stretching his legs out in front of him. "You have something you want signed and you have something I definitely need. How about a trade?"

"You're not getting another quarter out of me. I made that decision in September when you walked out on Kyle. So, Reynolds, if you need money I strongly suggest you look elsewhere."

"No problem." George quickly rose to his feet. "The boy's going with me. I don't want to ruin the kid's holiday, so we'll leave the day after Christmas."

"Not likely. I'm the one with temporary custody, remember? Or have you forgotten that I had to go to court to get it? Did you even stop to wonder how in the hell I was going to enroll him in school or have him treated if there was a medical emergency?"

Gavin's mouth tightened even more when he went on to say, "You walked out and didn't look back until you were in need of a place to stay. That's the only reason you came back. If you refuse to sign over full custody, make no mistake, you will be seeing me in court. Kyle's future is worth fighting for."

"You can't mean that."

"I'm dead serious. Kyle deserves to be happy, to grow up in a home with a brother who loves him."

"You don't know what you're getting into." George snickered.

"Like you know more than I do? Where were you when I was growing up? You weren't around when I started school. You weren't around to attend any of my elementary school assemblies or teacher conferences. My mother attended those alone."

Gavin hadn't expected to tell his father any of these things, but suddenly he couldn't keep the old hurts inside any longer. "You weren't there to see any of my junior high or high school games or track meets. Yeah, that's right, I ran track back then. You sure as hell weren't at my high school or college graduations.

"You think I want that for Kyle? No way. You sorry bastard, you didn't attend my mother's funeral. And she loved you to her dying day."

Gavin struggled for a calm he didn't feel. He was fighting the urge to go after his father with his fists. He prided himself on being a better man. He had to prove that to himself by hanging on to his temper.

Eventually he said, "My brother deserves better than I had it. And I plan to see that he gets it."

"I never knew those things bothered you."

"You never bothered to ask. Eloise Mathis was both mother and father to me. And she did a damn good job of it." He admitted, "When I was little, I used to ask her why. Why didn't my daddy love me?"

He swallowed the hurt that had never gone away. "She tried to assure me that you did love me, but I stopped believing. I finally realized she was protecting me from the truth."

Gavin moved to stand in front of his father. "I remember asking you once why you were never around. I was about seven. Do you remember your answer?"

George cleared his throat. "How am I supposed to remember what happened when you were a kid? That was over twenty years ago. I don't remember what I did last week." He couldn't meet his son's unwavering gaze.

"Twenty-four years ago. I remember your exact words. 'I don't have time. Now you run along. I got business to keep track of.'" Determined to get his emotions under control, Gavin paused before he went on to say, "The business you were talking about was playing the ponies. It was always something to do with gambling. That was more important than me or my mother."

"Look, I made a few mistakes—"

"A few? Try more than I can even count. The only time you bothered to show up for my sake was when I was drafted into the pros. You were there the day they cut the check, looking for your share. And because my mother loved you, I've always given you what you asked for.

"No more. Understand this, you lost your cash cow when you brought Kyle here and left him. Any money I would have given you will go to Kyle. I've set up a trust fund for him. His college is paid for. Whatever he needs to start his career will be there. And you can't touch it. I've made sure of that."

"What kind of man do you think I am?"

Gavin said candidly, "That's the problem. I don't know you at all. What's worse, Kyle doesn't know you either."

He watched anger and resentment move across his father's features, but he didn't see regret or shame. If he had seen either one, he might have backed down.

"Yeah, I will admit I didn't do all the things I should have for you. But with Kyle, you aren't taking into consideration that it was his mother who turned his care over to her elderly aunt while he was still in elementary school. Then she got herself hooked on drugs and overdosed. When the aunt died earlier this year, I took him."

"Because there was no one else but you," Gavin said dryly.

"I took him in."

"What does that change? Nothing." Gavin went on to reveal, "If it weren't for my high school coach and later Anna's father, I wouldn't know what it means to be a man. They showed me by example. A man takes care of his own. Always. Lester Prescott has always been available to his kids no matter what." Gavin snapped, "Regardless of what Kyle's mother did or didn't do, still you are his father."

"I took care of him."

"Did you? It doesn't look that way from where I'm standing."

Both men were so focused on each other that neither noticed the boy standing in the doorway.

"For all I know, his drug addict bitch of a mother was—"

"Shut up! You shut the hell up!" Kyle hurled himself at his father with his fists clenched.

Gavin managed to catch him before he could let a fist fly. He whispered to his brother, "It's going to be okay."

"You heard what he said." Kyle was shaking as tears flowed down his cheeks and he fought to free himself. "Let me go."

"Not until you calm down." Gavin ran a soothing hand over his brother's slim shoulders. "It doesn't matter what he thinks."

"But he said . . ." Kyle wiped his face on a sleeve.

"I didn't mean for you—"

Gavin cut in, "You've said enough."

Whatever the older man was about to say, he stopped. He busied himself by draining his glass.

"Don't you think you owe him an apology?" Gavin asked their father, his jaw so tight he could hardly speak to the man. Kyle wasn't the only one furious.

"I'm sorry, son. I didn't mean for you to hear that."

"What's going on?" Anna asked. The tension in the room was so thick it was palpable.

"Nothing worth repeating. Come on, bro. We both need some fresh air."

Kyle nodded, turning to leave. He didn't spare his father a backward glance as he headed toward the staircase.

"You don't need to go up with me. I'm okay now."

"Good. I'd hate to have to break his jaw."

Kyle laughed. "I'd like to see that."

Gavin put a hand on his brother's arm, halting his progress. "He had no right to call your mother names. He's angry because he lost at the casino and was taking it out on anyone willing to listen. I'm very sorry you heard it."

Kyle nodded. "At least when you say you're sorry, I know you mean it." He took a deep breath before he said, "Gavin, he's going to try to take me back. I know he will."

"You're right. He might try, but he won't win. He has nowhere to take you. He no longer has that apartment in Dayton. I promise you, I'm going to do everything within my power to keep that from happening."

26

When Gavin returned to the living room, he was relieved to see it empty. He was so angry that he didn't trust himself not to go after his father. Scowling, he walked into his office and called his attorney.

Afterward, he found Anna working on her laptop at the desk in the kitchen. He didn't even ask if she knew where his father had gone. He walked over and pulled her out of her chair and into his arms, taking comfort from her woman's scent. He began telling her what had been said, all of it, including his own hurt and resentment.

"Oh, honey. I'm so sorry." She kissed his throat.

He nodded. Rather than being embarrassed by the lingering hurt, he was relieved to get it out in the open. There was no question that he trusted her completely.

"What are you going to do?"

"Whatever I have to do to get his signature on that paper. If that means money, then I have to do it, although it will be very hard to swallow. How can I put Kyle through a custody trial?" Gavin sighed heavily. "He's not strong enough emotionally to deal with all the garbage that is bound to come out during a trial. What if he had to testify against our father? I won't put that kind of pressure on him, not unless there is no other way. You saw what happened when Reynolds let loose on Kyle's mother."

"I don't blame Kyle for being upset. For what it's worth, I agree with you. You have to protect your brother."

"Thanks, sweetheart." He kissed her tenderly. "It helps knowing I have your support. Did you know that fool lost the entire twenty-five grand? I doubt he has enough left to play the nickel slots. Writing him a check will be like throwing good money after bad."

"Gavin, if you do that, you know he will only come back for more a few months down the road."

"There won't be a next time. After he relinquishes his parental rights he will have nothing I want." He brushed her lips with his kiss. "I'm sorry, but I can't get away tonight. I have—"

"Shush, I know. Kyle needs you."

"You're not angry?"

"Of course not." She slid her arms around his waist and gave him a squeeze. "But I should be going."

"Let me get our coats. I'll walk you to the cottage."

"You don't have to do that."

"Yes, I do. I need a few of your good-night kisses. It's the only way I'll get any sleep tonight."

"Look, man, I don't know what's going on between you and Prescott. Hell, I don't want to know."

"Then why bring it up?" Gavin frowned at Everett Long, the Lions' offensive coordinator.

"You guys have been tight for too many years to let anything come between you, especially a woman, even if she is family."

"You're right, Long. It isn't your problem." A muscle jumped in Gavin's jaw.

"It'll be everyone's business if you two don't get it straightened out by game time. Nothing and I mean nothing is going to keep us from winning this one, and that includes you and Prescott."

Suddenly a well-dressed man walked up to them. "You Mathis?"

Gavin paused barely a hundred yards from his van. "Yes?"

"I'm an associate of your old man's," the man said, glancing nervously over his shoulder.

Gavin turned to Everett, "Excuse me. I'll see you tomorrow at the game."

"Right," the other man said, before continuing on to where his own truck was parked.

Gavin said, "Whatever kind of business you have with George Reynolds is between the two of you."

The other man managed to step in front of Gavin, blocking his path. "I'm sure you don't want Reynolds's gambling debts to be made public. He came to me for a loan. I gave him five grand, which he understood came with restrictions. He now owes me fifteen thousand. I want my money."

"And how does this concern me?"

"That huge contract you signed last year was in all the newspapers. I'm sure you don't want one of the tabloids to get a hint of this story."

Gavin's eyes narrowed as he studied the other man. "Are you threatening me?"

"Not at all. But make no mistake, I'm a businessman. I don't believe in throwing my money away."

"Ah, Mr. . . ."

"Matthew," he supplied.

Gavin nodded. "Mr. Matthew, I don't believe in throwing money away either, but that's what you did when you tossed Reynolds five grand. I'm not about to give you a penny. As far as calling the tabloids . . ." Gavin reached into his jacket and retrieved his cell phone. "Knock yourself out," he said as he tossed the other man the phone before he walked away.

As Anna and Kyle drove toward the new football stadium on Brush Avenue, she described how spectacular downtown Detroit had once been, all lit up during the Christmas season, while she was growing up in the city. When she and her brothers were kids, they couldn't wait to see Hudson's Department Store's display windows, not to mention the Thanksgiving Day parade.

The Lions' new stadium was across from Comerica Park, where the Detroit Tigers held their baseball games. Ford Field had been open only since the beginning of the season. Judging by the enthusiasm of the crowd it was an undeniable success. Despite the weatherman's forecast of an additional two inches of snow to go along with the four inches already on the ground, the stadium was packed.

Anna knew nothing could dampen the crowd's excitement, because the Lions were having a record season, and there was a great deal of talk about the upcoming Super Bowl. Many Detroiters viewed the new stadium as a good luck charm since the Lions were finally back home in Detroit.

Nearly every seat was taken, including the team's family section of the stadium. Anna and Kyle waved to her family when they came in. Anna and Kyle's seats were a couple of rows behind the Prescott family's. Everyone was there except Devin and baby Kaleea. Anna's cousin Ralph, as usual, was with a new lady. Kelli switched seats with Kyle so that he and Wayne could sit together.

Anna had been relieved when Gavin's father had gone to the GreekTown Casino rather than the football game. There had been a steady increase in tension around the house since the day of George Reynolds's arrival.

Everyone rose to his feet when the home team ran out onto the field. Detroit, unlike many professional football teams, didn't have cheerleaders, but their mascot, Roary the Lion, was there to rev up the crowd. By half-time, the Lions were trailing the Chicago Bears seven to thirteen. The second quarter was barely under way when Kelli sent Anna a questioning look.

"You have barely said two words to the family. Is something wrong?"

Careful not to be overheard, Anna said, "It has been a stressful week. I'm just glad to see Kyle relaxed and happy for a change."

"What happened?"

"Gavin and Kyle's father has come for the holidays. I'm surprised Mama didn't mention it to you."

"From what Wes has told me about the man, he isn't much of a prize. The man walked out on his fourteen-year-old son without a word to anyone."

"You can't imagine how stressful it has been with him in the house," Anna confessed. "You would think he would be proud of Gavin and want to see one of his games while he's in town."

"Where is he?"

"GreekTown Casino." Anna jumped to her feet along with the crowd when Detroit recovered the ball. When they were seated again, she told Kelli about the custody papers. Careful to keep her voice down, she said, "I don't know what's going to happen if Gavin can't get him to sign those papers. Kyle deserves better than what George Reynolds has to offer."

Kelli whispered back, "You really sound scared. Surely

the court won't take him away from Gavin? Reynolds deserted him."

"I hope not. Gavin doesn't want Kyle to testify against his father. And I agree with him. Kyle would be devastated."

The two women exchanged a troubled look.

"Maybe it won't come to that," Kelli tried to reassure Anna.

"I hope not. Gavin has been so worried. He can hardly concentrate on anything else." Anna watched as Gavin fumbled the football. "He's not playing anywhere near as well as he should. Those kinds of mistakes can get him hurt."

"Don't I know it. Wesley's game is off too. Do you think it was the fight they had?" Kelli asked with a frown.

"I don't know, but the team cannot afford having its two best players make stupid mistakes." Anna frowned.

"Are you and Gavin going to the party at Stanley's house tonight after the game?"

Both women were suddenly on their feet, shouting when Detroit made a first and ten.

"Aw right now. Kelli, tell your man to get that arm working." Shirley Jackson, wife of one of the offensive guards, Cal Jackson, shouted from where she was seated two rows back.

"You tell Cal to hold that line," Kelli shouted back with a wave.

"You got it."

Everyone laughed. The third quarter provided Detroit with a field goal opportunity that they missed.

"It doesn't look good," Kelli said anxiously, and then shouted, "Gavin, get your feet moving."

Anna whispered, "If those two knuckleheads would work together we could win this one. This feuding is certainly not doing either one of them any good. Gavin hasn't said anything, but I know he misses Wesley. I love them both and I hate feeling as if I am in the middle."

"It has been especially hard on you. Wes is pretending it

doesn't affect him, but I know better. Gavin is coming to Christmas dinner, isn't he? Your mom told me that your dad invited him."

"I don't know. He believes if he comes he will spoil my mother's holiday. There is bound to be an argument. And I haven't changed my mind. If he doesn't come, then neither do I."

"Anna, that will spoil everyone's holiday."

"It can't be helped. Kelli, I didn't start this, but I won't leave Gavin at home alone either."

"This is so hard on you."

"Whatever I do, someone will be hurt."

"Look!" Kelli jumped up.

It was in the fourth quarter with less than five minutes on the clock. Detroit's offensive line managed to hold Chicago's defense long enough for Wesley to get into the pocket. He spotted Gavin in full motion as his long legs ate up the Field-Turf the team was so fond of.

Gavin dodged yet another defensive back by turning his body and stretching his legs even more as he flew past the fifteen-yard line while reaching over his left shoulder for the football. The crowd went wild as he caught the ball and tucked it into his side. With an explosive burst of speed he moved toward Detroit's end zone. Gavin was close to the line when Brad Coleman, the Chicago Bears outside defensive linebacker, charged into him from his right side while Jack Howard, the cornerback, hit him from the opposite side. The jarring force sent him forward and down as two other men piled on top of him. All together over a thousand pounds of sheer force pinned him in place.

It appeared that Detroit had made the touchdown. From what could be seen of his upper body, he appeared to be in the end zone. The hometown crowd was in an uproar. Yet when the last man rose, Gavin didn't move. Even though he was surrounded, Anna could see that he wasn't moving. A hush fell over the stadium as they waited to find out how badly he was hurt.

Anna, like everyone else, was on her feet, hands covering her screams as she waited to see if Gavin was all right. Kelli held on to her as they watched Wesley take off down the field. Somehow her brother reached Gavin before the team doctors or the Lions' staff and was down on his knees removing Gavin's helmet, talking to him.

Anna had no idea that she was screaming his name until Kyle grabbed her and buried his wet face against her shoulder. She was too busy praying to offer the boy more than a word of reassurance. Suddenly, she was surrounded by her family, and their unwavering support as they all waited an eternity for word.

Everyone in the stadium knew that while football was a game that could bring tremendous joy, it could also bring horrendous physical risks to its players. There was always the possibility of severe injury, head trauma, paralysis, or the very real threat of death.

"He's going to be all right, baby girl," her father insisted.

Ralph said nothing, but Anna felt the steadfast comfort of his hand on her back.

"Please God," Anna prayed.

"Look," Donna shouted.

"He moved! I saw him move!" Kyle whooped.

Anna and Kyle hung on to each other as they watched Gavin sit up on his own. He was being helped to his feet. And then he was able to walk off the field on his own. Evidently the wind had been knocked out of him. The crowd roared. Not only was Gavin all right, Detroit had made the touchdown. The score was tied.

As the team moved into place to try for the extra point, Anna's family went back to their seats. Everyone settled down to watch the remaining minutes on the clock being played out.

Kyle whispered in Anna's ear, "You don't think Wayne saw?" He referred to his tears.

Hiding a smile, she shook her head. "He was too busy watching the field." She smoothed a hand against his cheek. "You okay?"

"Yeah. You?"

"I need to sit down." Anna's legs were trembling so badly she had no choice. Kyle helped her into her chair.

"You okay?" Kelli asked.

"I will be once I know he's okay. Can you see what's happening? Is he still on the sideline?"

Kyle said, "He's sitting on the bench. The team doctor is checking him out."

Kelli patted Anna's hand, "If it was serious they'd have taken him to the hospital. They don't play around."

Anna nodded, trying to collect her scattered wits. She glanced at Kyle who didn't look much better than she felt. "Want to sit here with us?"

He nodded, taking the empty seat on the other side of Anna. He said, "I never thought much about him getting hurt."

"It's a rough game, but he's going to be fine," Kelli volunteered, and then whispered to Anna, "There was some good that came out of this. Wesley was right there beside him."

"You're right." Anna smiled. After Kyle and Wayne went off to get ice cream, she swallowed before she told her sister-in-law, "I was so scared. I thought I'd lost him."

Kelli squeezed her hand. "But you didn't. He's going to be fine."

Ann nodded. Kelli knew only too well what every woman who loved a football player knew. His life could end out there on that field he loved so much. Kelli also prayed that when her husband went out on the field, he would return to her alive and whole.

"I need to see him, look into his eyes to know he's all right." Anna confessed. "I love him, Kelli. I didn't plan to but I can't help it."

Her sister-in-law surprised her when she said, "I know. Why else would you ignore your family's disapproval to be with him? Does he know how you feel?"

Just then the crowd went wild as the Lions made the extra point with less than two minutes on the clock.

"No. I can't tell him."

"You don't believe he returns your love, do you?" Kelli said, close to her ear.

"I know he doesn't. We want different things from life. For now, just being together has to be enough." Anna said no more. There was nothing more to be said. She'd like nothing better than a good cry, but knew it was pointless. It would solve nothing and leave her with swollen lids and a headache.

Although Gavin had called while they were on the way home from the game to let them know he was fine, Anna still felt unsettled. She moved restlessly around the kitchen, waiting for him to come home, while Kyle enjoyed a snack, though Anna had no idea how he had room for it. He looked calm, his gaze on the small television set on the counter.

Anna soothed her nerves by making one of the hero sandwiches that Gavin enjoyed after a game. She was wrapping the huge sandwich in plastic wrap when they heard a key in the lock.

Anna laughed when she saw Kyle grab his brother and give him a hug before he was barely in the door.

"I'm okay, bro," Gavin said, returning the hug.

"Good. Don't scare us like that again," he ordered.

Gavin chuckled. His eyes locked with Anna's over the boy's head for a long moment before Kyle let his brother go.

"Yeah," she said, going over and encircling his waist. She buried her face against his chest as she blinked back tears.

"Sweetheart, I'm fine . . . honest. Just got the wind knocked out of me." He gave her a gentle squeeze, kissing her temple.

Eventually she had collected herself enough to ask, "Hungry? I just finished your sandwich."

"Sounds good."

Kyle was clearly enjoying his Christmas vacation from school. He grabbed a half-eaten bag of chips. "I'm going up to my room. I have a phone call to return."

Gavin lifted a brow. "Oh?"

"Her name is Anita," Anna teased.

"Really. How old is she?" Gavin wanted to know.

"Fourteen. She's in my homeroom," Kyle volunteered around a grin as he dashed out of the room.

"Maybe I should have that talk with him?"

"I thought you two already had that talk," she said as she retrieved a carton of milk from the refrigerator.

"Never hurts to repeat it." He came up behind her, pressing a kiss to the side of her neck.

She turned to face him. "Kyle is right. You really scared us." She moved a caressing hand over his unshaven cheek.

"I'm sorry, Anna." He held her close. "These kinds of things happen. It's part of the game."

"Coming from a football family you know I understand, but that doesn't mean I have to like it."

When she would have backed away, he tightened his hold. "Come back here. Let me hold you a little longer." He urged her closer until her breasts were cushioned on his chest, her legs tucked between his.

Anna released a deep breath as her arms moved up to encircle his neck. "I couldn't stand it if you'd gotten hurt."

He ran a soothing hand down her spine. "It's over. And I'm only a little sore, that's all."

"I'm fine, now that you're here. I didn't expect to see Wesley going to help you."

"You aren't the only one surprised." He swallowed hard. "It hurts knowing that Wesley no longer had my back. It's been like losing a member of my own family." He pressed a kiss against her lips. "Do you still want me? As much as I want you?"

Anna shivered but would not let him change the subject. "Did the two of you have a chance to talk?"

"Not really." He took yet another kiss. "Wes knows that I'm not about to give you up."

"Well, well." George laughed as he entered the kitchen. "Should I come back later?"

"Of course not." Anna put some distance between them. "Would you like a hero sandwich?"

"Yeah." He grinned, eyeing Gavin wearily.

"Take mine. I'm not that hungry," Gavin offered, and then added, "When you're finished, you'll find me in my office. We have a few things to settle." Before his father could respond, he walked out of the room.

Gavin was seated on the edge of his desk, rereading the contract his lawyer had sent over. He had to convince their father to sign. Kyle's future was at stake.

"What's up?" George asked as he walked through the open doorway.

The walls were paneled with rich cherry wood, and Gavin's football and track trophies were displayed in floor-to-ceiling cases behind his desk. Framed photographs of Gavin on the field were mounted on the wall in front of the desk.

"Please close the door and have a seat." Gavin motioned to one of the leather chairs in front of the desk.

"What's this about?" George looked uncomfortable. "If this is another go at how I failed both you and Kyle, I'm not interested."

"This is about Kyle making his home here with me. As you know, I've been granted temporary custody. Both Kyle and I would like me to permanently take over his guardianship." Gavin handed over the papers. "My lawyer has drawn up the necessary papers. All it takes is your signature."

George didn't bother to read the papers. "You know what I want. Get your checkbook out, then we'll have something to discuss."

Gavin reached into the desk and took out his checkbook, and quickly wrote out a check and passed it to his father.

"A thousand dollars. Are you nuts?"

"That's should get you an airline ticket and somewhere to stay for a few days."

When George moved to tear it up, Gavin warned, "I wouldn't, if I were you. That's all you're getting." Before his father could respond, he said, "I met your business associate. He stopped me outside the team's headquarters."

"What?"

"Mr. Matthew, I believe he said his name was. You owe him money and he didn't see any reason why I shouldn't pay your bills."

George straightened in his chair, the check in his pocket. "Look, I had nothing to do with that."

"He threatened to take your gambling problem to the tabloids," Gavin explained.

"What did you do?"

"I gave him the use of my cell phone. I don't like threats." Gavin's voice was hard with anger. "I suggest you take care of it and quickly."

"I don't have that kind of money." George ran a hand anxiously over his hair. "Not unless you—"

"Forget it. I had nothing to do with getting you into debt. Nor will I have anything to do with getting you out of it. You lied to me. You said you'd handle it. What if this Matthew character had approached Kyle and not me? Where is your head? Only a fool would play around with these people, especially if he valued his body parts."

George swore. "I told you I'd take care of it."

"Your gambling problem caused this. You could get help. There are organizations willing to help."

"Gamblers Anonymous? Hell no."

Gavin shrugged before he picked up a heavy folder from the desk. "Everything I need to prove what kind of man you are is in here." He tossed the folder over to his father. "A detailed accounting of where you've been and how much money you've lost during the time Kyle has been here with me. There is more of that, and it goes back years."

George flipped through the report. "You've had me followed."

"I had you investigated by one of the best firms in the country. As you can see, nothing has been overlooked."

"But why?" George looked genuinely hurt.

"I can't believe you're asking me that." Contemplatively, Gavin's long fingertips touched. "Surely you are not that dense? I don't want to make that file public by taking you to court for custody of Kyle, but I will."

"You didn't have to go to so much trouble. I told you I'd sign for a price."

"No. I've given you all I plan to give. So if that's what's holding you here, you can leave tonight, but without Kyle."

"Kyle is mine."

"No, he isn't. He may only be fifteen, but he knows who he wants to live with. If you would like, I'll invite him in. I'll let him tell you what he thinks of your parenting skills." Gavin reached for the telephone with the in-house line.

"Don't bother." George shifted in his chair. Spotting the crystal glasses and decanter on a shelf in the built-in bookcase adjacent to the desk, he rose and crossed to it. He didn't ask but poured himself a drink.

Gavin said nothing as he waited.

"I am not going to let you do this. I'm taking Kyle with me." George headed to the door.

"The hell you are." Gavin reached the door ahead of him, blocking it. "Haven't you done enough? Why are you so determined to force my hand? You can't win. I'll have you locked up in court for years to come."

"You have all these big-shot lawyers and financial advisers at your disposal," George raged. "You think that all you have to do is snap your fingers, and you can have anything you damn well please."

"What I know is that you're a lousy father. What's more, I can prove it."

George tossed back the contents of his glass. He snapped, "Damn it. I'll sign, but I want the right to see Kyle."

"Agreed."

George went back to the desk and quickly signed the papers without reading them. When he finished, he said, "Call me a cab. I'm leaving tonight."

Gavin said nothing as he watched the man who had fathered him and his brother toss Gavin's car keys and then walk out. He couldn't stop wondering why he felt nothing but sadness. After calling the cab, he rose and started toward Kyle's room.

Later that night as Gavin lay with Anna asleep in his arms, he recognized that he had his mother to thank that he wasn't like George Reynolds. Gavin could never turn his back on the people who mattered most to him. For some time he'd suspected that he hadn't let himself get serious about a woman for two reasons. He not only doubted his ability to commit, but he also longed to be valued for himself, not his income. Those concerns had disappeared, thanks to Anna. No woman deserved to be treated the way George had treated his mother.

Over the past few weeks, he'd gradually faced a few hard facts. He wanted all the things his father had dismissed as unimportant. Gavin longed for a family and a home brimming with love. He yearned to be the father his own father had never been interested in becoming. And he wanted these things with the special woman in his arms. Anna was beautiful in ways that went far beyond her physical attributes. It had to do with the beauty deep inside her.

27

Holiday preparations were complete. Anna had done her Christmas baking with the realization that she would be spending the day with Gavin and Kyle, not at her parents' home with her family. Even though it made her sad, she had given up trying to persuade Gavin to join them.

On Christmas Eve, the house was filled with Gavin's employees and their families. He threw the party every year. There were gifts and bonuses for everyone attending, courtesy of Gavin.

The major difference this year was that Wesley and Kelli had sent their regrets, as had Anna's parents, brothers, and cousin. It was the third year that Prescott and Raye Catering Company was handling the food preparation and clean-up. It was always an important job for them, but this year Anna wouldn't be helping. She was acting as Gavin's hostess. The party was in full swing when Anna went into the kitchen.

"What are you doing in here again?" Janet scolded.

She was handing over yet another tray of hors d'oeuvres, this one filled with hazelnut and shrimp wrapped in endive leaves, to a formally dressed waiter. He was one of the five who had been hired to serve tonight. The bar had been set up in the dining room, where the bartender was mixing up blackberry champagne cocktails, rosemary gin fizz, and spiced red wine punch. Krista was busy filling a tray of Alsatian potato and bacon tarts, while Lori was taking a pan of meatballs out of the oven that would be served in a mint sauce. There were also crab cakes, spicy chicken wings, and a variety of cheeses to round out the menu.

Anna put her hands on her hips in exasperation, drawing attention to the lovely hunter green velvet slacks that she had teamed with a pale green vee-neck cashmere sweater trimmed in sequins at the neck and hem. Her long hair had been pinned up into a simple chignon and diamonds sparkled in her ears.

Anna reminded her, "I do own half of this business, or have you forgotten, partner?"

Janet shook her finger at Anna. "You're a hostess tonight, or have you forgotten? So get your butt out there, before Gavin catches you trying to fix something. You know what he said."

Anna whispered, "I'm not used to this. How long does he expect me to do nothing but smile and chat?"

"Get on out there, girl, and at least look like you're having a good time."

Anna spoke so quietly that Janet had to lean forward to hear over the activity in the kitchen. "He keeps introducing me to people as if we were an old married couple. It's driving me crazy. I need to keep my feet flat on the floor and not off in some cloud. I don't need to be wishing for something I can't have."

Janet took her aside, down the short hallway between the guest restroom and the laundry room. "What's wrong with that? You are a couple."

Fighting back tears, Anna admitted, "Janet, I don't know what's wrong with me. Lately I'm not sure of anything. All I know is that Gavin doesn't feel the way I do, and sooner or later, it's going to matter."

"Anna . . ."

"There is nothing you or anyone can say to make him love me."

"Honey, I thought you were happy with the way things were between you two."

"I was happy. Now I'm just plain scared and getting more so every day."

"Scared of what? What brought all this on?"

"Something is bothering Gavin, and he won't talk to me about it. Maybe he's regretting what our relationship has cost him. He lost the friendship that he values. And I keep remembering what Daddy said. He didn't ask me how I felt about Gavin, because he already knew. And he's right. Gavin and I want two different things in life. And I don't know how long I can go on pretending otherwise."

"This is your life and you're letting your fears get the best of you. I'm sure he will share what's bothering him, when he's ready. Be patient."

"That's easy for—" Anna said, then stopped abruptly as she noticed Gavin approaching.

"There you are." Gavin walked up and placed an arm around her waist. "She's not working, is she, Janet?"

Janet laughed. "I won't let her."

"Good." He smiled down at Anna. "I've been looking all over for you. There are some people I want you to meet."

"Excuse us." Anna forced a smile as he took her away. "Who?" she asked when they reached the central hallway.

"Dan Winters is here with his wife. He oversees the foundation's scholarship program." He paused to study her face. "Is something bothering you, sweetheart?"

Anna reached up to smooth his mustache. He was devastatingly handsome in his black custom-made tuxedo. "I'm fine. Now let's go meet the Winterses."

Romantic music flowed from the speakers and couples began dancing in the large, marble foyer. Anna had had only one dance with Gavin. The party was still going strong. No one seemed inclined to leave. Around ten-thirty, Kyle came up to her and whispered, "Are these people ever going home?"

Anna laughed. "Doesn't look like it. You don't have to stay. If you'd rather duck out, go ahead. I'll cover for you."

He gave her a quick hug. "I owe you. Night."

"Good night."

Kyle was a different boy since his father had signed over his parental rights to Gavin and left town. Just knowing that he was where he was loved and wanted meant the world to him. He was a carefree teenager. The resentment and anger were gone.

Anna stopped to talk with Mrs. Tillman and her gentleman friend. Both were widowed. She smiled at the man and pretended she hadn't heard everything there was to know about "dear Mr. Murdock" from Mrs. Tillman the past few months they'd been keeping company.

Vanessa was there with her teenaged sister. Vanessa was so shy that she didn't even smile at a few of Gavin's teammates who dropped by.

Anna had turned toward the kitchen when Gretchen slipped her arm through Anna's. "The house has never looked better. The food is fabulous. I'm having a wonderful time. How about you?"

"Oh yes." Anna had to raise her voice to be heard over the music. The dancing was in full swing.

"How did Gavin manage to keep you out of the kitchen?" Gretchen teased.

Anna laughed. "Every time I head that way, he comes after me. He must have spies watching me."

"Gavin is right. You look great tonight." Gretchen asked, "Is that new?"

"Yes, and thank you. You're looking awfully good yourself. Uh-oh, let's go talk to that gorgeous husband of yours. He looks like he needs rescuing." Anna nodded toward the good-looking redhead who was grinning up at him as if he was the answer to all her prayers.

It was nearly two by the time the guests finally began saying their good nights. Janet and her staff packed away the leftover food and cleaned the kitchen. Anna was exhausted by the time they called good night.

"Where is Kyle?" Gavin asked, closing the door behind the very last of his guests.

"He asked to be excused over an hour ago. He's probably asleep by now."

Looking around, he noted that everything seemed to be put back where it belonged. Smiling, he said, "It's good to have the house to ourselves again. Did you enjoy yourself, sweetheart?"

"It went well. Janet and the ladies outdid themselves. Everyone seemed to enjoy themselves."

"That doesn't answer my question. Did you enjoy yourself?"

She laughed, slipping her arm through his. "Yes and no. I'm not used to circulating at parties. I'm used to taking care of the food."

"Why, Anna?" He paused outside the entrance to the living room where a fire still glowed in the fireplace. "You knew just about everyone here."

She confessed, "I was a tiny bit uncomfortable. Everyone was watching me, speculating on our relationship."

"Sweetheart, it's only natural for them to be curious. A lot has changed around here in the last few months." He caressed her nape. "You were the most beautiful woman here. Why wouldn't I want you on my arm?" He teased, "They should be asking, What does an intellectual like you see in a dumb jock like me."

"That isn't funny." She tried to look really furious but couldn't help responding to the laughter in his brown eyes. "Stop it. Stop looking at me that way."

"I'm glad to finally have you to myself. Wait right here." Gavin went into the living room. He looked through the stack of CDs until he found the one he wanted—"Unforgettable."

"Dance with me." He didn't wait for an answer but pulled her into his arms. He said in a seductive whisper close to her ear, "Our favorite."

They swayed in time to the music as she followed his lead. She said softly, "I love that song."

"I know." He sighed, "I've wanted to do this all evening."

Surprised, she reminded him, "We danced earlier."

"It's not the same when there is only the two of us."

He shifted her along his long length. She shivered in response to his masculine appeal, melded her body to his. When the song was over, he tucked her hand over his arm and led the way into the living room.

They sat down on the loveseat, kicking their shoes off and putting their feet up on the wide ottoman. They relaxed and watched the fire burning in the grate.

"You look so handsome tonight, Mr. Mathis." She smiled up at him. "Of course, I wasn't the only woman who had her eyes on you tonight."

He quirked a brow. "Oh yeah."

"Yes. None other than Natasha Baker. Even though she came with a date, that didn't stop her from grinning up in your face."

"Don't tell me you still care what she thinks?"

"Not really." Locking her hands behind his neck, she pressed a kiss against the side of his throat. "I know better than to let another woman worry me. If you wanted to be with her, you wouldn't be parking your sneakers under my bed."

Gavin placed a lingering kiss on her lips. "Sweetheart, I value every moment we've spent together these past few weeks." Tilting her chin until he could look into her dark gray eyes, he said, "I know it hasn't been easy for you to move into the guest house, but I am so glad you did."

"Gavin . . ."

"Shush." He caressed her lips with his briefly before he said, "Let me get this out. I've been doing a great deal of thinking. Anna, I don't want what we have to end . . . not ever. You're so special to me. I wouldn't change what we share for anything or anyone."

Gavin's eyes searched hers, then he said, "I have something for you. I intended to wait and give it to you tomorrow." He grinned, "But I can't wait."

She stared at him, her heart suddenly racing so fast she could hardly catch her breath. She watched as he reached into his jacket inside pocket. He was smiling as he took out a small velvet ring box. He popped the lid.

"Anna Prescott, will you be my wife?"

Her eyes went wide in disbelief as she stared at the three-carat square-cut diamond solitaire, surrounded by small round pink diamonds and set in platinum. It was breathtaking.

The ring wasn't what caused her bottom lip to tremble or her eyes to fill with tears. Unable to bear their closeness, she tried to move away but he held her fast.

"What's wrong? You don't like the ring?"

"Please, let me up." Her voice trembled from her turbulent emotions, her throat nearly locked with tears.

Reluctantly, he dropped his arms. He placed the ring on the side table. "Please, talk to me. Tell me what's wrong? I thought you'd want to get married. It would certainly solve our problems with your family."

Anna quickly came to her feet and moved away from him. She shook her head vehemently. "You thought wrong."

When she turned to leave, Gavin moved so quickly that he reached the archway ahead of her. "You aren't going anywhere until you tell me why." His hands were clenched at his sides.

Fighting tears of humiliation, all Anna wanted was to get as far away from the man she loved with all her heart as quickly as possible. Determined not to embarrass herself even more by revealing too much, she whispered, "Move out of my way."

"Not until we've talked this over. Tell me what I said that upset you. Or is the thought of marriage to me what you find distasteful? I honestly thought you would be happy, that you'd want to be part of my family."

"Why would you think that?" She blinked hard to hold back the tears. "Do I look needy? Or is it that you just assumed I'm in need of rescuing? Well, I'm not."

Gavin said between clenched teeth, "All you have to do is say no and all will be forgotten."

"No." She poked her finger into his chest. "I don't want to marry a man who wants a wife to help him take care of his little brother. Or a man who wants to marry me to heal the split in my family. I deserve more and so do you."

Gavin's features had suddenly gone cold and withdrawn. "My apologies. I certainly didn't mean to insult you."

"You haven't."

"Then why won't you look me in the eye?"

Anna forced herself to look up into his dark gaze. "We evidently want and need two different things."

"Evidently," he said dryly. He smoothed a hand over his hair, then asked, "What have we been doing these past few weeks but playing at being married?" The inquiry sounded more like an accusation than a question.

"I wasn't playing at anything. I thought we were having a mutually enjoyable, satisfying relationship."

"We did." He unclenched his jaw. "I mean we do. Anna, is it so wrong for me to want to make you happy? Or to want me and Kyle to be happy, as well as your family?"

She shook her head. "That isn't why people get married. There has to be more. If you had brought this up before my father came to discuss our living arrangement, then perhaps we would have something to talk about. But not now, after all that has happened. How can it work?

"It's not what you really want. You've never said one word about wanting to marry . . . ever. From the first you told me how you felt about commitment. It was never an option. Nothing's changed but your level of guilt."

"You want me to say I love you? Is that what this is about? I do love you."

What she wanted was for him to mean it. Forcing back tears, she lifted her chin. "Gavin, I know. I know you are doing this because of what my father said. How could I not know how much my father and Wesley mean to you? You've always valued Daddy's opinion. This isn't even about me and you."

"That's not true. How can you say that?"

She shook her head, thinking about how she'd worked so hard at not letting him guess how she felt about him. His declaration of love was a joke. He'd only said it because it was expected of him. If she were crazy enough to say yes, how long could it last? Six months? Maybe a year? Her family would be happy. Anna would be miserable.

"Admit it," she demanded. "This is about repairing your relationship with my brother and regaining my father's approval."

"Damn it." Gavin rested one hand on a lean hip. "Did you even listen to what I said to you? Yes, I would like to repair my relationship with your family. But Anna, what I want is you. I want us to be a family. I want a house full of kids someday.

"I can't imagine anyone but you carrying my child. If you're worried about my interfering in your catering business with Janet, forget it. I would never interfere in your career. If you want to start a restaurant, I'll back you."

She bristled. "My career isn't the issue. When I moved to the cottage, I did it because of the way I felt about you. I wanted to be with you as much as we could manage. My reasons had nothing to do with anyone outside of you."

He cradled her face in his large hands. "It's been more than good between us. I enjoy making love to you. And you can't tell me that you don't enjoy having me inside of you."

She pushed at his chest. "You're talking about sex!"

"Damn straight I'm talking about sex. It is a definite part of what we've shared. We're good together, in and out of bed."

"We're not getting anywhere with this conversation." Ready to throw up her hands, she tried to walk past him, but he held her against his chest. Her soft breasts were pillowed on his chest when she insisted, "Let go."

"Just answer one question. Are you telling me that you want what we have to end?"

Anna nearly screamed that it was over for her the instant he asked her to marry him, without love. "I'll stay for Kyle's sake, just until you find someone else to cook for you. I'll move back to my own place the day after Christmas."

As soon as the words left her mouth, Gavin dropped his hands. Although he didn't like her answer, he stopped fighting. There was a mixture of pain and anger in his dark eyes as he shoved his hands into his trouser pockets.

He said, "Tomorrow is bound to be awkward for all of us."

"If you'd rather I left tonight, I will." She lifted her chin another notch.

"I'm not pushing you out the damn door," he snapped.

"Kyle will expect us both to be as excited about the holiday as he is. This will be the first Christmas the two of you will spend as a family. If it's all right with you, I'll prepare breakfast and stay until after he has opened his gifts. I can excuse myself and go over to my folks'. You won't have to worry about your meal. It's all planned, and I should be out of your kitchen by no later than two."

Walking to the fireplace, he stood staring down at the logs burning to ash in the covered grate. "Kyle will want to be with Wayne on Christmas, that is, if you and your family have no objections."

Her arms were wrapped protectively around herself but her eyes were on her feet, which she suddenly remembered were bare. She went to recover her shoes.

He repeated, "If you and your family have no objection, can—"

She hastily interrupted, "Of course. He's more than welcome to come with me. Are you sure?"

There was no warmth in his voice when he said, "Thanks. He's going to know soon enough that something is wrong."

"Not tomorrow. We both want it to be a special day for his sake. Good night." Anna hurried out.

Somehow she kept her head held high and her shoulders back until she reached the kitchen. Thankful that he could not see the tears spilling down her face, she rushed on, pausing only long enough to retrieve her jacket before she raced along the lit path to the cottage. She was sobbing aloud by the time she had the door open. She collapsed onto the sofa.

She hadn't remembered to leave a lamp on or bothered to remove her coat. She had no idea how long she cried, but she couldn't seem to stop. Her head as well as her heart ached by the time she finally undressed and crawled into bed—the bed she'd expected to share with Gavin. He wouldn't be coming—not tonight, not any other night.

Tears seeped down her cheeks, slowly soaking the pillow as she wondered how it had all blown up in their faces. It happened so quickly, so unexpectedly. When she'd dressed for the party, her thoughts were filled with details of the party and the problems in their relationship.

Was it only a few hours ago that she told Janet she was scared that the difference in the way they felt about each other would someday matter? It never occurred to her that before the night was over, her heart would be broken because he'd proposed.

She hadn't seen it coming. They were dancing and talking about the party and then he was showing her the most beautiful ring she'd ever seen. She was still reeling from the shock that it was over between them.

After weeks of shared intimacy, she'd hungered for his love. After countless fantasies of a home filled with Gavin's babies and his love, he had offered what she'd once thought she wanted more than anything else in the world. But she had been wrong. She couldn't marry a man who didn't love her as much as she loved him.

It was nearly dawn when she glanced at the bedside clock. Christmas Day. She moaned unhappily. For Kyle's sake they had decided to pretend that nothing was wrong. How was she going to get through this day?

Tomorrow she would leave this place and move back into her own home. Yet the heartache was only beginning. She had no idea how long it would take for him to find a replacement. In the meantime she would continue to see him day in and day out, pretending that her life wasn't shattered.

She wasn't sure what was worse. Without a doubt, she was moving toward a life that didn't include Gavin. How could she bear it? What choice did she have but to learn to do without him in her life? He was such an attractive man that it wouldn't take long before he found someone to take her place.

Anna felt as if her heart had been crushed into a million tiny pieces that she had no hope of putting back together again. Would she ever feel whole again?

"Gavin, why? Why did you do it? You had to know I couldn't say yes," she whispered aloud.

They'd been happy, hadn't they? Or had she been walking around with her head stuck in some cloud? She was forgetting the nights she cried herself to sleep because she loved him while he didn't return her feelings. Or the numerous times she'd bitten her lip to hold in her true feelings when she lost control and climaxed in his arms.

"Doesn't matter anymore," she reminded herself as she hugged the pillow. "It's over."

28

It took all Anna's resolve to get herself over to Gavin's to prepare Christmas breakfast.

Kyle was downstairs before she'd finished making the pecan cinnamon sticky buns that both he and his older brother loved. He was so excited that he couldn't stop talking or sit still.

"I don't know what's taking Gavin so long. I'm sure I heard him moving around earlier. Why would he even bother to dress? It's Christmas."

With a forced smile, she said, "He'll be down soon enough. Want a cup of hot chocolate while you wait?"

She'd dressed in black denim leggings and a bright red sweater. Her long locks were held back by a ponytail. Even though she told herself it didn't matter how she looked, she'd taken care to disguise her swollen lids and the shadows under her eyes. Her lips were tinted with crimson red lipstick.

"I suppose. Wayne has already called to tell me what he's gotten for Christmas," Kyle complained.

"Don't believe him. Our family never opens gifts until after dinner. He just wants you to think he knows."

Kyle laughed. "Just wait until I see him."

"Are you upset that your father didn't stay for the holiday?"

He shrugged. "Not really. I'm just glad I didn't have to go back with him."

"Merry Christmas," Gavin walked into the kitchen wearing snug jeans that had seen better days and an old sweatshirt. His feet were covered by a pair of white athletic socks.

"It's about time," Kyle complained. "A guy could starve to death waiting on you to show up."

Gavin's laugh sounded forced. He grabbed his brother, looping an arm around his slender shoulder. "You don't look hungry to me. Does he, Anna?"

"I'm hungry, if you two aren't. Good morning." She barely glanced his way when she asked, "Coffee?"

"'Morning." He let go of Kyle. "I'll get it." He walked past where she paused to rescue the bacon and sausage from the grill before she began whisking eggs in a mixing bowl. Gavin avoided making eye contact as he picked up the carafe and filled a large mug with steaming hot coffee.

Kyle let out a moan. "Can you smell the cinnamon buns?"

"Without a doubt," Gavin said, before he asked Anna, "Sleep well?"

"Just fine." She made a point not to lift her gaze from the skillet heating on the stove. She didn't need to look at him to tell that he blamed her for their break-up. Instead she concentrated on putting piping hot rolls, bacon and sausage, a pile of fluffy scrambled eggs, and cheesy grits on the table, as quickly and efficiently as possible.

Gavin held her chair as was his custom, but she didn't send

him a ready smile, merely offered a polite thank you. She hoped that Kyle didn't realize that he was doing all the talking and that the two of them had said next to nothing to each other. It was painfully apparent to her that when Gavin bothered to look her way, his dark eyes were cold and distant.

When the meal ended, it was Kyle who urged both Anna and Gavin into the living room to open gifts. The word "torment" didn't come close to expressing the way Anna felt during that pain-filled next half hour.

By the time she accepted the beautiful cashmere sweater set that had to have cost the earth from Gavin, her nerves were truly shot. She gave Kyle a hug for the gold hoop earrings he had selected for her. Kyle gave Gavin a dark green turtleneck sweater. Apparently he'd been saving his allowance and was pleased with himself.

Although Gavin thanked Anna for the butter-soft, gray leather gloves and driving cap she had given him, he made no move to touch her. Kyle was thrilled with the video game from Anna and the costly leather jacket, CDs and sneakers Gavin surprised him with. Then Kyle hurried off to his room to call Wayne, thus leaving Anna and Gavin alone for the first time that morning.

"Excuse me." She practically jumped to her feet. "I have things to take care of in the kitchen."

"Today is not a regular workday. Leave the cleanup from breakfast."

"I have a turkey dinner with all the fixings to prepare." Her back was ramrod straight.

"Don't bother. Kyle will be with Wayne and your family."

"But what about you?" she blurted out.

"That's no longer your concern. Enjoy your day," Gavin said before he walked out of the living room.

* * *

Even though Anna had changed into a black tunic-length sweater trimmed in white and a long black skirt over black leather boots, her spirits hadn't lifted.

She and Kyle were loaded down with packages and baked goods. Anna offered no explanation but greeted her family warmly. She accepted her father's, brothers', and cousin's hugs without comment.

"Honey?" Her mother tried to draw her aside, but she shook her head no, whispering they would talk later. She kept busy in the kitchen helping Kelli and Kelli's mother, Clarice, with dinner. It was her father who asked the question that was on everyone's mind.

"Isn't Gavin coming?"

Anna shook her head and quickly asked Clarice about her arthritis. She did her best to pretend she didn't see the concerned looks her parents exchanged.

The last thing she wanted was to confess all and break down in tears. There was nothing that could be done. Her involvement with Gavin was over, but the lingering pain was excruciating.

"Is there anything I can do?" Kelli asked softly when she joined Anna in the dining room as she was setting the table.

"No thanks." Anna dredged up a smile, knowing that if she as much as said Gavin's name, she would be a basket case. "I'm all done."

She linked her arm through her sister-in-law's and headed back to the kitchen. "Come on. We could use your opinion on whether we need more cayenne or onions in the greens. Something is just not right."

Kelli refused to be moved. She whispered, "The problem is not food, and you know it. You're hurting, and I want to help."

"Food is all I can talk about without breaking down," Anna whispered back miserably. "Come on."

When they entered the kitchen filled with family and homey holiday smells Kelli briefly shook her head as she looked at the expectant Donna.

Ralph's latest lady friend, Candy Marshall, chose that moment to walk into the kitchen in a skirt that was too short and tight to be functional, teetering on extremely high heels.

"Need any help?" Candy offered. There was nothing subtle about her, from her heavily applied makeup to her nails that were so long they curled under like claws.

The women quickly shook their heads, assuring her that everything was under control.

"Surely I can be of some help?" She pouted prettily.

Anna grabbed the huge salad bowl from the refrigerator and handed over a long-handled fork and spoon. "You can put these on the side table. Then fill the water goblets, if you don't mind?"

Once she was gone, Donna whispered from where she gave the dressing one last stir, "Where does he find them? There's a new one every week."

Kelli shook her head, "Let's just hope she doesn't bend over in that postage stamp she's wearing."

"Shush, she might hear," Anna warned.

"I just wish that boy would find a nice young lady and settle down like you and Wesley, Kelli. I have just about given up hope on both Devin and Ralph. Devin is worse. He doesn't even bother to bring them home," Donna complained.

"Mama, the relish is ready. You want me to put another batch of rolls in the oven?"

"Yes, we're almost there, ladies. Clarice, that creamed corn smells wonderful. We are in for a real treat." Donna beamed at Kelli's mother, who frequently shared the holidays with them.

"I can't wait until you try this German chocolate cake my girl made. She's turning into a fine cook." Clarice smiled proudly at her daughter as she bounced little Kaleea on her lap.

"Why, thank you, Mom. I'll pour the gravy," Kelli volunteered.

When Candy returned, Donna asked her if she would ask Ralph to carry in the turkey and Wesley to bring in the ham. Kelli reminded Donna not to forget the chitlins.

Once everyone was seated around the table, Lester said grace before the family dug in. The meal was a resounding success. Anna was glad that Kyle felt so at home and equally relieved that he hadn't asked why Gavin had decided not to join them.

Gavin's name wasn't mentioned, even though it was obvious to Anna that she wasn't the only one missing him. Wesley hadn't said much, but his questioning gaze strayed time and time again to his sister. After dinner and after the gifts had all been opened and admired, everyone went into the living room where Donna, at the piano, began playing Christmas carols.

Wesley came over to Anna and whispered in her ear, "Let's go."

"Go where?"

He took her elbow and practically lifted her from her chair and guided her out of the room, then down the hallway into the family room. Devin was right behind them. Soon the door was closed with Devin's tall frame leaning against it.

"What's this about?" she said, crossing her arms under her breasts preparing herself to face down her brothers.

"It's time we talked," Wesley said.

"Why? Haven't you two done enough already?" She lifted her chin.

"Too damn much, evidently," Devin said with a worried frown. "Talk. What happened?"

Wesley demanded, "Why isn't Gavin here? And why are you looking as if someone died?"

She glared at them. "You two forgot Ralph, didn't you?"

"I'm right here." He was as tall and handsome as the rest of the Prescott men and equally as determined. He pushed past Devin and closed the door. "What's going on?"

Devin volunteered. "Trying to find out what's wrong."

"Haven't you three done enough already?" Anna glared, refusing to let them get the best of her. "Well, I have good news. You should all be thrilled. Gavin and I are now history."

"What happened?" Ralph questioned.

"It's over. We broke up last night. I will be moving back home tomorrow. And he will start looking for a new chef just as soon as the holidays are over. Satisfied?" She was so busy blinking back tears that she failed to notice no one seemed happy about the announcement.

"Wait until I get my hands on him," Wesley ground between his teeth. "Gavin had no business touching you if he wasn't willing to give you his name."

"The bastard. He won't get away with this," Devin promised, his hands balled at his side.

"Wait," Ralph shouted at his hotheaded cousins. "There has to be more going on here." He took her hands into his own. "What happened, cuz?"

"What difference does it make?" She snatched her hands away. "Why aren't you guys celebrating? It's what you all have been hoping would happen. Gavin is out of my life for good." Anna brushed at the tears that, no matter how hard she tried, she couldn't hold back.

"No one is celebrating, especially since you've been hurt," Wesley said softly. "What happened, little sis?"

"It's obvious that some sports groupie got in the way. You know how some of them act," Devin sneered "We've all had to deal with them."

Ralph pulled her over to the sofa and sat her down. "Anna? Was that it?" His concern was as evident as her brothers'.

"If you need me to hurt him the way he hurt you, I will,"

Devin offered, his temper getting the best of him. "No one hurts my baby sister."

"Will all of you stop it? This is not about anyone else, just Gavin and me." She jumped to her feet, hands clenched at her sides. "We couldn't make it work. There was just too much in the way, including the three of you. You didn't even want him here for Christmas."

"Wait a minute." Wesley followed. "Dad went to see you and Gavin. He said he smoothed things over. He and Mama both wanted him here. And we all accepted that, even if we didn't like it. We planned to keep our mouths shut."

"That's right," Devin growled impatiently. None of them wanted to see Donna and Lester upset, and that was exactly what would have happened if Anna hadn't come home for Christmas.

Anna nodded. "Daddy came by. And yes, he did have a talk with us. He let Gavin know he wasn't happy with our living arrangement." She hesitated, studying the tops of her boots.

"Daddy came right out and told Gavin that if he wanted me he should marry me. Well, you know how much Gavin respects Daddy. He's been more like a father to him than his own father."

She was silent so long that Ralph prompted, "What?"

"Evidently this time it made an impression on Gavin. Last night after the party, he asked me to marry him. He even bought me a ring." Anna began crying in earnest.

Wesley pulled her against his chest. Devin handed her a handkerchief. They waited until she calmed down somewhat.

Wesley asked, "So why aren't we celebrating your engagement?"

"Yeah, sis." Devin was clearly upset, unable to bear her tears. "I thought you were in love with him."

"That's obvious," Ralph insisted. "She wouldn't have let him touch her in the first place, if she didn't love him."

"Shut up, all of you. You're only making her cry harder." Wesley was doing his best to calm her.

It took her a few moments to calm down enough to even think straight, let alone explain. They soon had her settled on the sofa cradling a glass of brandy she didn't want.

"Drink some of it," Devin persisted gently.

Anna took a sip to shut him up, then wiped at the stubborn tear that ran down her cheek.

It was Ralph who asked, "Why aren't we planning a wedding, darlin'?"

"Because I turned him down."

Devin was the only who said what the others were thinking, "Why in the hell did you go and do that?"

"What do you mean, why did I do that?" Anna was on her feet, shaking and furious. "What woman in her right mind wants to marry a man who doesn't love her? Not me."

All three men looked at one another, clearly bewildered.

"Who says he doesn't love you?" Wesley asked.

She looked at them through watery eyes. "Believe me, as hard as this may be for you knuckleheads to understand, every man on this earth isn't in love with me. Gavin happens to be one of them. He only asked me because he believed it was the right thing to do."

"He does love you," Devin said, as if anything else was preposterous.

"He doesn't," she yelled back.

"Wait a minute." Wesley demanded, "Did you ask him how he felt about you?"

"No. I'm not that desperate." She took another sip of the brandy, then shuddered at the taste. She put it down before she said, as evenly as she could manage, "I know Gavin cares about me. I also know, as Kyle's guardian, he's determined to provide a stable home for his brother. None of that has anything to do with loving me."

Wesley cupped her shoulders, gently turning her to face him. "I repeat, did you ask the man how he feels about you? I know Gavin. Yes, he loves Dad, but he isn't about to marry to please someone else, not considering his family history."

Wesley paused for emphasis. "If the man asked you to marry him, he did so because he wants you. One thing the guy has always been is his own man. Just because he hasn't said he loves you, doesn't mean he doesn't feel it."

"Wes is right." Devin was thoughtful before he said, "Gavin wouldn't ask you to marry him to please Dad. There has to be more."

"Gavin tossed out an 'of course I love you,' as if it were an afterthought. And there is no doubt in my mind that he loves me, but he's not in love with me the way I am with him."

Frustrated, Devin snapped. "If he said it at all, he meant it. You'd never hear me saying it if I wasn't dead serious, that's for damn sure."

"When you say those words, hell will no doubt have frozen solid." Ralph laughed.

"And you would say them? Mr. New Woman Every Half Hour? Every time I come home, you've got some new babe on your arm. Give me a break," Devin snapped.

"At least I bring them home. What is your excuse?" Ralph shot back. "You got women in two states trying to run you to ground."

"I'll take that as a compliment." Devin smiled.

Wesley shook his head. "Will you both shut up? Neither one of you knows a thing about being in love. You'd both run like hell if a woman even looked like she wanted to get serious with one of you."

"The way I see it, that's not a bad thing." Devin laughed.

Anna snapped. "Now that we've gotten that out of the way, I'm leaving. This conversation is over."

"We aren't done," Wesley said. "Anna, what more do you want from the guy? He gave you a ring."

"I want him to mean it."

"He does," her brothers shouted.

Anna looked from one brother to the other before she turned to her cousin. "You think they're right?" Her heart raced from just the possibility.

Ralph nodded. "Sure I do. Ask him. How else will you know? Cuz, don't throw away the chance to have a future with the man you love. You can't walk away just because the man wants to make a family for himself and his brother."

Anna recalled the words Gavin used when he asked her to be his wife. There wasn't so much as a hint that he truly loved her.

"As much as I want to believe you're right, I can't." She bit her lip to hold back the tremors. She'd already cried an ocean of tears, more would change nothing. "If Gavin was in love with me, why didn't he come right out and say it?"

Devin groaned as if he were in pain. "Don't go all female on us, sis. The guy asked you to marry him. Believe me, he wouldn't have done that if he wasn't in love with you. No man would."

"That's for sure," his equally single cousin agreed.

Wesley shook his head. "Don't listen to those jocks. Neither one of them knows a blasted thing about being in love."

The other two swore at him.

"Sorry, sis," Devin apologized and Ralph nodded his agreement.

Wesley asked pointedly, "Does he know how you feel about him?"

"She slept with him. He ought to know," Devin put in.

"Please. How many women have you slept with that you didn't love or could care less if they loved you?" Ralph asked.

"Yeah, but that's different," Devin said sheepishly.

Ignoring the others, Wesley quizzed, "Did you even once tell him that you're in love with him?"

Anna wrung her hands. "I couldn't. I didn't want him to feel as if he were taking advantage of my feelings for him."

"The way I see it, you have a choice," Wesley surmised. "You can find out how he feels, or you can turn tail and run like a coward. Which is it going to be?" When she didn't respond quickly enough, Wesley urged, "Sis, Gavin has the means to hire a million chefs, but there is only one of you. No one can take your place."

"Just ask him," both Ralph and Devin said at the same time.

"It's a whole lot easier to say than do," she confessed unhappily. "You all could be wrong."

Wesley advised, "Not likely. But you're a Prescott. If he says no, then sock him."

29

Was she making a huge mistake by taking their advice, she wondered, as she followed the drive to the side entrance. She slowed the car to a stop beside Gavin's SUV, knowing that it didn't necessarily mean anything. He could just as easily have taken one of the other cars or a limousine.

She couldn't stop thinking about how angry and withdrawn he'd been that morning. The memory did nothing to ease her anxiety. All he wanted was to have her as far away from him as possible. And she couldn't blame him. He had gone so far as to sacrifice spending the holiday with his brother in order to see the back of her.

Wesley seemed so sure that Gavin was in love with her. The chances were just as good that he was wrong. The two men hadn't exactly been close in the last few weeks. One thing was certain. She had to find out the truth. How could she walk away if there was even the smallest bit of doubt in her mind?

Her entire future depended on his response to that one question. If that meant making a fool of herself, then she was willing to take the risk, because she just couldn't think of another option.

She got out of the car, automatically locking the door without thinking. Unfortunately, her excuse for returning early and without his brother sounded weak even to her own ears. When Kyle and Wayne asked if Kyle could stay overnight, she'd agreed and even offered to pack his bag, promising to drop it by later.

She considered going to the cottage first to freshen up, hoping to boost her spirits, but decided against it. Instead she let herself into the dark house. How she looked didn't matter. Another application of powder or lipstick wouldn't change how Gavin felt about her.

It was barely dusk, but although the outside lamps were lit, the house was dark. It was also silent, not a good sign. It looked as if no one was at home. Her stomach felt as if it were tied up in knots as she walked through the kitchen. It was a large house. He could be anywhere.

"Gavin?" Anna called, turning on lamps as she went. She checked the rooms on the first floor before she slowly mounted the stairs and walked down the long hall. She paused at the door to his suite before she knocked.

When there was no response, she tried again. Eventually she had to force herself to go inside. His sitting room was dark and empty. She crossed on unsteady legs to his bedroom. It was also empty, as was his bathroom. Anna sighed wearily. Unless he was hiding in the laundry hamper, he wasn't at home.

Disappointed, Anna stopped in Kyle's room long enough to pack an overnight bag, and then she hurried down to the main floor. She hesitated at the back staircase and flicked on the light before she went down. The gym, the indoor swimming pool, the sauna, the basketball, and the racketball courts were all empty.

Dejected and sad, Anna locked the house. When she got in her car, she realized she was not quite ready to face her family. She needed some time alone . . . time to think about what she was going to say to Gavin. She left the bag on the passenger seat and then followed the walkway to the guest cottage she'd been calling home the last few weeks. That might all end tomorrow. She wasn't quite ready to face the inevitability of the move. She'd been so happy when she moved in, so filled with dreams.

Anna's steps slowed as she approached the cottage. It too was bathed in darkness. She'd left earlier without a single thought of leaving on a light. Her heart had been too heavy with grief to think beyond getting through this one day.

She was facing another night alone and was unsure if she could bear spending it in the cottage, in the bed she had shared with Gavin. Maybe she should just go home tonight? Nothing could be worse than spending Christmas Day without him.

How could she bear it if he didn't love her? There would be no more nights of listening for his footsteps or long talks with the moonlight shining through the French doors. No more nights of sleeping in his arms or stolen moments and kisses.

How many times had she reminded herself that one unspoken word shouldn't matter? Could it be true that the sizzling hot kisses and the incredible love making were a thing of the past?

Had all her love been wasted on a man who could not or would not offer love in return? She was no closer to knowing the answer to that question than she had been when she left her folks'.

"No closer," Anna whispered to herself as she unlocked the cottage door and went inside. She moved absently to the nearby lamp. Turning it on, she jumped when she saw Gavin sprawled on the sofa. She hadn't noticed the fire that was burning in the grate.

He held a beer bottle in his hand. Judging by the two other bottles on the side table, he'd been there awhile.

Shielding his eyes from the light, he asked, "What time is it?"

"It's a little after seven."

"I didn't expect you back so soon." He swung his legs down to the carpet. His gaze slowly moved over her before he looked away. "Where is Kyle? At the house?"

"He asked to stay overnight with Wayne," she answered, her stomach fluttering with nerves. "Just for tonight. Is that okay?"

"It's a little late to refuse," he said dryly.

"I didn't think you would mind. I packed an overnight bag for him. I left it in the car while I came in to—" Recognizing that she was babbling she stopped. "Should I apologize?"

"No, Kyle is entitled to enjoy the holiday," he said tightly.

Realizing that she'd left the door open, she went back to close it. Leaning against it, she quizzed, "Gavin, why are you here?"

He rested his forearms on his thighs before he pushed himself up to his feet. "It doesn't matter. I'll get out of your way."

"No." she said quickly, then added, "Please don't go." Swallowing with difficulty, she took off her ivory wool coat, black velvet hat and scarf, and tossed them into the nearby armchair.

His dark eyes were devoid of emotions. "Why?"

"I'd like to talk."

"We've both said all that needed saying last night."

"Maybe you did, but I haven't." She walked right up to

him, even though her legs weren't as steady as she would like. "I can't leave things as they are between us. I have to know."

He carefully placed the unfinished bottle with the others. He quirked a brow, a hand braced on one lean hip. "What?"

"I had a talk with my brothers and Ralph before I—"

He interrupted sarcastically, "I just bet they were thrilled when you told them we've broken up. Something to celebrate."

"No one was celebrating." She bit her lip to hold back the tremors.

He grated harshly, "Look, say what you have to say, so I can get the hell out of here."

"Too many memories, Gavin?" she taunted.

He stiffened but he didn't bother to respond.

"Were they all bad?" she whispered unhappily.

"You know they aren't." He didn't look at her but over her left shoulder. Impatient to leave, he demanded to know, "Anna, what is this about? You wanted out, you got it. What more is there?"

Blinking back tears, she confessed, "I never wanted what we had to end . . . not ever."

"I was there when you gave back my ring." His eyes mirrored the bitterness in his voice.

"That was different."

"Pardon me for being dense, but what in the hell are you talking about? From where I'm standing N-O means just that."

He ran an unsteady hand over his unshaven jaw. Moving to the fireplace, he leaned a shoulder against the mantel, staring into the depths of the log-filled grate.

His voice was gruff when he accused, "The way I heard it, you didn't want a damn thing I was offering."

"That's not true."

Gavin's eyes moved from her cottony-soft hair to linger on her red-tinted full lips. He caressed her mouth with his dark hungry eyes. He sighed tiredly.

"Why are we even discussing this? Damn it, don't play with me like this, Anna, just say what you have to say, so I can get the hell away from you."

The tears she'd tried to hold back spilled from her dark gray eyes. She hastily wiped them away. "You don't even want to be in the same room with me anymore."

"What do you expect, Anna?" He gestured wildly. "You were the one who turned me down, not the other way around. I'll be damned, if I'm going to beg you to stay with me."

"You don't have to beg. You never had to do that. All I've ever wanted was your love."

Gavin's eyes collided with hers. He stood there studying her. Eventually he said, "I told you how I feel."

"You told me that I was special to you. And that if I wanted you to say you loved me then you would. It was an afterthought, and that hurt."

"I asked you to marry me."

"Why, Gavin? I came back early looking for you because I have to know . . ." She stopped, then forced herself to continue. ". . . if you're in love with me. Is that why you asked me to be your wife? Because that's my reason for refusing. I don't believe you're in love with me."

Her arms were wrapped around her waist as if she were protecting herself from even more hurt as she silently prayed. If he didn't love her, then they had zero chance of making it work.

A frown creased his brow, his hands hung loosely at his sides. "How can you not know how I feel about you?"

"Gavin . . . please. Just tell me."

He slowly crossed to her, placing a finger under her chin and tilting it up so that he could study her face. "Yes, I love you, Anna Prescott. I've been in love with you for some time." His hands were gentle as he cradled her face. "That's why I wanted you to share your life with me."

Anna slipped her arms around his waist and held on. It was several moments before she could speak or see past the tears obstructing her view. Resting her cheek on his chest, she leaned against him.

"Anna? How could you have doubts?"

"You never said the words. You said from the very first that—"

"I know, but I didn't see marriage as the answer for me. And you were right. Talking to your father made me recognize I wanted what your parents have shared over the years."

She hit him with her balled fist. "You should have told me how you felt."

He confessed. "I thought you knew I loved you."

His eyes closed at the sweetness of having her back in his arms again. She was crying in earnest now, as she tucked her face beneath his chin.

"Oh, Gavin. I love you so much, it hurts."

He sighed heavily. Bending his knees so he could gaze into her eyes, he whispered, "You don't tell a man you love him, then hide your face. I want to look at you, sweetheart." He rained kisses down from her forehead over her soft cheeks, her nose, to her soft generous mouth. As he savored her, he tasted her tears.

"I should be furious with you. Look what needless agony you put us through," Anna scolded as she cradled his unshaven cheeks.

"I won't make that same mistake again. I'm in love with you, so much so it hurts." He kissed her tenderly. "I'm sorry I didn't make myself clear last night. How was I supposed to know those words meant so much?

"I'm a jock. What do I know about these things? I never

felt this way about anyone before. I certainly never wanted to marry."

She warned, "I suggest you memorize those three words."

Anna was kissing Gavin when she gasped as she felt him lifting her off her feet. She quickly wrapped her arms around his neck. He sat down on the couch with her in his lap.

"Sweetheart, I spent a terrible night without you. I couldn't sleep. I kept replaying our argument. I hated every minute of it."

When he pressed his lips to the highly sensitive place on her throat, she shivered in response, whispering his name.

"I love you so much."

He stared into her eyes before he confessed, "You were right. I needed to hear those words just as much as you did. I didn't fully understand how much it meant to me until just now."

"I was miserable without you. Just ask my cousin and brothers."

"Uh-oh. Now the Prescott men are really gunning for me, especially Wes."

"No, they aren't. Wesley is still your friend. He stood up for you today." When Gavin looked doubtful, she quickly explained, "It's true. As soon as I told him that you proposed, his entire attitude changed and he insisted that he knew the reason why."

"Honest?" Gavin grinned.

"Yes. Wesley told me straight out that I was wrong. He told me that you were your own man, and you wouldn't ask me to marry you to please someone else, even Daddy. Both Devin and Ralph encouraged me to come here tonight and find out the truth."

"So that's why you came back?"

"Partly." She placed a kiss against the warm scented base

of his throat. "I was such a mess that everyone knew something was wrong. Wesley ushered me into the family room, wanting to know what was going on. Devin and Ralph followed. They were all so sure you loved me. It took all three of them to convince me to at least try to find out why you asked me to be your wife."

"Then I have them to thank." He ran a soothing hand down her back.

"I thought I knew why. I was wrong."

"None if it is your fault, Anna. You're not a mind reader. I did a lousy job of proposing."

"Honey, no. Don't say that."

"It's true. If I hadn't messed up, we would have spent last night and today together instead of apart."

"We both made mistakes. I should have told you why I was so upset."

"You are going to marry me, aren't you?"

"I haven't been asked today." She smiled.

"Don't tease. It's too important." Gavin's eyes locked with hers when he asked, "Will you marry me, sweet Anna? Will you be my wife and my lover?"

"Yes, my love." She sighed heavily as he kissed her with all the pent-up emotions that had been locked inside him. That kiss led to another and yet another.

"Thank you," he whispered gruffly, holding her close. "You have no idea how happy you've made me."

Her smile was warm, brimming with happiness. "Promise me that from now on, there will be no more secrets."

"You have my promise that it won't ever happen again. I believe in you and what we have." He revealed, "I just never expected to fall in love. My parents never married. What I knew about love and marriage has been gained from watching your parents and Kelli and Wesley."

He brushed her lips with his own. "I don't want to make any more mistakes, Anna. I want what we have to last for the rest of our lives."

"It will. Honey, tell me what you meant when you said that you've loved me for some time. How long have you known?"

He smiled. "I've always cared about you. My feelings for you started changing even before you came here to work for me. I noticed the changes you made in your appearance . . . you began wearing perfume . . . you wore your glorious locks down more often. I was thoroughly intrigued by the woman you'd grown into while I wasn't paying attention. Suddenly I stopped thinking of you as Wesley's little sister."

He smiled. "That's about the time I began to worry about who you were involved with, and I was convinced you were dating one of the guys on the team. And I didn't like it, not at all. Hell, you were in and out of their houses five days a week. Whenever I questioned you"—he paused to give her a hard kiss—"you told me nothing."

"Gavin, there was never anyone else. I made those changes because I was feeling differently inside. I wanted to look on the outside like I felt on the inside. For so many years I was so busy finishing school and getting the business established that I didn't take time to dress up or wear makeup. I looked in the mirror one day and didn't like what I saw. Honestly." She caressed his throat. "I am very glad, Mr. Mathis, that you noticed."

He chuckled. "I noticed all right. When you came to work for me, I couldn't keep my eyes off you. I was captivated by the way you smiled, the sound of your laughter. I was touched by the warmth and kindness you showed Kyle. You turned my house that was much too big for one person into what I wanted it to be . . . a home."

Anna smiled up at him, giving him a hard squeeze. "How many of those beers did you have?"

"Not that many. I'm stone-cold sober."

"I'd hate for you not to remember any of this in the morning." She laughed.

"That's not about to happen. I know exactly what I want. And that's you." He brushed her mouth with his. "No matter how hard Kyle tried to make things difficult, you never gave up on him. I think that's when I began realizing that I was falling in love with you. You have such a generous spirit. You were even nice to my father." He shook his head.

"The next thing I knew I couldn't keep my hands off you. Even though I knew, going in, how protective the men in your family were about you, it didn't stop me from going after you. What about you? When did you know?"

"Well . . ." she teased.

"Tell me."

She laughed. "That's easy. Even before I came to work for you full-time, I was attracted to you. Suddenly all I could think about was you. I started looking forward to seeing you, hearing the sound of your voice. I often lay awake wondering what it would be like to hear that sexy, deep voice of yours at night."

She confessed, "By then I was working for you full-time. I tried not to, but I couldn't help it. I wanted you. And I hated the idea of you being with anyone else. I was so jealous of Natasha. Just knowing that you two had once been lovers hurt. I hated that she knew things about you that I could never know."

"Natasha was never a threat. I got so tired of women who were after me not because of the man I am but for what I could do for them that I chose to do without for a year."

"You told me, but I couldn't quite make myself believe."

"Believe it. I'd gotten so that I rarely dated."

Anna was smiling when she said, "I longed for your touch . . . ached to have your kisses. Oh Gavin, I wanted you to make love to me for weeks before you ever touched me." She blushed before she said, "Then you started pursuing me, and I panicked. I knew nothing about pleasing a man like you. Yet I couldn't stay away from you. I adored your kisses . . . your caresses. And then my meddling brothers saw us kissing. That really threw me. Gavin, I was so upset, embarrassed, and furious."

"It wasn't your fault," he said, huskily as he held her close. "Sweetheart, when did you realize it was love?"

"Thanksgiving weekend, I knew beyond any doubt that I was in love with you." She quietly revealed, "It took all my control not to scream those words at you when you were inside me. You have no idea how many times since then I've bitten my lip to keep from saying those three little words, especially while we were making love."

"So that was what you said the other night against my throat."

She nodded. Gavin sponged Anna's soft lips with his tongue, then groaned deeply when she opened for him and stroked his tongue with her own. His hands moved down her back to her generous hips. He tightened his hold, cupping and squeezing her behind while she pressed her breasts into his chest. Quivering, Anna rubbed aching, hard nipples against him.

He kissed her hard before he revealed, "Suddenly all I can think about is being inside you and making you climax, again and again. I can't wait to hear you scream your love while you come."

Her cheeks were hot as she wrapped her arms around his neck. She scolded, "Shame on you."

"I will show you shame later, but for now there are two

things I have to do." His voice was husky with suppressed need. His hard shaft pressed against her side as his hand moved over her cloth-covered thighs. Suddenly he rose and placed her on the cushion beside him.

"What?"

"Just give me a moment." He shoved his hand into his back pocket and pulled out the ring box. "I bought this over a week ago, and I've carried it around with me trying to find the right time to give it to you." He dropped down on one knee. "Will you accept this as well as my heart, sweet Anna?"

She nodded, cradling his unshaven cheek. When she held out her left hand, he grinned, placing a tender kiss on her ring finger before he slid the ring onto it. Anna's arms went around his neck and they shared a sweet kiss. Once more she was cradled in his arms.

Recalling what he'd said, she asked, "What was the other thing you needed to do?"

"Talk to your father. I want to ask his permission to marry you."

She tilted her head back to search Gavin's features. "Seriously?"

"Absolutely."

Anna smiled. "What if he says no?"

"I wouldn't be happy about it, but I'm marrying you no matter what. Ready to go?"

"You want to go tonight? Everyone is still over there."

"Right now. I've waited a long time to have you. I want it settled tonight."

She smiled. "Let's go."

It was a cold, starry night with the ground covered by a new blanket of snow. Gavin didn't feel the cold as they walked hand-in-hand. It was Anna who insisted they stop for him to get his jacket and boots.

"It will take too long," he complained, his arm around her waist.

"We're in a hurry?" she teased.

"You bet. The quicker we get there, the faster we'll get back and," he said against her lips, "I can make you scream."

Blackboard bestselling author
Beverly Jenkins

NIGHT SONG
0-380-77658-8/$5.99 US/$7.99 Can

TOPAZ
0-380-78660-5/$5.99 US/$7.99 Can

THROUGH THE STORM
0-380-79864-6/$5.99 US/$7.99 Can

THE TAMING OF JESSI ROSE
0-380-79865-4/$5.99 US/$7.99 Can

ALWAYS AND FOREVER
0-380-81374-2/$5.99 US/$7.99 Can

BEFORE THE DAWN
0-380-81375-0/$5.99 US/$7.99 Can

A CHANCE AT LOVE
0-06-050229-0/$5.99 US/$7.99 Can